BARRANCA

TROON McALLISTER

Also by

TROON McALLISTER

Scratch

The Kid Who Batted 1.000

The Foursome

The Green

RuggedLand

RUGGED LAND | 401 WEST STREET · SECOND FLOOR · NEW YORK CITY · NY 10014 · USA

RuggedLand

PUBLISHED BY RUGGED LAND, LLC

401 WEST STREET · SECOND FLOOR · NEW YORK CITY · NY 10014 · USA

RUGGED LAND AND COLOPHON ARE TRADEMARKS OF RUGGED LAND, LLC.

PUBLISHER'S CATALOGING-IN-PUBLICATION
(Provided by Quality Books, Inc.)
McAllister, Troon.
Barranca / Troon McAllister. -- 1st ed.
p. cm.
"An Eddie Caminetti novel."
ISBN 1590710444
1.Golf--Fiction. 2. Golf stories. I. Title.
PS3557.R8B377 2004 813'.54
QBI04-700076
Library of Congress Control Number: 2002117829

Book Design by Hsu + Associates

RUGGED LAND WEBSITE ADDRESS: WWW.RUGGEDLAND.COM

MARCH 2005

1 3 5 7 9 10 8 6 4 2

FIRST RUGGED LAND TRADE PAPERBACK EDITION

BARRANCA

PART I

THE BEGINNING OF THE STORY

If somebody tells you a coin is going to come up heads,

and it does, it doesn't mean he knew what he was talking about.

—Eddie Caminetti

CHAPTER 1

It used to be called the Oval Office in the White House, but that was before the world's largest appliance maker forked over $11.5 million to restore the mansion to its former glory and William H. Gates chipped in another two mill for the president's office. There was some carping at first, but the budget watchers in the Ralph Lauren Senate Building got over it quickly.

"What I'm saying. . . okay, not exactly *saying*, per se, so much as, uh, well okay, I guess I *am* saying it—stating it, you might say—but not, as it were, *averring* it. What I'm not averring, just trying to put across without quite stating it, is that we have a situation. Well okay, not a *situation*, as such, since that might require you to become actively involved in . . . wait a minute. Wait a minute. I'm not saying there *is* such a situation . . . or that there is not a situation . . . I'm not saying there *is* something that requires your involvement and that you're not getting involved. No, nothing like that at all. In which case, I guess there really isn't a situation, just a, well, just a *thing*, as it were. Doesn't even rise to the level of needing to be stated. Or averred, for that matter. Which is to say, it would seem that there's really nothing going on at all. That's it! That's it! There's nothing going on at all! Alright, then? Alright! Except . . . well . . . I really ought to tell you about, um, what it is that isn't going on. Or not, as it were . . ."

As CIA officer Joffrey Hayne's voice trailed off miserably and National Security Advisor Anatoli Kropotkin rolled his eyes ceiling-ward, President Thomas Madison Eastwood, patrician head resting comfortably in his thickly veined hand, stared at Hayne with the same withering gaze that had paralyzed opponents in all three debates during the last election campaign, the kind of ambiguous look a rhinoceros might give to a rabbit that had inadvertently wandered in front of it: *Are you worth the effort it would take to crush you into a red-brown skid mark or should I just move on?* "Is Marguerite out again today?"

Hayne, acutely aware of his two assistants sitting behind him, and already half-undone by the ocean of bad blood between himself and Kropotkin, drew a shuddering breath and let it out slowly as he nodded wretchedly. "Flu."

Hayne, somewhere in his late forties and with a pasty-complected face and shapeless body that painted him as clearly not a field agent, was a senior analyst (SA) in the Office of Current Production and Analytic Support (CPAS) in the Directorate of Intelligence (DI) of the Central Intelligence Agency (CIA), reporting directly to the Deputy Director for Intelligence (DDI). CPAS was the office responsible for preparing the President's Daily Briefing (PDB), a six- to twelve-page summary of critical intelligence matters delivered either in writing, to presidents who were fast studies and liked a lot of detail or who simply didn't believe that it was necessary to meet face-to-face six mornings a week, whether or not there was anything critical going on; or in person, to presidents who found reading burdensome and time-consuming. It was also delivered in person to presidents who could often tell more from the way a message was delivered than from the content of the message itself.

Eastwood was of the latter persuasion, although, in this particular situation, he couldn't tell from Hayne's delivery whether World War III was imminent or the price of tulips was about to rise in Holland. "Be sure to give her my best, okay?"

"Certainly, sir."

The Marguerite in question was a thirty-five-year veteran of CPAS who'd been doing a single job all that time, and who did it so well that her rare absence was keenly felt by the president and those among his senior security advisors who also received the PDB. Marguerite's job was to take the final intelligence summary and, in the two hours prior to the briefing itself, rewrite it in its entirety so that nothing of its content was actually stated, just implied, and to do so in a way that would afford the president complete deniability should anything in it ever threaten to come back and haunt him. The president never actually knew anything as a result of the daily briefing; he just had, as Marguerite herself had first stated it during the Nixon administration, an "inkling."

Right now, though, President Eastwood didn't even have that. "Tell me something, Joffrey," he said to Hayne. "Is it true you've got little vibrators on your windows over at CPAS?"

"Yessir," the senior analyst said, daring to come back to life, however slightly. "To make sure nobody can eavesdrop on us using laser or microwave acoustical detectors."

"How's that?"

"If you can sense the vibrations in a glass window from a distance, you can reconstruct the sounds that made them. Like people talking inside the room or dialing telephone numbers. By shaking the windows with these vibrators, we drown out those signals."

"Huh. Very clever."

Brightening noticeably, Hayne said, "Thank you, sir."

"You think of that yourself?"

The brightening dimmed. "Uh, no. No, that's been done for some years now."

"I see. Well, good idea anyway, because I'd sure as hell hate for anybody to get wind of what you just told me."

Hayne seriously considered grabbing the ceremonial sword from behind the president's desk and jumping onto it, belly first, but rejected the notion because it might be taken as a hostile gesture toward the president if Hayne didn't impale himself on it fast enough. Or, worse yet, he might not die in the attempt but only wound himself, although, come to think of it, slowly bleeding out on the carpet might be preferable to the conversation he was currently having. "Yes, sir."

Yes sir, what? Why were they always doing that? What if I stick my thumb in his eye . . . he buys me dinner and flowers? "Joffrey, why don't you worry about protecting the country instead of me and just tell me what's going on. What do you say, kid? Just to be different for a change."

Nothing in reply.

"Come on . . . whaddaya say?"

Nada.

"Pretty please?"

Zip.

"You know," Eastwood continued, "if it ever got out that it took a presidential order for an intelligence officer to tell the truth, it wouldn't look too good for the Company, now would it?"

"No, sir, I suppose it wouldn't."

"Fine, then. Let's have it. Something about this guy in South America. . . ?"

Hayne, who had enough of an "inkling" to know he'd been given a presidential order, implied or otherwise, set his briefing book on a chair and motioned his two assistants out of the room. When they were gone, he said, "It's getting worse."

"So I gathered. What'd he do now, rob a bank?"

"No sir. He robbed a country."

"How's that again? What country? And what'd he rob them of?"

"Brazil. And what he robbed was four hundred thousand acres' worth of real estate."

"Where?"

"Parana, Goias and Rondonia."

Eastwood called up his mental map of the region. "Now what the hell kind of sense does that make?"

"Damned if I know." Reddening slightly—not because of his mild profanity, but because, in the pantheon of career-limiting verbal gaffes, an intelligence officer saying "I don't know" to his president was like a Marine recruit saying "Bite me" to his drill sergeant—Hayne hurried on. "Didn't make any more sense when he grabbed Bucaramanga and Popayan in Colombia."

"They grow dope there?" the National Security Advisor asked.

Hayne jumped at the chance to stick a small knife into Kropotkin. "No. It was the most obvious first thought, but no, they don't. Fact is, we don't know what this guy is doing. Or, more correctly, we know what, but we don't know why."

Eastwood mulled it over for a few seconds. "You run it past Dalton?"

Hayne stiffened, and tried to ignore Kropotkin, who he was sure was gloating over the question. "Mr. Galsworthy is no longer with the Agency, sir."

"I know that, but why not ask him anyway?"

"We have a vast array of resources at our disposal, so I don't see any reason why we need to go outside and —"

"Any'a your vast array know what this . . . what's his name, anyway?"

"Barranca, sir. Manuel Villa Lobos de Barranca. And—"

"Any'a your vast array know what this Barranca's game is?"

"No," Hayne fairly spat.

"Well, there you go then." Eastwood threw his hands in the air. "Pick up a phone and ask Dalton what he thinks. Okay?"

"Of course, Mr. President."

Eastwood eyed him suspiciously. "And you'll give him all the background, right?"

"If you wish."

"I wish." The implication that Hayne wouldn't have done so had this part of the conversation not taken place was not lost on the president. He stood up and rapped a knuckle on the desk. "That pretty much wrap it up, then?" Kropotkin started to get up as well.

"Not quite, sir." As the two other men sank back slowly, Hayne said, "There's the matter of Jez Rama'am. The Pentagon brass are coming unglued over that air base they've been asking for, and —"

"Thought we had that one sewn up. We build the sultan a port, he gives us the base a few years later."

"Yes. Yes, well, that's the thinking, yes. Except . . ."

Eastwood stared at him, unwilling to prompt the guy any more.

"Except there's a problem."

And what might that problem be, Joffrey? Eastwood thought.

"Rather a serious problem."

Uh huh.

"Inside the Pentagon." And then Hayne went quiet.

Eastwood kept silent. For nearly a full minute. Then he stood up. "Well, I guess that does about wrap it up then."

"But sir, there's this problem."

"What problem?"

"The one I've been trying to tell you about!"

Eastwood came around to the front of the great desk. "I didn't see you trying to tell me anything, Joffrey. I saw you sitting there saying nothing. In fact, I'm kind of curious: How long would you have sat there? Five minutes? An hour?"

"Sir, I—"

"Do you have any idea how my day is scheduled? Any idea how precious every minute is? How does this work, Hayne: You go back to the Agency and brag about how much time you spent with the president, is that it? Do you give them some notion of the signal-to-noise ratio along with it? Like everything you had to tell me could have been sent in on a postcard?"

"Sir—"

"Meeting's over, Joffrey. And unless there's a ballistic missile eight minutes away from hitting one of our cities—a major city—I don't want to see you back here today." Eastwood held up a finger to indicate that Hayne was not to answer, and when he was sure the beaten man understood, Eastwood pointed the finger to the door of the Gates Office, out which Hayne slunk as though to his hanging.

When he was gone, Eastwood turned to Kropotkin. "We need to put him on suicide watch?"

"*Nyet*," the National Security Advisor advised. "Let him kill himself."

"Good thinking. Now what the hell's going on in Jez Rama'am?"

"What is going on is that we are going to spend a billion dollars on a gift to the sultan right now in exchange for his permission to build an air base later. Some of the Pentagon *apparatchiks* do not think he can be trusted."

"Can he?"

Kropotkin grunted. "One of those questions that demands to be answered, but which cannot be, which we answer anyway and then either suffer or get rewarded for, even though it was nothing more than a coin toss. There is no way to know, Thomas. You know that."

"But I have to make a decision nonetheless."

"The price you pay for getting to ride around on the Blockbuster."

Eastwood walked to the window and looked out at the peaceful garden beyond the colonnaded balcony. Less than a minute later he turned back to his NSA.

"You decided?" Kropotkin asked.

"Yeah." Eastwood walked back to the desk and dropped onto his chair. "Get me Eddie Caminetti."

CHAPTER 2

The place looked like a miniature Grand Canyon into which an ocean's worth of green paint had been poured, running down ravines and side canyons and pooling here and there into rolling fairways and flat greens. It was one of the most stunning golf courses in the world, but all of that meant nothing to the CEO of a very large corporation who was standing over his putt on the sixteenth green and sweating because of more than just the desert heat. He was down by one with three holes to go and if he didn't make this birdie he was one hole closer to losing a significant chunk of the yacht he'd had his heart set on.

He exhaled slowly and tried to focus, blocking out all external stimuli except for the soft *whurf-whurf-whurf* coming from somewhere in the direction of the clubhouse. He tried to block that too but the sound was not only out of place in this wild, raw landscape, it was also getting louder. Reluctantly, he backed off the putt, stood up and turned toward the clubhouse.

A spec was visible in the distant sky and quickly grew larger as the massive helicopter approached. Players elsewhere on the course looked up, and then prepared to forget about it until it turned sideways to circle the course and they read UNITED STATES OF AMERICA painted in crisp white letters along its side, just below larger letters reading GAP JEANS in fluorescent red and blue.

The CEO's friend and playing partner, who was also the chairman of the board of the CEO's company, pointed to the seal painted on the door of the chopper. "Hey, look at that," he said.

"I'll be goddamned," the CEO responded.

"Fuck me, not again," Eddie Caminetti muttered as he turned away.

The helicopter finished its circling maneuver and hesitated slightly before angling in toward the sixteenth green and beginning a slow descent. Players in the vicinity grabbed their hats as the downdraft from the giant blades threatened to tear the grass right off the ground, and then turned away when sand from the natural desert terrain got swooped up in the building typhoon and was shot sideways at high speed.

The pilot skillfully set the machine down less than fifty yards from the green and feathered the blades, reducing the blast somewhat but not the noise. No sooner had the wheels touched down than a small stairwell dropped from the door and a uniformed Marine officer hopped out and strode toward the foursome. Behind him, two armed corporals emerged and took up station at the bottom of the stairs.

The Marine officer's steely eyes scanned the group of golfers and settled on Eddie, who was lightly resting his folded hands on top of his putter. The Marine saluted smartly and said, loudly, above the roar of the engines behind him, "Mr. Caminetti?"

Eddie didn't return the salute, nor did he move in any other way, and he didn't raise his voice to be heard. "Who wants to know?"

The officer finished his salute but didn't seem to otherwise notice the impertinence. "Like you to come with me, sir."

"Why . . . am I under arrest?"

Now the officer faltered slightly. "Are you—no, sir, you're not under arrest."

"So what, then?"

The officer was seriously nonplussed. It had never occurred to him that there would be anything short of full, unquestioning cooperation if you set the goddamned presidential helicopter down in the middle of a goddamned golf course, pranced out of it in full military splendor, threw a thoroughly professional salute and requested of a citizen that he accompany you. Who in the hell wouldn't jump at the chance for a ride in goddamned Marine One, for chrissakes! "The president requests your presence in Washington, Mr. Caminetti. He—you are Edward Caminetti, aren't you?"

"That's me, alright. Request denied."

"What the—*request denied*?"

"Yeah. I'm in the middle of a round here. Got a lot of money riding on this one."

The CEO had recovered enough by now to think maybe Eddie was pushing this just a little too far. "Jeez, Eddie. Maybe you oughta—"

"You forfeiting the round, Harold?"

"What?"

Eddie turned toward him. "You giving up?"

But business was business. "Hell, no. You leave, you lose."

"What I figured." Eddie turned back to the Marine. "Got two more holes after this one, son, and then I'll go with you."

"Sir, I don't think you under—"

Eddie pointed over the officer's shoulder toward the chopper. "And get that damned thing outta here. How's a man supposed to putt, all that noise whacking him in the head?" He twisted on a heel and walked away, leaving the Marine standing at attention with no idea whatsoever what to do.

"You'll come with me after the round's over?" the soldier yelled out above the din.

Eddie stopped and turned. "You got beer on board?"

"Fully stocked bar, sir."

Eddie nodded and continued walking away. "Okay, then."

The foursome waited until the helicopter lifted off and rose gracefully away, and didn't comment on the fact that the officer had remained behind. "Mind if I stick around?"

"Suit yourself." Eddie motioned for the CEO to putt, watched him miss his birdie, then sank his own for par.

The CEO, now in real trouble and miserable, jammed his putter into his bag and said to the Marine, "No room in the carts."

"No problem, sir. I'll walk along."

Eddie stored his own putter, then indicated to his partner that he'd walk to the next hole, too.

The Marine removed his cap and ran a hand through his hair, grimacing up at the fierce sun as he and Eddie walked down a steep concrete path. "Heard you were a curmudgeonly prick, Caminetti, but didn't think it was true."

"Well, now you know different."

"What've you got on this game?"

"Low six figures. I'm up two and one."

The officer replaced his cap. "This guy any good?"

"Better'n I thought. So what's your Commander in Chief want with me?"

"Damned if I know." The officer looked around, apparently noticing the spectacular golf course for the first time. "Man, this is one awesome track." He looked at his watch and seemed to be doing a mental calculation.

"They rent clubs," Eddie said. "Good ones. I'll treat you."

The helicopter was slowly circling the golf course. The officer reached for a microphone on his collar, pulled it close to his mouth and said something into it too softly for Eddie to hear. An answering crackle of static came back, then the Marine spoke once more, sharply, and let the mike snap back into place. A few seconds later the helicopter slewed around until it was facing away from them and began receding into the distance.

"You up for another eighteen?"

Eddie shrugged, then tried to size up the Marine from the corner of one eye as they walked. He scratched the bottom of his chin with his thumb.

"For how much?"

CHAPTER 3

GATES OFFICE—G.E. PRESIDENTIAL RESIDENCE

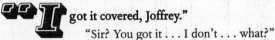I got it covered, Joffrey."

"Sir? You got it . . . I don't . . . what?"

"I'm handling it."

"But . . ." CIA officer Joffrey Hayne put a hand to his head and rubbed his brow. "Sir, how could you possibly —" He was interrupted by a knock at the door, which snapped him out of his momentary disorientation. *Nobody* interrupted the President's Daily Briefing. Not ever. Something terrible, something *awful* must have—

"Sorry to disturb you, Mr. President, but Mr. Cami—"

"Ah, yes!" Eastwood jumped to his feet. "Tell him I'll be right with him."

"But sir . . . !" Hayne protested.

"I think we're done here. Don't you, Anatoli?"

"Quite done," the NSA responded.

As Eastwood came around the desk, Hayne reached clumsily for his briefing book, dropping several papers as he knocked it off the chair. "I really . . . we have to . . ."

"Here you go," the president said as he stooped to help the senior intelligence analyst retrieve the errant sheets.

"But—"

"Hey, don't worry. Let's do this again tomorrow, okay?"

The joke was wasted on Hayne, who began stepping backward, clutching sheets of paper to his chest even as Kropotkin put an arm across his shoulders and helped usher him on his way.

"Jez Rama'am . . ." Hayne said to Kropotkin. "The sultan . . . this is heating up, don't you see?"

"I'm sure it will be fine, son."

"He's been avoiding it for days!" Hayne squeezed out between clenched teeth. "I'm telling you—"

"Stating or averring, Joffrey? Ah, I'm just kidding."

By then Kropotkin had him in the secretary's anteroom, where Hayne was able to see the source of the unprecedented disruption, a quite ordinary-looking man about whom there was something quite out of the ordinary. Hayne wouldn't put his finger on it until he was already on his way off the G.E. Residence grounds, which was when it hit him: Whoever he was—and he couldn't be a somebody because Hayne didn't know who he has—the nondescript guy was the only human being he'd ever seen waiting outside the Gates Office who was completely relaxed and at ease.

"You look like shit," said Eddie Caminetti, which in and of itself wasn't a noteworthy remark, unless you consider whom he'd said it to.

"I'll remind you that I'm the president," Eastwood said.

"Sorry. You look like shit, Mr. President."

"That's better. A little goddamned respect around here."

"So what'sa matter?"

"What's the matter?" Eastwood stood up and ran a hand through his thinning hair as he began pacing around the Gates Office. "I'll tell you what's the matter."

Eddie waited without saying anything until Eastwood turned and faced him, his hands now on his hips.

"What's the matter is that in the next two weeks I have to decide whether to commit eight hundred million bucks' worth of civil engineers, machinery and materials to build a full-scale commercial shipping facility in Jez Rama'am in exchange for Sultan al Ahmadi's promise to let us build an air base there three years from now."

Eddie waited to see if anything else was forthcoming, which wasn't. "I know al Ahmadi. Met him a few months ago." Which, of course, the president would already know. "Is it a good deal?"

"Hell, yes, it's a good deal! Pentagon's been trying to get this done since the Carter administration."

"So what's the problem?"

"The problem," Eastwood replied, walking slowly around his massive desk, "is that we can't put anything in writing. We have to build the port first, then wait three years, at which point the sultan will invite us to establish the air base."

Eddie nodded. "Can't look like the port was part of the deal."

"Right. Otherwise, it looks to the rest of the Arab world like the sultan sold out to infidels."

"It'll look like that anyway. Because he did."

Eastwood shook his head and stared out the bay window overlooking the Miracle-Gro Rose Garden. "We'll create some kind of pretext, invent some threat to Jez Rama'am. Make it look like we're doing al Ahmadi a favor."

"Clever. So now what's the problem? Mind if I smoke?"

"Very funny." Eastwood turned around, his face grim. "What if he doesn't hold up his end? What if he changes his mind or gets cold feet? With nothing in writing . . ." Eastwood lifted a hand and let it drop to his side.

"So what you're telling me, you don't know if you can trust the guy."

"Exactly."

"Well . . ." Eddie thought it over for a second. "If he stiffs you, just nuke the capital."

"Thought of that. In fact, I'm thinking of doing it tomorrow."

Eddie lifted a pack of cigarettes out of his jacket pocket and waved it toward the balcony. Eastwood nodded and motioned him to the french door, but as Eddie rose an aide entered from the secretary's anteroom.

"Mr. President, the undersecretary from Agriculture has been waiting for ten minutes, and he—"

"And he what?"

"Sir?"

"And he what? Has he got something more important to do?"

"Well, I don't—"

"I'm in the middle of something here, son."

"I understand, sir. Should I tell him—"

"I don't give a rat's ass what you tell him."

"Yes, sir. Thank you, Mr. President."

The kid scooted out like he'd been on death row and had just gotten a reprieve.

"Still can't figure out why they always say that," Eastwood muttered. "Thank me for what . . . busting his balls?"

"For letting him bask in the presence." Eddie walked to the door and held it open, then followed the president onto the balcony. Once there, he shook out two cigarettes. Eastwood took one and waited as Eddie lit it for him, then blew out a thick blue cloud.

"What about all those guys in the CIA?" Eddie asked as he lit his own. "The NSA, too. Don't they have reams of shit on all these guys?"

"Oh, yeah. Whole office, called Leadership Analysis." Eastwood inhaled again, then leaned against a white pillar. "I can tell you what al Ahmadi had for breakfast this morning, how much he lost in Monte Carlo last month . . . Hell, I can tell you his daughter's grades in home economics. What I can't tell you—what nobody in this entire god-damned bureaucracy can tell me—is whether I can trust him to keep his word."

"Is that all?"

"Is that all?" Eastwood looked at him, incredulous. "What are you, fucking kidding me, Caminetti? The stability of the entire region might depend on this deal!"

"Pretty important, huh?"

"Chrissakes . . ."

"And you're asking me because . . . ?"

Eastwood turned to Eddie and drilled him with his eyes. "Because, Eddie, you know how to read people better'n anybody I ever met, all those spook fucks in the CIA included."

"What about that poster boy from Covert Ops? Whatshisname, I read about him . . . something to do with that rebel in South America."

"Hayne, yeah. Good man. One of Dalton Galsworthy's boys and thinks just like him, too. Galsworthy was the best ever, but he's taken early retirement."

"How come?"

"Found himself starting to think like Hayne."

What Eastwood couldn't tell Eddie was that, some years before, Hayne had put into place a brilliant counterintelligence strategy after a Soviet mole had been discovered in the rarefied upper echelons of the

CIA. Hayne suggested promoting the man and then providing him a constant stream of disinformation to feed back to his Russian control. It had so excited intelligence higher-ups that they'd neglected to put in place the standard kinds of checks and balances to ensure that all was going according to plan, deeming it too burdensome, too expensive and wholly unnecessary. The lone dissenter had been Dalton Galsworthy.

Everything seemed to be going beautifully, despite a series of spectacular intelligence failures whose sources nobody could trace, until Galsworthy, using the sorts of unofficial back channels every good officer set up as a safety net, discovered that the mole had fallen head over heels in love with the Grateful Dead, Ray's Pizza, the poker pit at the Agua Caliente Indian casino in Palm Springs, an Eighth Avenue hooker named Chesty Moran and democracy, in precisely that order. His devotion to all things American was so passionate that—without telling anybody, because who was he going to tell?—he turned and became a double agent, determined to do everything in his power to safeguard the interests of the United States and undermine those of the Soviet Union. He decided that his most effective course of action was to feed his handlers as much disinformation as possible. Of course, blinkered as he was to the true nature of his position in the CIA, he had no way to know that the data he was altering and passing on to his Soviet controllers had already been altered by the CIA before being given to *him*. In effect, what he ended up giving to the KGB was a tidal wave of information that all too often contained accurate intelligence other officers were routinely risking their lives to protect.

By the time Galsworthy's analysis of the situation was complete, the damage estimate was staggering. Among other things, the monumental backfire had delayed by nearly two years the reunification of East and West Berlin. Hayne couldn't be blamed, really, because his plan had passed muster throughout the Company and been approved at every level, but he was taken out of Covert Ops and parked safely in the Office of Current Production and Analytic Support. His state of mind was not helped when the former Soviet mole, Anatoli Kropotkin, became the president's national security advisor.

"Look, Eddie, I can't use any of those guys because al Ahmadi knows all the good ones. But he won't suspect *you're* up to anything except a golf hustle. So I'm asking you—" Eastwood dropped his cigarette, crushed it out with the toe of his shoe and leaned in closer. "Will you go play some golf with this sonofabitch and find out if I can trust him or not?"

Unintimidated, Eddie said, "You think I can find out?"

"I know you can."

"What makes you so sure?"

"You once told me you can learn more about a guy in a single round of golf than you can living next door to him for six months. "

"And this is important, right?"

"Eddie . . ."

"Alright, then." Eddie crossed his arms, then raised a hand and rubbed the bottom of his chin with his thumb. "For how much?"

Eastwood blinked and straightened up. "What?"

"For how much?"

"What do you mean, for how much?"

"I mean, how much will you pay me to tell you if you can trust al Ahmadi?"

"You're kidding me, right? Tell me you're just jerking my chain."

Eddie shrugged. "You just told me that it's critically important and that I'm the only guy in the world who can tell you. So I'm asking you, what's it worth?"

Eastwood's eyes narrowed slightly. "This is your country we're talking about here, fella."

"No kidding. But that's no reason I should do it for free."

"Aren't you a patriot?"

"Hell, yes. Aren't you?"

"You're damned right I am!"

"Well, aren't you getting paid?"

"That's different!"

"The hell it is."

"Now look here . . . !"

"See you on the links, Mr. President." Eddie turned and began walking back toward the Gates Office.

Eastwood, his jaw literally hanging open, was speechless, but only for a second. "Goddamnit, Caminetti! You can't walk out on me!"

Eddie disappeared through the door.

Eastwood blew through it a second later. "Okay! What the hell do you want?"

Eddie stopped and turned, looked at the ceiling, then back down at the president. "A hundred grand."

"You're nuts."

"Maybe, but it's irrelevant. You want to know if you can trust the sultan, it'll cost you a hundred grand."

"Fifty," Eastwood shot back.

"A hundred."

"Seventy-five!"

"A hundred."

"Dammit, what kind of negotiation is this!"

Eddie cocked his head slightly. "What gave you the idea I was negotiating? My fee's a hundred large. Take it or leave it."

Eastwood fumed for a few seconds, then hissed, "I suppose you want expenses, too."

"Won't be necessary."

The president pretended he was thinking it over, even though both of them knew he had no choice. "Agreed," he said through clenched teeth. He walked behind his desk and sat down. "So? When will I have an answer?"

"Right now."

"What?"

"Right now. I already know."

"And . . . ?"

"Yes, you can trust him." Eddie turned and began walking toward the door the shaken aide had recently shriveled through. "So long."

Eastwood jumped to his feet. "Hold on a goddamn second!"

Eddie inhaled deeply and let it out noisily. "Now what?"

"That's it? *Yes?* That's what I get for my hundred grand?"

"That's it. I told you; I already met the guy. I'll tell your secretary where to send my check." Eddie put his hand on the doorknob and twisted it.

"You're saying I can trust him."

"Yep."

"You sure?"

"Absolutely. Hunnerd percent, no doubt about it. Now——" Eddie jiggled the doorknob. "Can I go?"

Eastwood eyed him slyly. "What if you're wrong?"

"Huh?"

"What if you're wrong! What if the sultan goes back on his word?"

Eddie pursed his lips and shrugged. "I'll give you back your dough."

He pulled open the door, walked through and turned one last time before closing it behind him.

"Thank you, Mr. President."

SIX MONTHS EARLIER

It wasn't like Eddie Caminetti to sweat, but it had nothing to do with the heat of the deep Rama'amian desert, nor with the unusually high humidity that resulted from the moisture coming off the deliriously lush golf course upon whose eighteenth green he was now standing.

It had to do with the fact that he had a $150,000 bet going with Sultan Aliwa al Ahmadi who, although now in an ugly sand trap, was nevertheless up by one going into the last hole. And, like many of his desert-domiciled Arab brethren, al Ahmadi was very, very good in sand traps.

The bunker was so deep Eddie couldn't even see the sultan, but he saw the two other members of the foursome and all four caddies watching and knew from their eyes when al Ahmadi had swung, then he saw a golf ball float up over the lip of the high trap, settle gently onto the green and roll within six feet of the cup. Eddie eyed his own ball some twenty feet away and realized that, even if he sank it and al Ahmadi two-putted, the sultan would win. Eddie walked to his newly irrelevant ball and leaned down to pick it up.

"Fuck!" came a guttural utterance from the vicinity of the bunker. Al Ahmadi, grim-faced and eyes blazing, came tearing onto the green.

"Hell's a matter with you?" Eddie said. "That was a terrific shot!"

Al Ahmadi pointed to Eddie's ball. "Putt it!" he commanded.

"Putt it?" Eddie stopped in mid-bend. "Jeez Louise, Aliwa: Even if I sink the thing, all you have to do is two-putt to win."

"I said, putt it!"

Confused, Eddie straightened up and put his hands on his hips. "I'm giving you the goddamned putt. What do you want to do, drag out the agony? All's I want right now is a cold beer."

"By the beard of the Prophet . . . will you just putt the goddamned ball, Eddie? And we don't drink beer here, remember?"

"Yeah, right. Okay, keep your turban on."

Eddie took in the slope of the green and the grain of the grass, then got into position, held still for a second and gently tapped the ball toward the hole. It looked at first like it wouldn't even get halfway there, but Eddie had accurately gauged the slight downhill grade and the speed of the grass that had been drying for hours. The ball eventually slowed, approached the lip of the cup, hung there for a second . . . and dropped.

"Fuck!" al Ahmadi repeated, with even greater venom.

Then he missed his putt.

As al Ahmadi tapped in, Eddie held his arms out to his sides. "You happy now, your highness? Can I get that freakin' beer you don't have eight hundred cases of in your cellar?"

"Not yet. We have to play it off." Al Ahmadi pointed to the bunker. "I double-hit in there."

Eddie stared after him as the sultan threw his putter to his caddy and walked off the green in disgust. What he'd meant was that, owing to the slow speed of the ball coming off the sand and the high speed of his swing, the club head had caught up with the ball after it had been struck and touched it a second time, which counted as another stroke. His two-putt had then put the match dead even.

Al Ahmadi was the only one who had known about the double-hit, his hands having sensed the second impact even though there was hardly any sound. Had he not said anything, nobody would have suspected, including Eddie, and that would have been the end of the match and an uncontested victory for the sultan.

Instead, he and Eddie had to play sudden death, continuing on until one of them won a hole and thereby the entire match, which Eddie did on the very next hole. A few minutes later he had a check for $150,000 in his pocket and six months after that the hundred grand the U.S. government would pay him for confirming al Ahmadi's near-pathological honesty. President Eastwood was an honest man, too, at least when it came to paying off his obligations using the government's money.

CHAPTER 4

QUAKER OATS CRISIS CENTER
(FORMERLY THE WHITE HOUSE SITUATION ROOM)

It's getting serious."

President Eastwood look inquiringly at his director of Central Intelligence. "What was it before?"

"Before," DCI Baines Gordon Wainwright replied, "it was just another wannabe Che Guevara pulling fraternity pranks in shitholes I can't even pronounce."

"And now?"

Wainwright hitched up his shoulders and folded his hands together. "Now, the frat house has some serious ordnance and, even worse—"

"A following," Secretary of State William Patterson answered. "People who think he's another Bolivar."

Eastwood nodded his understanding. "Think we should do something?"

"Problem is," Patterson said, "that might be just what he wants us to do. To get his ticket punched."

Eastwood knew what State meant: A reaction of any kind from the U.S. government meant instant certification and credibility. It was the first step toward the *sine qua non* of external validation, coverage by the GNN news network. But while an American response wasn't that difficult to achieve, commentary by a GNN superstar required much more effort, usually in the form of gruesome atrocities against large groups of (white) people, a threat to the supply of oil or the possibility of terrorist attacks. White people being in even shorter supply in South America than oil, that left terrorism, but South Americans didn't have much of a beef against their northern neighbors, so it wasn't immediately clear why the U.S. should be interested at all.

"Why should we be interested at all?" Eastwood asked the room.

"Because he's operating cross-border," Wainwright responded.

"Something we haven't seen since Al Qaeda."

"Cross-border? How many countries is this guy in?"

"Three, so far: Brazil, Colombia and Peru."

"And there's noise he might be in Costa Rica and Guatemala, too."

Eastwood whipped his head around to face Defense Secretary Harold Fortesque. "Wait a minute: You telling me the guy is all the way up in Central America?"

Fortesque held up his hands, palms outward. "Just a rumor so far."

Eastwood picked at his lower lip for a few seconds, then said, "Let me see that list of all those regions he's gone after." When it was handed over, Eastwood reached inside his jacket, pretended to scratch his chest and pressed a button on a small pager in his pocket.

A few seconds later a uniformed Marine entered the Crisis Center. "Begging your pardon, sir . . ." he said, then handed the president a note.

Eastwood read it to himself. It said, "India and Pakistan have gone to nuclear war, someone has blown up the Grand Coulee Dam and your grilled cheese is getting cold."

"Damn," he said quietly, then stood up. "Gentlemen, I need a moment."

The others rose as Eastwood turned and followed the uniform out the door. Just outside the Gates Office he said "Thanks" to his secretary, then, "Get Galsworthy on the phone." The retired CIA officer was on the line by the time he got to his desk.

"Dalton, whaddaya say, whaddaya know?" Eastwood said cheerily as he picked up the phone.

"I'm an intelligence man," Galsworthy answered. "I don't know anything. And even if I did, it's not important, but I won't tell you anyway. What's up?"

"Western civilization is in deep trouble."

"Well then, thank God you called me."

"Got a riddle for you. What do the following places have in common? You ready?"

"Shoot."

"Okay. Popayan, Cuzco, Narino, Magdelena, Espirito Santo—by the way, this is in no order except by what's easiest to pronounce—

Chanchamaya, Medellin, Rondonia— and don't say drugs because I already—"

"Coffee."

"What? Coffee what?"

"Those are places they grow coffee."

Eastwood dropped the sheet of paper and frowned at the phone. "Coffee?"

"Yep. Why? What's going on?"

Eastwood didn't hesitate before letting his old friend in on the situation. "You ever hear of a guy down in South America named Barranca?"

"Manuel Barranca? Sure. Actually knew him a little. Nice guy."

Eastwood smacked his forehead lightly. Should have realized . . . "Harvard. You know him from Harvard."

"Right. Cuban Guy. He was in the MBA program. Serious fellow, tops in his class, but friendly. Except at poker. At poker, he was a great white and Bruce Lee rolled into one. Lost track of him some time ago, and . . . hey, wait a minute: Did you say South America?"

Even over the phone Eastwood could hear the gears in Galsworthy's head turning, and he gave the legendary spook his time.

"Whoa," Galsworthy breathed. "Whoa, whoa, whoa! Jesus Christ!"

Eastwood grimaced and bent forward slightly as something ugly gripped his belly. He'd known Galsworthy for thirty years and had never seen him react to even the worst of situations with anything more than, "Well, my goodness, I suppose we should address that, eh?" So what the hell could be going through the man's mind?

His secretary stepped through the doorway and held a cup in the air, rocking it back and forth as she mouthed, "Coffee?" at her boss.

TWO WEEKS LATER

Wayne Chemincouver, five feet ten of outwardly directed self-loathing exacerbated by the newly identified caffeine-deprivation unremitting psychosis syndrome (CUPS), let the door of the Starbucks swing closed behind him, narrowly missing the elderly woman he'd just hurried ahead of in the parking lot. "Sorry," he muttered, not to her but to the people standing in a snaky line so long it nearly reached the door. "Din't see you."

He sauntered up to a stand holding a stack of newspapers and pretended to look at one while he casually inched closer to the line, about twenty people forward from the back. The half dozen employees in the store, already bored to tears even though none of them was more than six weeks into their exciting, challenging careers as part of the dynamic Starbucks family of customer-oriented "partners," seemed more intent on carrying on loud, mindless across-the-room, conversations amongst themselves than on serving the patrons or maintaining an orderly queue.

"So I'm, like, hello?" yelled the cappuccino-machine partner. "And he's all, what? And I'm, like, yeah, whatever, knowmsayin?" She pulled a handle and a loud steaming sound erupted. "Whuwuzzat, low-fat?" she asked a customer, who'd already told her three times she wanted cream.

"Totally," called back the loose-beans-packing partner. "You go, girl."

"Uhh-ight," agreed the pastry partner.

Wayne picked up a paper and tried to hold it as steady as his badly shaking hands would allow. He opened to a random page and fumbled with the fluttering sheets, angling closer to the line as he seemed to struggle to organize the paper.

"Whuwuzzat again, half-and-half?"

Just as Wayne was nearly home free, a voice called out from behind him, "Hey, buddy . . . you waiting for coffee?"

Wayne, now facing forward, pretended not to hear.

"Yo! Hey!"

"Excuse me . . . !" said the woman he'd just cut in front of.

"Huh?" Wayne looked around, as if to ascertain where the voice was coming from, and could it possibly be directed at him?

"I said, excuse me. I've been waiting on this—"

She was interrupted by the looming presence of a man the size of one of the larger models of SUV who'd just come forward from the back of the line. "I said, are you waiting for coffee?"

Wayne, offering a look of innocent surprise, glanced around, blinking in apparent confusion. "Wh—huh? Me? Oh, hell no!" He held up the newspaper, grinned and stepped back. "Just readin the paper. Musta forgot where I—nope, just readin." He turned to the lady behind him. "Sorry. Din't meana cut you—"

He noticed the distinctly unfriendly stares boring in on him, and his voice grew petulant. "Hey, excuse the shit outta me, okay? Big fuckin deal. I mean, shit . . ."

He walked to the back of the line, his posture daring anybody to stare at him as he did so. Two big guys did, and Wayne stared back at them, his head bobbing like a gamecock's spoiling for a fight, but without stopping to push the point. Despite his obvious cowardice, a goodly majority of his nerves were crackling and buzzing like high-tension power lines, making it unclear to onlookers whether he might just snap anyway, if sufficiently provoked by a real or imagined slight.

Once ensconced in his rightful place in line, Wayne watched the activity at the counter with all the patience of a speed-freak humming-bird, huffing and rolling his eyes if any customer dared ask a question or took more than three seconds to specify exactly how she wanted her coffee. "Oh, f'chrissakes, lady! Yer buyin coffee, not a goddamn car!"

Half an hour later he reached the counter. The counter partner was looking toward the cappuccino machine. "And I'm like, gimme a break, knowmsayin? Give. Me. A. Freakin. Break!"

"Totally," the cappuccino partner answered.

"You mind?" Wayne said, earning him a tight-lipped, vauntingly contemptuous sneer.

"May I help you?" the sneer snarled.

"Coffee."

"What kind?" The unsuspecting counter partner had no idea that it was Wayne's first visit to a Starbucks, the AM/PM mini-mart—and just about every other place in town he was used to—being completely out of coffee.

"What kind? A cuppa coffee! Whaddaya mean, what kind?"

"You want the coffee of the day?"

"Yeah, sure. What's the coffee of the day?"

The counter partner, professing enormous reserves of patience for dealing with idiots, inhaled deeply and exhaled loudly. "Brazil Ipanema

Bourbon with Serena Organic and Conservation Colombia."

Wayne stared at her for a second. "Yer shittin me, right?"

"You want it or not?"

"What's it taste like?"

"Folgers."

"Okay, gimme a cup."

"What size?"

"Large."

"We don't have large."

"What the hell do you mean, you don't—okay, what sizes you got?"

The counter partner gritted her teeth, having been through this some five hundred times in her exciting, challenging career as part of the dynamic Starbucks family of customer-oriented partners. "The smallest is tall."

"The smallest size you got is *tall*?"

"Hey, you wanna hurry it up there, pal?" somebody called out from the line.

"Hold your damned horses," Wayne shot back. "Waited half a god-damned hour."

"Coulda read the sign while you were waitin," someone else pointed out.

"Yeah, right, the sign. And what am I supposed to make outta *tall*, asshole?"

The counter partner held up a cup and jiggled it. Wayne pointed to a larger cup. "What's that?"

"Grandé."

"Okay, grandé, okay. So that's the big one."

"No, that's the middle one."

"So what's the big one?"

She said something that sounded vaguely Italian but which made no sense in English. Or Italian either, for that matter.

Wayne shrugged.

"You want it?" the counter partner insisted, refusing to move until Wayne gave his assent, however grudgingly.

"That the biggest?"

"Yeah, it's the biggest."

"Gimme two."

As she poured the coffees she looked at the pastry partner, then at the ceiling and shook her head. Wayne watched as she slapped the cups down in front of him, sloshed coffee coating the top and sides of the plastic caps.

"Anything else?"

"No." Wayne opened his wallet and pulled out three one-dollar bills. "How much?"

"Sixteen-fifty," the counter partner replied. "Plus tax."

The paramedics arrived about ten minutes later, the police some ten minutes after that, the national guard about an hour later. It was the scene of the first—and second and third—fatalities directly attributable to the crisis.

When Osama bin Laden launched the 9/11 attacks, Americans had a week-long group hug, then decided to get revenge by buying more Chevies ("Let's get America rolling again"), then pretty much forgot about him altogether and went after someone more catchable instead.

When India and Pakistan resumed live-fire testing of nuclear weapons, it was page twelve news and the administration punished the two rogue nations by eliminating *samoʐas* from a State Department lunch for the Bangladeshi Minister of Agriculture.

When a quarter million Yugoslavian Muslims were slaughtered in the most horrific wave of ethnic cleansing since the Holocaust, a minute of silence was observed in a preseason exhibition basketball game between the Sacramento Kings and the Los Angeles Lakers. The Cleveland Cavaliers and the Charlotte Hornets did the same for half a million dead Rwandans.

It was only when Americans found out that their coffee supply was threatened that all hell broke loose.

The first major consequence was a downgrade in Moody's rating of City of Seattle muni bonds, which led nine days later to the complete collapse of that city's economy. Frenzied hoarding of existing coffee supplies resulted in nationwide riots as citizens bridled first at grocery store owners trying to limit purchases to individual customers, then at each other for trying to buy more than their fair share, and quickly spread to include the hijacking of delivery trucks and raids on retail distribution centers. The fourth through seventh riot-related deaths occurred in McMinnville, Oregon, where one Wayne Chemincouver, already badly injured in a previous altercation, was beaten to death by a mob as he tried to fill a five-gallon Coleman cooler with coffee from the self-serve counter at a Dorky Don's Minimart. It was followed by a rash of similarly spontaneous melees after a jury in an Oregon circuit court acquitted all twenty-two of Chemincouver's alleged murderers based on their attorney's successful crafting of a "caffeine defense."

The Eastwood administration's first attempt to quell the disturbances took the form of public pleas for calm. This tactic was doomed to inevitable failure given its target audience, making it roughly akin to asking a strung-out heroin addict to please be patient for a few days while they hunted up some aspirin for him. The FAA took the extraordinary measure of banning all domestic flights prior to 11:00 AM each day after passengers on a Southwest Airlines early-morning flight from Oakland to Portland, upon noticing a flight attendant carrying two cups of java into the cockpit of the fully-loaded 757 just before take-off, stormed the door and caused over $200,000 in damage when the steamy joe spilled onto the control panel of the plane's digital flight controls. (In the subsequent indictment proceedings, the presiding judge was unpersuaded by a front-page photo from the *Oregonian* that showed one of the passengers trying to rectify the damage by licking the coffee off the still-glowing red and green indicator lights.)

In the greater scheme of things, though, at least in the minds of the Republican-controlled congress, the rioting and mayhem were inconsequential in comparison to the impact on the corporate bottom line. Following an impassioned floor speech by Senator Elmore Scruggins (R-Kentucky) in which he described the nearly overnight transformation of the beginning of the business day as "nothin more'n two hours'a unproductive ball-scratchin," both houses voted overwhelmingly to extend the official working day to ten hours, with two mandated apple juice breaks and the hours of 8–10 AM to be supervised by armed guards recruited from the ranks of purportedly non–coffee-drinking Mormon and Muslim federal workers. State governments and private corporations were strongly urged to follow suit, although the Mormon/Muslim angle quickly faded after a hijacked Maxwell House delivery truck, hastily repainted, was tracked by a reporter to an LDS cathedral in Provo after it had unloaded half its cargo at a Shiite mosque in Evanston, Wyoming. By the time the reporter found the completely empty vehicle in a ditch off the nearby interstate, another hijacked truck, this one carrying Maxwell House, was spotted leaving the parking lot of a church in Armuchee, Georgia, with "Big Bill's Radiator Repair" handwritten on its side.

There were also consequences of a deeper, more profound cultural nature. As the price of coffee from Jamaica and Kenya rose to over $200 a pound on the black market, class distinctions began to reassert themselves with a vengeance, as only the very well-off could afford to indulge. "We have coffee!" began appearing in ads for the most exclusive hotels and cruise ships. Employee "perks" became the pun-of-the-day as preferred parking spaces and corner offices gave way to company-sponsored coffee as a premium benefit. Hotel prices in Hawai'i tripled when that state's governor Leilani Ohana declared a state of emergency and, under the special powers granted her in times of civil stress, decreed that no coffee grown on the high slopes of Kona could leave the state. Within two weeks the Big Island's airport became the nation's fifth busiest, despite its only having a single runway, one (outdoor) baggage claim area, four skycaps and two bathrooms.

It was when Jamaica and Kenya demanded—and got—seats on the U.N. Security Council that Thomas Eastwood decided maybe it was time to do something.

CHAPTER 5

What President Eastwood wanted most at this moment— more than world peace or re-election or the immediate death of his Secretary of the Interior—was fifteen minutes alone in the bathroom to finally rid himself of the Swedish meatballs lovingly prepared for him by his twelve-year-old daughter as part of her first homework assignment in seventh-grade Home Economics, an antiquated, retro-sexist course much beloved by the fabulously rich swells who'd been sending their daughters to the William Penn School for Young Women since before the Earth had fully cooled.

But fifteen uninterrupted minutes with the *New York Times* crossword puzzle in the only room of the West Wing in which he could truly be by himself was not to be.

"We're talking about a potentially dangerous destabilization of an extremely volatile region of the world, Mr. President," the Secretary of the Interior proclaimed imperiously.

President Eastwood turned to him incredulously. "Well, no shit," he said. "After two goddamned hours *that's* your penetrating political insight? Telling me what we all already know? Why the hell do you think we were all here at five in the goddamned morning! And why in God's name is the country's goddamned chief tree watcher even in a meeting like this in the first place!"

At least that's what he would like to have said. What he said instead was, "Good point," as he nodded thoughtfully, pretending to absorb the Secretary's profound wisdom.

"Stating the blindingly obvious hardly constitutes a good point," the characteristically blunt Secretary of Defense Harold Fortesque opined. "You actually got any *suggestions*, Mr. Secretary?"

"He was just level-setting," Housing and Urban Development threw in. "Providing a contextual framework within which to effectuate decision making."

The defense secretary leaned in toward the president and whispered, "She's still getting in touch with her inner bitch, Tom. Can we clear the room and move on here?"

"What was that?" HUD demanded.

"State secret," Fortesque responded. "Eyes only, hush-hush, need to know . . . that sort of thing."

"I'm a member of the president's cabinet, Mr. Secretary, and I have a right to—"

"Okay, okay," Eastwood said, pumping a palm toward the massive conference table. "Let's everybody settle down here."

CIA director Baines Gordon Wainwright, after getting a look of pure pleading from Fortesque, jumped in. "Mr. President, I've got some Alpha-51 clearance material here . . ." He let his voice trail off.

"Alpha-51?" Fortesque breathed. "Damn."

The president furrowed his brow meaningfully and heaved an apologetic sigh. "Well, then, I'm afraid everybody without Alpha-51 clearance will need to leave the room. We'll be back to you all later."

"What's Alpha-51?" HUD asked Interior as they shuffled out of the Cabinet room.

"Are you serious?" Interior arched his eyebrows in surprise, pointedly underscoring how out of the loop HUD was. "High as it gets."

"Wow."

Soon only State, Defense, the CIA director and the president remained. "Alpha-51?" Eastwood asked.

Wainwright shrugged. "Best I could do at a moment's notice. Thought it sounded pretty heavy."

"Least we got rid of em," Fortesque said. "Will . . ." He turned to Secretary of State William Patterson. "What's the latest from our embassy down there?"

"It's not good." Patterson opened a manila folder and laid it on the table in front of him. "This Barranca character really is threatening the stability of the whole region, and his grass-roots support is growing faster than we can track it. Some rogue military elements are getting restless, and not just in one country, either."

"Military elements?" Fortesque's eyes grew wide, then narrowed. "You telling me the armies are hooking up with this guy?"

"Might be starting to," Patterson replied, fingering some of the documents in the folder. "And while a revolution here and there is usually no big thing, well, a bunch of them at one time, under the control of a single individual?" He sat back, folded his hands across his chest and let the question hang in the air.

"I don't think we can let that happen," Fortesque said. "Another major power in South America? I can tell you in detail how it's going to shape up over the next few years."

"Your psychic abilities hardly give us a rationale for moving troops in, Harold," Patterson chided gently.

"Look, you know as well as I do that—"

"What I know and what we can prove are two—"

"Hold it, guys," Eastwood intervened. "I hope this decision doesn't have to come down to a choice between invading and doing nothing. There've got to be some less dire alternatives." Murmurs of grudging assent were layered with undertones of skepticism.

"What do we know about this guy, this Barranca?" Fortesque asked.

"A great deal," the Secretary of State said as he leafed through several more papers. "Our intel is superb."

"He's ex-military," Wainwright said. "Squad leader in Unit 53, equivalent of our Green Berets."

Patterson found what he'd been looking for. "Also been in the diplomatic secretariats of three different countries with postings in Moscow, London and Saudi Arabia. Master's from Harvard . . ." Patterson looked up. "The man doesn't have anything against the United States, Mr. President. It's strictly a local matter."

"Except that he might have gotten hold of a couple of missiles," Fortesque countered. "Maybe more."

"But he never lifted a finger against this country."

"Neither did Saddam Hussein, and look what we—"

"You were saying, Bill?" Eastwood prompted.

"Huh?"

"What we have on Barranca . . ."

"Oh. Yeah. Well —" Patterson held up a single sheet of paper and repositioned his reading glasses. "Majored in English literature as an undergrad, the usual campus protest involvement, well liked by his classmates, excellent grades . . ."

Eastwood frowned. "So what turned this guy into another Guevara? What's he trying to prove?"

"My opinion?" Patterson said, setting down the sheet of paper. *No, Genghis Khan's.* "Please."

Patterson cleared his throat. "I don't think he's trying to prove anything."

Everybody else waited, but Patterson stayed quiet, waiting to be begged.

"Meaning?" Eastwood said, playing along.

"Meaning, he honestly believes governments in the region are all corrupt, especially Brazil's, and the people are suffering because of it. He thinks it's his calling to do something about it."

Eastwood looked to Wainwright, who nodded his concurrence, then back to the rest of the table. "Shit," he spat forcefully, and everybody understood: There was nothing more dangerous than a revolutionary who truly believed that he was doing God's work. Same went for a president. "What else?"

Patterson consulted his file again. "He's traveled extensively, written essays for some prestigious journals, enjoys classical music, nuts about baseball, donates to the ASPCA, reads *The New Yorker, Science News, Newsweek*—"

"Sounds to me," Eastwood interrupted, "that we really don't know shit."

Patterson gulped, but was at a loss only momentarily. Calling on his vast reserve of experience in diplomacy to cover his butt, he turned to Wainwright. "Has there been any more G-2 since you gave us this information?"

"Well, he's got links to Al Qaeda . . ."

All eyes turned to Wainwright.

"Just kidding," the CIA director said.

"Do we have anything we can actually use?" Eastwood asked

nobody in particular.

"Yeah," Defense said. "We got an army."

"Very funny."

"I'm not kidding. You think the American people are going to object?"

"You want me to go to war over coffee?"

Fortesque shrugged. "At least it's a real issue. Not like anybody's going to demand more evidence."

Eastwood, his bowels in an uproar, surreptitiously pressed a button on his watch. Several seconds later his secretary came in.

"Mr. President . . . ?"

"Huh? Oh, yeah. Damn." Eastwood put both hands on the table and stood up abruptly. "Bill and I are late for a meeting. Why don't you guys stick around and see if you can come up with some kind of strategy."

Wainwright, licking his lips, looked longingly at the secretary. "Could we, um . . ."

"Right away, Mr. Director," she replied, then turned to her assistant. "Have some coffee brought in."

"How much?"

"Half a pot," Eastwood said as he and Patterson brushed quickly past them. "Fifty billion a year in combined budgets and all they can tell me is that the sonofabitch reads *Newsweek*."

Once in the safety of his Chief of Staff's office, Eastwood said, "I don't see where we have a choice, Bill."

"No, sir. Me neither. We've got to respond publicly, give this pain in the ass his day in the sun."

"We've seen what happens when one of these low-life banana-brains gets our attention and ends up on GNN. We've got to keep some kind of control on this, not let it get out of hand."

The Secretary of State understood perfectly. "What we do, we nail it all down before the official response. Guy'll be so berserk waiting for the whole world to know he shook us up, he'll agree to damned near anything. I'll have a couple of the lower-downs on the South American desk handle it. Don't worry."

"That's what I like to hear." Eastwood picked up a phone and punched a button. "Those guys out of my office yet?" he said into the handset.

MAUNA LANI RESORT, KONA COAST, HAWAI'I

Semiretired tournament referee Desmond Grant and fully retired U.S. Golf Association president Edmond "Knuckles" Sternwhistle stared at the television showing the leader board of the Acme Freeze-Dried Chipped Beef Classic. It showed Albert Auberlain tied for fourth place, two shots behind the leader after forty-eight holes of the seventy-two-hole tournament.

"I say," Grant observed, "young Auberlain is doing splendidly, is he not?"

"He is not," Sternwhistle replied. "Most everybody else is playing like shit. Looks to me like Fat Albert's brain is on hold."

As the image gave way to a news update, Grant rose and reached for the remote. "True enough. I fear he is somewhat distracted."

As he aimed the remote and prepared to turn the set off, Sternwhistle raised a hand. "Hold it a second!"

Grant held off. "It's just another update about this troublemaker chap in South America. I doubt there's anything new and—"

Sternwhistle, who'd been lounging on a sofa, sat up. A black-and-white photo was being shown.

"Same photo they've been showing all day, Edmond. Why the sudden—"

But Sternwhistle had jumped up and was grabbing the remote away even as he strode to the cabinet below the television, opened the door and began scrambling around to find a videocassette.

"My word! What on earth—"

"What the hell is this?" Sternwhistle said, holding up a cassette to read the label. "Béla Bartók Memorial Concert in Copenhagen?"

Grant beamed appreciatively. "A most excellent rendition of the String Quartet Number—"

"I'm sure it is," Sternwhistle said as he slammed the cassette into the VCR and hit a button on the remote.

"Oh, dear," Grant moaned plaintively.

"Too late anyway." The photo was no longer being displayed on the television.

As Sternwhistle left through the lanai, Grant jumped to rescue the videocassette before following him out. "I'm sure they'll show it again, Edmond," he called out as he walked. "Do you know the gentleman in question?"

"Not sure," Sternwhistle said.

A few minutes later they were in the office of the head golf professional. One wall consisted of ceiling-to-floor bookcases, and Sternwhistle ran his thumb over some volumes, mumbling to himself until he found what he was looking for. Grant read over his shoulder as Sternwhistle pulled the book off the shelf and laid it on the desk: *Great Golf Photos of the Twentieth Century.*

"Ah," Grant said in mock understanding. "A former touring professional who decided to go into the rebellion business, is that it?"

"No," Sternwhistle replied. "A former caddy."

THIRTY MINUTES LATER

The three Cabinet members stared down at the grainy photograph on the great desk in the Gates Office as President Eastwood and his chief of staff, Conchita Ortega, looked on.

"Holy shit," Secretary of State William Patterson said.

"Holy shit," Defense Secretary Harold Fortesque said.

"It's bullshit," CIA director Baines Gordon Wainwright declared.

"No, it isn't," the president informed him.

"In a pig's eye. Who told you it was authentic?"

"Friend of mine," the president answered.

"Inside the Company?"

"Not exactly. Inside the USGA."

"Huh." Elbowing his two colleagues aside, Wainwright bent down for a closer look.

The photograph had been taken on the green of a golf course, one of apparently tropical location judging by the palm trees in the background. It showed a group of seven men looking on as a golfer putted from about three feet away from the hole. Another man holding a club was also watching, from the other side of the hole. A caddy with a bunch of clubs in his hand stood to the side holding the flag. That a group of seven men was standing on the green while a twosome was putting out was unusual enough, but what made the photograph truly remarkable were the identities of the two golfers, each clad in standard-issue military plus-fours and combat boots.

"Are you telling me," Fortesque said, "that Che Guevara and Fidel Castro played golf together?"

"So it would seem," Eastwood responded.

"Bullshit," Wainwright said.

Eastwood dropped another photo on the desk. It showed Che striking a jaunty solo pose with a golf club. Then another, this one showing the legendary revolutionary with his club still in the air after punching out of some rough surrounding a stand of young trees, watched by a farmer on a tractor.

"This is the important one," the president said as he set down the last photo. It showed Fidel, in glasses with thick black frames, anxiously following his ball after a fairway shot, the future Cuban dictator still poised at the end of a truly ugly follow-through.

"Why's it so important?" Patterson asked.

Eastwood abruptly scooped up the photos and put them into a manila folder. "I'll tell you later. Right now, we need a strategy for moving forward on this."

The CIA director began talking, and the others followed suit within seconds, the voices rising as in a single chorus, the decibel level in inverse proportion to the merit of what was being said. Nobody had any good notion of what ought to be done, so they hid their fears behind displays of bravado, outrage, indignation, empty sagacity and raw bluster. Eastwood didn't hear any of it, until a particularly ominous rumble in his lower intestine brought him back to reality and the cacophony wailing all around him. He said something barely audible.

The caterwauling ended. "Sorry, Mr. President," Patterson said. "What did you say?"

Eastwood folded his arms across his chest, as he always did when he'd come to a decision. "Looks to me like Barranca wins round one."

Wainwright, instantly suspicious, said, "What the hell does that mean? Sir?"

"It means, one way or the other, we have to deal with the guy. Or at least acknowledge his existence."

At which the caterwauling re-reached its prior intensity, everyone trying to outdo everyone else with the passion of his outrage. "Appeasement! Caving! We can't roll over . . . the United States doesn't deal with . . ."

Eastwood waited patiently until breaths demanded to be taken, then said, "What's your suggestion, Harold?"

Fortesque straightened up as he bristled with indignation. "We don't give in! We can't look weak. We don't negotiate with—"

"I didn't ask you what we don't do. I asked you what we do."

"If we acknowledge this guy, if we're seen to—"

"What's the next step?"

"Harold's right, sir," DCI Wainwright said solemnly. "This country cannot—"

"I already got that part, Baines. What I'm asking is, what do you think we ought to do?"

"Sir," Secretary Patterson intoned as professorially as he could, which was a lot, "I think we're agreed that it's imperative we refrain from in any way legitimizing—"

Eastwood held up a hand, silencing Patterson. "Is there anybody else who insists on telling me what I shouldn't do?"

"Mr. President . . ." Patterson folded his arms across his chest. "I'm not completely sure you understand the gravity of this situation."

"Yeah, maybe you're right. Always been kind of a slow study. Pretty clear to you fellas, though, I can see that."

The others nodded sagely. "So what are you going to do, Mr. President?"

"Well, for damned sure, I'm not giving in to this guy."

"Excellent!" Wainwright barked, pounding a fist into his palm.

"That's the spirit!" Fortesque applauded.

"Bullshit," Chief of Staff Ortega coughed into her palm.

"What was that?" Fortesque asked.

"Bully, sir. Bully for you."

"Uh, yeah," Eastwood said smoothly. "Okay, fellas, that about wraps it up. I'll get moving on this ASAP."

The Cabinet secretaries slapped each other on the back as they filed out happily, doubtless repairing to the nearest watering hole to congratulate themselves on beating some sense into this wet-behind-the-ears president.

"Think I'm gonna puke," Ortega said when they were gone. She was five feet four of compressed energy, with skin the color of a double-shot latte, extraterrestrial cheekbones and eyes reminiscent of a minor deity in a classical Indian painting. Her face was arresting and accusing at the same time, but all of the hard edge she would like to have projected was utterly undercut by a spray of freckles that wanted only for a ponytail and a set of pom-poms to achieve their true potential.

"At least somebody'll be doing something. Okay, you know what we have to do."

Ortega scratched the back of her head, dislodging a pencil from behind her ear and catching it as it bounced off her shoulder. "I'll call the South American desk at the Agency and find a back-channel to Barranca."

"Better yet—"

"I'll have somebody at State do it, right. What are we looking for here?"

Eastwood walked toward his desk. "A simple conversation. Just let him know we heard him, nobody's panicking—"

"Everybody's panicking."

"Not in the G.E., though. And you know why?"

"Because we got plenty of coffee?"

"You betcha. We're just trying to find out where he stands. What's the point of his revolution, let him rant for a while about the working masses and justice and righteousness, and have two analysts listening in so they can tell us what's under the bullshit and how much it's going to cost us."

"Roger." Ortega took notes as the president spoke in his familiar *ex cathedra* style. "Boy, is this mouse going to roar when they put his mug on national television."

"Once in while you gotta toss a few crumbs to the downtrodden. Let him enjoy it while he can."

"We're going to have to tell the Secretaries something, and soon."

"You're right. What do you suggest?"

"Tell them we're holding fast and not giving an inch?"

Eastwood nodded his approval. "And emphasize that we've got the whole staff doing it twenty-four seven."

CHAPTER 6

AN EMBASSY ON M STREET

plendid party! You Yanks are quite good at this sort of thing."

"Thank you, Mr. Ambassador. Did you get enough coffee?"

"I certainly did. Most appreciated. 'Fraid I must dash and—"

"It's from Colombia."

"Indeed. Well, I must be—"

"We still have a few back channels of our own, if you get my drift."

"Ah, yes. Wonderful. Still, I have a most urgent—"

"Your people aren't bothered by this Barranca fellow, are they?"

"Bothered? Well, I—"

"I hope your people realize the U.S. has the situation well in hand."

"In hand? What do you mean by—"

"Which is not to say we've got it knocked, by any means, but—"

"Knocked? I'm afraid I don't—"

"But we're on top of it." A wink and a nudge.

"Is that a fact. Now that's interesting. How is it that—"

"Really sorry to have kept you, Mr. Ambassador. You mentioned you had an important, ah . . ."

"But—"

"Whoa, there's my man! Just walked in! Sorry, I've got to . . . you'll assure your people, won't you?"

"Assure . . . but what exactly—"

"Glad we had this chat and got it all straightened out. I'll report to my people that you're on board."

"On board? I say, hold on just a . . . would you wait a minute, please? Don't—"

"Sorry to have kept you. And hey, try the salmon dip: It's the tits."

The State Department beehive went into buzzing overdrive, as it always did whenever a new diplomatic overture was launched into the geopolitical ether. Foreign leaders were consulted with the kind of informality that, over the decades, had been honed into the strictest of formalities. No phone calls about the matter were initiated, in order to preserve the illusion that the situation didn't of itself warrant a contact. Instead, carefully worded asides were delivered during calls or meetings already on the schedule, the kind of zero-content comments that would enable diplomats to later assert that notice was indeed given even though no information was actually conveyed.

Most importantly of all, though, a significant portion of the beehive's energy was dedicated to assuring reporters and visiting dignitaries that absolutely nothing out of the ordinary was going on despite the obvious increase in corridor foot traffic, decrease in available parking spaces, increase in the number of closed office doors, decrease in the availability of "unidentified spokespersons" and increase in the vehemence of the denials that anything of note was afoot.

The networks were put on notice to stand by for a foreign affairs "development" of vital interest to the nation. Three military aircraft were made ready to carry the news contingents, all except Fox, which was on unofficial out-of-the-loopness for having broadcast a clip of President Eastwood breaking wind during an excruciatingly boring memorial service for an opposition senator who had died the previous week, ostensibly of a cerebral hemorrhage but actually of a massive heart attack while *in flagrante delicto* with a congressional page in the Ralph Lauren Senate Building cloakroom. G.E. Residence aides tried to leak that the gastrointestinal *faux pas* had in fact been committed by the First Dog, Fluffy, but Fox hadn't bought into it and ran the clip, asserting the rationale that a) it wasn't much different from a former president puking up his sushi during a Japanese state dinner, and b) Fluffy, had in fact been back in Washington at the time of the alleged flutterbuster.

"We get Barranca while the GNN cameras are still dazzling his brains out," Secretary of State Patterson told his aides during a planning meeting. "We praise him to high heaven for his humanity and his desire for peace, shove an agreement under his nose and tell him to sign it in front of a billion adoring viewers, then get a shot of him shaking hands with the president before his flight to a triumphant return home. Whole thing shouldn't last more than a morning, and by dinnertime the mocha java is flowing again."

Cargo ships from the merchant marine fleet were dispatched to half a dozen ports in South America, each with a coffee company executive on board duly authorized to enter into on-the-spot, short-term contracts, the funds guaranteed by the full faith and credit of the U.S. government. Hotlines were set up to the leaders of the involved countries—Brazil, Colombia, Costa Rica, Guatemala, Peru—to get their quick approval of whatever the U.S. diplomats managed to negotiate with Barranca. Of course, what they would "negotiate" had been decided in advance and would be dictated to Barranca, and the approvals were purely pro forma, to give the citizens the impression that their leaders were fully in command of the situation and equitably represented.

At 11 AM Washington time, Eastwood had his secretary place a call to the State Department.

"What the hell's going on, Bill?" he barked at Secretary Patterson. "I got a tee time at noon."

"Cable is just coming in from South America, Mr. President," Patterson answered, followed by some muffled mumbling in the background. "Seems to be in two parts."

"Two parts? Read em to me."

"It's not here, sir. Heading straight for the analysts. I'll call down there and get right back to you."

CHAPTER 7

A FOURTH-FLOOR OFFICE, COLGATE-PALMOLIVE STATE DEPARTMENT BUILDING

shen-faced and sick to his stomach, career diplomatic bureaucrat Arnold Sharefsky had to use both hands to set the phone back down so the receiver wouldn't rattle off its cradle. The sight of his hands shaking that badly scared him, so he kept them wrapped around the phone for a few seconds.

"What the hell?" asked his office-mate, Robert Cooper.

Sharefsky tried to answer but it came out as a cross between a gurgle and a croak, so he took a moment to compose himself before trying again. "He's coming down."

"He? Who? He? You mean, *he?*"

Sharefsky nodded dumbly.

"You mean *now?*"

Right *goddamned* now, as a matter of fact, which was how the Secretary of State himself had put it just moments before.

Cooper looked around the cramped office, wondering how they might get it ready for this unprecedented visit. He figured they had maybe three or four minutes until the Secretary finally reached —

The door flew open and slammed into the wall. "Do you mean to tell me—" The Secretary's first words made it into the room before he did. "—that this greaseball spic bastard *blew us off?* Blew off the only goddamned superpower left on this shit-ass planet? Is that what I'm hearing?"

"Well, sir," Cooper squeaked, "I wouldn't exactly characterize it as —"

"Listen, you Ivy League pansy turd, I don't give two squirts'a piss how you'd characterize it! Just tell me what he said!"

Sharefsky, not about to let his fear interfere with the one chance he'd probably have in his entire life to address the Department's *capo di tutti capi* face to face, ventured forth boldly. "He declined to meet with any of the representatives from State we'd suggested."

"Is that what he said? He said, I decline to meet with blah blah blah, is that how he put it?"

"Not exactly. No."

Patterson stepped slowly toward Sharefsky. "Son, I'm going to tear your heart out through your nose if you don't tell me exactly—"

"I'm sorry, sir, but the translation, it was, uh, a bit difficult, owing to the liberal use of the local vernacular, which in that part of the—"

"Then givvitame in Portuguese!"

"Spanish, sir. I don't know why, but—"

"Whatever!" The secretary leaned forward to listen.

"Right. Roger. Okay, it was *Péguelo en su oído*."

"Whuwuzzat?"

"Do you speak Spanish, Mr. Secretary?"

"Not a word, but at least now you can't dick me around anymore. What's it mean?"

Sharefsky reddened and shrank back against the wall. "Umm . . ."

"Stick it in your ear," Cooper said to the Secretary of State.

"I beg your pardon?"

"That's what it means: Stick it in your ear."

Anger quickly drained away from Patterson's face, and his expression turned to one of amazement as he straightened up. "He told me to stick it in my ear?"

"Well, not you, sir," Sharefsky said cautiously. "Not you personally, that is. You see, this particular form of the expression is nonspecific as to recipient, and is more or less intended to denote—"

"He told the United goddamned States of America to stick it in its ear?"

"In a nutshell," Cooper responded, causing Sharefsky to wince. "Not much ambiguity there."

"Huh." Patterson put one hand on his hip and with the other scratched his ear. "I'll be damned." A note of admiration seemed to tinge the secretary's voice. "So what's he want . . . guns? Planes? Money?"

"Seems not," Sharefsky replied. "It's not about what, it's about who."

"Ah." Here at last was something Patterson could relate to. "A higher-up, is that it? Somebody at the ambassador level?"

"No, sir," Sharefsky answered.

"Christ, don't tell me he wants an undersecretary! The nerve of this sonofa—"

"No. Not an undersecretary." Cooper inhaled deeply. "Not a Cabinet secretary, either, or even the president himself."

Patterson frowned in confusion. "I don't get it. Who the hell does he want?"

Cooper scrambled to retrieve the piece of notepaper Sharefsky had fretfully twisted almost into its constituent fibers. Straightening it out as best he could and fixing his reading glasses on his nose, Cooper squinted at the scrawled words, then looked up and read them to the Secretary.

A slight hint of nausea welled up somewhere inside Patterson. He turned, grabbed the doorknob for support, then slowly began walking out.

"Fuck me twice" was all the two bureaucrats could make of his muttering as they watched him leave.

"Okay," the president said, "the first sentence is pretty damned clear. But why'd he write it in Spanish? Barranca went to Harvard, for Pete's sake."

The two stiff shots of thirty-year-old scotch Secretary Patterson had poured into himself prior to calling his president did nothing at all to settle his nerves, but he was happy to forestall reading the rest of the cable for as long as possible. "He did, but you know that man-of-the-people crap with these guys. Thinks he's making history."

"I suppose. So what's the second part?"

No getting around it now. "It says, Get me Eddie Caminetti."

CHAPTER 8

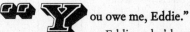ou owe me, Eddie."

Eddie, who'd walked through the Gates Office door only seconds before, regarded the president curiously. Both of them were standing. "Owe you for what?"

"You told me I could trust Sultan al Ahmadi, for which I paid you a hundred thousand of the citizenry's money."

"I did, and you could. So what's your problem?"

"The problem," Eastwood replied icily, "is that al Ahmadi gave up his position as sultan in order to marry an American actress, and his successor, who knew nothing of my agreement with Ahmadi, isn't going to let us build the air base in Jez Rama'am."

"Yeah, so?"

"What do you mean, so! We just awarded a billion in contracts to build their goddamned shipping facility just so we could get that air base, and now we don't have dick!"

Eddie flipped up a hand and let it drop to his side. "I knew that already. What I'm asking, what's that got to do with me?"

"You said I could trust him!"

"And I was right. But who guaranteed the guy was going to stay in office?"

"Stay in office? Chrissakes, Caminetti: It's not like he was elected. Sultans don't leave office unless they're dead!"

"Well, in that case, I guess you didn't see it coming, either. So how could you expect me to?"

"Listen—"

"What are you telling me, Mr. President . . . you want your hundred grand back?"

"That would be nice, for starters."

"So sue me. Anything else?"

Eastwood hadn't invited Eddie to the G.E. Residence to grouse about the money, an argument the president was destined to lose anyway. He'd just thought that starting off with the Jez Rama'am problem might soften Eddie up a little, make him feel guilty and set him up for the real matter at hand. Instead, Eastwood had only succeeded in getting his guest's hackles up. Or at least that's what he'd thought he'd done, until he reminded himself that Eddie didn't have hackles, at least not in the normal sense. The veteran hustler not only didn't have hackles, he didn't have much of an ego, either, and cared a good deal more about what he thought of himself than what other people thought of him. Unless, of course, what other people thought of him could be worked to his own purposes. Then it mattered very much, like if he could convince a high-stakes poker opponent that he was the bluffing type when he really wasn't, or that he never bluffed when he'd been doing it all night. Whether Eddie was actually a bluffer or not was beside the point, which was the only real point there was. He was whatever the situation dictated he be.

All of that flashed through Eastwood's mind in about the time it took him to realize that he'd accomplished nothing at all with this preliminary chitchat and he might as well get down to business and stop trying to bullshit the man who was not only probably the world's greatest bullshitter, but the most honest one as well. "We've got troubles in South America."

"No kidding," Eddie replied as the president returned to his desk.

"I mean real troubles, more than what you read in the paper."

"I've got guys on my island ready to trade their Gulfstreams for a cup of coffee. I hear tell national productivity is down seven percent and violent crime up fourteen. So what else is going on?"

Eastwood picked up a manila folder from his desk and sat down heavily. "Aside from caffeine addicts not getting their fixes," he said as he tapped a corner of the folder on his knee, "there's the economy of half of South America to consider, and the political destabilization that would result if some country went under. Took decades to get that continent halfway peaceful, and the whole damned thing could go up in smoke in a matter of weeks if it doesn't get straightened out."

Eddie mulled it over before responding. "Bummer."

"Bummer. Right. That pretty much sums it up. You should've been in government service."

"Not if wild crows were pecking out my eyeballs. So what's any of this got to do with me? And do I get to sit down yet?"

Eastwood motioned him to a couch in the middle of the office, then stood and walked toward the one opposite. He was still holding the manila folder. "Well, Eddie, right now you may be the most important person in the whole United States."

Eddie, who had emitted signs of showing some interest for the first time during this meeting, now stowed any such budding enthusiasm. "Holy Hannah, Mr. President," he chortled. "Don't you know by now that my ass is that up which smoke like that can't be blown?"

"I do."

The president's expression had a sobering effect on Eddie. "What's going on? This have to do with me owing you something, or you thinking that I do?"

Eastwood veered away from the couch and sat on the antique wing chair next to it. "We made a back channel approach to Barranca yesterday. You know what that is?"

"Yeah. It's when you use a *shabbos goy*."

"Use a what?"

"Jeez, I love politics. Every time you're in a campaign you put a yarmulke on your head and eat pastrami on the Lower East Side but you don't know what a—"

"You lecturing me, Eddie?"

"Okay, look: Orthodox Jews aren't supposed to operate lights on their Sabbath, or use pen and paper or rearrange chairs, because all of that is work and it's supposed to be a day of rest, right?"

"Right . . ."

"Well, that makes it kinda tough to operate the synagogue. So what they do, they hire a non-Jew, a *goy*, to do all of that for them. That's the *shabbos goy*."

"Beautiful story. But what's it got to do with —"

"So when the government needs to talk to some guy who doesn't officially exist because we don't recognize him, instead of three hundred

State department yahoos negotiating for six months on how to do it, you get some foreigner or business executive to do it for you. That's your *shabbos goy*. It's how the government talks to arms smugglers, terrorists, the Mafia, whatever, without really talking to them."

Eastwood thought it over. "Okay, so you do understand. What we figured, this gaucho would be so thrilled to have gotten the attention of the world's only superpower, he'd pretty much fall down and roll over."

"And he didn't."

"Sonofabitch wouldn't even talk to us."

"Really?" Eddie's eyebrows rose as he tried to assess the implications. "Now that surprises me. You woulda thought the guy wanted something from us." He leaned back on the couch and stared into the distance trying to make sense of it.

Eastwood let him have a moment, but Eddie quickly snapped out of it. "Wait a minute. What's this got to do with me?" He pointed to the president's hand. "And when are you going to tell me what's in that folder?"

Pretending to have forgotten about it, Eastwood set it down on the coffee table in front of the couch, placing it so that Eddie could plainly see TOP SECRET—EYES ONLY emblazoned in red at the top. When he saw that Eddie's eyes were firmly riveted on it, he said quietly, "Barranca asked to see you."

The normally unflappable Eddie flapped. "Me!"

Eastwood nodded. "You're the *shabbos goy*."

"You must be . . . *me*? What the hell for!"

"Tell you in a second. But first have a look at what's in that folder."

Eddie hesitated, then reached for the folder but didn't open it. "Hold it a second. You said he asked to see me?"

"That's right."

"Thought you said *you'd* made a back channel approach to *him*."

"That's how we're logging it. Makes it sound more like we're the ones in control. Now have a look inside that folder. And trust me," Eastwood assured him, "that photo is real."

Eddie opened the folder and stared down at the photo of Fidel Castro looking on as Che Guevara putted a golf ball toward a hole.

"Yeah, so?"

Now it was the president's turn to be surprised. "Yeah, so? That's all you have to say?"

Eddie peered more closely at the photo. "There something in here I'm missing?"

Eastwood looked like he was going to blow an artery. "That's two of the most famous revolutionaries of the last century playing *golf*, f'cryin out loud!"

"Well, obviously. So what're you getting all heated up about?"

"Don't you find that just a tad surprising?"

Eddie lifted the photo to find the three others, which he looked at only quickly before dropping the folder back onto the coffee table. "Mr. President . . . this ain't exactly new news."

Eastwood discovered that his mouth was hanging open and he tried to shut it without giving away his shock. "You telling me you've seen it before?"

"Hell yeah, I've seen it before. It's famous. Albert Korda took it in, I don't know, '58 or '59?"

"Right," Eastwood answered idly, his thoughts currently preoccupied with why the intelligence apparatus of the United States hadn't known about the pictures. Then something occurred to him: Maybe they had, because the existence of the pictures wasn't the point here. And he doubted Eddie had any idea who—

Eastwood bent forward and reached for the folder. Flipping it open he pointed to the man holding the flag and some golf clubs in the first photo. "You know who this guy is?"

Eddie didn't need a long look to answer. "The caddy? No idea."

Eastwood pushed the photo aside and pointed to the one showing Castro holding his follow-through, his caddy standing beside him. "Here he is again."

Eddie picked up the pictures and examined them carefully. "Still don't have any idea. Should I know?"

"No." Eastwood sat back on his chair. "But I do. That's Manuel Villa Lobos de Barranca, and he has a proposition for you."

"Fuhgeddaboudit."

"Eddie . . ."

"Mr. President, don't you have to take, like, a mental competency test before you assume office?"

"Actually, no. The people can elect a flat-out psychotic if they want to." Eastwood sat back on his chair. "And have, on several occasions."

"Okay, let me guess." Eddie jumped to his feet and stuck a finger behind the painting over the fireplace mantel. Wiggling it slightly, he said, "There's a camera back here and I'm going to be on Presidential Pranks, right?"

"It's not a joke, Eddie."

Removing his finger from between painting and wall, Eddie leaned against the mantel. "You want me to play golf with some guy I never even heard of?"

"Yes."

"For a million bucks?"

"Yep."

"In the middle of a revolution?"

"Right."

"Just so you can get a little discussion going?"

"You got it." Eastwood stood up and stretched his arms over his head. "Although he hasn't said that. Just that he wants to play you for a million dollars. We're kind of guessing it's a first crack at a back channel approach."

"Baloney. You think it's more than that. For one thing, back channels are secret and there's no way to keep my trip quiet. So tell me."

Eastwood folded his arms, and seemed to consider how much to share with Eddie. "There's not a thing in Barranca's background to indicate that he's got any military orientation at all, or even the stomach for violence. We think he wants to work out a deal for our backing, and he wants someone who isn't a professional diplomat acting as go-between."

"And he thinks I'm that guy?"

"You're who I'd pick, Caminetti."

Eddie, who could read people like a geologist could read stratified layers of rock, believed him. "I assume you'll be covering my losses, if it comes to that."

"Sorry. Can't do that. The United States government doesn't sponsor professional gamblers."

"Got it. Have I completely lost my marbles, or do you really expect me to parachute down into the middle of a jungle so I can risk a million bucks of my own money playing against a guy whose game I've never seen?"

"Thought you'd go just about anywhere for a money match."

"Not to the middle of a goddamned war zone!"

"It's for the good of your country, Eddie." Eastwood let his arms down and shrugged. "Besides, we don't know for sure that there's any actual fighting going on down there right now. So—" He looked at his watch. "What do you say"

"Told you already."

"What?"

"Fuhgeddaboudit."

CHAPTER 9

RONALD REAGAN INTERNATIONAL—WASHINGTON, D.C.

nd what is your business in the United States, Mr. Rivera?"

Carlos Rivera, the man who'd just stepped up to the Immigration and Passport Control booth, looked to be about sixty-five, but his Brazilian passport said he was ten years older than that, which gave the immigration officer just enough pause to ask a question or two, fully expecting an utterly undecipherable accent to deliver a timid reply.

"I have no business here."

The officer, who'd bent forward to the documents on his desk after asking the question, looked up. "Then what are you doing here?"

"Visiting family."

The officer looked back down. "Then that's your business."

"This is not business. It is family. I told you."

"Where's your family?"

"Excuse me?"

"Where is your family? What city?"

"What difference does it make?"

The officer didn't care where the man was going. He didn't care if he was going to go on welfare, run for governor of California, dance naked in Times Square or hang himself. All he cared about was making sure that, if some passport control officer was going to fuck up, it wouldn't be Earl Duncan Maynard, which was the name on his badge. Every time a terrorist bastard blew up a building, there was always some poor schmuck official who'd failed to notice that he'd entered the United States carrying a billfold made out of a certain kind of leather only tanned in Damascus or spoke with an accent identical to Osama bin Laden's or walked with a limp from an injury sustained during some holy friggin struggle or other or had gotten two traffic tickets in three weeks, a dead by-God tip-off that he was about to commit mayhem on a grand scale, and if that schmuck official had only been more alert and doing his job properly, none of this would have happened.

Well, that wasn't going to happen to Earl Duncan Maynard, nosirree. The officer leaned back on his chair, the better to regard the man before him: Despite the weather-beaten face, his eyes were remarkably clear. "The difference is that I asked you."

"Yes, but what for? Are you going to put me back on the plane if you disapprove of the city? And of which American cities do you in fact disapprove, might I inquire?"

"Listen, I—"

"I have already a visa. See?" The man pointed to the passport that lay open on the officer's desk, the large red and blue visa stamp occupying nearly an entire page. "It says I can come into this country. They asked me all these questions already."

"And I'm asking them again! Now what city is your family in?"

Rivera smiled, showing perfect and perfectly cared for teeth. "What are you going to do . . . look them up? Phone them?" Getting no response, he added, "Fine. Dubuque. This is in Iowa. My sister's name is Smith, my brother's is Jones."

"May I see your return ticket?"

Sighing audibly, Rivera handed it over.

"Says you're leaving in a week. Short visit?"

"It is a week."

"Kind of short, isn't it?"

"It is a week. Call it whatever you wish."

Maynard stood up. "You better answer my question, Mr. Rivera."

"What question!" Rivera, rather than be cowed by the officer's size, leaned forward. "I told you I will be here a week. You want to know if I consider a week to be short? Is that the information you require? Well, fine. Yes, it is a week, and *caramba!* is that short! Now what? You want to know if I think a month is long? Okay, good: It is long. Next question?"

The customs officer, who made an effort not to take things personally, sat back down, stamped the entry logo into the passport, and handed it back to Rivera. Carlos Rivera may have been a world-class pain in the ass, but he was no terrorist.

Besides, Maynard recognized his accent as Cuban, and the last time a Cuban had pulled any funny stuff, it was to hijack a plane to Havana thirty years ago, an activity that had become so commonplace and benign, Americans were known to book travel on especially vulnerable flights on the off-chance they might be diverted to the Caribbean capital and get a glimpse of a city otherwise forbidden to them, all expenses paid courtesy of Mr. Fidel Castro and the U.S. State Department.

"That is all?" Rivera asked in surprise as he took his passport and ticket back.

"Don't push your luck, buster. Next!"

Rivera raised his hands in mock surrender and walked off. By the time he made it around the booth, Officer Maynard had already forgotten him.

CHAPTER 10

DESERT FALLS COUNTRY CLUB—PALM DESERT, CALIFORNIA

Charles "Chuck" Stevenson, chairman and CEO of MagnaDyne Industries, unzipped a pocket on his golf bag and pulled out a cloth sack of tees. "Hope you don't think I'm going to roll over and play dead just so I can say I played a money game with the great Eddie Caminetti."

Eddie had been watching as Stevenson found a ball marker, opened a sleeve of balls, took out a Sharpie and wrote a big "CS" on each one, wetted the end of a towel, put on sunscreen, found his divot repair tool, put on his hat, got out his sunglasses, put ice in a cup and filled it with water, retrieved his cell phone and put it in a cup holder, positioned a scorecard in the steering wheel clip, stuck a pencil in the holder next to it, took off his watch and, just now, got out his bag of tees. "Wouldn't be playing you if I thought that, Chuck."

"Just so we understand each other. You really going to carry that bag all eighteen?"

"Keeps me fit."

"Suit yourself. You want to ride, just say so."

"I'll do that."

"I'm going to head over to the range. You coming?"

Eddie shook his head. "I'll stay here and stretch a little. Haven't played in days and I'm stiff as hell."

"Good idea. See you on the tee."

Eddie waited until Stevenson had driven off, then went inside the clubhouse and up the stairs to the lounge, where he poured himself a cup of tea, grabbed a newspaper from a rack and sat down at a window table that gave him a view of the path leading back from the practice range.

He'd barely opened to the sports section when he sensed a presence behind him. "Can I help you?" he said, without turning around.

"I doubt it," a carefully modulated and mellifluous voice replied. "But perhaps I can help you."

Eddie twisted around, and was struck first not by the man's Caribbean appearance, which comported well with his tone of voice and accent, nor by the blue eyes that were set off so boldly by his olive complexion, but by his relaxed, alarmingly peaceful demeanor, which Eddie knew, without knowing how he knew, would remain the same even if the clubhouse were to be hit by an asteroid in the next few seconds. "I take it we don't know each other."

"No." The man extended his hand. "My name is Carlos Rivera."

"Eddie Caminetti." As they shook he added, "But you knew that already."

"Certainly. May I offer you a cup of coffee?"

"Very funny." Eddie motioned to a seat across the table.

Rivera reached into his pants pocket and withdrew a fabric pouch held shut with drawstrings. "I brought my own."

Eddie stared at the pouch, then at the self-serve coffee brewers on a table along the far wall. Hanging from urns like necklaces were hand-drawn signs that used to say things like "Colombian," "Mocha Java" and "French Roast" but now said "Oolong," "Orange Pekoe" and "Earl Grey."

"Come," Rivera said, then began walking toward the former coffee bar.

Eddie followed, then watched as Rivera took a clean filter from a stack atop one of the urns, placed it in a basket and set it over an empty pot. He pulled open the drawstrings on his pouch and upended it over the basket. Rich brown grains of what certainly looked like coffee spilled out, and the aroma that blossomed upward from the small cascade confirmed it.

"I'll be goddamned," Eddie said. He couldn't tell if he was smelling the greatest coffee he'd ever come across or if he just missed the aroma so much even instant would strike him like that.

Rivera held his makeshift rig under the hot water tap of a brewing machine and pulled the lever forward very slowly until a trickle of steaming water began running out. As he moved the filter basket around underneath it so the water sprinkled over all of the coffee's surface area, the aroma exploded, and it wasn't thirty seconds before heads began turning elsewhere in the lounge.

"You might be starting a riot here, Carlos."

"I've enough for an entire pot. What do you think . . . twenty, thirty American dollars a cup?"

Eddie smiled, then tried to stay calm as Rivera patiently nursed the hot water through the coffee until the entire pot was filled, which took nearly ten minutes. He then poured two large cups completely full, put caps on them and handed one to Eddie. As they walked back to their table, some twenty people stared in their direction with the kind of looks a starving grizzly might give a plump salmon.

Rivera jerked a thumb over his shoulder and said, "Help yourselves," then he and Eddie quickly got out of the way of the resultant stampede, trying their best to ignore the shouts and threats that began flying around among people who, seconds ago, had been the best of friends.

Rivera pushed down the cutout pour spout in the lid of his cup, then held the cup up in the air. "Cheers," he said to Eddie, and took a sip.

"No, thanks," Eddie said by way of return toast. "Never touch the stuff. Now why don't you tell me what's on your mind?"

"It is decaf."

"Really?"

Rivera nodded. "That is all I drink. Please; try it. You will not be able to tell it from the real thing."

Eddie did, and he couldn't. He inclined his chin toward the mob still fighting over the pot of coffee. "What'll happen when they find out?"

"They will not. The placebo effect is as strong as any drug. They will swoon in delirium and speak of it for days."

"Interesting." Eddie took a long look at his watch. "Listen, this has all been a lot of fun, but I've got a round of golf coming up in just a few —"

"Yes. With the strong-chinned, steel-haired businessman I saw a few minutes ago. He looks to be a very formidable opponent."

"He is. And I —"

"I would like to caddy for you, Mr. Caminetti."

"Eddie. And I don't need a caddy."

"I did not say you did. I just said I would like to caddy for you."

"Why?"

"I need the money."

"Now, why would I pay you if I don't need your services?"

"But you do need my services."

"Listen." Eddie reached for his newspaper and began folding it up. "This is all very charming and mysterious, and I liked the performance with the coffee, but I'm not paying for something I don't need or want, so have a nice day, okay?"

"You have not even asked me what I would charge for being your caddy."

Eddie stopped folding. "Doesn't matter."

Rivera turned toward a large bay window. Not a frond was moving on any of the hundreds of palm trees visible on the golf course. The sun beat down mercilessly, and even the birds had called it quits in the harsh midday heat. "It is quite hot out there. Think how much more pleasant it would be to walk without the burden of that heavy bag on your shoulders."

"Right. Meaning no offense, you look to be what . . . sixty, sixty-five? "

"Something like that. But I am quite used to heat, as well as carrying heavy bags."

"Like I said, it doesn't matter. I walk because I like to walk. I could ride a cart if I wanted to. And that's why I don't need a caddy. At any price." Eddie stood and gathered up the newspaper. Not wishing to be rude or to offend, and thinking maybe he'd overdone it a little, he said, "Which is what, by the way?"

"One hundred thousand dollars," Rivera said evenly. "American."

Which stopped Eddie in his tracks. "A hundred grand?"

"Yes."

"For carrying my golf bag?"

Rivera turned and looked up at Eddie. "Do not be absurd. Who would pay such an amount to have his golf bag carried?"

"But you just said—"

"The money is not for carrying your bag. That is free."

"Then what's it for?"

"For helping you beat Manuel Barranca." Rivera took another sip and licked his lips appreciatively. "Ten percent of your winnings. How is your coffee?"

GATES OFFICE—G.E. PRESIDENTIAL RESIDENCE

"Uh huh. Yeah. Yeah? Really? Great work, Baines. I'll take it from here."

Chief of Staff Conchita Ortega hung up on the CIA director and speed-dialed Secretary of Homeland Security Mahmoud al Kahlil. "Moody?"

Kahlil recognized the voice immediately. "Connie. How you doin?"

"Good, good. Listen, we've got a little situation, hope you can help us out."

Kahlil was happy to do anything, as his was as thankless a job as any to be found on the planet and he was always on the lookout for things, however small, that might earn him some slight hint of recognition or gratitude. Like people who cleaned toilets or maintained computers, his success was utterly dependent on absolutely nothing bad happening, and when it didn't, nobody noticed. It was only when the plumbing backed up or the operating system wiped itself out or a building got blown up that anyone paid any attention, and then all manner of hell would pour down and the trouble-free years up to that point wouldn't even be a rounding error in the balancing of recriminatory accounts. So if Kahlil could do a favor for the president's chief of staff, he was only too happy.

"I just got a call from CIA," Ortega explained. "There's this photo we've had for a while, an old one. It's a picture of—get this, now— Fidel Castro and Che Guevara playing golf."

"Yeah, sure," Kahlil said, nodding even though Ortega couldn't see him. "I know it. Which one've you got . . . Che putting? Connie? You there?"

"Yes, I'm here." She'd just taken a moment to close her eyes, rub the bridge of her nose to stave off a headache and wonder why the CIA seemed to be the only entity in the western hemisphere that hadn't known about these pictures. Then another thought occurred to her, and she decided maybe she'd better present this to Kahlil slightly differently than she'd planned. Just in case there were other things the intelligence service should have known but were just getting around to finding out about.

DESERT FALLS COUNTRY CLUB—PALM DESERT, CALIFORNIA

"Who the hell are you?" Eddie asked.

"I told you, I am —"

"Yeah, I know. Carlos Rivera. What I'm asking—"

Rivera smiled and held up a hand. "I know what you are asking, Eddie."

He reached into a pants pocket, opposite the one in which he'd carried the coffee, and pulled out a worn manila envelope about the size of a large postcard. He opened it and withdrew what appeared to be an old photograph, carefully folded into quarters. He unfolded it, smoothed it out with his hand and turned it so it faced Eddie. "Have you seen this before?"

"There's one of Che right after he's hit," Ortega said to Mahmoud al Kahlil. "The guy who moved a tractor out of his way is still standing up on it, watching Che as he—"

"Sure. That's Carlos Rivera. Connie? Hello?" The phone had gone silent again, and Kahlil thought he'd heard Ortega groan something like *Fuck me*, but he couldn't have heard it right. "Connie, you okay?"

Fuck me, Ortega groaned. "Yeah, I'm fine. Couple of people trying to get my attention here, is all. Sorry, Moody."

"No problem."

"What I'm wondering, now that you've got so much information centralized in your department, can you tell me something about this guy, like where he lives, is he on any watch lists, that kind of stuff?"

Kahlil practically licked his lips. After the passage of the third version of the Patriot Act, his computer engineers had gone into an overdrive mode not seen since the Manhattan Project, building a system that consolidated information from the CIA, NSA, FBI, DIA, state, county and city crime information systems, bookstores, universities, telephone companies, credit card providers, casinos, day-care centers, ISPs, banks and virtually every other enterprise that ever requested so much as a customer's name. Could Mahmoud al Kahlil tell Ortega anything about this guy? Hell, he could tell you when his third cousin twice removed had her last acne breakout.

Even while Ortega spoke, Kahlil had been punching buttons, and he had her answer by the time she finished her last sentence. "Got him," he pronounced, braggadocio clearly lacing his voice.

Ortega gripped the phone so hard her knuckles turned white. "Tell me."

"Certainly. He's dead."

"What?"

"He's dead."

"What?"

"Connie . . ."

"I'm sorry. He's dead? Are you certain?"

"Died in a Havana hospital in 1977. Ruptured spleen and a punctured lung, following a farm accident in which —"

"No, no. That's okay." If Ortega could sense Kahlil's disappointment at not being asked for more details—he knew the make, model and even the serial number of the tractor Rivera had been driving when it turned over—she didn't show it.

DESERT FALLS COUNTRY CLUB

"You were their caddy?" Eddie asked in amazement.

"Usually just Che's. I only carried for Fidel when Barranca was not available."

Eddie sat back on his chair and regarded Rivera with newfound respect. "How the hell did you get into this country? And when?"

"When, a few days ago. And I got in because they think I am dead."

"Who thinks you're dead?"

"Your intelligence services. They think I died in a farming accident. I have been coming here for years."

"Using your real name?"

"Of course. It is a very common one, and besides, when they think you are dead, they remove your name from all the watch lists. Quite convenient, actually. Also, whenever I pass through Customs and Immigration, I raise a considerable fuss, making myself as loud, obnoxious and irritating as possible."

"Why?"

"Because no one with evil intent would dare call such attention to himself. Their suspicions melt away even as they wave me through in great haste to be rid of me."

Eddie turned as something across the room caught his eye. It was the assistant pro waving to him, telling him that he was supposed to be on the first tee already. Eddie nodded his acknowledgment, then turned back to Rivera. "How did you know I was playing Manuel Barranca? Which, by the way, I haven't agreed to do."

"I know because I have been Barranca's caddy for many years. And I know you haven't yet agreed to play him, but you should. I can help you."

"Is that so."

"Yes."

"And why would you do that?"

"For the same reason you would play him. Money, if you thought you could win. And my price is ten percent. Now . . ."

Rivera stood up and held a hand out toward the door. "May I carry your bag today? I will explain on the way."

"A caddy? Eddie Caminetti using a caddy?" Chuck Stevenson's voice was shot through with suspicion.

"Unless you have an objection," Eddie replied.

Stevenson turned his head slightly, as though regarding the two men in front of him from the corner of his eye would help him suss out a scam. "Just wasn't expecting it, is all. When we made our bet."

"Not a problem." Eddie hoisted his bag onto the back of Stevenson's cart. "I'll just ride."

"Thought you said you were gonna walk."

"That was *after* we made our bet." Eddie had been threading the retaining strap through the handle on his bag, but now when he paused.

"You want to call it off, it's fine by me."

Eddie could read what was going through Stevenson's mind as if his thoughts were written in flaming neon. There was nothing about their bet requiring Eddie to walk; Stevenson just knew he liked to. And on a hot day like this one, it had to take a physical toll, so he was happy to let him.

But Eddie had every right to take a caddy, and if Stevenson objected Eddie would ride, which would reduce the fatigue factor considerably. Then again, with a caddy carrying his bag, that fatigue would be greatly lessened. Of course, Eddie would still be walking eighteen long holes under the midday desert sun, which has to wear on a guy.

But why would he want to take a caddy in the first place? "Why do you want a caddy?"

"I don't. But he looks like he needs the money, and he offered."

"You mean you don't know the guy?"

"Never met him before in my life. I don't even think he's ever seen this course before."

"Guess he's not going to be reading too many greens for you, then." Like Eddie needed it. "What are you paying him?"

"A hundred thousand dollars."

"I see. Well, that oughta put a few tacos on his table." The last thing Stevenson wanted to do was call the match off, so he shrugged his acquiescence and watched as Eddie unhitched his bag from the golf cart, set it down and waved Rivera over.

The older man immediately began opening zippers and inventorying each compartment. "You have only four golf balls."

"Only gonna need one," Eddie said. He watched approvingly as Rivera found a ball mark repair tool and dropped it into his pocket, then took the dirtier of two towels hanging off the bag and went off to wet it down.

"I'll meet you on the tee," Stevenson said, and drove off.

Rivera came back, wringing out the towel, then hanging it back on the bag. "How large is your wager?"

"Ten grand."

"Strokes?"

"I'm giving him one a side. He's scratch and I figure I'm about a plus two."

"You *figure*?"

"I don't post scores. You ready?"

"Ready." Rivera made several quick strap adjustments and hoisted the bag onto his shoulders with one fluid motion. He didn't do any shaking or wiggling to get the bag comfortable, but seemed to like it just where it had settled. Eddie noticed that his posture, despite the weight of the bag, remained as upright as it had been before he'd strapped it on.

"We're playing the back nine first," Eddie said as he led the way. "Less crowded that way."

As they walked, Eddie made sure Rivera knew how he liked to play. "I don't need club advice and I don't need the greens read for me. I already know the yardages, too, and can take my own clubs out of the bag. You can clean them and put them back. And the most important thing of all . . ."

Eddie stopped walking suddenly. Rivera, who'd been walking slightly behind him, had to scramble to keep from stumbling into him. "However my conversations go with this guy," Eddie said, "don't assume you know the play and jump in to help me. A, you don't know the play, and B, I don't need the help. Got it?"

"Understood, Eddie. You need not worry."

"Okay, then." They resumed walking. "You play the game, Carlos?"

"Oh, yes! I love it. But playing for ten thousand dollars . . ." Rivera shook his head. "A great deal of money."

Eddie smiled. "Ten thousand to Chuckie Stevenson is less than pocket change. The money has nothing to do with it."

"Oh? What, then?"

Eddie pointed to a silver limousine in the parking lot near the tenth tee. A uniformed chauffeur was polishing the hood with laconic swipes of a white cloth. "That's his car. And that poor sonofabitch is going to be rubbing down the finish for the next four hours so that everybody in the whole club knows that Stevenson came here by limo."

"Ego, then."

Eddie pulled out a pack of cigarettes and offered one to Rivera, who waved it away. "Stevenson thinks he's a Big Swinging Dick, and spends most of his energy trying to prove it."

"MagnaDyne Industries, correct?"

Eddie eyed Rivera with renewed interest, then pulled a cigarette from the pack with his teeth. "How'd you know that?"

Rivera ignored the question. "I would say it is fairly clear he *is* a Big Swinging Dick. To be running such a corporation, after all . . ."

"That's just my point." Eddie lit the cigarette with a Bic and took a deep pull, then spoke around the smoke that poured out and slid around his head as they walked. "Guy's got more money than God and runs a Fortune 500 company . . . what the hell's he got left to prove?"

They were nearing the tee box, where Stevenson, despite having spent half an hour on the practice range, was loosening up with a few easy swings. "But he keeps trying to prove it every day anyway," Eddie finished. "Whaddaya say, Chuck . . . you bout ready to tee em up and hit?"

"Hell, yes. Want me to go?"

"Be my guest."

They both parred the first hole and got off good tee shots on the second. Eddie and Rivera walked off the tee box together as Stevenson drove ahead by himself. "So what is it you want to tell me about Barranca?" Eddie asked.

Rivera was still wiping Eddie's driver as they walked. "He plays off eight, same as me," he answered, using the British expression for indicating an eight handicap. "He is fairly consistent, at least on the courses he knows, and is scrupulously honest as well."

"Is that so?"

"Yes. Same as you, Eddie. And unlike our friend, Mr. Stevenson."

"Who just kicked his ball out of a divot. You have good eyes for an old guy. What else?"

Rivera provided an analysis of Barranca's game that would have done a psychiatrist proud. How Barranca liked to fall into a rhythm, and how easily that rhythm could be disturbed by seemingly innocuous occurrences. How he liked for his opponents to putt out before he himself began to putt, and how it rankled him when they refused to comply, as was their right. How he liked to alter, with prior agreement from the other players in his group, rules he felt were unfair, such as being forced to play out of a divot that some lazy golfer earlier in the day had failed to repair. Same for a footprint in a bunker or a cart rut that the maintenance staff hadn't yet gotten around to marking as ground under repair.

"He does not like to discuss business during a round," Rivera said, and Eddie thought it wise not to ask him what constituted shop talk for a revolutionary. "He considers golf to be an escape, a kind of psychic oasis, requiring such concentration as to divert one from even the most dire of woes."

"And he plays for money?"

"With great passion it sharpens the mind, and brings a certain level of consequence to one's actions."

"Is that you speaking, or Barranca?"

Rivera grinned. "Sometimes, it is difficult to know the difference. I have been playing with him, and carrying for him, nearly all my life."

By the ninth hole, which was actually the eighteenth of the course, Eddie and Stevenson were dead even.

"Is it not yet the time to delve into your bag of tricks, Eddie?" Rivera asked.

Eddie reached for the dry towel on the bag and bent over to wipe his brow. "It would be, except that I haven't got any."

"So I thought. You are both playing splendidly, and if there has been any—how do you call it?—*soft-pedaling* on your part, I certainly have not seen it."

"Hasn't been any. I'm playing the best I know how."

They watched as Stevenson teed up on the difficult par four and hooked his drive over a bunker and into a stand of trees, uttering an expletive when the ball disappeared from view.

"Tough break, Chuck," Eddie said, then hit a three-wood to a safe landing zone. "Rough's a little deep over there. We'll help you look if you haven't found it by the time we get there."

Stevenson sped ahead in his cart, and when Eddie and Rivera reached the fairway just abeam where they'd last seen the ball, he called out, "Got it! Pretty good lie, too." Indeed, the ball was sitting well up in the grass just a few feet from where Stevenson was standing.

"Good for you!" Eddie called back, then said softly to Rivera, "Is it my imagination, or was that—"

"Not your imagination," Rivera confirmed. "We would have been able to see that lie from the tee." Meaning that Stevenson had found the ball and moved it before they'd gotten there. "But I assume you are not going to accuse the chairman and chief executive officer of a Fortune 500 company of cheating."

"No, but not because he's the chairman, etc."

"Why, then?"

Eddie eyed the green from his spot in the middle of the fairway. "What do you think here . . . six-iron?"

Rivera looked toward the flag. "Seven, if you do not overswing. Better to be well below this flag." He handed over the club. "Why not confront him?"

"Because," Eddie said as he took the iron, "there's no percentage in it. We exchange words, we call off the match, I don't win any money and my pigeon has flown the coop."

"Yes. I see. What is your plan, then?"

Eddie hit his shot before answering, a high, curving beauty that left him five feet below the hole. "Good call on the club. And the plan is to get old Chuck unnerved."

Rivera took the seven-iron back and ran the damp towel over the face of the club head. "How?"

"Damned if I know. Got any ideas?"

Rivera looked over at Stevenson just as he brought a seven-wood down and sent the ball flying toward the green. "I do, if he hits at least one more bad shot."

It came on the number twelve par-5, when Stevenson hooked his tee shot again, this time sending it into the vicinity of several bunkers bordered by trees.

"Oh, dear," Rivera said to him. "That could be difficult to find. I should go help you."

"Not necessary," Stevenson said quickly and amiably. "I'm sure it's in plain view."

"No matter. I am happy to assist."

"Trust me, I'm sure —"

"Can you take your own bag, Eddie?" Rivera asked as he headed for Stevenson's cart.

"Look, there's really no reason to —"

"Absolutely," Eddied assured his caddy. Before Stevenson could protest any further, he had the bag on his shoulders and was already walking toward the fairway.

Rivera, already waiting in Stevenson's cart, thumped the driver's seat and said with a smile, "Let us go look."

When they arrived at the trees and bunkers, Rivera was first out of the cart. A few seconds later he pointed down and announced happily, "Found it, Mr. Stevenson!"

The ball was up against a root, and was the kind of lie that could easily result in a broken wrist if the man playing it decided to use his balls instead of his brains. Stevenson looked over to where Eddie was unshouldering his bag, right in the middle of the fairway and about 240 yards from the green. Eddie had a good chance of getting on in two and two-putting for birdie, or even one-putting for eagle.

One option for Stevenson was to hit a soft punch to get the ball over the traps and back into play, but that root made the outcome very uncertain.

There was also another option. "You might consider declaring it unplayable and taking a drop," Rivera suggested.

Unthinkable. "No. I'm going to play it. Go ahead on back to your man, and thanks for finding it."

"No problem." But Rivera didn't move.

Stevenson turned toward his cart to get a club. "Really. I got it from here. Go on back."

"I shall watch your shot, Mr. Stevenson. As long as you wish to play it as it lies, there is no sense losing it if you cannot see where it goes."

"I'm just gonna punch it out. It'll be okay. Really."

"I do not mind waiting."

"It's not necessary."

"I am happy to help out. It is not a problem. What have you got there, a three-wood? This is what you will punch out with? Curious . . ."

No, it was not what he was going to punch out with, as Rivera well knew. It was what he was going to thwack onto the green with as soon as this Hispanic busybody got the hell out of here so he could kick the ball away from that root.

And they both knew that Rivera's presence wasn't necessary, that there was no way Stevenson could lose sight of the ball if he hit a little punch, yet there Rivera was, standing on a little hillock above the trees, staring unflinchingly at the ball sitting on the root, and why would he be doing that unless he thought there was a chance Stevenson might move the ball and improve his lie if he wasn't watching, which could only mean that Rivera thought that this was something he might actually do, and why would he think that?

Because he saw me do it before. And so did Eddie.

The thought ricocheted around in Stevenson's mind and made him dizzy. Had he been found out? Had the steely-haired corporate titan, the architect of MagnaDyne's industry-leading ethics policy, been caught cheating at the one game the honest playing of which practically defined a man's character in the circles of the Biggest Swinging Dicks in the world?

Impossible. Unthinkable. How dare anybody—!

But there was the leathery little banana republic bastard staring at him, Jos´e or Hose B or what the hell ever, and as Stevenson replayed the tee box conversation in his mind, he knew that Eddie had sent him, and that could only mean they thought he'd committed the worst sin in sports.

Or maybe they only thought he had, hadn't actually seen him do it but only surmised it. The par-four number nine hole, that's where it must have been.

Shit.

No way in hell could he move that ball, not with that wizened greaseball staring at him like that, and trying to play it made no damned sense at all. Punching it out, what would that buy him, twenty yards? Thirty at the most? That wasn't much help, and there was a good chance he'd squeeze the ball between the club head and the root and not move it at all, in which case he'd be right back in the soup and down one more stroke on this hole.

But he'd already told the little prick he was going to play it out, and he'd already carried a three-wood to the ball, so now what?

Play to the sonofabitch's ego, that's what.

Stevenson stood over the ball for almost a minute as he pretended to line up the shot. Then he straightened up. "Damn, José, you know what? I think you're right. This is not a high-percentage shot."

"That is using your head, sir!" Rivera cried happily, then watched as Stevenson picked up the ball, carried it back about ten yards while making sure he kept its previous location between himself and the flag, and dropped it.

Still hyper-aware of Rivera watching him, Stevenson wound up, choked and sent the ball skittering right into the sand the drop was supposed to help him avoid.

Rivera had only one word when he rejoined Eddie a few seconds later and pointed back toward Stevenson:

"Tostada."

"A ten thousand dollar payday," Rivera said admiringly as they came off the eighteenth green. "Not at all bad, if I might say so."

"Not as good as twenty thousand," Eddie replied.

"Pardon? Was there an additional bet of some sort?"

Eddie glanced at Stevenson, who was morosely dropping his putter back in his bag. Then he looked over at the clubhouse and saw a handful of well-dressed executive types looking their way and waving. "Twenty bucks says I get another ten grand out of him."

"And there was no other wager?"

"None. I promise."

"Then I will accept your wager."

"Okay. You stay here."

When Stevenson saw Eddie approaching his cart, he reached into a pocket of his golf bag and pulled out a checkbook in a leather cover.

"Put that away," Eddie ordered.

"Huh?"

Eddie pointed forcefully to the golf bag strapped to the back of the cart until a confused Stevenson complied. "But I owe you ten grand."

"I know," Eddie said, reaching for his wallet, slowly, so that everyone at the clubhouse could see it. "But instead of writing me a check here for ten large, why don't you send me one in the mail for twenty?"

"Twenty! Why in hell would I do that?"

"Simple." Eddie jerked a thumb toward the clubhouse. "For another ten Gs I tell all those guys you beat me."

Shock, revulsion, outrage and indignation all competed for primacy on Stevenson's features. For about a second. "What about José?"

"His name's Carlos. Tip him a grand and he's not a problem." Eddie took a piece of paper out of his pocket and began writing something. "Now smile, and slap me on the back like you're bucking up my beaten spirit."

Stevenson did so, a broad grin plastered on his face, then he took out his wallet, counted out a wad of hundreds, expansively waved Rivera over and magnanimously slapped them into his hand. Eddie then gave him the piece of paper, on which he'd scribbled *For whipping my sorry ass, IOU $10,000*, and signed his name. Then he hung his head and began slowly helping Rivera wipe his clubs as Stevenson jaunted his way back to the clubhouse.

Rivera, when he was sure he could be seen from the clubhouse, patted Eddie's back consolingly. "There, there, my boy. How am I doing?"

"Terrific. I'm ready to cry."

"So it is true, then," Rivera said as he resumed wiping the clubs.

Eddie leaned over to pull his cigarettes from one of the golf bag's many pockets. "What's that?"

"You truly do not care how you look to other people."

"You're wrong there, Carlos."

"How so? We made it look to those men up there like you were just soundly beaten by their boss."

"Exactly. Which is what I want them to think. So you see?" Eddie stuck a cigarette between his lips and held his hands out to his sides. "I truly do care how I look to other people. It's critical in my line of work."

As Eddie flicked his lighter and held it to the tip of the cigarette, Rivera said, "That is not what I meant. I was referring—"

"I know what you meant. Come on, let's get out of here and drown our sorrows in a couple'a brews."

"Not just yet, Eddie. There's one last thing."

Eddie replaced the pack in the bag and folded his arms. "You already told me plenty. What else is there?"

"Barranca is concerned about his grandson. It seems the boy is having some difficulty finding his place, and could use some assistance."

"How old is he?"

"Fourteen."

"Fourteen!" Eddie turned and began walking toward the clubhouse. "Luvva Pete, Carlos. He's just a kid. He's got plenty'a time."

Rivera stood his ground, forcing Eddie to stop in order to carry on the conversation. "The boy is troubled, because he is not athletic."

"So what do you want me to do?"

"Whatever you can. Barranca would be immensely grateful. It would soften him considerably, and make your task easier."

Eddie took another drag on his cigarette and scratched the back of his head. "I'm no coach, Carlos. I wouldn't have any idea how to —"

"You have many friends, Eddie. In all walks of life. Surely you know athletes who might be called upon to provide the boy with some —"

Eddie was already waving it away. "I don't know any babysitters, and I wouldn't dream of asking one'a those guys to—"

"Just have a look at the boy. So you can say you saw him, that you made some small effort."

"He's here? In the States?"

Rivera nodded. "Boston. That is a secret, Eddie. As you might imagine, his life would be endangered should anyone learn of his true identity."

"I don't know . . ."

Carlos finished wiping the last club and stuck the damp rag through an eyelet on the bag. "I spent the last four hours advising you how to get the better of Barranca, and you seemed to trust me."

"Well, yeah, I suppose I did."

"Fine." Rivera got ready to hoist the bag onto his shoulders. "Then trust me on this as well."

"Hang on a second," Eddie said, motioning for Carlos not to pick up the bag just yet. "Tell me something: How did you meet Castro and Guevara?"

Rivera hesitated, as if deciding whether to answer, then said, "Fidel came to me for lessons."

"You're kidding."

Rivera shook his head. "He is a very determined man, and does nothing by halves."

"So what was it like? When they played, I mean."

The smaller man removed his hat and smiled as he wiped his brow with his sleeve. "They were both new at it, of course, and the idea was that they would compete on equal terms as neither had ever so much as held a club before."

"And how'd they take to it?"

"As you might expect. Fidel rebelled immediately, and wanted to change inconvenient rules. Interestingly," he said as he wiped the sweatband of his hat and put it back on, "Che did not, as he was quite taken with the inherent purity of the game. He felt that the course was not just the smooth fairways and manicured greens, but everything about the land, including roots, bare spots, fallen leaves and branches, pools of rainwater and even divots left by previous golfers. Castro was of a more practical bent, and felt that those things that were unfair or inequitable should simply be changed."

Eddie grinned. "Kind of figures, dudn't it?"

"I suppose."

"What I don't get, though, who were all those guys standing around and watching? On one hole they were right up on the green."

"Ah. Yes. The group of men was there to arbitrate rules. Castro called it the Central Committee and populated it with a majority of his most loyal followers."

"Were they actually keeping score?"

"Oh, indeed. Che and Fidel were both fiercely competitive, each in his own way, of course. And while they stood shoulder to shoulder facing great danger together many times, their greatest intensity was when they were pitted one against the other. History tells us that they agreed to play golf only to see what all the fuss was about in the developed capitalist countries, but I assure you, they played with no less ferocity than had they been tied for the lead at Augusta."

"And they brought their own rules committee with them." Eddie chuckled at what it must have looked like, that bunch following the two revolutionaries around all day. "Sounds like they took things a bit too seriously."

"Perhaps. But the Central Committee worked out so well, that is likely where Fidel got the idea to make the Cuban revolution a socialist one."

"Didn't it start out that way?"

"No. Fidel and Che were mostly intent upon getting rid of Fulgencio."

"Ful—"

"Batista. Fidel didn't declare the revolution to be socialist until nearly two years later."

"Huh. Didn't know that. Anyway, the rules guys, you were saying . . . ?"

"One member of the committee was named Raul," Rivera explained, "and he was one of three men running the new government, along with Fidel and Che. It never occurred to Che that Raul, his intellectual kindred spirit, might not be impartial, even though he was Castro's brother. It was part of Che's trusting nature, which eventually got him killed."

They stopped talking and waved to the group behind them that had just driven up. After the four got out of their golf carts and headed for the green, Eddie said, "So how'd they play?"

"Fidel got into a sand trap on the first hole and could not get out," Rivera said. "He slashed angrily at the ball over and over. Che, looking on in amusement, asked him if he was remembering to count his strokes. Castro picked up the ball and threw it out of the sand, and shortly thereafter Che hit four balls in a row into a freshly manured cow pasture. As neither one had finished the hole, they agreed to call it square, and so informed the Central Committee, as well as me. I was keeping score, you see.

"Unfortunately, one member of the committee, a former golf professional from an exclusive club that had flourished under Batista, protested. He said that the rules of golf, specifically one-dash-three, were quite explicit in that players were not permitted to change any of the rules. Che, relishing the possibility for debate, engaged him eagerly, and asked what would happen if two players agreed to change rule one-dash-three itself. Because if the rule against rule changes were itself changed, he explained, then it was no longer in effect, and one could pretty much change anything, right?"

"Interesting point," Eddie allowed, noticing one of the assistant pros coming out of the clubhouse and walking toward them, in no particular hurry.

"The former professional did not think so, and pointed out that the rule itself was not changeable. According to what? Che asked him. Well, he responded, according to the rule itself. So it is the rule that says you cannot change the rule? Che asked, and when the professional confirmed that, Che said, Fine . . . then I suggest we amend it. But you cannot! the man said, and Che responded, Certainly we can, and then he called out to Castro: Fidel! May we waive rule one-dash-three? Fine by me, Castro answered. The rule was no longer in effect, and any attempt to invoke it was no longer valid. But you had no right to change it in the first place! the man protested."

Rivera smiled at the memory before continuing. "You are quite right, Che told him, but now that we have, it no longer applies. Helpless now, the poor man turned to Castro, who said, What Ernesto said goes for me, for he is my brother in the revolution!"

Eddie, laughing, said, "I'm going to have to try that one out in my next match."

"Che won many of the rules debates that day, sometimes by quoting obscure passages from Kierkegaard and Epictetus in defense of his often dubious logic. By day's end he and Castro were playing something, but any resemblance to golf was purely coincidental."

The assistant pro had reached them by now. "You got a phone call, Eddie."

"Who from?"

"Some asshole says he's the president of the United States. Buddy a'yours?"

"Yeah, we're old pals."

"Says your cell phone's not answering."

"That's cuz it's off. Alright, I'll get it. C'mon, Carlos."

"You will consider what I said."

"Yeah, sure."

Eddie walked back with the assistant, who said, "So who is it on the phone?"

"The president."

"Yeah, right. Guess I shouldn'ta told him to keep his shirt on, huh?"

"Nah, it's cool."

CHAPTER 11

A GOLF COURSE WITH VERY GOOD SECURITY— ARLINGTON, VIRGINIA

n the par-4 number three, President Eastwood teed off with an iron.

"You keep using your head like that," Eddie said as he replaced him on the tee box, "I'm going to have to take back some strokes."

"Learned at the feet of the master." Eastwood had long prided himself on big, powerful drives that occasionally topped 280 yards and elicited admiring oohs and aahs from onlookers. More often than not, though, they crossed four fairways doing it, so he'd learned from Eddie that there were no videos on a scorecard and all you had at the end of the round was your score . . . and your won or lost bets. The subsequent change in his golf game was also reflected in his foreign policy, which had originally consisted largely of blustering threats and histrionics that only increased the enmity of other nations, but had of late morphed into a quieter and more skillful kind of diplomacy that achieved more lasting and peaceful results.

Eddie hit his usual drive, 250 yards straight down the middle. Unspectacular but extremely effective.

"You're such a bore," the president chided him.

"In golf, boring is good." Eddie bent to retrieve his tee. "You're either showing off or trying to win. Hard to do both at the same time."

"In politics it's practically mandatory."

As they walked together down the fairway, caddies and Secret Service agents in discreet tow, Eddie said, "You were supposed to tell me why sending an ordinary citizen to negotiate a peace isn't grounds for impeachment."

"It may be. I don't know. But here's the thing." They were approaching Eastwood's ball, and he motioned to the entourage to stay back, out of earshot. "Uprisings almost always involve astonishing amounts of bloodletting. People get killed by the thousands, infrastructures get destroyed, entire societies get torn apart . . . the amount of violence committed in the name of peace and justice is beyond imagining. And once the shooting starts, any thought of compromise is right the hell out the window."

"Isn't it sometimes justified?"

"Sure. Every time the uprisers win, the force was reasonable and necessary. Every time they lose, they were a bunch of bloodthirsty, greedy troublemakers who deserved to get wiped out. Either way, a lot of people get killed, and there's never any assurance that the winners were the ones who deserved to win. It's all kind of a coin toss."

As Eddie went quiet thinking about it, Eastwood waved to the caddies, who came forward and set their bags down. "Which normally doesn't bother the leaders," the president continued. "They either wind up as heads of a new nation, like Fidel Castro in Cuba, or as adored martyrs to a failed cause, like Che Guevara in Bolivia. Most of them are in it to get their rocks off anyway, and getting martyred or run out of town is a helluva lot easier than actually having to run a country. The big shot marches in triumphant and pretty soon he's just another politico who can't even keep the water and electricity running."

Eastwood still had his four-iron and worked his hands around the grip then waved for the others to catch up. "Lot damned easier to fight for a cause than to manage the result once you've won. The smart ones turn over the reins right away and blame the inevitable chaos on inept politicians." He hit a fairly decent shot to within 30 yards of the green. He gave the iron back to his caddy, pulled a sand wedge and putter out of his bag, then they headed off to Eddie's ball.

"So if I get this right," Eddie said as they walked, "you're telling me this Barranca character may have figured out a better way? Pin the whole thing on an economic boycott, work out some kind of settlement face-to-face with one guy and avoid the bloodshed?"

"What I'm thinking about Barranca starting talks this early, and with not a lot of leverage on his side other than the coffee thing, I'm thinking—*hoping*—he's looking to compromise. No hard-line take it or leave it bullshit. Do a little give and take, you know—" Eastwood looked at Eddie slyly "—like you're doing right now."

"I am?"

"We're talking, aren't we? Trying to come to terms?"

Eddie looked away and put his hands on his hips. "Sounds good on paper, Mr. President, but I don't know . . ."

"Think about it, Eddie. It's a crapshoot to begin with, so why lead your followers into a bloodbath on a fifty-fifty proposition?"

"But if Barranca counts on the United States to back him up, it's still fifty-fifty."

"Except no one gets killed!" Eastwood stopped suddenly, which caused the phalanx behind him to do the same. "Don't you see? This guy has worked his cause up to the point where he's forced the world's only remaining superpower to pay attention, and he hasn't fired a single shot. Now why would someone like that risk the lives of his loyal followers in a shooting war, especially when it's not fifty-fifty, it's more like ninety-nine to one, because he's got half a dozen countries in South America pissed off at him in addition to all the caffeine addicts in the western hemisphere?"

He waited to make sure Eddie was taking in all the implications before walking again. Eddie, lost in thought, hesitated, then walked a few paces behind. "And this is okay with you? This is better than fighting him for it? Because he may be armed with pitchforks and shovels but we wouldn't have to put a single man on the ground, the kind of technology we got."

"We can't fight him. Looks to me you got about one-forty to the green, What're you gonna use?"

"Pitching wedge. How come we can't fight him?"

"Because he isn't in one place. He's all over the map, and his people are scattered all over the place, too, and even if we knew where, we couldn't identify them, which doesn't matter anyway, because even if they were all crammed into Yankee Stadium we couldn't lay a single finger on them. You'll never reach with a wedge; it's uphill."

Eddie pulled out a wedge. "What the hell are you talking about?"

"Go ahead and hit."

"Twenty bucks, I get inside of fifteen feet."

"You're on."

Eddie lined up, swung with everything he had and stuck the ball less than six feet from the pin.

Eastwood sighed. "I'm supposed to be a pretty savvy guy. Why the hell am I still making bets with you?"

"The failure of logic against experience. Why couldn't you touch him?"

Once again, Eastwood motioned for the entourage to stay well back. "For a reason nobody seems to be noticing amid all the hubbub."

"And that is?"

Eastwood, grimacing slightly with the kind of pain only a helpless politician understands, said, "Well, I'll tell you, Eddie: He hasn't done anything wrong." They'd reached Eastwood's ball, which was lying deep in an unrepaired divot. Looking at it, he said, "Don't suppose you'd let me —"

"Forget it."

The president grunted, handed his putter to Eddie and set up over his ball with the sand wedge. He scooped it neatly and got it to within the same distance from the flag as Eddie's. "With my stroke here, we're lying even."

"Only statistically. Realistically, you lost the hole already."

"Bullshit." Eastwood took his putter back from Eddie.

"Twenty bucks?"

"Up yours. Let's go putt."

After Eddie won the hole with one putt against Eastwood's two, they began the long walk to number four.

"Fact is," the president explained, "Barranca hasn't done anything illegal or certifiably threatening to the U.S."

"What about the impact on our economy?"

"What about it? Every time OPEC raises the price of oil it hurts our economy. Airbus drops the prices on their planes below their costs because of government subsidies, U.S. airlines go out and buy them, which hurts like hell, but what can we do . . . raise tariffs on red wine and hope they see the light?"

"We went to war against Iraq over oil, didn't we?"

"Ha!" Eastwood clapped his hands, and the sound echoed from the thick stands of poplars lining the walkway. "That's because that schmuck Saddam gave us the perfect excuse! He goes and invades

Kuwait, and we get to ride to the rescue and save the oil at the same time. Hell, we do stuff like that all the time."

"I meant the second time."

"There was no second time. First time just took eleven years, with an intermission."

Eddie pulled out a pack of cigarettes, shook it and offered one to Eastwood, who looked around guiltily and took it. "So what you're saying, Barranca's not giving us any excuses to hit him."

"Right." The president stuck the cigarette between his lips and bent forward to take the light Eddie was holding up in his cupped hands. "Being damned careful about it, too."

Eddie then lit his own. "What if I lose the golf game?" he said as he shook out the match. "You said you won't cover me."

"You're thinking small, Eddie. There's a lot more at stake here than your crummy golf match."

"Not for me, there isn't. Suppose I don't play him at all and just go down there to work out the deal?"

"No good."

"How come?"

"Because if you don't go down there for a big money match, you have no other reason to be there. Everyone'll know you're representing us, and that can't happen. Besides, we're just guessing about the back channel thing. What happens if you show up down there, refuse to play and that's all he really wanted from you in the first place?" Eastwood looked away from his Secret Service detail and took another surreptitious hit from his cigarette. "This is not a guy we'd like to get mad right now. Not until we know him better."

At the par-5 fourth, they sat on a wooden bench next to the tee box. The caddies and Secret Service agents kept a respectful distance back. "So what do you say, Eddie, will you go?"

"Sure. For five million bucks."

Eastwood laughed. "Yeah, right."

"That's my price, no matter what I work out. And that's take it or leave it."

"This is your country we're talking about!"

"We been through that before, Mr. President."

Eastwood nodded at the tee box, and stood up. "Let's hit."

Eddie teed off first. As they came away from the tee, Eastwood said, "First of all, paying you the same for a good or bad deal is bullshit and you know it. For all I know you might not say a word to the guy and come right home to collect."

"Then what you're saying, you don't trust me. Barranca does, but you don't, is that it?" When the president didn't answer, Eddie said, "You throw me into the middle of a nasty situation like that, ask me to risk my own money, I get five million for putting together a deal."

"No."

"Then I'm not doing it."

"Goddamnit!" Eastwood thundered, then took an angry step toward Eddie, but stopped when he saw his bodyguards already readying to go into protective mode, an eagerly anticipated boredom breaker in which no bystander was innocent or safe, including the president himself, who was liable to get a rib or two broken as the Secret Service agents raced each other to see who could protect him the most.

Eastwood raised a hand to stop them, then shook his finger at Eddie. "You can't extort me like this! I'm the goddamned president, goddamnit!"

"And you get so eloquent when you're angry. Take your shot."

Still shaking, the president took a mighty wallop with his three-wood and barely reached the ladies' tees. "Now look what you made me do!" He threw his club to the ground and stormed off as his caddy retrieved it, wiped it down and put it back in the bag.

Eddie remained silent as he followed.

"I'm not paying you five million dollars to play a game of golf and then hand Barranca our balls on a platter," he said when Eddie had caught up.

"Don't blame you. That'd be completely nuts."

"Now you're talking. So?"

"So what?"

"So what's it going to be?"

"I told you. Five million."

"But you just said that was nuts!"

"Nuts for you to pay it. Not nuts for me to ask."

"Well, I'm not going to do it."

"Then I'm not going to Brazil."

"Ecuador."

"What?"

"We fly you to Ecuador, and Barranca will pick you up there."

"How come?"

"Because that's the way he wants it. And the hell you aren't going!"

This time, it was Eddie's turn to stop. "The hell I am, Mr. President. What are you going to do . . . audit my tax returns?"

"For a start."

"Then you should know I keep impeccable records. Including all the dough I've taken off'a you."

"You wouldn't dare!"

"Dare what? Hand my records over to a government official who came armed with a properly executed subpoena?" Eddie eyed Eastwood and took a step back. "Say . . . you wouldn't be asking me to tamper with evidence, would you?"

"Oh, fuck off and die, Caminetti. I'm not paying you five million, or two million or two goddamned cents."

"Of course you're not. You'd be an idiot if you did." At a reproving look from Eastwood, Eddie quickly held up his hands. "And nobody's sayin the president of the *You*-nited States is an idiot."

"Alright, then."

"Yep. Stick to your guns, damnit."

"You bet."

"Uh huh."

Eastwood took a ball from his pocket and prepared to tee it up.

"Sir, what are you doing?"

"Taking a mulligan."

"You had one on the first tee."

"Whatever." Eastwood stood over the ball, inhaled, let it out, then straightened up and put the driver up on his shoulder. "Did you really think I was going to fork over five million bucks?"

"Hell, no."

"Then why'd you come up with a number like that?"

"Because I knew you wouldn't go for it."

"Okay, you were right. You made your point, and I made mine. We're both tough guys, so let's not bullshit each other. How much do you want?"

"So now we're agreed I'm going to get paid, and it's just a matter of price?"

Eastwood scratched his nose and looked at Eddie reprovingly. "Bad negotiating to rub your opponent's face in it when you win, Eddie. You should know better'n that."

"Yeah, you're right." Eddie grinned sheepishly. "Sorry."

Eastwood waved it away gracefully. "Not a problem. So, what's it going to be?"

"Five million."

It's as much the job of a Secret Service agent to stop the president from impulsively doing something stupid and self-destructive as it is to stop others from doing it to him, so three of the agents guarding Thomas Madison Eastwood wasted little time in pulling him off the much smaller and much less volatile Eddie Caminetti, while the remaining two helped the flabbergasted caddies understand how breathing even a word of what they'd seen would without question change their heretofore ordinary lives into something considerably less comfortable.

CHAPTER 12

The president's a gambler, I'll tell you that."

National Security Advisor Anatoli Kropotkin waved away Director of Central Intelligence Baines Gordon Wainwright's assessment. "You do not know what a gambler is, Gordy."

"Oh, is that so? And I suppose you're a real gambler, is that it?"

Kropotkin shook his head. "*Nyet.* But I will tell you who is."

"And that would be?"

"Our Mr. Caminetti."

Secretary of State William Patterson *harrumphed* angrily. "Haven't even met the sonofabitch and I hate him already. Thousands of people in my department and the president's really going to let some two-bit, low-life golf hustler deal with Barranca? Hell kind of sense does that make!"

"Why's Caminetti a real gambler, Anatoli?" Defense Secretary Harold Fortesque asked. "Just because he's going to Brazil for a big money match?"

"No. It is a certain state of mind." Kropotkin enjoyed the curious looks at the enigma he'd just tossed into the pot, then realized it wasn't curiosity at all, but impatience with his hammy, old country style of self-indulgent storytelling. "Okay, look: I will give you an example."

Kropotkin settled himself comfortably. "I had occasion to meet Eddie, at the prestigious Augusta golf course. He was a guest of mine and Bradford's. We played in the morning, then Eddie went off to the horse track. It was a glorious day, full of warm sun, and —"

"Gonna take all goddamned afternoon if we let Pushkin here tell it." The interruption came from FBI director Bradford MacArthur Baffington. "Caminetti bets two bucks on a hundred-to-one long shot in the first race. Sure enough, the nag wins, and now Eddie's got two hundred bucks, which he lets ride on another long shot in the second. That four-legged piece of crap wins, and now he's got about four grand in his pocket, which he proceeds to place on another long shot, and then another and another, until he's got over four hundred thousand dollars after the eighth race."

"And that means he's a gambler?" Fortesque said with some derision.

Baffington held up a hand. "I'm not finished. In the ninth he puts the whole wad on a sure thing and damned if the horse doesn't come in third, wiping out everything Eddie'd won on the first eight races."

The FBI director picked up his drink, which he'd been ignoring since taking over the story from Kropotkin. "That night he comes into the clubhouse and Anatoli here yells out, Hey, Caminetti! How'd you do at the track?" Baffington took a long belt of his drink and smacked his lips. "And Eddie calls back, swear to God, he shrugs and says: I lost two bucks!"

Baffington lowered his glass, banged it on the table twice and pointed at Fortesque with his forefinger. "Now *that's* a gambler."

The Secretary of State *harrumphed* again. "Very impressive, and big fucking deal. What's this gambler going to do about Barranca's revolution? Man doesn't know the first thing about global politics!"

Baffington waved him down. "Take it easy, Bill."

"Take it easy? We've got half a trillion dollars' worth of trained diplomats waiting on ice for a situation like this and we're sending a golfer? Why should I take it easy?"

"It's not that simple," Wainwright said.

"Fine!" Patterson wrapped his arms across his chest and slammed his elbows onto the table. "I'm ready for the complex details!"

Wainwright signaled to the waiter for another Cutty, then sniffed and frowned a few times, as though trying to determine how best to explain the situation. He pursed his lips in concentration and tapped his fingers idly on the table before coming to a decision and sitting up straight. "Now that I think about it, I guess it really is that simple."

"Now listen —!" Patterson had enough brains to hold himself in check when the waiter arrived with Wainwright's drink.

The waiter picked up the empty glass and carefully set the fresh drink down, then said to Baffington, "Begging your pardon, Mr. Director, but there's a fellow opposite who would be very appreciative if you would indulge him with a photo."

"Which fellow?" Baffington asked.

"Just there," the waiter said, pointing. "With the pink-and-ochre aloha shirt, Bermuda-length shorts and black socks with sandals. The young lady beside him, she with the three Target totes and handbag of no small capacity, is likely his wife."

Baffington didn't bother to look, but pulled a pen from the waiter's breast pocket and scrawled his name on a napkin. "This will have to do, Peter."

"Very good, sir. Shall I deliver a message?"

"Yeah," Baffington said as he handed the waiter the pen and napkin. "Tell them if either one of them comes near this table I'll have them both killed."

"Splendid. Thank you, sir. Sorry to have disturbed you."

"Jesus H. Fucking Holy—!"

"No need to go ballistic, Bill," Wainwright said calmly.

"No need to—of course there's a need to go ballistic!" Patterson bellowed. "What is this, the goddamned Twilight Zone?" Patterson paused for breath, then something new occurred to him. "Hey . . . how come all you guys know about this and I'm just hearing it?"

Fortesque shrugged. "President figured you'd go ballistic when you heard it."

"That sonofabitch!"

"But he was right," Baffington pointed out.

"That's beside the point!" Patterson was beyond stunned at the seeming unconcern of his compatriots. How was it possible that they were not even slightly rattled by something this bizarre and preposterous? These were, after all, some of the smartest people in government service. Which could only mean . . . "I take it this guy has no authority, formal or otherwise. Come to think of it, he's not really representing us at all, right?"

Wainwright inclined his head. "Nothing written down, if that's what you mean."

Patterson began to see it. "So if Caminetti blows it, as far as the U.S. is concerned, no talks ever took place."

"Never happened even if he doesn't blow it," Wainwright corrected him. "Barranca just lives up to his end of whatever he agreed to and nobody knows why."

"What if he doesn't?"

Baffington shrugged. "Then we're no worse off, and we know the guy's a lying, cheating bastard who can't be trusted."

"And if he muscles Caminetti and we renege, nobody knows that we're lying, cheating bastards who can't be trusted."

"Exactly."

Patterson thought about if for a few seconds, then nodded. "I like it," he said, calming somewhat. "You get right down to it, Caminetti's just some nobody on a golf trip."

"Exactly," Baffington affirmed.

"No authority whatsoever."

"You got it," Fortesque likewise assured him.

CHAPTER 13

ABOARD THE BLOCKBUSTER PRESIDENTIAL EXEC-O-LOUNGER

Despite the name change owing to that corporation's underwriting of all operating costs for the duration of President Eastwood's term of office, air traffic control still referred to it as Air Force One. Air traffic control referred to *any* plane the president was on as Air Force One, even if it was a Piper Cub doing touch-and-gos in Opalocka.

It was still the same fabulously appointed Boeing 747-200, just like any other 747 if you didn't count $200 million in advanced communications equipment, a self-contained baggage loader, built-in front and aft stairs, an executive suite with dressing room, lavatory and shower, a conference and dining room, a medical facility complete enough to do a heart-lung transplant (unwritten policy considered every passenger on board except the president and the surgeon a potential donor, even if they were still alive) and the capability to refuel in-flight. Interior spaciousness was best described by noting that, whereas the crew/passenger capacity of a commercial 747-200 can exceed 500, on the Blockbuster Presidential Exec-o-Lounger the max is 120, and forty of those are press representatives crammed into a single cabin configured like an ordinary Vegas Express, all passengers in perpetual, knee-to-chin emergency landing position. The presidential suite alone could hanger a four-passenger Cessna.

And it was a comfort to the passengers that the bright blue-and-yellow Blockbuster logo splattered all over the fuselage, complete with "Three Nights for Three Bucks!" in four-foot-high Day-Glo letters, could not be seen from the inside of the plane.

"Some bird, eh?" President Eastwood said to Eddie as they sauntered past the press area.

"I seen better."

"Bullshit. Whose?" As opposed to "Where?" or "When?"

"Donald Trump's."

Eastwood waved it away. "Quarter the size of this baby."

"Which is why he can land it in twice as many airports."

"Yeah, but he can't pick up a phone and blow up Moscow."

"Good point. Hadn't thought'a that." They'd reached the executive suite. A uniformed Marine stood at attention with his back to the door.

"Hiya, Randy."

The Marine saluted smartly at the president's greeting and stepped aside. Once inside, Eddie said, "Was that a guard?"

"Of course."

"What the hell is he guarding against? Don't you, like, check IDs or something before you let people on this thing?"

"Yeah, but with all the guests, press, celebs and the like riding around with us, he just makes sure nobody messes with my stuff."

"Your stuff. Like . . . ?"

"Ah, you know: nuclear codes, shit like that."

"I see. Well, I sure feel better knowing your shit is safe."

"Eddie . . ."

"Mr. President, don't you think it's about time we talked about what it is you'd like me to get done with this Barranca guy once I get down there?"

Eastwood motioned Eddie to one end of a leather-covered couch, and sat himself down on an easy chair angled away from it. "What would you like to drink?"

"What time is it?"

"Damned if I know. Depends on the time zone."

"Ginger ale'll be fine."

"Sounds good." Eastwood punched a button on the intercom built into the arm of his chair and gave the order to whoever picked up at the other end. He'd hardly gotten his hand off the button when the door opened and a uniform brought in a tray with glasses, ice in a silver bucket, sliced lemons and limes, napkins and two bottles. "What the hell took you so long?" Eddie noticed that the president hadn't spoken until the uniform was looking directly at him.

"Had to send out for it, sir. No ice on board."

"Okay, just set it down. We'll get it from here."

After the waiter left, Eddie said, "So how does this work: Guy joins the Army dreaming of glory in battle and winds up serving drinks on an airplane? That supposed to look good on his resume?"

"Air Force."

"Whatever."

"Allenby was a pilot trainee. Lost most of his hearing and part of his left foot when an engine quit on him and he had to bail out. Could've wound up a homeless junkie on a Santa Monica beach but instead he's serving his president on Air Force One."

"No shit?"

Eastwood shook his head. "Besides, he's a three-handicap and owes me over eight hundred bucks so I own his ass. But let's talk about Barranca."

The president picked up a remote control from a holder built into the side of the easy chair and pointed it at a wall. A panel rose to reveal a map of South America, political boundaries shown in thin white lines, topography in pale colors and large brown blotches scattered in a swath stretching from the northwest to the southeast.

"That brown stuff is the coffee plantations he took," Eddie guessed.

"Right. And I'm not prepared to start a war against an enemy I can barely identify who's scattered across half a dozen countries and mixed in with an innocent civilian population."

"We did it against the Baathists . . ."

"I rest my case. Next question?"

"What's he want?"

"We don't know for certain."

"Alright then, what do *we* want?"

"We want the coffee to start flowing again, at the old prices, with no further destabilization in South America."

"Well." Eddie slapped the leather arm of the couch. "I once hit a ball two hundred yards out of an ice cream cup, so I don't see how this is going to be a problem for me. Anything else?"

Eastwood laughed, then reached for a bottle and twisted open the top. "Problem here is, you're asking me questions like I have the answers and I'm just holding out on you. But I don't and I'm not."

Eddie leaned forward and picked up the second bottle. "So you don't have any idea what Barranca wants? Aside from a million bucks of my money?"

Eastwood upended the bottle and burbled the contents into a glass. "I'm guessing what he wants is an acknowledgment of the legitimacy of his revolution, maybe even some assistance."

Eddie stopped, the bottle only a few inches off the tray. "Assistance? You mean, like, military?"

Eastwood frowned before answering. "If he's as smart as everyone tells me he is, he can't really be expecting that. What are we going to do. . .send in troops to fight against Brazil? He'd have to be a total loony to think we'd do that, and I don't think he's a loony. For all I know, he might be the smartest revolutionary in history."

Eddie brought the bottle the rest of the way up and twisted it open. "Okay, so let's say he's looking for acknowledgment and assistance. What I don't get is, who, exactly, do we assist?"

Eastwood, trying to suppress a knowing smile, asked, "Meaning?"

Eddie tonged a few ice cubes into his glass. "Meaning, how do you even identify who you're dealing with? You said he hasn't attacked anything, isn't trying to overthrow an administration, there aren't any coup attempts, he's mixed in with the civilian population . . . aside from Barranca himself, what's—I don't even know how to put this—what's the *thing* that's asking for recognition and assistance?"

Eastwood picked up his glass and leaned back on the lounger. "What you're saying is, you can't draw a line around Barranca's organization and say everything inside the line is in, and everything outside, isn't."

"Exactly. If you reached some kind of agreement, and he signs it, who else is committed by it?"

Eastwood grew thoughtful as he took a few sips of his ginger ale and stared off into the distance. "I don't know."

"Well, don't you think somebody ought to find out?"

"Of course I do. But Barranca won't talk to anybody but you." Eastwood took one more sip and set his drink down, then folded his hands in his lap. "Given everything he's seen, he doesn't trust governments, ours or anybody else's."

"What an odd concept."

"He thinks that everything governments do is suspect, that there's always a hidden agenda, whether it's making more money, or getting ahead politically, or saving your ass or getting more ego points. He doesn't believe we do things just because they're the right thing to do."

"Do you?"

"That's beside the point. What's important is what *he* thinks, and that brings us to you."

"This is going to be good."

"More ice?"

"Sure."

Eddie held out his glass as Eastwood picked up an ice cube with the tongs and dumped it in, then another. "What I'm guessing, you being about the biggest bullshit artist in the world—"

"Don't sell yourself short, sir."

"But that's my point, Eddie. All your bullshit is right out in the open. You practically stand up on a lectern and say, 'Listen to me! I'm not kidding! I'm gonna take you to the freakin cleaners and don't say I didn't warn you!' Whereas everything a governmental administration does is exactly the opposite. We say, 'Don't worry. We're here to help. All we care about is your welfare, and you can trust us.'" Eastwood scratched the side of his nose. "Then we fuck em up the ass nine ways from Sunday. And if we did our jobs really, really well, they say 'Thank you' and vote us right back into office."

Eddie, lost in genuine wonder, had to blink several times to clear his head. "*A salut,*" he said, holding up his glass. "Best damned explanation of politics I ever heard."

"Thank you."

"So I'm supposed to go down there with a vague notion of what we want and no notion of what he wants and work out a deal, is that it?"

"I wouldn't have put it quite that way, but . . . yeah, that's pretty much it."

"Are you sending some people down with me to do that?"

Eastwood took a deep breath and let it out slowly. "Sure. Whole planeful of all kinds of experts. To advise you and back you up when you need it." Then he just stared at Eddie.

Who realized there was something he was supposed to be figuring out. Eddie watched his president for some sign of what that might be, but got nothing back from the legendary poker face other than the sense that it was something important. The intercom on the president's desk buzzed but it didn't cause even a flicker on his features, and he ignored it.

"You said Barranca wanted only me."

"He did."

"So he might not like all these other guys."

"He might not."

"He might not even like that they're around."

"Possibly."

"Which leaves only me."

"So it would seem."

"Mr. President," Eddie said after a long pause, "are you giving me authority to represent the United States?"

"You see any other way?"

Eddie, who was not used to being thrown for a loop or intimidated, was now both. "But I don't know what I'm doing!"

Eastwood smiled broadly, then chuckled as he shook his head and slapped the arm of his chair. "Goddamn, Eddie. Do you think even the president knows what the hell he's doing when he's doing something nobody ever did before?" When Eddie didn't respond, he went on, "You think JFK 'knew what he was doing' when he was handling the Cuban missile crisis, or Truman when he had to decide whether to drop the Big One?"

"Never thought of it like that."

"Nobody does! Everybody expects us to know everything, in advance, and never make a mistake. But we don't get elected because we know all the answers; we get elected because voters think we're the kind of people who can figure it out. And the truth of the matter is, we don't get paid for flying around in the Blockbuster and making speeches and riding herd on legislation. Hell, any schmuck with a good staff can do that and look like a statesman."

Eastwood leaned forward and pointed a finger toward Eddie. "The only time we ever really earn our pay is when the shit hits the fan and we make it go away, at least temporarily, and without too many people getting killed in the process." He leaned back and set his hands on the chair arms. "All the rest is pure bullshit, and anybody who tells you different is either kidding himself or kidding the citizens."

Eddie stared at him for a long few seconds, then said, "Fine. You go down there and handle Barranca, because sure as hell nobody voted for me."

"I told you already: I can't."

"Because he doesn't want to see you?"

Eastwood grunted. "Don't be stupid. If I wanted to meet with him, I could have him brought here in manacles. No. The reason is that the leader of the free world can't be seen to be bullied by a seat-of-the-pants, wannabe Guevara who thinks he's holding the nation hostage."

"But you are being bullied. And he does have us hostage."

"I said 'seen to be.' You think I'm planning to tell the New York Times I'm giving some low-life hustler presidential authority to negotiate on behalf the United States?"

Eddie knew full well that Eastwood was doing no such thing, that he would be operating within a tight set of parameters dictated by a policy worked out by scores of advisors, and that if things ultimately went bad the administration would substitute ordnance for diplomacy and worry about the consequences later.

But he also knew that it was in everybody's best interest to get this worked out quietly and with minimal damage, which was why Eastwood and his closest advisors were willing to play out this absurd farce based on the possibility that more drastic measures might be avoided. "So what am I authorized to do . . . give him Rhode Island? Make him chairman of the Fed? Get him Lakers tickets?"

Eastwood shook his head. "You're acting on my authority, so you can do only what I'm allowed to do."

"Wow! Can I call down an air strike? Damn, I've always wanted to call down an air strike. Or maybe strafe some shit. Yeah, that'd be—"

"Will you be serious, f'chrissakes?"

"No air strikes?"

"Actually, you can. It's called an emergency police action. But you really can't."

"Rats. Okay, so what can I do?"

"Depends on what he wants."

"Which is . . . ?"

"I don't know. But I've got some very smart people working on it, and they're preparing some role-playing scenarios."

"Huh?"

"They'll try to anticipate as many possibilities as they can, then you'll rehearse all of them according to scripts they'll prepare."

Eddie thought it over for a few seconds. "Sounds like a smart idea."

"Yeah."

"Not gonna do it."

"Sorry?"

"Not gonna do it."

"What?"

CHAPTER 14

"What the hell do you mean, he's not gonna do it!" thundered Secretary of State William Patterson, unmindful of the spittle that he'd just ejected onto the collars of an aide from the office of the Assistant Secretary for Diplomatic Security and Foreign Missions (DS) and an analyst from the office of the Director General of the Foreign Service & Director of Human Resources (DGHR), both of whom didn't dare do anything about it but simply stared straight ahead, hoping that nobody else saw it and knowing for sure that everybody did and would be talking about it for days.

There were few things President Eastwood relished more than staying as calm as a Buddhist monk when someone else was in the process of going off the deep end. Not acknowledging someone else's anger or giving him the leeway to be human and blow off a little steam, but instead behaving as though he were a nine-year-old having an attack of hysteria, was a cheap but effective way of asserting your innate equanimity and level-headedness, not to mention your superior crisis-management skills. There was also, of course, the risk of communicating that you just plain didn't give enough of a shit to get excited, but if you were the president, that risk was acceptable.

"He won't do it, Bill," Eastwood said with maddening tranquility. "Says that unless you're right there with him and doing the work, getting briefed and prepped will only cramp his style. And there's a good possibility Barranca won't deal with anybody except Caminetti, so he's likely to be on his own."

The thirty-odd State Department underlings sitting around the massive conference table that had been carved from a single California redwood each tried to outshrink everyone else into their seats. Sitting in the presence of the chief executive was enough in itself to terrify any bureaucratic suit into near-catalepsy, but watching their own department head—and a Cabinet-level one, no less—devolve into a blustering ouch-bag of uncontainable indignation at the same time was overload akin to swallowing a grenade. Only the president's preternatural tranquility prevented two or three of them from imploding entirely and throwing up all over their ruled yellow writing tablets and crisply sharpened number-two pencils.

In one of those career-defining moments so feared and yet so yearned for by upwardly mobile government service professionals, inflection points from which flowed either the mother's milk of rising stardom or the bitter sludge of a downward spiral even Jesus Christ couldn't reverse, Jarred Leffington Wapcaplit III, newly promoted section supervisor in the political analysis department of the office of the Assistant Secretary for Western Hemisphere Affairs, cleared his throat and said, "Why don't we just make him do it?"

The silence that ensued could be heard four offices away. It was later ventured that even most of the heartbeats in the room had momentarily ceased, lest any of the assembled call attention to him- or herself by virtue of an overactive ventricle.

Eastwood looked over at the adventuresome young man who had just tossed a four-hundred-pound coin nine miles into the air and whose metabolic functions had effectively ceased pending said coin's return to earth in one of only two possible configurations. "And your name would be?"

The coin had reached its apex, paused for a split second, and was now starting downward. "Wapcaplit, Mr. President." Was that enough? Did he want a full name? Did he want his department, job title, shoe size?

Eastwood nodded, then looked down at his fingernails. "Wapcaplit, uh huh."

The coin was picking up speed now, accelerating inexorably, so much mass moving so fast it would obliterate anything that dared try to stop it. Wapcaplit could feel the full weight of it in the lining of his stomach.

"Well, I'll tell you something, Mr. Wapcaplit. In a democracy—" Eastwood looked up at the newly promoted section supervisor in the political analysis department of the office of the Assistant Secretary for Western Hemisphere Affairs "—the highest rank is citizen."

Wapcaplit, undergrad from Stanford, MA in diplomacy from Harvard, felt the coin crash into the earth only after passing right through his skull.

"I can't make him do anything," Eastwood finished, as though it were lost on anybody in the room that young Wapcaplit's career had just been definitively consigned to the deepest, darkest, dankest cellar of the deepest, darkest pit of federal bureaucratic hell, the likes of which existed nowhere else in the civilized world.

Which was too bad, because his suggestion wasn't a bad one. The notion that the president of the United States couldn't coerce a private citizen was absurd. He could start by putting the IRS on him, and no matter how careful and honest Eddie was with his taxes, it didn't matter, because the U.S. Tax Code was so insanely complicated, and in some cases so blatantly self-contradictory, that no human being on earth could possibly file a return of even modest complexity that didn't have something wrong with it somewhere.

Besides, if all else failed, Eastwood always had the Patriot Act. Using it, he could get a court order to tap into Eddie's Web surfing just by telling a judge that such spying was relevant to an ongoing investigation, and if Eddie had ever entered a word like "fertilizer" into a search engine—a likely possibility considering that he owned a golf resort with over two square miles of tended grass—he could be detained, indefinitely and without benefit of counsel, because of the potential assertion that he spent more time on his resort island than he did in the United States and was therefore in actuality a foreigner. Whether that could be demonstrated was another story altogether, but he could be held while it was being contested.

So Wapcaplit's suggestion that coercion be brought into play to get Eddie to sit through some briefings before going to Brazil was not bad in and of itself. What was bad was that he'd voiced it out loud, and in front of the president, who had no choice but to smack it down in the strongest possible terms because any semblance of "plausible deniability" had been effectively denied him.

All of which Secretary Patterson saw in a flash, right along with the end of the young lad's career, but he was not to be deterred. "We have resources, Mr. President," he persisted. "We know things and have expertise that this Caminetti guy hasn't clue one about."

"Good point," Eastwood said. "Maybe we can reason with the man. After all, he's neither stupid nor close-minded. So, let's see what we've got."

"Excellent!" Patterson, responded, and the room exploded with the sudden racket of unclasping briefcases, withdrawing manila folders, clattering paper clips, shuffling sheaves of documents and the clicking of ballpoint pens. Only Wapcaplit, whose small and large intestines had by now fused into a single undifferentiated mass, remained immobile.

"Okay!" Eastwood rubbed his hands together. "Let's start with a little history. When did Barranca start his campaign?"

Patterson pointed to an analyst from Western Hemisphere Affairs.

"We don't know, Mr. President."

"No problem! What else has he taken aside from the eighteen coffee-growing regions?"

Patterson nodded to a researcher from Economic and Business Affairs. "We don't have complete information on that, Mr. President."

"I'll take partial information. No? Alright, then: Where's the coffee harvest being stored in the interim?"

Patterson shot a glare at a technical specialist from the office of International Information Programs, who shook his head morosely and said, "Hasn't been compiled yet, sir."

"Casualties in the field? Results of local surveillance operations? Names and locations of his key lieutenants, ordnance supplies, vehicle distribution, food and water stores, base and distributed field operations? Okay, then, how big's his army?"

"At least two hundred thousand men, Mr. President!"

This last came from Monroe Zeidwick, who worked for the Undersecretary for Arms Control and International Security, and to whom every eye in the room had just turned.

"How's that again, son?" Eastwood asked.

"Two hundred thousand, minimum, sir." There was nothing tentative in Zeidwick's voice, no hesitation in his delivery, no sign that he was anything but confident and eager to strut his stuff. He'd had only the one analytical assignment since this Barranca business began, had worked on it night and day, and had come into this meeting praying fervently to be asked the one question he was completely capable of answering. Since the president had begun has barrage of questions that everyone now understood he'd known all along to be unanswerable, Zeidwick was so eager to share his hard-won knowledge that, had Eastwood not brought it up himself, Zeidwick would have either figured out a way to finesse it into the conversation or just plain blurted it out.

But he hadn't had to do either of those things, and now he had everyone's attention, the secretary's and the president's included, and from this moment forth he'd command some goddamned respect in this man's bureaucracy.

"How do we—what was your name?"

"Zeidwick, sir. Monroe Zeidwick, Arms Control and International Security."

"Zeidwick. Okay. So how do we know he's got two hundred thousand troops? Minimum?"

Not how do we *know, by God,* Zeidwick thought. *How do* I *know. None of you knows shit yet, and you won't until* I *tell you!* "Force-resistance analysis, Mr. President." He was smart, Zeidwick was. Don't tell them more than they wanted to know, don't show off, don't kill them with details they don't need. Give them the top level, then the next level only if they asked for it, then the next only if asked again.

"What's that?"

Zeidwick started to put his elbows on the table, then thought better of it. "We may not know anything specific about Manual Barranca or what he's done —" He could feel two dozen of his colleagues bristle almost visibly "—but we know quite a bit about what he was up against when he did them. We know the size of the land seizures, the protective facilities that were in place, the capabilities of local law enforcement as well as those of relevant military forces . . ." He let his voice trail off, Monroe Zeidwick his own self prompting the president of the United States to fill in the blanks.

"So you backed into what it would take for Barranca to succeed."

"Precisely, sir."

"Huh. Well, I'll be damned." Eastwood tapped his fingers on the table for a few seconds. "What's your margin of error?"

Oh, bliss! "Plus or minus thirty-five thousand, sir."

Eastwood nodded approvingly. "Nice piece of work there, son."

"Thank you, sir," Zeidwick replied, even as he began mentally picking a color scheme for his new corner office.

"Anything else?"

"You'll run this past Caminetti?" Patterson asked.

"Run what past him?"

"Zaftig's analysis. About the size of the army. So he lets us prep him."

"Prep him with what, Bill? We don't know shit that he can use. And besides . . ." Eastwood stood up, followed by thirty-odd others. "He's already been briefed."

"By who!"

"That's classified. I'll tell you in your office. We're done here."

"Hang on a second. When's he leaving to go down there?"

"Day after tomorrow."

"Why the delay?"

"Said he had something to do."

SECRETARY'S OFFICE, COLGATE-PALMOLIVE STATE DEPARTMENT BUILDING

"Who the hell is Carlos Rivera?"

"Manuel Barranca's caddy."

Patterson looked at Eastwood disdainfully. "Bullshit, Tom. He's been dead since '77. Wainwright already told us."

"Yeah, well, his corpse showed up a few days ago and told Caminetti damned near everything there is to know about Barranca."

"So you already knew all the answers to everything you asked in there?"

Eastwood laughed. "Jeez, I'm not that devious, Bill. What I meant, he told Eddie everything about Barranca's golf game. Eddie figures now he can beat him."

Patterson, incredulous, slumped onto his plush leather executive chair. "You mean that's why Caminetti agreed to go? Because he thinks he can win a golf match?"

"Look at it from his point of view and it's not unreasonable. Besides, what do I care? I just want him down there, get some dialogue going."

"But —"

"Don't worry about it." Eastwood waited to make sure his secretary of state stopped objecting, then considered whether to tell him the really bad news or not. "We've been friends a long time, Bill."

"Oh, shit."

"Oh, shit what?"

"Oh, shit, the last time you said that we bombed Tunisia."

"This isn't as bad."

"Oh, shit."

Eastwood got up and opened the office door. "Hey, Evelyn," he said to Patterson's lead assistant, "you got any coffee squirreled away somewhere?"

She got up and walked to a mahogany filing cabinet on the wall opposite her desk. "The G.E. sent some over when they found out you were coming, Mr. President," she said as she pulled open a drawer.

"Not for me." Eastwood jutted his chin toward his shoulder. "For him." Then he looked at his watch: 5:30 PM "You might want to spike it a little, too."

"He's got a reception with the Belgian ambassador at seven, sir."

"Right. Make it a double shot."

"Let me have it," Patterson said when Eastwood came back into the room. "And is this on the record?"

"Up to you."

"If it is, then you know the rule."

Eastwood did: Patterson wouldn't let friendship stand in the way of his responsibilities and obligations as a public official. He'd made it very clear when originally asked if he wanted the Cabinet-level job that he wouldn't participate in anything even remotely resembling a cover-up or an illegal operation, and that everybody had better know from the get-go not to assume he'd play ball with any shenanigans.

"Okay, off the record." Eastwood resumed his seat. "It's a bit more than just starting some dialogue. I've authorized Caminetti to negotiate terms on behalf of my office." He winced in anticipation of the explosion sure to follow, but he'd underestimated Patterson, and not for the first time.

"Goes without saying, if you really do send him."

Eastwood held his surprise in check. "I need for you not to make waves on this, Bill."

Patterson thought it over. "Then you and I never had this conversation."

The assistant came in carrying a cup of coffee in an elegant cup and saucer. "Are you sure I can't get you something, Mr. President?"

"Yeah, you can. Coffee and a shot. And forget the coffee." He waited for her to leave and close the door behind her. "Covering your ass, Mr. Secretary?"

"Call it what you want, Mr. President." Patterson took a small sip of the hot coffee. "But if you expect to me to sit quietly and not say a word after you tell me that you're letting a professional hustler represent the United States with full executive authority, then either you didn't tell me in the first place or I meet with the congressional leadership tomorrow morning and convene an impeachment committee."

Eastwood's face grew cold. "I'm entrusting you with a national security secret."

Patterson, mid-sip, broke it off and set the cup down with a clatter. "Not off the record, you're not! And while we're at it, let me tell you something." He pulled a handkerchief from his pocket and dabbed at his lips. "The reason I don't blow it open right now is that I don't for one second believe you'll honor anything that low-life commits us to that would be detrimental to our interests. Should that change, all bets between us are off. I mean it, Tom."

"I know you do. Okay, then." Eastwood stood up. "Just stay the hell out of the way."

"What if he screws it up?"

"He's not going to."

"How can you be certain?"

"Don't worry about it."

PANTRY OF THE G.E. PRESIDENTIAL RESIDENCE
—EARLIER THAT DAY

"All I'm saying, Mr. President, I might have to paint outside the lines a little."

"And all I'm saying, Eddie, I'm not sure I like the sound of that."

"Little late to be having this conversation, isn't it?"

Eastwood rose from his stool imperiously, so that he could stare down at Eddie, who was not only still planted on his own stool but was considerably shorter than the president to begin with. "Try to bear in mind that you're representing not just your country, but the integrity of this office as well!"

Rather than respond, Eddie took another bite of his tuna salad sandwich.

"Are you listening to me?" Eastwood looked over at Romaine LeClaire, a black woman in her late fifties who'd run the G.E. kitchen since the building had still been called the White House, and lowered his voice. "We're not rug merchants! There are rules, protocols, certain formalities . . ."

Eddie chewed slowly as Eastwood boiled, then took a slug of milk to wash it down. "You through fumigating now?"

"Through what?"

"Getting all heated up and blowing off steam?"

"You mean *fulminating*. And no, I'm not."

"Uh huh."

"You can't embarrass us, Eddie, and you can't break the rules!"

"Yeah, right." Eddie took another bite, but before swallowing lifted his glass toward LeClaire. "Triffith sanitch, O-ay."

"Glad you like it, Mr. Caminetti," she replied. "More milk?"

"Nyarnk."

As LeClaire went to get the milk, Eddie swallowed and turned to Eastwood. "Who're you kidding, Mr. President?"

"What about my reputation? What about *yours!*"

"First off, I don't give a rat's sweet patoot about my reputation, and second of all, who you plannin on tellin if you think I screwed it up?"

"This is not how I do —"

"Oh, f'cryin out loud: We're off the record, so who're you talking to? You want to put in your memoirs that you agonized and tried to convince me to behave like one'a those three thousand diplomats you're *not* sending? Is that it?"

"Listen, Eddie. What I'm saying—"

Eddie wiped his hands and threw down his napkin. "I know what you're sayin, and it's complete bullshit."

"Just a —"

"What are we talking about here, Mr. President?"

Eddie turned to make sure none of the kitchen staff was in earshot. The sun hadn't even risen yet and there were only one or two others in attendance, and that many only owing to the president's habit of sneaking downstairs for a quick bite at all hours of the night. LeClaire started back into the room holding a container of milk, but at a barely perceptible head shake from Eastwood, the experienced kitchen master veered off to the side and waited.

"This isn't some tea party you're talking about," Eddie continued, "and I'm not some embassy toastmaster who drinks sherry with his pinkie in the air. If some chest-thumping sonofabitch has a knife to our throats, are you really telling me there's some rulebook I gotta follow? I mean, what am I supposed to say when the whole country is counting on me? Sorry, folks, we had it all worked out but page four hundred, paragraph nine says I can't agree to let him ship more than three sacks of Colombian on a non-U.S. merchant ship so now your kids have to starve to death?"

"Ah, c'mon, Eddie . . . don't overdramatize here."

"Oh, yeah? What happens if I don't come back with a deal?" When Eastwood didn't answer immediately Eddie said, "You're probably going to start a little war, right? That's what everybody thinks."

"Not because of anything we've said."

"Sure. Haven't said anything to make em think otherwise, either."

"Rumors like that can sometimes be helpful. Maybe they'll help loosen Barranca up a little, make him more agreeable to playing ball."

"Maybe it'll just piss him off."

"Maybe. But what you're really telling me," Eastwood said, "is that you're not about to risk your five million dollar fee by going in with your hands tied."

"Damned straight." Eddie signaled to LeClaire that it was okay to come in now. As she walked over, he said, "That's why I won't let those diplo-yahoos brief me, see? I don't want to find out about the eight thousand things I can't do." Eddie held up his glass and LeClaire poured. After she left again Eddie said, "No way I take on a job without the juice to get it done."

"What are you going to do?" Eastwood asked.

"How the hell should I know? I don't even know what we're up against yet." Having made his point, Eddie saw no need to rub the president's face in it. "I'm just letting you know, sir: If it sounds reasonable to this ordinary citizen, it's on the table."

Eastwood had had enough trouble just getting Eddie to go on the trip, and as this argument was getting nowhere anyway, he didn't want to chance making him change his mind. "So why the delay? What's so important you can't go right away?"

"Little business to take care of first."

CHAPTER 15

A NEIGHBORHOOD BALL FIELD IN WABAN, MASSACHUSETTS

The kid tried to pretend he couldn't hear them, but to a fourteen-year-old, schoolyard taunts were about as ignorable as grenades going off in your pants.

"Yer a joke!" one barely pubescent voice rang out in strident alto.

"Should be playin hopscotch!" another chimed in.

The kid stared straight at the pitcher, who shook his head disdainfully and launched another fastball straight up the middle. The kid swung and missed, which set off a fresh round of whoops and hollers from the nearby group of eighth graders a few hundreds credits shy of their sensitivity certification.

Up in the stands, Albert Auberlain grimaced and looked down at his shoes. "Gittin worse by the minute."

Eddie Caminetti nodded slightly, but kept his eyes on home plate.

Another fastball whiffed by as the kid swung ineffectually.

"Pitcher's not even putting anything on it," Auberlain observed. "Throwin creampuffs my grandmother could hit."

"Your grandmother's dead."

"My point exactly."

The next pitch was outside, and the kid let it go by for a ball.

"Least he can see," Auberlain admitted grudgingly.

"That he can," Caminetti agreed.

The surly group of budding Gehrigs was in full vigor now, shouting over each other to see who could hurl the most pointed barb.

"Send yer kid sister out here, ya moron!"

"I think I hear yer mother callin, doofus!"

The kid didn't react to the latest round of insults, but as soon as the pitcher got the next sign and straightened up, he stepped away from the plate and held up his hand.

"Time!" the ump yelled, raising both arms.

"Oh, yeah...time!" someone called out sarcastically. "*That'll* help!"

"Get it over with, you dork!"

"Yer wastin *our* time!"

Eddie watched as the kid scooped up some dirt and rubbed it on his hands, the bat cradled in his elbow. The young boy took his time, looking around to assess the situation. One ball, two strikes, the fielders barely paying attention, secure in the knowledge that the odds of the next pitch ending up anywhere but in the catcher's hands were about the same as one of them getting hit by a de-orbiting satellite.

Eddie watched as the kid adjusted his batting helmet, kicked a piece of nonexistent dirt off the bat, rolled his neck around a few times to loosen it up, then stepped back to the batter's box, grinding his spikes into the ground as he resumed his stance. He took a couple of easy practice swings, then set the bat just above his right shoulder and his eyes on the pitcher.

Then he went still. Completely, like a cobra poised to strike. Steely determination beamed from his face, and the pitcher's former insouciance gave way to a new tension at the same time that the noise from the onlooking players died down slightly. Maybe one or two of them noticed that the heel of the kid's forward foot was barely touching the ground, that he was holding the bat so far around it was pointing straight at the left field bleachers.

Straight at Eddie and Auberlain, whose eyes shifted back and forth between the kid and the pitcher.

The boy on the mound got another sign but waved it off, waved it off again, then stood up as the catcher punched his glove once and held it out to receive the pitch. The gang of self-impressed future big-leaguers was quiet now. With no men on base threatening to steal, the pitcher could take his time winding up.

The kid at bat didn't move as the windup got under way. There was no reason to; he'd gotten himself coiled into the exact place he wanted to start his swing from, and there was no need to adjust. He just waited. Watched and waited, weapons radar on full alert.

The pitcher whipped his arm over his head, threw his weight forward and snapped his wrist, using every ounce of his hundred and twenty pounds to send the ball rocketing toward the plate, and had barely enough time to notice a slight narrowing of the batter's eyes as they locked in on the ball heading right for the very heart of the strike zone, barely enough time to recover from his forward momentum and try to duck because about ten milliseconds before the ball arrived over the plate the scrawny batter released every last iota of the energy he'd stored up in his back, legs and shoulders and focused it down into the bat, which was knifing around so fast there was hardly any time for the air in front of it to get out of the way. At the exact instant the ball reached the plate the bat got there, too.

And passed harmlessly beneath the ball.

"Strike three!" the ump yelled, and the eighth graders revived their momentarily dormant jeering with even more gusto than before.

"You suck, Je-*rome*!" they screeched with glee, the irony of berating one of their own teammates utterly lost on them. "You stink!"

Auberlain cleared his throat and slapped his hands on his thighs. "That's about the ugliest damned swing in the game'a baseball."

"Yeah," Eddie said, his eyes still glued to the kid, who, downcast and thoroughly defeated, was walking disconsolately back to the bench. "But it's the most beautiful golf swing I've ever seen in my whole life."

CHAPTER 16

President Eastwood hated diplomatic receptions. In fact he hated cocktail parties altogether, except for the private ones he threw himself, and for which he got to handpick all the guests.

But this. This was a chaotic mishmash of invitees selected by five different committees from State, the G.E. Presidential Residence social office, the CIA, the DIA and the executive board of the Association of American Oil Companies. There were only two people in attendance that Eastwood actually liked and enjoyed talking to, but one was making *flan* in the kitchen and the other was carrying a tray of drinks to the second-tier functionaries on a different floor. State had assured the president, on many such occasions, that spending his time with the kitchen help would not sit well with the functionaries upon whom he was supposed to be spreading royal jelly, not to mention that it would interfere with the serving of food and drink. For a while Eastwood had taken refuge with the children of his hosts, playing video games and otherwise having a good old time to the immense pleasure of their parents, but that was early in his administration before he had fully grasped the Washington obsession with the intensely competitive game involving who could get closer to the real seat of power. Shaking hands with the president carried a few points, being called by name was worth a few more, getting photographed in conversation with him got you a huge bonus, etc., etc. If the president holed himself up down in the playroom for a few hours of Donkey Kong and s'mores with the kiddies, the people upstairs tended to get a little snarly at being gypped out of their much-anticipated round of Power Poker.

It should have been a pleasant occasion for Eastwood. Such gatherings were often a litmus test of how the president was faring, and right now this president was faring extremely well. America suspected he was on the verge of sending troops to rid the western hemisphere of the scourge called Barranca, and it had been carefully leaked that he was awaiting only the perfect confluence of weather, tides, enemy troop positions and confirmed intelligence before his minions in the armed services pounced like starving cats and accomplished their mission with an absolute minimum of American lives lost. Peace and stability would return to the neighbor continent and, of much more immediate concern, coffee would once more begin flowing northward, in anticipation of which prices had already started dropping on supplies hoarded by speculators intent on making a Schadenfreudian killing in the marketplace.

America at large was tickled to death. At last, the crisis looked like it might come to an end. Because of the expected swiftness of the confrontation and Manuel Barranca's perceived inability to mount any serious resistance, the realities of war and its attendant atrocities weren't being discussed by anybody. There was only joy that the arrogant, disruptive, upstart revolutionary was about to go down in clean, surgical flames, and the air at the party was filled with the kind of bonhomie normally attendant to those whose own good fortunes were entirely dependent on their proximity to the good fortunes of others.

"A pleasure to meet you, Mr. President," said the ambassador from Lichtenstein, pumping Eastwood's hand furiously with both of his own.

Eastwood had his drink in his left hand, and held it away from his body in a practiced maneuver designed to minimize the shock waves threatening to slosh it onto his sleeve. He looked around for the official photographer, knowing that the jackhammering wouldn't cease until the ambassador got his picture taken. Spotting the lensman, Eastwood nodded for him to come over. He knew that when the ambassador saw the camera he'd let go of his hand, which he did right on cue, quickly cupping an elbow in his own hand and touching a finger to his chin in an attitude of contemplative discourse, staring straight at Eastwood in apparent disregard of the camera. The president complied, opening his mouth as if actually speaking, holding up a finger in front of the man's face. When the picture finally appeared in a newspaper or, more likely first, the diplomatic pouch back to Lichtenstein, it would look as though the ambassador had been absorbed in something profound and portentous the leader of the free world had seen fit to share only with him, and right in the midst of all the other important people he was ignoring in favor of the ambassador. By the time the evening was over, a hundred such photos would be zipping around the world in diplomatic pouches and on the Internet, with printed copies ready to be framed and mounted on highly visible wall space all over town.

Dutifully accommodating the superannuated bureaucrats for whom such displays of access were their daily bread and butter was the price Eastwood had to pay to accomplish the one important task he'd come for, a task he could have done in a three-minute phone conversation but that the diplomatic formalists at State, for whom placing the salad fork on the wrong side of the plate was cause for a U.N. resolution of condemnation, assured him was absolutely the wrong way to go.

"Would you excuse me for one moment?" Eastwood said to the ambassador, holding his drink aside to accommodate a resumption of the two-handed fist shake.

"Of course, Mr. President!" the ambassador assured him vigorously, as though he'd just been asked to address both houses of the U.S. Congress simultaneously. In a voice loud enough to be heard on K Street, he added, "A pleasure speaking with you! I look forward to the further exchange of views on these important matters!" He waited for the telltale flash of a strobe light to bounce off the walls before finally, reluctantly, surrendering the president's hand.

Conchita Ortega smiled brightly at the ambassador as she steered the president to another corner of the room. "What important matter?" she asked. "The price of Beluga in Vladivostok?"

"Damnit, you were eavesdropping!" Eastwood squeezed through clenched teeth.

"Sorry. There he is." She pointed to a dark-skinned man fully bedecked in flowing Arabic robes. "Advance made him leave his scimitar in the gun safe."

"Probably saved him from cutting off one of his own fingers. How do you pronounce his —"

"Ali *Ach*-med bin Ka-ud," Ortega replied, emphasizing the guttural first syllable of the middle name. "Make like you're clearing your throat."

"Thought it was *Ah*-med."

"That's how it's written."

Ka-ud, upon seeing their approach, waved away the people he'd been engaged in conversation with, but stood his ground and didn't step forward in greeting. Eastwood sighed inwardly, knowing he was in for some power-tripping of the first order. But that was the great thing about being the president: For everyone else in the world, such childish displays were of critical importance, and if you made the wrong move it was interpreted as a sign of weakness. For the president, though, the same moves were always seen as signs of admirable humility, because he *was* the seat of power, and that was never in doubt and never needed to be affirmed.

Eastwood strode forward purposefully, underscoring that the mountain was coming to meet Ahmed, and he enjoyed the slightly uncertain look in the Middle Eastern potentate's eyes. Ka-ud's ground-standing tactic would only work if the president limped toward him uncomfortably, as though he'd just conceded a critical battle to a superior enemy. Instead, it now looked as though the player with the clear upper hand was deigning to confer a singular honor upon only one in a vast multitude of eager inferiors for whom such displays were of paramount importance, and about which the president himself couldn't give a tinker's cuss.

"*Ach*-med!" Eastwood called out with a smile of intense delight at seeing an old and dear acquaintance.

Ka-ud reached for the outstretched hand. "Mr. President. Such a sincere delight. We are so very pleased you could join us this evening."

"Wouldn't have missed it for the world," Eastwood said, stepping to Ka-ud's side to face the camera. They held the handshake for the time it took the photographer to snap off a dozen motor-driven shots, moving as he held the shutter button and automatically bracketing the exposures to make sure he got at least a few usable pictures to frame for the Sultan.

Eastwood patiently shook hands with each of the two dozen embassy officials and hangers-on Ka-ud introduced him to, most of whom seemed to have last names consisting of "Ka-ud" with another syllable tacked on, which was interesting considering that the last time the president had attended a diplomatic reception at the embassy, most of the last names had contained some variation of "Ahmadi," the previous sultan. When at last there were no more third cousins left, Eastwood said, "I need to speak with you for a few minutes. In private."

"Cer-tain-ly," Ka-ud said, drawing the word out slowly, knowing full well why the president was here. He held a hand out toward a corner of the large room.

"In private."

"I assure you, Mr. President, we shall not be disturbed."

Ka-ud led the way, the president following behind. Two senior diplomats from State's Middle Eastern section fell into step with them, but Eastwood waved them away, which brought looks of horror to their eyes. They'd spent many hours briefing the president on how to handle this critical conversation, in the process outlining their own roles with great precision. They'd scripted out in forty pages of branching decision-tree diagrams exactly who was going to say what depending on who said what first.

But that was several weeks ago, and a lot had happened since then.

With a slight jerk of his head, Ka-ud cleared the area under a Moorish tapestry so that the two of them were alone. Following standard anti-eavesdrop protocol, Eastwood waited until Ka-ud was settled and comfortable, then said, "Let's move down a couple of feet," and did so himself without waiting for a response. Ka-ud had no choice but to follow him, and any listening devices that might have been planted beneath the wall hanging were thus rendered useless. "You know why I'm here, Ahmed."

The sultan smiled indulgently. "I am assuming it is to do with the shipping center your government is so generously providing assistance with."

"Not assistance. We're building it for you."

"As I said, most generous."

"Yeah. Thing is, we had an off-the-record agreement with —"

Ka-ud held up two fingers and waited for the president to stop speaking. "I feel compelled to point out, sir, that whatever informal arrangements my distant cousin might or might not have entered into are, for reasons I am sure you can appreciate, not necessarily binding upon the newly installed legitimate government of the people of Jez Rama'am."

"Does that mean you don't intend to honor that agreement?"

The still-smiling Ka-ud let his eyelids half drop as he rocked his head back and forth. "We shall see, Mr. President. Situations change, as you yourself well know." He looked heavenward. "Who among us can say what the future will hold, or what turn of events might conspire to compromise even the most well-intentioned of plans?" He folded his hands across his ample belly and let his words hang in the air. Ka-ud was well aware that the ceremony announcing the building of the shipping center had been seen live on television by fifty million people in the region and had been front-page news all over the world. Work had already begun on the project and was in full swing. Regime change aside, he had the U.S. president by the short and curlies and he knew it.

Eastwood ran over the State Department script in his mind, thumbing through the various branches and links he was supposed to follow, then glanced at the two diplomats chewing on their fingernails who were waiting to be summoned to assist, as they'd planned so carefully. Eastwood's next mental image was of the script—and the two diplomats—flying out the fifth floor window trailing three distinct lines of smoke. "You know something, sultan?"

Ka-ud turned to him slowly. "Mmmm?"

Eastwood heaved a great sigh and scratched the side of his head. "I've had a really rough couple of weeks, you know what I mean?"

"So I understand. We ourselves, being Islamic, do not of course drink coffee, but I do sympa—"

"Yeah. Which kind of makes me wonder what the hell you do with the two hundred pounds of Kona mountain blend trucked over here by Safeway every month."

Ka-ud lost his smirk. "I assure you I have no —"

"Or the weekly two cases of Johnny Walker. Black Label, is it?"

"Again, I —"

This time it was Eastwood who held up a hand, immediately stopping the sultan. After waiting to make sure the man was going to stay quiet, he said, "Ahmed, I've been dealing with nothing but assholes and hucksters for the last three weeks, all on account of one slimy sonofabitch in the middle of a rain forest who thinks he can hold the world's only remaining superpower hostage."

"It would seem he can," Ka-ud said, trying to regain some lost ground.

"Right. What you don't understand, fella, is that the only reason he can is because we're really nice guys over here in America. We treat our enemies with more respect than our own citizens. We don't call them names, we pretend to respect their religions and their customs, we honor their leaders, we buy their art and their labor and their wines and caviar while they dump shit on us."

"I don't see what—"

"Even when they violate the very things we hold most dear, we're still nice guys. Like, say, their country is run by an iron-fisted dictator nobody elected, who holds power only because of his last name. He may be dressed up like a king or an emir or . . . well, a sultan . . . but the fact is he's still a dictator. Now, I hate dictators. I mean I really, truly detest them. But I do business with them, because they have stuff we need. So no matter how badly they treat their own people, we look the other way, because it's sometimes in our own best interest to do so. You see what I'm saying here?"

Ka-ud's face had gone ashy. He didn't know whether to be afraid, outraged or both. Both is what he landed on as the most appropriate. "See here, Mr.—"

"You need to stay quiet for a few more minutes here, Ahmed. Trust me. You don't want to say anything before I'm finished."

Ka-ud elected to stay quiet.

"Good. Now I'm as nice a guy as the next fella, and I've learned how to play the game. But I'm only human, see? There's only so far I'm willing to go. And, like I said, it hasn't been an easy few weeks for me, getting pushed around by this asshole in South America. So to tell you the truth, I'm getting a little sick and tired of it. Because I'm the goddamned leader of the goddamned free world, and the goddamned leader of the goddamned free world isn't supposed to get pushed around by power-obsessed pieces of shit posing as respectable leaders of men!"

Eastwood felt himself getting strident, and didn't like the expressions on the faces of the two representatives from State who seemed as though they were getting ready to organize a recall election. He threw an arm across Ka-ud's shoulders and gently turned him around. To the rest of the guests, it looked as though he was about to take the sultan into his deepest confidence. "So let me tell you how it's going to be, Ahmed. You listening?"

Ka-ud, not trusting himself to speak, could only nod.

"Good man." Eastwood leaned in closer, until their faces were side by side. "You're going to sign an official document, postdated two years from now, that gives us permission to build an air base on your soil. You're going to allow our engineers to start laying the infrastructure right away. I mean this week. It'll look like an irrigation project, but it's going to be the underground portion of the base, including water and electrical lines, sewer pipes and weapons storage, as well as the mother of all parking lots that will eventually be a pair of runways. You following me so far?"

Ka-ud nodded dumbly.

"Okay. Now I know what you're thinking. You are thinking you'll get through this little conversation, then you'll go back home with your dander up and send me a wire politely telling me to stick it in my ear. And that's cool. Not sure I'd do anything different in your place."

Through the arm he still had on Ka-ud's shoulders, he felt the man starting to relax. That was good.

"But if you do that, here's what's going to happen, Ahmed. First, Jez Rama'am is suddenly going to become a hive of terrorist activity."

"What! But we've never . . . you have no evidence whatso—"

"Doesn't matter. We've invaded countries on less. Now where was I? Oh, yeah. Personally, I have no problem with you consorting with hookers. Hell, you have diplomatic immunity, so we can't even arrest you for it. But you have to wonder what they're going to think back home when they find out about it, complete with graphic testimony from the hookers in question, given in exchange for their own immunity."

Ka-ud's eyes narrowed. "You wouldn't dare! Besides, as you said, I am not elected. I rule by virtue of the well-established lines of descendancy that have—"

"And then we're going to halt construction of the port. That'll throw, what: two, three thousand of your citizens out of work? Think that might be enough to start a democratic revolution, with a little help from CIA covert op's?"

"You wouldn't dare!"

"They won't pull your statue, down, Ahmed. They'll tie a rope around your neck and pull *you up*."

"This—this —" Bits of foam flecked the sultan's lips. "This is beyond outrageous! This . . . this is blackmail!"

"Yeah," Eastwood said calmly. "But mostly it's extortion."

"But . . . but you're the president of the United States! The *United States!* You don't do these kinds of things! Everybody knows it! The whole world knows it!"

Eastwood patted Ka-ud's shoulder, then withdrew his arm. The two of them were now side by side with their backs still to the rest of the room. "You're right. And that's the whole goddamned trouble, don't you see? It's why we get kicked around so often. Well I'm sick and goddamned tired of it, I'm going to change it, and unfortunately for you, *Ach*-med, Jez Rama'am is where I've decided to put my foot down."

Ka-ud was too confused and angry to trust himself to respond. He wanted to go home and think about it, speak with his trusted advisors, consult with other leaders in the region and knock back a few stiff shots of Johnny Walker Black Label. But he was right here, right now, one on one with the president himself, and he knew with depressing certainty that he was standing at a crossroads that would go down in history. What he said in the next few minutes would be critical beyond his imagining. And he had absolutely no idea whatsoever what the correct course of action was, which was the problem with inheriting leadership for which you were utterly unqualified.

"Lot to absorb, isn't it?" Eastwood asked solicitously.

Ka-ud, totally lost and not even making a pretext of having a handle on the situation, could only nod.

"I understand. So let me get to the other side of the coin before some mailroom clerk decides to give me his views on the state of health care in Kentucky."

The other side of the coin? Ka-ud was dumbstruck at how fervently he jumped to grasp at whatever straws the president might be offering.

"We're not bullies or thugs, Ahmed. And we don't like being heavy-handed. Now I know full well we can beat you into submission and there's not a damned thing you can do about it, but . . ." Eastwood scrunched up his face into an expression of severe distaste and shuddered. "*Brrrr!* Not our style, you know? I don't like that sort of thing. The carrot is much better than the stick, eh? You understand?"

Ka-ud nodded.

"What?"

"I understand!" It came out a little louder than Ka-ud had intended.

Eastwood pretended not to notice. "So: If you sign the document," he said, "we keep working on the port. You yourself get invited to a full-scale state dinner at the G.E. You become the rising voice of cooperation and enlightenment in an historically troubled region, a great friend to the world's last superpower and . . . wait. That's a problem, isn't it? Yeah. You'll be seen as betraying the Arab cause, sucking up to the godless infidels, and so on and so forth."

Eastwood glanced surreptitiously at Ka-ud, seeing the man's face fall and the hope start to fade from his eyes.

"Well, fuck em, Ahmed," Eastwood said brightly. "By the time that port is finished, you'll be the most powerful leader among the Arab nations since the Prophet himself. All of Europe will adore you, you'll be admired by freedom-loving people everywhere. You might get a little flack from your fellow nations, but here's the best part—"

Eastwood sensed a puppy-dog eagerness in the sultan, and sidled closer to take him into his deepest confidence. "Who's going to mess with you when you've got a full-scale U.S. military base ready to pound the living shit out of anybody idiotic enough to take you on?" He nudged Ka-ud in the ribs. "With friends like us, *fuck* your enemies."

Ka-ud, nearly in tears at the picture the president had just painted, hadn't even felt the playful poke.

"So what do you think, Ahmed? We got a deal or what?"

Ka-ud didn't trust himself to speak, so powerful was his relief-laden elation, and Eastwood didn't rush him. The sultan tried to compose himself, but still kept his back to the room for fear his sloberringly grateful expression might give him away.

Finally, he gulped a few lungfuls of air and turned to Eastwood. "I could use a shot of something strong."

Eastwood turned and snapped a finger at the State Department reps. It was all they could do not to trip over themselves as they came running forward. "This is Tweedledee and Tweedledum . . ."

"Edgerton and O'Malley," one of them said as they held out their hands, which Ka-ud smothered in both of his at the same time.

"Tweedledum here has some pieces of paper in his pocket for you to sign," Eastwood said to Ka-ud. "Tweedledee has a flask of Johnny Walker. Why don't you boys go off into a back room and start signing and drinking, and I'll join you in a few minutes. And oh, by the way . . ." Eastwood reached around and grasped all three of them as best he could. "Laugh like hell."

All of them joined in a highly visible expression of mirth and affectionate camaraderie that brought the rest of the room to jealous silence.

Then Eastwood left them to handle the formalities while he went off to finally do what he'd really come to do.

He spotted the decrepit old man pretty much where he thought he would, parked in a hideaway corner of a side room, fully engaged in conversation with the most interesting person he could find.

" . . . can't be affected by outside electrical forces or magnetism," the earnest young man was saying.

"So it can't be jammed?" Dalton Galsworthy asked, staring at him through his Coke-bottle glasses.

"No."

"What about with more light?"

"No! That's the amazing thing about a beam of light, see? You can shine a thousand other beams right through it, and nothing happens. It still gets to where it's going, with no interference. Isn't that something?"

"Sure is," Galsworthy said, scratching the side of his mouth through his thick beard.

"So what are we talking about?" Eastwood asked as he came up behind them.

The young man gasped, took a step backward and nearly tripped over a chair. Eastwood reached out and grabbed his arm, the one not holding a drink. "Easy there, fella. Maybe you ought to cut back a little."

Uncomprehending at first, the engineer quickly caught on. "It's just soda, sir. President Eastwood, I mean. Um . . . Mr. President?"

"Any one'll do. So what were you guys talking about?"

Galsworthy, who'd been leaning casually against a wall, still was. He jutted his chin toward the stunned engineer. "Eckert here's been regaling me about the virtues of optical computing."

"Optical computing? What the hell is that?" Eastwood directed the question toward Eckert.

"It's, um —" Eckert cleared his throat "—it's computing using light instead of electricity."

"No shit?"

"No sh—" Eckert grimaced. "Yes. Yessir."

"You can actually do that?"

"Oh yes, sir . . . Mr . . . yes. We're doing it now. In the lab, of course."

"Huh. What about EMP?" Eastwood was referring to the intense electromagnetic pulse given off by a nuclear blast.

Eckert brightened at the question. "No! Doesn't affect the circuit at all!"

"Unless the blast itself is close enough to fry the whole goddamned thing, right?" Galsworthy said.

Eckert blanched at the easy profanity in front of the president, despite the president's own use of it earlier. "Well, sure. That goes without saying. But, um—" He wasn't certain how much he should go on about his beloved topic. Was the president just being polite or was he really interested? "If a command and control facility is targeted by nuclear weapons and it's other than a direct hit, the optical computer will keep working inside a much smaller radius than a conventional device."

"Huh." Eastwood folded his arms across his chest as he thought about it. "So if we had one of those on an AWACS, or the Blockbuster, they couldn't knock out our comm with a nuke, right?"

"Long as the plane was still flying," Galsworthy pointed out.

"Exactly!" Eckert exclaimed exultantly. "That's exactly right!"

"I'll be damned. Have to look into that. What's your first name, Eckert? And where do you work?"

"It's Presper, sir. I'm at the National Bureau of Standards."

"Good. Do me a favor, would you?"

"A fa—sure. I mean, certainly, Mr. President. What —"

"See that lady over there?"

Eckert looked over to where the president was pointing. "Miss Ortega?"

"Yeah. Go on over there and tell her how to get in touch with you, okay?"

"Well, gee, I uh . . ."

"She'll know I sent you. Trust me."

"Trust you. Oh, of course, sir. Trust you, sure. I didn't mean to—"

"Fine. Now I need a minute or two with the professor here, so if you don't mind . . ."

"Not at all! Pleasure meeting you!" Eckert didn't know whether he should hold out his hand, so Eastwood did, and was pleased that the young man didn't try to linger but took off right away. He was even more pleased when, from a few steps away, Eckert returned to shake hands with Galsworthy, who waved off an apology for having been forgotten in the wake of Eckert's disorientation.

"Nice kid," Galsworthy said when the engineer was out of earshot.

"Anything to this computing with light business?"

Galsworthy shrugged. "There is if you can figure out how to wire up the rest of the plane optically so it doesn't get pulsed and crash with a perfectly functioning computer on board. But yeah, it's real. So how've you been?"

"*Mezza mezza*. You?"

"The same. How's the asshole doing?"

"Hayne? Still an asshole. I need you to go down to South America."

"When?"

"Tonight. Car's out in front. They've got your kip and the details."

Galsworthy sighed. "Christ a'mighty, Tom. You got me working harder than I did when I was on the payroll."

"You didn't do shit when you were on the payroll."

"Only proves my point. I'm babysitting that golf hustler, right?"

"Yep."

"Okay." Galsworthy finally pushed off the wall. "What's so important about him?"

"He owes me money."

"You're a riot. What's my job?"

"Your job is to get me out of this fucking mess. We may to have to get military if Caminetti doesn't make headway with Barranca and I'll be damned if I'm going to start anything until someone I trust gives me something other than forty acres of primo bullshit."

"Heard Barranca wants him alone. No entourage."

"I'm sending one anyway, and I want you in it, but nobody's to know it's you."

Eastwood left it at that, and when Galsworthy realized no more was coming, he gave a half-salute and started for the door.

But Eastwood called him back. "Say Dalton . . . you know anything about that golf match Fidel Castro played with Che Guevara?"

Galsworthy let out a grunt. "We knew a lot more about those two guys than anyone knew we knew."

"So what was that round like?"

Galsworthy leaned back against the wall again. "Lotta crazy shit happened, I can tell you that. What I heard, their styles of play pretty much matched their styles of starting revolutions. Castro relied on his size and strength and liked to whack monster drives and fairway shots, but Che, a bit more of a contemplative sort, had some pretty good finesse around the greens. Somehow it was lost on Castro that a two-foot putt could be the equal of a huge tee shot in terms of scoring, and they say he seemed surprised when he lost a hole after he'd actually managed to keep one of his drives from going out of bounds, like it should have counted for more or something."

"Either of them ever play before?"

Galsworthy shook his head. "The idea was, they'd play against each other and neither one of them had ever picked up a club before."

"You said it got crazy . . ."

"Yeah. Started out pretty courteous but went rapidly down the tubes. On the second hole, Fidel was down in eight and Che had a putt of less than a foot to make seven. He looks at Fidel for a while until Fidel finally says, What? And Che says, You telling me I actually have to putt this? Betcher ass, Fidel tells him, or whatever the Spanish equivalent is. Che thought that was kinda chintzy, that he should've conceded the damned thing, but Castro wouldn't budge. Even said he was surprised at Che, the big purist, wanting to get a score he didn't properly earn."

"I know some guys like that," Eastwood said. "So what happened?"

"Che was so shaken he missed the putt. Interesting part is, he was all pissed at Castro, while Castro insisted it only proved his point: There were no guarantees in golf. Anyway, it put Fidel up by one after only two holes."

"Then what?"

Galsworthy smiled maliciously. "On the very next hole Fidel putts to within an inch and he's lying six, right? Steps up and he's a little too casual. One-hands the thing, toes the ball and misses."

"Serves him right."

"Yeah. Except Che's not like that, see, so he says to the caddy, who's keeping score, that he conceded the putt, and it should go down as a seven. Not another word, doesn't make a big deal of it, doesn't even look at Fidel, who should have been pretty damned embarrassed."

"Maybe he was."

"You think? Because two holes later Che has a six-inch putt and Fidel makes him putt it."

Eastwood laughed at that, encouraging Galsworthy to continue.

"So after that their course etiquette goes straight down the shitter. I mean, they start stomping on each other's lines and flicking cigar ashes on them, fidgeting and talking in the middle of backswings, rattling clubs at the worst possible moments, you name it. But they keep apologizing to each other whenever they get called out, and at one point Che goes cuckoo and demands a do-over after Fidel passes some wind with truly awesome timing and makes Che screw up a shot. Fidel tells him to get stuffed, the caddies agree he doesn't get to play it again, and after that it's open warfare between the two.

"Eventually, Che starts to kind of retreat within himself, so focused he seems oblivious to what's going on around him, but it was bullshit: The guy knew exactly where the match stood at all times, and while Fidel bullied and thundered his way through each hole and each shot like he was hunting elephants, Che kept making adjustments depending on how well Fidel was hitting."

Eastwood, paying rapt attention, didn't hear Connie Ortega come up behind him. "Mr. President . . ." she said, pointing to the ambassador of something-or-other.

Eastwood nodded, and after Ortega walked away, he shook hands with Galsworthy and said, "You best get going."

Wearing a fake beard, thick glasses he didn't need, a wig with a pony tail and lifts in his shoes, Galsworthy would leave the crowd wondering who the man was who patted the president on the arm, said "See you in the funny papers" and melted into the night.

CHAPTER 17

Where's that dick from hair!" demanded ace TV reporter Mona Bertram without turning away from the in-studio monitor showing the outgoing feed. On the fifty-two-inch plasma screen was a photo of Bertram herself, with her familiar toothy grin, her name superimposed underneath. From a nearby speaker a voice-over was saying, "Wake up with Mona Bertram! Spend the morning in bed with America's number one newscaster!" The on-screen photo was replaced with another of Bertram, identical except that she had one eye closed. "Bright, talented and just your type!" Then the first photo came back, then the second, giving the impression that she was winking seductively. "She's got her eye on you!" the announcer finished.

A disheveled and beleaguered-looking man in his early thirties hurried to Bertram's side, combs and brushes in hand, scissors clamped between his teeth, terror in his eyes.

"I look like a fucking raccoon," Bertram snarled at him.

"Doing your hair isn't going to fix that," he muttered.

"What did you say!"

"Going on air in six flat." He nodded toward the production assistant, who was counting down with his fingers and silently mouthing, "Five, four three . . ." The hairstylist, who hadn't actually done anything to Bertram's hair, patted a nonexistent stray wisp into place and stepped smartly away.

Bertram, who'd been wearing an expression that would have suited Quasimodo's inquisitor, suddenly smiled brightly, widened her half-shut, heavily made-up eyes and said into the camera, "And finally, to close off this Sunday broadcast, a sad note from the little town of Armuchee, Georgia . . ."

Bertram's face was replaced on-screen by a panning shot of a tall chimney standing naked amid a pile of smoking rubble. " . . . where the Church of Our Lord of Infinite Mercy burned to the ground yesterday." As the camera homed in on a small white cross lying askew against a charred fence, the picture dissolved back to Bertram's face, now smiling even wider. "The cause of the fire was unknown, but the parishioners have vowed to rebuild. Pastor Jonathan Billingsley spoke with GNN earlier this morning."

A quick cut to Pastor Billingsley, surrounded by some of his flock. The in-studio monitor was soundless, but was set up for closed-captioning. "Thing is," the crawl indicated the pastor was saying, "our congregation has grown remarkably in the past few weeks, and I think this is just God's way of telling us He needs a bigger house to hold all His faithful, and we're only too happy to oblige Him." The captioning software automatically capitalized "God" and His various pronouns, a programming change made at enormous expense following a threat to organize a national boycott made by three powerful religious lobbies, the only thing they'd agreed on in over twenty years.

There was a freeze and dissolve from the pastor's resigned smile to Bertram's less beatific one. "That's it for this morning," Bertram said. "From all of us here at GNN, have a great day out there." Practically giggling now, she added. "Please stay tuned for the GNN morning news and the latest information on an awful mudslide that may have buried up to twenty thousand people in eastern Pakistan."

Then she gave her trademark wink, waved cheerily and said, *"Ciao!"*

OFFICE OF CONCHITA ORTEGA—THE WEST WING

"I heard that's not what really happened."

Chief of Staff Ortega's annoyance was readily apparent over the speakerphone in the office of Lance "Sparky" Kroeger, president, chairman and CEO of Global News Network. "It was a hundred percent accurate, Ms. Ortega." He pronounced "Ms." as though imitating a bee on an extended reconn mission around a rhododendron.

"Was it."

"You bet."

"So the cause of the fire isn't known?"

"I'm not saying there aren't some suspicions, but that's all they are at this point."

"Is that so."

"Sure. We don't care to speculate until the official report is in. Wouldn't be professional."

"And when will that be?"

"Hard to say; two, three weeks, maybe."

Ortega closed her eyes and fought to keep her voice steady. "Less than thirty minutes after TWA 800 went down you had a former FAA official on the air saying there was no doubt it was a terrorist attack."

"That was different. Quite different."

"How?"

Ortega could hear Kroeger rising out of his chair, could practically see him leaning belligerently over the speakerphone as he growled, "Is there a point here, ma'am?"

"Yes, there's a point." Ortega sat up straighter in her chair, as if to go long distance toe-to-toe with the powerful media magnate. "The point is that I don't give a damn if you needed a heartwarming story to cap off the Mona Bertram love-fest, but I need to know what went on in that church so I can brief your president properly. Now I don't have the time or the inclination to send people down to Armchair, Georgia, to—"

"Armuchee."

"Whatever. I want to know what your on-site guys know."

"Well, gosh, ma'am." Kroeger's voice went oleaginous, causing Ortega's face to scrunch up as if she were in physical pain. "You know there's journalistic privilege involved here. Integrity, ethics, protecting sources and that sort of thing . . ."

I could shove all your integrity up a flea's nose and still have room for your brain, Ortega thought, but withheld the infamous Levantism in order not to get distracted from her objective. "There's no such thing as journalistic privilege, Kroeger, and we both know it. We also both know you have something and you're working it into a feature for one of your deeply intellectual magazine shows."

She waited for a reaction but got none, which was all the reaction she needed to know she was on solid ground. "So let me make this clear: You tell me what the hell's going on, which I'll keep off the record, or the next interview any of your ace reporters ever gets with the president—and I mean *ever*—will be about his pet llama having a baby."

"He doesn't have a llama."

"He plans to get one when he's ninety."

QUAKER OATS CRISIS CENTER
(FORMERLY THE WHITE HOUSE SITUATION ROOM)

Secretary of State William Patterson drummed his fingers impatiently on the table. He was nervous to begin with, but CIA officer Joffrey Hayne, sitting several seats away with his knee pumping up and down furiously and his jaw muscle threatening to pop out of his cheek, was making him even more jittery. "It's not that I'm unfeeling about such things, Connie, don't get me wrong. I have deep sympathy for those poor people who suffered such a senseless tragedy."

"What poor people?" Ortega, all sweetness and innocence, asked him. She was well aware of the literalness with which he approached matters spiritual.

"Why, the parishioners whose house of worship was so abruptly and cruelly taken from them!"

Ortega furrowed her brow. "But the pastor said it was a welcome sign from God. So it was a good thing, from the Lord's own hand. Why would you —"

"Connie," Eastwood interrupted her with tired resignation, "are you going to bust his balls again or just tell us what you have to tell us?"

Ortega arranged her hastily scribbled notes in front of her. "It wasn't God paving the way for a new church. It was a riot."

"How's that?" DCI Baines Gordon Wainwright asked. "A riot? Who the hell rioted?"

"Some of those new congregants the pastor was talking about on GNN." Prompted by a glare from the president to get on with it, Ortega said, "Seems the sudden spurt in the church's growth came about as a result of their Saturday morning Bible study class. They used to get maybe fifteen, twenty people tops, and about three weeks ago it began to get really popular."

"How popular?" Wainwright asked.

"Three hundred and fifty people last week."

"But that's wonderful!" Patterson exclaimed. "All of those people waking up to the Word! How could that possibly —"

"They served coffee." FBI director Bradford MacArthur Baffington, sitting stonily, hadn't moved a muscle prior to offering his analysis.

"How's that?" Patterson asked. Hayne's leg-pumping had ramped up to a new frequency somewhere in the gigahertz range, and Patterson was seriously contemplating jamming a letter opener into his knee.

Baffington's eyes flicked toward Ortega. "Didn't they? Coffee, for all those troubled souls seeking the Word."

"They did indeed," Ortega affirmed. "And while the church elders thought it was the coffee that brought them in but the Word that kept them coming, that theory pretty much evaporated at about the same time as their coffee supply, most of which they'd been selling on the black market to fund a new extension to house all the new believers."

"So what are you saying?" Eastwood asked hesitantly. "They really rioted?"

"Burned the place to the ground," Ortega answered.

"A church?" Patterson asked, horrified. "They burned a church over coffee?"

"They burned it for being misled," she said.

"Jesus H.," Wainwright said. "I got misled by a stereo salesman once but I didn't burn the friggin place down."

"You don't get addicted to consumer electronics, Mr. Director."

"My wife would beg to differ."

Ortega turned to Eastwood. "It's all going to hell, Mr. President."

Eastwood ran a hand through his thinning hair and tried to look presidential, but of all the things his ardent readings of history had prepared him for, this wasn't even close to being one of them.

PART II

THE END OF THE STORY

Bad weather is never the cause of the crash. Flying into bad weather is.

—Eddie Caminetti

CHAPTER 18

ZAMORA CHINCHIPE, ECUADOR

The plane carrying Eddie Caminetti to South America was a newly refurbished Boeing 707 belonging to the United States Air Force. In addition to Eddie, its completely filled cabin contained five deputy undersecretaries from State and three from Agriculture, two stenographers from Justice, four CIA covert ops officers masquerading as foreign attaches-in-training, eight Pentagon officials with an equal number of aides and assistants, two aircraft maintenance men, a three-man backup flight crew, two chefs, three flight attendants, a physician and a dentist, a forensics specialist from the FBI, two members of the Senate Select Committee on Foreign Affairs and a radio technician named Lester Ausgespielt.

After receiving landing clearance in the form of a battered orange flag waved by the airport's sole employee, who was standing on the alarmingly short runway as the 707 did an exploratory flyover, the plane banked gracefully, made another circle and touched down with smoke streaming from its updated carbon-fiber brakes as it screeched to a shuddering halt with less than two hundred feet of asphalt remaining. After it taxied clear of the runway, one of the flight attendants unlatched the door, pulled it inside and swung it out of the way, then stepped aside to let one of the maintenance men unhook a telescoping air stair and deploy it down to the ground. As the entourage began to disembark, those in front saw a large group of men in camouflage starting to swarm in their direction from the far end of the runway where, well off to the side, an aging Lockheed-Vega twin-engine plane sat like a museum piece. Some of the soldiers were riding in a pair of old jeeps, but most were on foot. Wary at first, the men leading the way down the air stair relaxed when they saw that the soldiers were laughing, shouting and waving their arms in greeting as they approached.

"Natives seem friendly," a full-bird Marine colonel said to an Air Force captain, who stuck his head back inside the plane and urged the rest to follow them out.

Each person stepping off the bottom of the stairway with his luggage was greeted with a smile and a handshake, the welcoming soldiers practically tripping over themselves to convey their happiness at their visitors' arrival and to take their luggage and set it on the ground, including a golf bag with the letters EC stitched on one side. When no more passengers emerged from the plane, one of the soldiers said, *"Estos son todos?"*

"Si," someone from State confirmed. Everybody was now out of the plane.

"Good," another, paler soldier said, then pulled an AK-47 assault rifle from inside his jacket. It was followed immediately by the appearance of some forty other identical weapons, which sounded like a truckload of ball bearings dropping onto slate flagstones as their cocking handles were pulled back and released. In short order, everyone from the 707 found at least one rifle aimed in his or her general direction.

The pale soldier, his own rifle aimed skyward, walked forward and scanned the passengers until his eyes alit on one in particular. "You," he ordered. "Step off to the side."

Eddie Caminetti held his ground, but the full-bird colonel disabused him of any notions of resistance. "Those are guns, fella. They have them and we don't, so get going."

As Eddie began to obey, one of the soldiers spotted the golf bag and jogged toward it. Grinning, he slung his rifle over his shoulder, bent to pick it up, and started to walk off with it. One of the backup flight crew pilots shouted "Hey!" and took a few steps toward him, but the soldier dropped the clubs and had a handgun pointed at him almost before the bag hit the ground.

Radio technician second class Lester Ausgespielt reached out a hand to stop the would-be hero. "Let it go," he ordered, and the unusually confident command in his voice had its intended effect immediately. The pilot glared at the soldier, but he didn't try to advance any further, even when the man re-holstered his handgun, picked the golf bag back up and began walking toward the end of the runway.

By that time three other soldiers had Eddie separated from the rest of his fellow travelers and loaded into one of the jeeps, which took off down the runway. The pale soldier who'd spoken in English climbed into the second jeep and followed. The remaining airplane passengers, surrounded by the rifle-wielding soldiers and trying hard to cope with various levels of terror, watched helplessly as Eddie, hanging on to the roll bar of the wildly bouncing vehicle, was driven away.

Radioman Ausgespielt, ignoring the rifle pointed at him, tried to use the time to take in and commit to memory every detail he possibly could. The first thing that struck him was that the top of the tail of the Lockheed Vega at the end of the runway was covered with a piece of burlap. He didn't understand why until he looked around for the plane's registration number but couldn't spot it.

"They covered up the N number," he heard one of the Air Force men whisper to another, and that was it: Without a visible number, they couldn't identify the plane.

As soon as Eddie and the soldiers who'd taken custody of him stopped in front of the plane, other hands reached up and dragged him out of the jeep and set him up with his back to the fuselage. The pale soldier jumped out of the other vehicle, reached into his back pocket to pull out a black bandanna, and handed it to Eddie.

"Ohmigod!" one of the flight attendants back at the 707 cried out, her hands flying to her mouth. The Pentagon officials tried not to betray their own alarm as they watched Eddie defiantly shove the bandanna away. Admiration crept into their eyes as the pale soldier held out his hand to offer a handshake and Eddie made no move to take it. Some conversation then seemed to take place between the soldier and Eddie, but there was no way for onlookers that far away to figure out what was being said.

Suddenly, two large men who'd been standing slightly behind Eddie and leaning against the plane gripped his arms. A third man reached between his legs and seemed to be frisking him. The pale soldier stepped back, turned and waved to one of the men guarding the 707 passengers. The man lifted his rifle into the air and shouted, *"Vuelta! Inmediatamente!"*

The passengers who understood Spanish quickly turned around, the others soon following suit. They were too afraid and powerless to disobey. The flight attendant who'd earlier cried out began to whimper pitiably. Others winced in anticipation of a shot ringing out from down the runway.

It didn't come. Instead they heard the thud of a closing door followed by the sound of a pair of large piston engines creaking to an uncertain ignition. By that time the soldiers guarding them had moved to the front of the group, one of them warning in broken English not to turn around as his comrades wandered among them to ensure their compliance.

Soon the Lockheed's props were turning with enough speed to move the plane onto the runway, where the pilot held the brakes as he cranked the engines up to full power. The noise of the old power plants bringing the props up to speed was deafening, and grew even louder as the brakes were released and the plane started forward. A blast of wind hit the 707 passengers as the Lockheed lumbered past their position and picked up more speed. Soon the rumble of the engines steadied into a smoother roar, and after another minute could no longer be heard.

The soldier apparently in charge of the guards lowered his weapon, and the others did the same. They soon arranged themselves into a column about eight feet wide, terminating at the bottom of the air stair. Heeding the clear signal, the passengers entered the gauntlet and re-boarded the 707. The last up the stairs was Radioman Ausgespielt. "*Adios*, assholes," he said with a wave.

"Up yours," one of the soldiers answered. "And have a nice flight home."

By the time the 707 was airborne and had passed through six thousand feet, the soldiers had stopped watching it and were drifting back into the jungle. None of them saw the solitary figure that popped out of the plane's rear door or the square black parachute that blossomed open above him a few seconds later.

Aboard the plane the senior CIA operative unbuckled his seat belt and strode forward to a radio set mounted near the galley. On the way he passed a stunned pair of flight attendants in the front row who'd just watched their radio technician jump out of the rear door of the plane. Seconds later the intelligence officer was giving someone on the receiving end of the radio a brief but thorough description of what had just occurred, but he was wearing headphones and they couldn't hear what was coming back.

"Yes, sir, it was very bad, sir," he said deferentially when he'd finished. "Yessir, I understand. Well, Dalton Galsworthy parachuted down as soon as we were out of sight."

The two flight attendants exchanged startled looks. "'Galsworthy?'" one of them said. "I thought his name was Ausgespielt."

"It was," the other said. "I saw it on his shirt."

"Yessir. Yes, Mr. President, there's a sat phone in Caminetti's golf bag—"

More startled looks; was this guy really talking to the president? *The* president?

"—but I have a bad feeling he's never going to see that bag again. Um, sir, Galsworthy left a message for you. Yessir. He said, um, he said you should give Caminetti's sat phone a try every once in a while." There was a pause. "Well, I asked him that, Mr. President, and he said, well, he said you just never know, and don't give up. Right. Right. Thank you, Mr. President."

CHAPTER 19

BILL AND MELINDA GATES OFFICE— GENERAL ELECTRIC PRESIDENTIAL RESIDENCE

"Nothing at all from Caminetti?" FBI director Baffington asked uselessly as Joffrey Hayne's leg pumped up and down furiously a seat away.

Wainwright shook his head. "Total silence. I've got my guys monitoring the frequency but, other than that, not much we can do. We've got no people down there at all." He looked at Eastwood. "Your predecessor signed a few agreements that tied our hands."

"So we're doing nothing?" William Patterson asked. "How about repositioning some satellites, at least see if we can get some pictures? Maybe Barranca's on the move."

"Can't," Wainwright said, seeming to take some pleasure in his negative responses, none of which he viewed as his own fault. "To get a KH-11 over central South America we'd have to shift its orbit, which would make it pass over Russia, Georgia and Tajikistan." Another look at Eastwood. "Got some treaties about that, too."

Eastwood, trying to keep his irritation in check, failed. "Well, why don't we just shut down your whole agency, what do you say? You can't tell me shit, you don't know dick, your hands are completely tied . . . what are we spending twenty-six billion a year on, tell me?"

"Well, Mr. President . . ."

"Don't Mr. President me, Baines! I get a daily briefing full of information I can't use about things I don't care about—" Hayne's leg stopped pumping "— and the one time I need some serious G-2 you can't give me anything!"

He let it hang in the air, and the others, who by now knew his style well, were savvy enough not to disrupt the awkward silence he'd created. Eastwood waited until Wainwright's upper teeth were nearly through the skin of his lower lip, then said cajolingly, "Now level with me, Baines: You mean to tell me we don't have a couple'a three unofficial, off-the-books assets down there, some eyes and ears nobody else knows about who can give us some skinny without tipping anybody's hand? That what I'm hearing?"

Hayne had his eyes lasered in on Wainwright, and when he sensed the first nanometer of a nodded answer to the president's question, came out of his seat, his hands in the air, heedless of what the CIA's *major domo* might think of his reaction but fairly certain that, in the fullness of time, the wisdom of his actions would be self-evident.

"No!" Hayne fairly screamed, which in combination with his fear-somely aggressive posture would have looked to a Secret Service agent like a full-frontal assault on the chief executive, were there any such agents in the room. "No, Mr. President, we certainly do not have any such assets!"

Too shocked to rebuke his underling, Wainwright said, "But—"

And had barely gotten the single syllable out before Hayne resumed his aggressive assertion. "Rest assured, Mr. President, that we have absolutely nobody or anything even remotely construable as back channel or poisoned assets. Nothing, sir! And you can take that to the bank. Isn't that right, Mr. Director?"

Wainwright had by then caught on to Hayne's attempt to preserve plausible deniability on the part of the president, and actually felt gratitude to the little twerp for saving him from a potentially career-threatening faux pas. "Joffrey is quite correct, Mr. President. All our assets are a hundred percent above board. However . . ." He kicked it to Hayne.

Who ran with it. "We've got some inquiries out, sir. Nothing beyond phone calls to some, uh . . . friends! Yes, that's it! Friends. The kind of people with whom we come in contact on a daily basis, and whose love of freedom and America extends beyond any petty notions of national borders or, um, the kind of decorum normally practiced by seasoned diplomats. Their positions are, ah, a little less, uh—"

"Delicate?" offered Eastwood.

"Delicate!" Hayne yelped in relief. "Oh, yes! Delicate! A bit less delicate and, therefore, they're more inclined to be of service."

"We expect to hear from them shortly," Wainwright added.

But something tugged at the corners of Eastwood's attention. "How come shortly? Why not now?"

"Seems, that, uh, well . . ." Hayne began.

"Well, what?"

"Well . . . we haven't exactly been able to contact them." Hayne stepped back miserably and flopped onto his seat.

"How's that again?"

"Seems they've gone incommunicado."

"When?"

Hayne exhaled, and wondered if it was actually possible for someone to commit suicide by neglecting to breathe, and how long it would take. "Shortly after Mr. Caminetti did."

Wainwright sniffed. Twice.

"Okay, we're adjourned," Eastwood said, picking up on his DCI's signal. "Connie, Baines . . . stick around for a few minutes."

"Our 'friends,'" Wainwright said after the others had left, "appear to have flown the coop. What I meant by 'shortly' was that we're working on getting them back."

"Who are they?" Eastwood asked.

"One or two people you don't want to know about, sir. Hayne was right on that."

"When will we hear something?"

"Soon. When I know, you'll know ten seconds later."

Momentarily assuaged that at least something, however puny, was being done, Eastwood leaned back and set his gaze on the ceiling. "What about you, Baines?"

"Sir?" Wainwright knew perfectly well what he was being asked.

"What do you think is going on?"

The DCI didn't answer right away, wanting to make sure he had the president's full attention. When Eastwood finally redirected his eyes toward him, Wainwright said, "I think he's dead, sir. Caminetti, I mean."

Eastwood harbored the same fear, but it had been nameless and undifferentiated until Wainwright decked it out in words that seemed to seal his friend's fate.

"Are we keeping a lid on this?" added Ortega, ever the political protector.

"They're not hearing it from me," Wainwright assured her.

Eastwood, alert to nuance, caught one now. "*Who* isn't hearing it from you, Baines?"

JIMMY BUFFET CHAMBER—RALPH LAUREN SENATE BUILDING

Senate majority leader Orville Twickham (R-NC) was who wasn't hearing it from Wainwright, except that he'd heard it *all* from Wainwright.

"It's a black day in American history," he intoned stentoriously on the floor of the great chamber, "when a pipsqueak from a third world, one-horse dorp can hold the world's only remaining superpower hostage! When a two-bit, low-life terrorist can brutally murder an innocent citizen of our fair nation, a veritable goodwill ambassador, and we choose to sit back and let it happen! A black day, sirs!" Whether Twickham was aware that there were madams among the sirs, or was deliberately ignoring the former, no one could tell. It had been thirty years since they could.

"Will the Senator yield for a question?" asked the newly elected tyro, Garrick Preston (D-ME), rising slowly in anticipation of a positive response.

"I will, sir!" Twickham replied, adding, "For a question," as a pointed reminder to Preston to make sure it was a question and not a speech of his own.

"Thank you, Senator. It's a simple question. What is your evidence that this citizen was in fact murdered, or that he is even dead, and that Manuel Barranca is a terrorist?"

"Why, the evidence is self-evident!" Twickham retorted, as though insulted that the question had even been asked. "He has committed economic terrorism upon us, leading to loss of life, property and basic freedoms, and our intelligence resources are convinced that our fellow citizen is dead! At the hands of Barranca and his murderous thugs!"

"But—"

"Might I remind the Senator that I am the ranking member of the intelligence committee," Twickham said, "and in matters of national security I —what? What?"

An aide was tugging at his sleeve. Twickham bent to listen.

"I'd go easy there, Senator," the aide advised in a whisper.

"Easy? Easy?" Twickham started to straighten back up. "Son, the fate of our fair —"

"Yes, I know." The aide looked around nervously, then tugged Twickham back down. "Thing is, you're either going to have to reveal your source or stand trial for exposing vital secrets."

"What the hell are you talking about!"

"You can't just pick and choose what's a matter of national security and what isn't, based on the point you're trying to make. You open that door, and anybody can walk through it and demand the rest of what you know."

"But what did—"

"You said this Caminetti guy was murdered and you said Barranca was a terrorist."

Twickham was a blowhard and a grandstander, and like all blow-hards and grandstanders, put self-protection at the top of his priority list. "Damn! You're right. How do I fix it?"

"Go with the terrorist thing. That's a matter of opinion because there's no definition of a terrorist." *Thank God*, the aide chose not to add, being well aware that Twickham had in the past twenty-four months labeled as a terrorist everyone from the DoJ attorney who'd tried to indict him for bribery to the plumber who'd overcharged him for unplugging a clogged drain. "Accuse the man of murder and you're going to have to come up with some hard evidence." *Like a body, you old fart.*

Without acknowledging his assistant's wisdom, Twickham turned back to the chamber. "In time, the truth will at last be told. But this is not a court of law, Senator," he said directly to Preston, "and the strict rules of evidence do not apply." He then turned back to the full chamber. "The citizens of our fair land depend on the collective wisdom of this august body to act on their behalf in those situations whose very ambiguity and lack of detail make our insights and leaps of judgment all the more important and vital!"

"Will the Senator yield for a question?" said Dolores del Vecchio (D-NJ).

The aide nudged Twickham, whom he feared would reply to del Vecchio as he would to a housemaid. "Yes!" he hissed.

"With pleasure," Twickham announced.

"Thank you, Senator." Del Vecchio, a small woman in her late sixties, stood. "Do I understand the Senator to be saying that we should be less diligent in justifying the use of military force in South America than we would in incarcerating a petty thief in Brooklyn?"

"No!" Twickham declared. And left it there.

"But then how do you —"

"I yielded for one question, Madame Senator, not a follow-up." He waited until del Vecchio sat down, then turned his attention back to the chamber at large. "Far be it from me to additionally burden a president in time of crisis—" He pointedly ignored the snickers snickered by forty-eight of his colleagues "—but it would be irresponsible of this esteemed body to ignore its responsibilities with respect to the irresponsible direction being taken by the current administration that is responsible for the current crisis."

"Well said," muttered the aide.

"Thank you," Twickham replied. He wasn't at all senile, just self-absorbed and contemptuous of any sensibility—political, cultural or ethical—other than his own.

The aide glanced at his watch—one PM on the dot—and looked up at the gallery in time to see the single S-GNN "Senate Cam" swing into position toward the dais, where the president pro tem of the Senate was fiddling with some papers. The aide waited exactly sixty seconds, during which he knew the S-GNN on-air announcer was doing his intro, and when he saw a red light come on just under the camera's lens, looked toward the fourth seat in the second row and touched the side of his nose.

"What do you suggest we do?" called out Paul Stillwell (R-UT) at the signal.

"Are we hot?" Twickham asked the aide, who nodded. "Thank you for the question, Senator!" Twickham put one foot in front of the other, planted his hand on his hip with his suit jacket flipped open, and raised his chin toward the gallery. "I'll tell you precisely what we must do!"

He waited for the Senate Cam to swing away from the dais and toward him, then placed a hand on the lectern and said, "We must take bold and decisive action to end this crisis once and for all and demonstrate to the rest of the world that the United States of America will not be bullied by second-rate terrorists fronting the forces of evil!"

Fifty-one of his colleagues burst into lusty and sustained applause as the president pro tem banged his gavel with little enthusiasm and to even less effect. Forty-eight others, dumbfounded, glanced at one another to see if anyone else had noticed that Twickham hadn't actually said anything substantive.

"We should say something!" Garrick Preston whispered to del Vecchio.

"Like what?" she answered. "Go on GNN and declare that the president shouldn't take bold and decisive action to end this crisis once and for all?"

Preston leaned over and replied, "Why don't we just point out that the esteemed Senator's remarks were equivalent to 'We should have world peace'?"

Del Vecchio smiled indulgently at the rookie. "Don't do that."

"How come?" protested her colleague.

"So somebody else doesn't do it to you the next time you say something dopey." It was one of the unwritten rules of the most exclusive club in the world.

"I'd never say anything that transparently idiotic."

"You just did." Del Vecchio considered Twickham as he held the Lincolnesque pose he'd struck. "But that's not our biggest problem right now."

"No? What is?"

"That the Twickster is no dope." Del Vecchio idly tapped her lower lip. "And he's seriously trying to get us into a shooting war."

CHAPTER 20

"**W**hat the hell time is it down there?" Eastwood demanded of no one in particular.

"Depends where he is," answered National Security Advisor Anatoli Kropotkin.

"Well, shit. He's in South America, isn't he?"

"It's several time zones wide, sir," offered Joffrey Hayne.

"Is it," Eastwood responded icily. Before anyone could respond he called out to his secretary, "Try Caminetti again!" He then turned back to Hayne and Kropotkin. "So what do we think?"

"He might be dead," Hayne observed, "because if he were alive and had his phone, he would have called in as soon as he could. On the other hand, if he's in an especially precarious situation, he might not want to give away that he even has a satellite phone." Thus having predicted that Eddie was either dead or alive, Hayne, immensely pleased with his trenchant analysis (his first career was as a stockbroker), sat back and mistook his president's look of disbelief for admiration.

"I think I've got him, sir!" the president's secretary said from the doorway in a voice choked with excitement. "The connection's not very good, but it sounds, at least I think it—"

Eastwood punched the speakerphone button. "Caminetti!"

They were greeted by a loud burst of static. " . . . you, Mr. President?" emerged from the sonic mist. "Can hardly . . . it's not . . . I don't think I can . . ."

Eastwood put his mouth closer to the speakerphone. "Can you hear me now?" he shouted. "Can you hear me now?"

"Barely . . . trouble . . ."

"What's that, Eddie? What'd you say?"

"Terrible . . . major problem . . ."

Eastwood, Hayne and Kropotkin looked at each other in alarm. "Eddie! What the hell's—"

More static. "Can't talk long . . . no good . . ."

"Stay with me, Eddie!" Eastwood said loudly, panic lacing his voice. "What's going on?"

"It's falling apart . . . can't hold it together much longer . . . running out of . . . oh, shit . . . help me . . . !"

"Eddie! Eddie?"

"Barranca's coming . . . !"

"Caminetti!"

The static suddenly ceased, leaving the three of them staring at the speakerphone.

The president's secretary reappeared in the doorway a few seconds later. "I'm afraid the line's gone dead, sir," she said softly.

"Dead?"

She nodded. "Tech services reports a complete loss of signal."

CHAPTER 21

The room was somewhere on the same lower level as the swimming pool JFK ordered renovated in the early Sixties, not too far from the entrance to the tunnel through which LBJ purportedly embarked on a few late-night excursions. Rumor had it that the room was once a storage facility for hazmat and other defensive gear in case of a chemical or biological weapons attack, but it wasn't much of a rumor, since less than two dozen people even knew of its existence. The barely legible, water-stained sign mounted on the single doorway said RESERVE OFFICE SUPPLIES, just in case somebody wandered by, but since nobody but the two dozen were even authorized to be on that level, should such a wanderer be caught down there he would quickly find himself with much more pressing concerns than finding out what was in there.

It was a small room, not much bigger than a suburban living room. A single, octagonal, baize-covered table with eight plain chairs dominated the middle, and was overhung with a large, square-bottom chandelier. Arrayed along the walls were a refrigerator, a few shelves, two small cupboards and an air vent. A narrow doorway led to a tiny bathroom with a toilet and sink but no bath or shower. On a wall opposite the main door was a roll-about cart containing glasses of various sizes along with an impressive assortment of ultra-high-tech communications devices quite out of synch with the spartan adornments in the rest of the room.

At present, only five of the eight chairs were occupied.

"Raise it up," said President Thomas Madison Eastwood, tossing a ten-dollar chip into the middle while trying not to get potato chip crumbs on the sleeve of his tuxedo. He was dressed for a cultural exchange concert at the Kennedy Center and was trying to squeeze out a few hours of personal enjoyment before descending into the tedious hell of ethnic dancing from Outer Zipnoid or some such obscure Portuguese possession.

"Baloney," said FBI director Bradford MacArthur Baffington. Only in this room, where not only the physical space but the time spent in it had been ordered officially nonexistent by the president, was such apparent disrespect permitted.

"Ditto that," dittoed Defense Secretary Harold Fortesque.

"Apparent" because, in the world of poker, such openly expressed sentiments weren't at all disrespectful. Bravado was expected and encouraged and, like all manner of deceit, fraud, intimidation, bluster and bald-faced lying, was a necessary and integral part of the game.

"Then call the bet," Eastwood suggested.

"Damn straight I'll call," Fortesque replied, pushing two chips into the pot.

If the president wanted to play poker, then he had no choice but to temporarily suspend the diplomatic niceties of his office; otherwise, the very nature of the game would have precluded its being played. When it came to poker, the leader of the free world carried no more weight than a petty officer on a gunboat, a thought Eastwood tried to keep out of his head owing to a particularly painful trouncing he'd taken during a goodwill tour shortly after his election, from a petty officer on a gunboat.

"He's got em," Chief of Staff Conchita Ortega said as she threw her hand into the muck.

Which left the next betting decision to Director of Central Intelligence Baines Gordon Wainwright, who picked at his lip and stared from his cards to the community cards face up in the middle of the table, then to Eastwood, then back to his own cards, and so on, seemingly *ad infinitum*.

After about a minute, Fortesque said, "Criminy, Baines: All the money you make selling those Cuban stogies your guys stole from Batista . . . what the hell's another ten bucks?"

"Money's not the point, Harold," Baines said, without taking his eyes from the cards or his finger from his lip.

"Oh, yeah? So what is?"

"Winning," Baffington suggested. "Money's just the score card."

"Being smarter than the other guy," Ortega added. "Being the biggest swinging—"

"Hey!" Eastwood admonished.

"—pendulum on the block. Baines, I'm growing old waiting for you to —"

"Re-raise," Wainwright said at last, adding two more chips to the ten dollars he already had in from his opening bet.

"Goddamnit," Fortesque said as he forfeited his hand.

"Gee whiz," Baffington agreed as he mucked his own.

"Shit," Eastwood groaned as he gave up his own cards. He watched Wainwright let go of his now-unnecessary hand and reach over the table to rake in the pot he'd just won without showing his cards. "So what did you have?"

Wainwright paused in his raking and shot Eastwood a look of withering contempt. "You want to see, you pay."

"I'm ordering you as a matter of national security to tell me what you were holding."

"If you put it that way . . ." Wainwright picked up his cards, melded them into the deck and began shuffling. "Three aces," he said as the others laughed.

Eastwood looked at him and shook his head. "How'd you ever get to be DCI anyway, Wainwright?"

"You appointed me."

"What the hell were you smoking, Tom?" Fortesque asked.

"Same stuff he must've been smoking when he sent that Camel-Betty character down to South America," Wainwright answered.

"Caminetti," Ortega corrected him.

"That's what he said." Fortesque rose and stretched his arms over his head. "I need a break."

"I need a loan." Baffington rose to join the defense secretary at the rolling drinks cart.

Fortesque reached for a bottle of Chivas, then looked back at his dwindling supply of chips. He noticed that the normally hard-swigging Wainwright was pouring himself his third glass of cranberry juice, and wondered if there might be a connection between the DCI's temporary but disciplined sobriety and his considerably higher stack of chips. At the moment, though, the thought of that golden nectar flowing icily down his throat was more appealing to Fortesque than any reversal of fortune he might be able to engineer in its absence. Besides, if he was going to forswear booze in favor of better play, the time to start would have been two hours ago, not after he'd already knocked back three, maybe four glasses of scotch and let that ship sail out of the harbor. "Clock's running out on us, Tom," he said as he poured a healthy shot over the ice cubes already loaded into his glass.

Eastwood grunted as Ortega reached past him to lasso a bottle of Jack Daniel's. "He's right about that clock," she said.

"We're starting to look like a bunch of pu—I mean, uh, wimps," Wainwright added. "Getting some whiffs here and there from international cable traffic."

"Potty mouth," Ortega scolded as she poured.

"Hey, I caught myself in time, didn't I?"

"Interesting how you won't offend a lady's sensibilities but you've got no problem pounding the bejesus out of a bunch of third world nomads."

"Not the same and you know it, Connie." Wainwright took a long sip of his juice, and waved away Fortesque's joking attempt to pour a large dollop of scotch into his glass.

"I'll give you twenty bucks if you drink a glass," the defense secretary offered.

"I'm going to get about two hundred from you for not drinking it, Harold."

Baffington grabbed one of the beers that had been supplied especially for him. "Things sure are heating up on the domestic front, Mr. President." A product of Princeton and Grosse Point, the FBI director had never been able to address Eastwood, or his predecessor, any other way. "Lot of people thought we'd get over it in a hurry, but it's just getting worse."

"For heaven's sake," Ortega said. "Isn't it time to regain a little perspective? It's just coffee!" The other four looked at the non–coffee drinker but said nothing. Eventually she turned away, flapping her free hand at them, and her absurd comment died aborning.

"Ever notice," Baffington said, "how we can get attacked by terrorists and people shake their heads and move on, but if somebody gets cut off at a freeway exit he's ready to jump out of the car and commit murder?"

"True," Fortesque said. "I know guys who get shot at all the time and take it in stride, but light up a cigarette at the next table and they turn into pit bulls."

"Nothing surprising about that," Wainwright said. "One's personal, the other isn't."

"Getting attacked by terrorists isn't personal?" Ortega said.

"Nope. Personal is some inconsiderate sonofabitch getting right in your face in a way that affects you directly. It's why you'll lash into your husband or wife for things somebody else wouldn't even notice."

"You spent too much time in psy-ops, Baines," Fortesque chided.

"No, he's right." Baffington grabbed a handful of beer nuts from a crystal bowl. "I never got mad when bad guys robbed banks, but let somebody saunter into a meeting late without apologizing, I go nuts."

"This is all very enlightening," Eastwood said, "but what's it got to do with Barranca?"

"Everything." Wainwright topped off his glass and turned back to the table. "Every morning some construction worker doesn't get his cuppa, it's like Barranca is standing right in front of him taking the coffee pot out of his hands. It's not some shadowy religious nut strapping bombs to himself eight thousand miles away he reads about in the paper. No, coffee is something he can relate to; twenty people dead in a distant bus station isn't."

"You're right," Baffington observed. "Worst anti-Arab sentiment we ever tracked was when gasoline first topped a buck a gallon."

"Fine." Eastwood uncorked a previously opened bottle of Romanian cabernet and waved it in the air. "So what are you telling me?"

"We have to go after Barranca," Fortesque said.

"Over coffee?"

"No," Wainwright replied. "Over his ability to generate so much disruption."

"With no perceived consequences," Baffington added.

"And for kidnapping and probably killing an American citizen," Fortesque finished up.

Eastwood looked at his chief of staff. "Connie?"

"Yeah, we want the women's view," Wainwright sniggered.

"Bite me," Ortega said, picking up her half-smoked cigar and flicking a gold lighter at the same time. "My concern," she said as she held the flame to the tip and took in a few puffs, "is that our lack of response might encourage other upstarts to try some similar tactics."

"Over something far less benign than coffee," Wainwright added.

"Thing is, Tom," Fortesque said, "this business of Camel-Betty disappearing, it gives you all the excuse you need to order military action."

"I agree," Wainwright said. "You get right down to it, Barranca practically called a truce by inviting a U.S. citizen down. Then to turn around and snatch the guy, well . . ." He shrugged and left it at that.

"We don't know what he did with Eddie," Eastwood argued feebly.

"We all heard that last sat-phone call, sir," Baffington said. "Something nasty was about to happen to him."

Wainwright, lost in thought at Baffington's comment, idly fingered one of his many stacks of chips. "I hear he's some kind of character, that Caminetti," he said. "Brad, you've played golf with the guy . . ."

"So've I," Eastwood said with a wistful smile. "Swear to God, the guy pulls a con, sometimes you don't even know you've been had."

"Now how is that possible?" Ortega asked.

Baffington poured some beer into a glass and took a slug. "This one time," he said, "we were playing at Augusta, and on the third hole he asks me, all innocence and childlike curiosity, if I inhale or exhale on my backswing."

"He did that to you?" Eastwood exclaimed. "Sonofabitch!"

"I don't get it," Ortega said.

"I do." Wainwright set down his glass so he could gesture with both hands. "He got them thinking about something they'd never thought about before. Something that didn't actually need any thinking, but once you get it in your mind, it suddenly seems important. Like you should have been paying attention all along."

"Then you start trying to figure out what it is you do," Baffington threw in, "but you really can't tell, so you get hyper-self-conscious about it and start to worry about whether you've been doing it wrong all along, and whether whatever it is you try to do right there on the spot is correct or not."

"Totally destroys your concentration," Eastwood explained. "All you can think about is your damned breathing."

"But what's worse—" Wainwright spread his hands "—you don't even realize you were conned until you find out he's done it before." He let his hands drop, then looked at Eastwood. "Clever, I'll give him that."

"All very touching," Ortega said, "this male-bonding bullshit, but there's business we have to discuss. Harold, you said we now had a perfect excuse to launch an action."

"Helluva point, Tom," Wainwright said. "If we needed a pretext for launching something military, we've got it now. Does Barranca really think he can hold Caminetti hostage in exchange for major concessions without dire consequences?"

"Doesn't even make logical sense," Baffington offered. "Barranca behaved so dishonorably, he couldn't be trusted to hold up his end even if he did manage to squeeze some agreement out of us. So you have to wonder why he did it. Until we figure that out . . ."

"Are we definitely ready to go?" Wainwright asked.

Fortesque nodded. "Been in place for two days. We can launch on four hours' notice."

The talk continued, but if there was one thing Eastwood knew for a dead certainty, it was that he didn't have enough information to make a final decision, and he wasn't going to get it from advisors whose opinions he could predict in advance. He needed a private source, and he had one, but what he didn't have was time.

Three hands later Ortega said, "God, these suck," and threw in her cards. Eastwood instantly did the same, even though he was holding ace-king suited, and rose from the table. Once at the wet bar, he jerked his head slightly and Ortega rose to join him. She reached for a glass and leaned in.

"You have to buy me some time from Congress," Eastwood whispered.

Ortega knew enough not to ask why. "You mean from Twickham."

Eastwood nodded. "This is serious, Connie. I don't care if you have to promise him a new military base in friggin Raleigh, just get him off my back."

"What do you need?"

"Forty-eight hours. Twenty-four at the very minimum. I have to give Dalton a chance to find Eddie."

"I know he's your friend, and I hate to be hard-hearted, but he's just one guy, and —"

Eastwood shook his head vigorously. "It's not that. I don't want to start shooting until I know why Barranca would do something this dumb."

"Hey," Baffington called from the table as he pointed to his watch. "Shouldn't you be going?"

Eastwood looked at his own watch. "Damn . . ."

"Hold it, " Wainwright said, and began poking through the president's chips. "Okay, you're losing. You can go."

CHAPTER 22

Fatigued, disoriented and under pressure, it was all Dalton Galsworthy could do to fight down the impression that the overwhelming vegetation was consciously trying to pull him down and strangle him to death. The steamy, oppressive heat didn't help, and the sweat constantly running into his eyes and down his back and chest reminded him of Vietnam, where he'd done three tours as the Company's covert op's officer in Saigon. But at least in Southeast Asia he'd had some support, hundreds of people at the other end of radios, dozens of base stations in friendly villages, a wide assortment of contacts and the admittedly suspect backing of the local government.

Here, wherever the hell *here* was, he was alone, and somehow not knowing exactly where he was added to the overall feeling of dread. He'd damaged his portable GPS unit after parachuting down and landing awkwardly on a tree stump, but the device probably saved his life, deflecting a sharp protrusion of dried wood but getting smashed to pieces in the process. The only electronics he had left were a tracking receiver and a sat phone.

The tracking receiver was tuned to the frequency being emitted by a transmitter disguised as a pack of cigarettes he'd stashed in Eddie Caminetti's golf bag next to the sat phone. It was in the same zippered pocket that had hit the ground when that asshole of a pilot had tried to object to a soldier taking the bag. Somehow it had survived, and was still transmitting, although Galsworthy had no way to know if he was actually tracking it to Caminetti or would find himself emerging from the jungle at some exclusive golf course in western Brazil because the soldier had really stolen the golf bag and pawned it to raise a few more *reals* for Barranca's annoying revolution. Galsworthy had been in the jungle for thirty-six hours now, it was growing dark for the second time since he'd landed and thoughts like those were threatening to drive him crazy, and it was why he was so relieved that his earpiece was whistling away at top volume, which meant he was very close to the transmitter.

He noticed that the vegetation was thinning rapidly and then he stopped, wiping furiously at his eyes to make sure he wasn't seeing some fatigue-induced mirage. Out beyond a final berm of downed palms was what appeared to be a factory complex of some kind, or a small, enclosed town or military outpost. It consisted of a series of two- and three-story wooden buildings within a clearly defined perimeter, and it was occupied: In the dying light he could see men walking here and there in the main yard.

The whistling in his earpiece had reached its peak volume and was now pulsing rapidly: The transmitter was within a hundred yards of his location. He reached down to his belt and turned off the power, and at the exact instant his hand touched the switch a light came on in a small hut on the very edge of the perimeter boundary closest to him. Galsworthy unlatched a leather case hanging from his shoulder, withdrew a compact pair of binoculars, trained them on the hut's single window and tried to suppress a gasp as Eddie Caminetti's face filled half his field of vision.

Eddie seemed to sway unsteadily, confusion on his face as he strained to see something. Suddenly two men appeared behind him. One drew up his hand and appeared to push Eddie, who disappeared from view, then the other raised a rock high above his head and brought it crashing down. Galsworthy distinctly heard a dull, sickening thud and tore the binoculars from his eyes as he stepped back and fought to keep from getting dizzy.

His foot caught on a vine and he stumbled, making a loud crunching sound. He whipped his head around and brought the binoculars back up to his eyes. Sure enough, the man who was wielding the rock had stopped, his head up. He was listening, swiveling his head slowly back and forth, ready to locate the sound if it reoccurred. Galsworthy held his breath and didn't move, and soon the man looked back down, probably having dismissed the disturbance as the skittering of a jungle animal. Galsworthy forced himself to shift the binoculars away from the window so he could use the light spilling from the hut to check out the surrounding situation. He was dismayed to see dozens of men with automatic weapons patrolling the yard and the perimeter. Seconds later the light went out and Galsworthy heard the sound of a wooden door being slammed shut.

Sweating now from more than the heat, Galsworthy turned and began heading back into the jungle, setting his feet down slowly and carefully, backing off and trying a different spot if he felt himself stepping on something hard that might snap and make a noise. It took him almost twenty minutes to go far enough to feel safe, and then he unhooked his satellite phone and punched the button connected to the encoding chip.

"Smith," a voice at the other end said.

"Jones," Galsworthy replied to the president. They were using code names in case anyone was monitoring the satellite or cellular frequencies, something that was very difficult to do unless you had twenty bucks' worth of gear from Radio Shack. "I found Eddie. He's alive."

"Thank—"

"But he's in serious trouble."

"Can you get him out?"

"I don't know. It won't be easy, not without a way to communicate with him."

"Dalton," the president said, "I can't hold off the pressure to launch an assault much longer."

"How much time do I have?"

"I don't know. Connie's working on something that might buy us some time, but you can't bank on it."

Galsworthy bit his lip as his mind raced through a series of possibilities, but none popped up as particularly attractive. "I need to scout around a bit more."

"Tell me about Eddie."

Galsworthy closed his eyes and tried to put the hut out of his mind. "I think he's okay for now—" *if he doesn't bleed to death* "—but there's nothing I can do about it. I'll phone you back, say . . ."

"An hour?"

"I'll try."

CHAPTER 23

"**L**et me put it as plainly as I can, Ms. Ortega," Orville Twickham said calmly, although without being able to keep traces of a smirk away from his mouth.

"As plain as you put it on the Senate floor?"

"There're no cameras around now, Connie. No point getting huffy." The smirk traces transmogrified into something considerably less benign.

He was right, and she knew it. "Shoot."

"Apt choice of words." As Senator Paul Stillwell and two aides sat back content to let him handle the load, Twickham leaned forward and folded his hands on the vast table. "Your president—"

"*Our* president, Senator." Ortega was capable of lowering the temperature herself when the situation warranted it.

Twickham unfolded a hand, waved it in the air, said "Whatever," then refolded it. "The president is blowing a perfect opportunity to bomb a terrorist back into the Ice Age."

"Is he."

"Yes, ma'am. Barranca kidnapped and probably killed a U.S. citizen he himself sent for, and which the U.S dispatched in good faith, all as part of a trap. Not only did Eastwood—"

"President Eastwood."

Twickham stopped, unwrapped his hands again and leaned back on his chair. "Tell me something, Connie: You're new at this, right? Been in the job, what . . . less than a year?"

"You know very well that's true."

"Right. Well, here's a piece of advice: Save the bullshit for *The Mona Bertram Show* or for those go-get-em college students you lecture to who like that kind of sophomoric mind game, okay? Because the only purpose it serves when nobody else is watching is to piss the other guy off, and trust me when I tell you, you don't want to piss me off."

"And why is that?" Ortega said brittlely.

"Because we're negotiating, that's why." Twickham waited to see if further explanation was necessary, then decided it was. "The object in negotiating is to get what you want. It isn't to be right, or to win an argument or come off smarter than the other guy." He tapped two fingers on the table. "It's to get what you went in to get. Business 101, Ms. Ortega."

"Thanks for the lesson. You've still got no call to insult my president."

"I thought he was *our* president."

Ortega's dark brown skin turned a shade lighter as the three men behind Twickham turned away—gleefully, it seemed to her—from the flogging.

"See what I mean?" Twickham said affably. "I play some bullshit mind game, you get your dander up . . . and what the hell's the point of it all?"

Well put in her place but unwilling to acknowledge it, Ortega said, "Are we getting close to the part where you tell me what you want?"

"You bet." Having made his point, Twickham, heeding his own counsel, saw no need to push it further. "As I was saying, not only did *the* president do something abysmally stupid in sending this what's-his-name down there, he—"

"Caminetti." Ortega held up a hand to forestall another lecture. "Just telling you his name. It's Eddie Caminetti."

"Fair enough. So not only did the president let himself be trapped by an amateur revolutionary, he may have gotten a citizen killed."

"How was he to know a citizen was going to get killed?"

"Well . . ." Twickham laughed and shook his head. "How do any of us know what's going to happen? Except that when you're an elected leader, everybody expects you to be psychic, no matter how unreasonable that might be. If something you started goes down the can, it's your fault, even if you had no way to know. Fact of political life, Connie." He paused for a second. "Of course, if you don't think your president is going to suffer a barrage of shit for getting snookered and for getting Caminetti killed, well, hell . . .". He made as if to reach for his briefcase on the floor, but held his hand above it. "We can end this pleasant little confab right now."

Ortega looked away and tapped a pencil on the table , as though trying to come to a decision about whether to end the meeting. It fooled no one but they all played the game for the sake of tradition. "You're saying we should attack Barranca."

"Immediately," Stillwell said, seizing his opportunity to go on the record despite Twickham's considerable seniority. "Today, if possible."

Ortega returned her gaze to them, noticing that Twickham's hands were back on the table. "How do we attack an enemy we can't identify, much less isolate to a specific location?"

"Hey . . ." Twickham sat up straight and began buttoning his jacket. "Not my bailiwick, Connie. I'm just a senator."

"Separation of powers," Stillwell said as he stood up, motioning for the aides to do likewise. "Not for the legislative branch to dictate military strategy."

Ortega smiled and looked down at the table, confident she understood the play now. The majority senators were about to demand, publicly and loudly, that the Eastwood administration take military action against those holding the country hostage, knowing perfectly well that such action was a practical nightmare. They'd then blame the administration for the inevitable failure, or blame it for simpering inaction if it did nothing. "Pretty good thinking there, Senator."

Twickham, half out of his chair, hesitated in that position before standing fully erect. "Sorry? What was that?"

"I think you're right." Ortega began gathering her own papers. "And I'm going to go talk to him about it right now."

The two senators exchanged glances. "You are?" Twickham said, confusion and doubt in his voice.

Ortega stopped shuffling her papers. "That's what you want, isn't it? A hard recommendation to the president to get on down there and wipe this mess up?"

"Um . . . you bet."

"Well, there you go." She stood up and held out her hand, shaking firmly with both senators and their assistants. "Thanks for coming." She turned to go, then spun back. "Oh, one little thing?"

"What's that?" Stillwell asked.

"The president will want a set of specific recommendations from the Senate Armed Services Committee. You know, what assets to deploy, where to send them, optimum targets . . . that sort of thing." She turned away again.

"Wait a minute," Twickham called after her.

She turned again. "Yes?"

"That's not the purview of the Senate committee, and you know it."

Ortega waved her hand dismissively. "Old thinking, Senator. You said so yourself."

"I did?"

"Oh, yes! It was a brilliant speech. One of my favorites. In fact—" She pretended to fumble with her papers, but the sheet she wanted was right on top of the stack. She yanked it off, held it up, then set it back down and adjusted her glasses. "—I have it right here. The afternoon of the inauguration, if memory serves. You said, 'We can only hope that this president ushers in an era of bipartisan cooperation, involving Congress in matters of substance at an early stage, in detail, inviting participation in the very conceptualization and planning of major initiatives. We will not shrink before this obligation, nor will we hesitate in providing whatever assistance we can.'"

Ortega took off her glasses. "I'm going out on a limb here, but I'd say launching an assault in South America qualifies as a major initiative, wouldn't you?"

"Now, listen . . . !"

But she'd turned again and was walking toward the door. "I'll tell the president he'll have your recommendations by the end of the day." Hand on the doorknob, she turned one last time. "And he'll tell GNN how pleased he is at the bipartisan cooperation."

"Connie!"

"Yes?" She waited, knowing Twickham wouldn't have anything to say. But his lesson earlier had been a good and valuable one, and she wasn't one to ignore sound advice, regardless of what quarter it emanated from. "On the other hand," she said thoughtfully, "that's kind of short notice, isn't it?"

"Uh . . . yeah . . ."

"So what do you say we both sleep on it a little and get back, say, tomorrow afternoon?"

Twickham recognized the open door and shot through it. "That's very level-headed thinking, Connie. Paul?"

"Sounds good to me," Stillwell readily agreed.

CHAPTER 24

Yoshi?" Eastwood inquired into the phone, making sure he had the prime minister of Peru on the line and not the operator who had set up the phone call. He wished to avoid a repeat of a recent incident in which he'd asked Muriel Gannon, seventy-eight-year-old matriarch of the G.E. Residence telephone switching center, how her balls were hanging lately, thinking he had the senior weapons advisor to the Joint Chiefs on the line. (Muriel, showing the stuff of which a forty-five-year service career was made, responded that they were hanging just fine, thank you very much, and hoped the president's were doing equally well.)

At the other end of the line in Lima, Yoshi Noriyuki stood up abruptly, nearly tipping over his chair. "Yes, Mr. President! At your service!"

"Nice to speak with you, Yoshi. How's everything going down there?"

"Just fine, sir. Just fine. And you?"

"Wonderful. Never better." Connie Ortega slipped a piece of paper onto Eastwood's desk blotter. "And how's Mariella? Got that bit of pneumonia cleared up yet, has she?"

"Oh, yes indeed, Mr. President! Thank you very much for inquiring!"

"Not at all. And how are things shaping up for the elections? Got everything under control?"

"Well," Noriyuki said, trying to sit down and feeling around for his chair, "one never knows for sure about such things, does one? At times it seems—"

"Yes, well, I know exactly how you feel. Yessir. Could always use a little help from your friends, eh?"

"That is indeed true."

"Catching a little flak on account of this Barranca business, are you?"

"Catching . . . sorry, Mr. President?"

"Feeling the heat?"

"Heat . . . ah, yes! Yes, I am feeling heat. It is a bad business. You yourself know this well."

"True, but hey, to us it's just coffee. To you, well: The guy's hitting a little close to home."

Noriyuki had by now found the edge of his chair and pulled it under him. "Very close, sir," he said tiredly as he sank into his chair. "It is causing no small end of concern among my ministers."

"I bet. Well, listen . . . just called to make sure you're alright, and—Say, there's one thing I oughta mention."

"Yes, sir?"

"We're thinking of mounting a little operation against Barranca. Nothing major, you know, just kind of come on in there, blow him all to hell and leave quietly. Get me?"

Noriyuki was on his feet again. "Indeed I do, sir!"

"Okay then. 'Course, we don't know exactly where yet, so we might have to drop a few troops on Peruvian soil. Got any problem with that?"

"Problem? Ah, well, I suppose not, but I rather—"

"Good! That's what we like to hear! Couple of bits of ordnance to go with them, of course."

"I see. Yes. What sorts of—"

"Ah, nothing big. Some antiaircraft batteries, couple'a three missile launchers, maybe a MOAB or two . . . nothing that'll muss your hair, pardner."

"Muss my—?"

"You don't need to worry. When we're gone, you won't even know we were there. Get me?"

"Well, I don't know about—"

"And all that will be left is you getting your country back, for the good of your people, who will put you back in office next term so fast your opponent will wish he'd stayed in the army where he belongs. Are we on the same page now?"

"On the—yes. Yes! The same page, yes!"

"Attaboy, Yoshi. You take care now, hear?"

"I will, sir. And—"

"And give my best to your lovely wife. Tell her I hope she feels better."

"I will do that."

"Good man." With the prime minister now eating out of his hand, Eastwood was ready to end the call, awaiting only the final confirming response.

"Thank you, Mr. President."

Galsworthy ended his surveillance of the outpost about fifty minutes after he'd begun, to give himself some time to mentally prepare for the call he had to make to the president. Then he punched the button.

"Smith," the president answered.

"Jones. Did she do it?"

"Yes!" The president's voice was strong in the aftermath of Ortega's tactical victory over Orville Twickham. "Twenty-four hours. But that's probably it. Have you got a plan?"

Galsworthy nodded absently—it wasn't a great plan—then remembered it was a phone call and said, "If you can call it a plan."

"What are you going to do?"

"Let them capture me." To the answering silence he said, "It's the only way in without a division behind me, and all I've got is a sidearm." He knew he'd get no argument from the president, and he was right.

"Then what?"

"Damned if I know."

"Great plan."

"Knew you'd like it. Mr. President, if it goes sour, under no circumstances are you to bargain for my life. Or Caminetti's."

"You giving me orders, Dalton?"

"And I expect you to snap to."

"Roger. Listen, I've got some guys here, they want to see if they can narrow down your position. Hang on a second."

As he waited, Galsworthy took a scrap of paper and a penlight from his jacket pocket but had no time to read what he'd written before a new voice came on the line. "Hello? You there, Mr. Galsworthy?"

No, I stepped out for a burger. "I'm here," Galsworthy answered as he turned on the penlight and pointed it toward the piece of paper.

"Excellent. What I want to know, what time——"

"Sun's upper limb disappeared at exactly six-thirteen thirty-two my present position, horizon two degrees above actual. Headed niner-two degrees for thirty-eight hours, approximate average two klicks an hour."

There was no immediate answer, then a small voice said, "Well. Okay then. Um . . ."

"Anything else?"

"Uh, no. Not from me. But hold on, because . . ."

"What?"

"They want to know what kind of flowers you see there." It was the president's voice.

"Flowers?"

"Yeah. Something about the indigenous flora, I don't know. Hang on."

"But I don't know anything about——"

"Dalton? Baines Wainwright here." Galsworthy recognized the CIA director's voice, as well as the forced friendliness in the president's presence. "Look around and see what kinda flowers they got."

"I tried to tell the president, I don't know——"

"Okay, here one'a my analysts. You tell her the flowers, she'll write em down. Ready? Okay, here she is."

"Go ahead, Mr. Galsworthy," a new, young and very eager voice said.

Galsworthy sighed and began rubbing his forehead with two fingers. "Listen, is Hayne in the room? And don't say his name out——"

"Joffrey Hayne? Why, yes sir, he's right here! This was his idea! Did you want to——"

"No." Galsworthy gritted his teeth; it wasn't the young analyst's fault, and there was no sense giving her a hard time because of it. "Are you a flower expert or something?"

"Oh, no sir! Just taking down what you say. Are you ready?"

Yes. Ready to choke the living shit out of Joffrey Hayne. "Gimme a minute." Without lifting his head or even opening his eyes, Galsworthy said, "Okay, here goes. You ready?"

"Ready!"

"Okay. They got some catatonia . . ."

"Catatonia, right. Got it."

"Couple'a natatoriums, one or two pandemoniums . . ."

"Pandemoniums! Excellent! Keep going."

"You betcha. Whole bunch'a honoraria and calliopes, and . . . oh, whoa: hallucinogenia! Damn! You don't see that stuff every day!"

"Boy, you sure don't! What else?"

"Patagonias. Those are everywhere. Intelligentsia, too. You getting all this down?"

"You bet I am, Mr. Galsworthy!"

"Wonderful. Saw some indisposoria growing near the perimeter..."

CHAPTER 25

There had been no public announcement, of course, nor any official word at all from the G.E. Residence or the Departments of Defense or State. Not a single sheet of paper had been generated, and all discussions had been strictly classified according to the most restrictive national security protocols described in the Patriot Act. Any conversations not occurring within the confines of a secure room were held on scramble phones only, and the number of people to whom such conversations were confined totaled less than thirty. Which is why it took nearly an hour for it to appear on the Internet and almost the entire morning for the wire services to confirm it and get it out to every newspaper, television network and radio station in the country.

But it didn't really matter. It was shaping up to be the biggest no-brainer of an American military action since Pearl Harbor triggered the country's entrance into WWII. Aside from a few radical extremists who wouldn't have counseled armed resistance if their own homes had been invaded, everyone was on board for this one, including both sides of the aisle in Congress. Television talking heads, embarrassed and uncomfortable at not being able to viciously criticize broad policy, ignored the question of whether war was justified and instead concentrated on the details, ripping to shreds opposing points of view as to where the invasion should start, on what day, using what ordnance and directed specifically against whom. That no one in the military had divulged anything about any of those things didn't stop the pundits from taking them to task anyway, on the theory that, although no official had publicly advocated any particular course of action, doubtless such advocacies had been expressed somewhere in the corridors of power. When they eventually came to light, the criticisms would still be valid with respect to substance, and only the attributions would have been wrong, easily correctable minor lapses in no way impinging on the validity of the original observations.

Foreign allies, eager for an opportunity to affirm their friendship with America following their perceived betrayal of it during the previous war, clambered onto the bandwagon zealously, even offering supplies and manpower for the coming effort. That these displays of support would trigger critical anti-terrorist clauses—easing of barriers, reductions in tariffs, relaxed intellectual property restrictions—inserted into key trade agreements by the previous U.S. presidential administration was, of course, not even a remote consideration in light of the greater good to be wrought. The takedown of the villainous Barranca and his band of merciless thugs would be acclaimed the world over, the invading soldiers hailed as nonconquering, liberating heroes, America seen in a new light of justice, righteous retribution and the enlightened policing of the enemies of the world's helpless and downtrodden.

All Eastwood needed to let slip the dogs of war was a phone call from Dalton Galsworthy.

The phone rang.

"Relax, Mr. President," Chief of Staff Conchita Ortega said lightly with a dazzling *What could possibly go wrong?* smile as she reached for the phone on his desk. She popped off one of her earrings and held the receiver to her ear. "Ortega," she said into the mouthpiece. She listened for a few seconds, then closed her eyes, looked downward and began rubbing the bridge of her nose.

"What?" the president asked.

She hung up the phone without saying goodbye or otherwise acknowledging the caller. "You have to call it off."

CHAPTER 26

Like many major corporations, GNN chose its headquarters location based not on tax advantage, available local labor supply, transportation access or other such standard business criteria, but because it was where the founder had always hung his hat and he liked it there. In the case of Global News Network, by far the largest single news organization on the planet, Chicago was world headquarters because Lance "Sparky" Kroeger—president, CEO and the man who began it all—had a particular fondness for the bouillabaisse at Chez Couverture d'Poussière on the corner of Rush and Dearborn. There wasn't anything particular about the bouillabaisse, according to local food critics, most of whom found it pretentious, cloying or hinting of Gaelic arrogance, but Kroeger, who'd been assigned to the Marseilles office of the Associated Press for three weeks following an abrupt departure from college in his sophomore year, had lost his virginity in the kitchen of La Petit Outil to a lusty *sous* chef from Lyons who had bet an off-duty U.S. Marine that she could shuck enough clams for the evening's preparations while simultaneously graduating Kroeger from boy to man. As it happened, she'd barely gotten her knife into her third hapless but aptly named cherrystone when Kroeger, in his inexperienced and overly excited eagerness, cost her fifty dollars. In the sweet afterglow of his bivalve-bedecked rite of passage he'd barely noticed her rage despite a mixture of blood and clam juice running down his face from a newly-inflicted knife wound, but for the remainder of his life the perfume of simmering bouillabaisse impinged on his central nervous system like an opium cocktail without the felony implications.

Leonine and craggy, Kroeger was central casting's picture of a front-line Marine captain, right down to the scar that ran from his left eye almost to his mouth. The source of the original wound was the subject of endless speculation, fueled by a certain darkness that invaded Kroeger's face whenever he was asked about it and refused to discuss it. The bane of Kroeger's current existence was star reporter Mona Bertram, a toweringly self-absorbed, monomaniacal ball-buster who, for some reason that taxed the normally savvy Kroeger's ability to fathom, was adored by millions of viewers, primarily in the male nineteen-to-thirty-five demographic. That she was beautiful and sexy was undeniable, and in fact was the entire key to the promotional campaign GNN had mounted for her, in part to deflect attention away from the otherwise obvious fact that the most important element of every interview she conducted was Mona Bertram herself. But it continued to amaze Kroeger that her relentless and visible egotism was lost on the Nielsen families who kept her Q ratings somewhere north of the Arctic Circle. Kroeger would love to have dumped her long ago, but he knew full well that suits in the other, publicly held news organizations wouldn't care if she'd murdered her own children so long as she boosted their ratings, and so he kept her on.

From a business point of view it was the right thing to do for the bottom line, but lately Bertram had been making very loud noises about wanting to do some "real reporting," as opposed to simply reading out loud in front of a camera what others had written and conducting scripted interviews with people who knew in advance that they weren't going to get any serious zingers coming out of left field. Bertram had dipped a toe into those treacherous waters once by going off-script with a Southern senator from the Foreign Trade Relations committee, and it was only his sense of down-home graciousness and quick verbal timing that had kept mercifully low the number of people who'd noticed her reference to "The Gap" rather than GAAT.

"This is horseshit, Sparky, and you know it," Bertram shrilled, trailing slightly behind Kroeger as he walked rapidly down the main corridor of the second floor of the GNN building. "I sit on my ass in a goddamned studio all day while real reporters are running all over the world making news."

"Not making news, Mona. Gathering news." He saw no need to point out to Bertram one of the problems she'd have as a "real" reporter, her subconsciously ensconced sense that news—i.e., events that happened to real people and institutions—existed primarily to provide reporters with things to report. Like the proverbial tree falling silently in a forest, something deep in Bertram's psyche was half-convinced that anything that didn't make it to the seven o'clock report hadn't actually happened, or, at most, was of vanishingly small consequence. What she'd actually meant by "making news" was the magical transmogrification of a randomly selected event into something newsworthy, a kind of benediction lending it legitimacy and weight. It was how powerful news organizations were able to so effectively manipulate public perception, morphing a vice president into a court jester over a simple spelling error while excusing by virtue of its deliberate inattention a popular president's public—and publicly repeated—declarations that radiation came from the burning of coal, acid rain was caused by an excess of trees and buses had the same fuel efficiency as cars.

"Don't play semantic games with me," Bertram replied. "Just look at it from your bottom-line perspective: How long do you think I'm going to be able to keep pulling in those fantastic ratings reading from scripts all day?"

Simple, he thought. *Keep wearing tight sweaters, shiny lipstick and those fuck-me shoes we buy for you at a grand a pop, leer seductively at world leaders and throw that shit-ass wink at the horny masses who tune in every night like you're ready to get naked in the hot tub with them at the drop of a hat.* "It's what you're a master at, Mona. The way you put over a story . . . it's like Cronkite and Murrow all rolled into one. People believe in you; they trust you. When Mona Bertram speaks, they know that all's right with the world, no matter how bad things are." He stopped, and put a comforting hand on Bertram's shoulder. "You're the very best in the business, Mona. And I have to be truthful: I don't like the way you put yourself down like that, like what you do isn't important, maybe the most important thing that happens around here." He knew that speech would bite him in the ass come contract negotiating time, but what the hell: Bertram knew her worth to GNN with the same accuracy that a cat knows its body position while falling out of a window, so the only real negotiation that ever occurred with her agent was whether Kroeger was willing to pony up the number.

Bertram, chewing her lower lip, considered Kroeger's words. "You're right," she finally announced, the egocentric extremism of it utterly lost on her. "But you're missing the point, Sparky. Sure I pull in the ratings, but what about respect from my peers? People in our business? Before long they're going to start realizing that I'm not actually out there doing reporting."

Before long? Kroeger almost choked at the titanic density of his star reporter. "You're crazy, Mona," he said, and then touched another match to the parchment of his negotiating position. "Every other network out there would kill to have you on their team."

"That's not the kind of respect I'm talking about. How come I always get asked to judge beauty contests but nobody asks me to speak at news conventions or journalism schools?"

Let me count the . . . "Mona, you have to—"

"Sparky!" came a shouted call from far down the corridor. Kroeger and Bertram turned to see a production assistant running breathlessly toward them, then stop and beckon when he had their attention. Kroeger always insisted that everyone in the organization call him by his nickname.

"What's up?" Kroeger asked as he started forward, surprising deference to a lowly PA but in actuality a retreat from Mona Bertram.

"Something important," the PA answered, waving him forward again. "In Sports."

Kroeger halted his forward motion. "What the hell could be so important in Sports?"

"I don't know," the PA said as he turned to lead the way. "But Steve Farley said to find you, even—" He stopped when he noticed that Bertram, rather than continue on the way she'd been walking, had turned to follow Kroeger.

"Even what?" Kroeger prodded.

The PA seemed pleased that Kroeger had insisted on hearing the rest of the sentence, and even more pleased that he got to say it in front of Bertram. "Even if I had to drag your ass out of the can."

"I'm coming with you," Bertram said,

"Mona . . ."

"I said, I'm coming!" She then stared defiantly at the PA, who waited for a nod from Kroeger before turning once again and heading back down the hall.

They found sports reporter Steve Farley standing in front of a control console, phone pressed to the side of his head, a hand covering his other ear. He was hunched over, and periodically hunched even further, as though that might somehow make it easier to hear whatever it was he was having difficulty hearing over the phone.

"Who's he on with?" Kroeger asked the senior engineer on duty, who stiffened noticeably at the sound of that gruff voice from the back of the room. He'd never seen Kroeger anywhere near the sports department before.

"Miguel Sangeria," the engineer responded. When he got no reaction from Kroeger, he said, "A junior golfer who's been hanging around with Albert—"

"Albert Auberlain," Kroeger finished for him. "I know who he is."

Despite Kroeger's well-known lack of regard for sports reporting—he considered it entertainment and GNN was supposed to be about hard news—there was no way not to know about Miguel Sangeria, the fourteen-year-old phenom who'd popped onto the national golf scene out of absolutely nowhere less than six months ago. Apparently a protégé of pro golfer "Fat Albert" Auberlain, he was rocketing up the ranks of junior golf with dizzying velocity, mowing down other kids with established pedigrees, and nobody could quite figure out how he'd gotten there. When the question of his age was brought up by an investigative reporter whose network had gotten burned following its superhype of a fifteen-year-old Puerto Rican Little League pitcher who'd turned out to be a nineteen-year old Dominican, Auberlain had produced an unassailable birth certificate from a Colombian maternity hospital complete with a baby footprint that proved to be an exact match to Sangeria's own podiatric hieroglyph.

Kroeger watched Farley hunch even further down, but this time it was to scratch frantically on a pad of paper while squeezing the phone even more tightly to his ear.

"Lousy connection," the engineer explained. "Kid must be on a cell."

Farley straightened up, nodded vigorously, then said something into the phone and hung up. He picked up the pad of paper and began reading over his notes, arching his back to relieve some of the strain that had built up while he'd been bent over the desk.

Without waiting for Kroeger's permission, Mona Bertram strode into the control room, took up a position opposite Farley and said, "So what's the scoop?"

Farley, shaken out of his reverie, looked up and blinked, saw Mona, and blinked some more. Of all the thoughts running through his head, none had anything to do with explaining to her what "the scoop" was. He turned, looked around for something he could actually relate to, and spotted Kroeger. He held up the pad, waved it once and started for the back of the room. Bertram, stemming an insulted outburst, bit her lip and followed him.

"What's up?" Kroeger asked as Farley approached.

"Not sure." Farley tapped a finger on the pad of paper. "This kid— you know Miguel Sangeria?"

"Golfer, yeah. What about him?"

"Well—" Farley halted, as though deciding whether it made any sense to report on his conversation "—he says he spoke with his family in Brazil, and—"

"Thought he was Colombian," Bertram interrupted. At Farley's surprised expression she added, "I actually watch the station once in a while, jock-o."

"What about him?" Kroeger said.

"His family relocated," Farley explained. "I think they're in the coffee business. Anyway, Miguel says he's been unable to get in touch with them for the last two days, but this morning he spoke with a family friend and, uh . . ."

Kroeger, his impatience mounting, said, "F'chrissakes, Steve. You're the one who called me in, so—"

"He says there's a war going on down there."

The control room, which had continued its normal bustle even while every ear in it had been tuned to whatever it was that was going on that involved the big boss himself, suddenly quieted. "A war?" Kroeger said, trying to ignore body language from Bertram indicating that every antenna in her opportunistic sensing array had just gone to DefCon 4.

Farley shrugged and indicated the pad he was holding. "That's what the kid says."

"A war." Kroeger tried to process the information, but stopped halfway through. "He give you any specifics?"

"Kind of. Best I can figure, Manuel Barranca decided to take on the entire Brazilian army in one last-ditch stand."

"Holy shit," the senior engineer breathed, a sentiment shared, if not voiced, by everyone within earshot.

Except Kroeger. "Hold it a minute. There's a war going on in South America and the first anybody hears about it is from a sports reporter who got it from a snot-nosed fourteen-year-old golfer from Colombia?"

"Hey, don't shoot the messenger, Sparky. And, by the way, Sangeria's no snot-nose. He's more level-headed than half the pros on the circuit."

Kroeger knew Farley was neither an idiot nor a grandstander, and certainly not given to Chicken Little hysterics. Was it even remotely possible that GNN had just lucked into the greatest head start in news reporting history?

"There's one more thing, chief," Farley said.

"What?"

"The family friend Miguel spoke to. He's an American citizen. On site."

"Who is it?" Bertram asked.

Farley kept his eyes on Kroeger as he answered. "Eddie Caminetti. And he may be in trouble."

Without even looking away from Farley, Kroeger knew instinctively that Mona Bertram had just gone to DefCon 5.

CHAPTER 27

roeger considered the possibility of having Bertram physically removed from his office, but decided to ride it out for a while.

"Think about it, Sparky," she was insisting as she paced in front of his desk. "This could be the biggest exclusive since Charles Foster Kane started the Civil War!"

Was there anything to be gained, Kroeger wondered, by pointing out that it had been William Randolph Hearst, and the civil war had been Spain's, not America's? Probably not. "We have no confirmation whatsoever, Mona. All we know is that a notorious hustler calls a fourteen-year-old immigrant and says he's stuck somewhere in the middle of a war nobody even knows about yet. Now what the hell kind of sense does that make?"

"None," Bertram replied, coming to a halt in front of Kroeger's desk. She folded her arms defiantly and said, "Unless you find out that it wasn't Miguel Sangeria who Caminetti called, it was Albert Auberlain, his best friend, because he was on a satellite phone and it was the only phone number he could remember, except Auberlain wasn't home and the kid answered instead."

"So how come the kid called a sports reporter?"

"Because Steve Farley's the only reporter the little dickwad knows!" Bertram spread her arms as she made her point, then let them drop. "Who the hell else was he going to call?"

Not a bad point. Except . . . "Say: How the hell come you know all of this, Mona?"

"How come?" She dropped her arms and clasped her hands behind her back. "Because I checked the caller ID in the control room and phoned back, that's how come." *Like a real reporter,* she didn't need to add. "Auberlain answered and told me what happened. And he was worried sick to death about Caminetti."

Kroeger swiveled his chair around and stared out at the river moving slowly thirty stories below him. He pretended to be thinking but was in fact steeling himself.

"Let me run with this one, boss," Bertram said. She'd never called him boss before.

"No."

She'd been ready for that and didn't let her emotions carry her away. "Why not?"

"Because you don't know how. You have no sources, no contacts, no leads and no way to get them. We got maybe, I don't know, a day at the most before someone else gets wind of this. We have to confirm, and that includes getting something from a highly placed U.S. official, probably off the record. Then we need more specifics. I don't know if twenty of my most experienced reporters can get it done, so what makes you think you can?" It was harsh, but it was the truth, and Kroeger knew instinctively that it was the right tack to take with her, because she'd see the implications immediately: If she got in over her head and it ever came out that she'd been the cause of GNN's failure to capitalize on the story, the next time anyone saw her face it would be on a Frostee-Freeze employee ID badge.

Kroeger turned his chair back around to underscore the power of his argument, fully expecting to see a thoroughly wilted Mona Bertram. He was already searching for the words to ease the blow and deciding to let her take over the afternoon news show so she could at least be the one to break the story.

But there was no wilting to be found in Bertram's face or posture. "I can do it, Sparky."

Kroeger sighed inwardly. Was this going to be the end of their professional relationship? She had only eight months left on her contract, and could easily —

Hold it. Something was wrong here. There was no way the vauntingly self-centered Bertram would depart the network in a petulant huff. Prospective employers would know the reason within minutes, and if they even suspected that the temperamental diva had her mind set on doing investigative reporting in the field, she wouldn't be able to get a job in the mail room. And there was also no way she would risk her career by taking on a monster news assignment and blowing it in front of—almost literally—the entire planet. Which could only mean . . .

Kroeger flew up out of his chair, rested both fists on his desk and leaned forward threateningly. "What have you got!"

Bertram, to her credit, didn't take a single step backwards. "What do you mean?"

"Don't screw around with me, Bertram! I put up with your shit because I have to, but there's a line I won't go over, if I have to sink this whole fucking network!" Kroeger held out his hand and pointed a finger right at her eyes. "What have you got?"

For the first time, Bertram faltered, because she wasn't sure how to make the decision she had to make in the next few seconds. At least there was no doubt about one thing: Kroeger already knew she had something on the story. The only question was whether she was going to give it up.

"I asked you a question, Mona." His tone was menacing and not at all collegial.

"Do I get the story?"

A fair question. "If what you have is good enough."

An unfair answer: She'd have to trust him. But she was savvy enough to know she had no real choice. "Caminetti's going to call me in twenty minutes."

What she should have said was that Caminetti was going to *try* to call. He'd made it clear to Miguel Sangeria that his access to a sat phone was a hit-or-miss proposition, by no means assured. As of right now, twenty minutes had already stretched to forty.

In the control room with at least a dozen other GNN personnel, Bertram and Kroeger sat off to the side by themselves discussing the details of exactly how this story was going to be run. Having reluctantly granted her the lead on the assignment, and having made it clear that he could snatch it away at any moment, Kroeger had to switch gears and get his mind right to make sure the network came out of this situation farting in silk while every other news director went schizoid trying to figure out how they'd gotten out-gunned.

"You'd have to go down there, Mona."

Her eyes lit up, the glow fueled by visions of herself in a flak jacket, triple-A lighting up the night sky behind her with that nifty greenish glow, wincing and dodging as something exploded really close to the camera, gutting it out smack in the thick of it, never giving a moment's thought to what the actual point was of putting herself in harm's way, since it did nothing at all to enhance the value of the report to the viewer. Almost getting killed was how reporters in the field, like mountain climbers or crocodile wrestlers, earned their stripes, and this was Mona Bertram's chance to earn hers. Maybe she'd even get blown to pieces and wind up with a coveted spot on GNN's Wall of Greatness commemorating company personnel killed while covering a story. That would sure as hell show them, alright. But it would also be a bummer career-wise, so maybe a small flesh wound would be better, something that wouldn't show up on camera. Could you get a small flesh wound from one of those rockets, or was it pretty much either getting killed or not getting a scratch? What kind of warning would you get? Does the thing come screaming in from a distance or just kind of explode with no notice, and was there a way to tell in advance where it was going to—

"*INCOMING!*"

Bertram shrieked and dove under the table so fast she split the seam on the back of her tight skirt and broke a heel off her shoe.

"Mona?" Kroeger dipped his head under the table and regarded the totally freaked reporter with a baleful stare. "You alright?"

Bertram, pupils wide as dinner plates and shaking, looked away from Kroeger and noticed that no one else in the control had had much of a reaction to the shouted warning. Her eyes eventually alit on an engineering intern who, with a slightly startled expression, was dangling a phone receiver from his fingertips.

"For you, Miss Bertram," he said.

"What?"

"Incoming phone call. Weren't you waiting for one?" He turned to Kroeger. "I think it's Caminetti."

Like an awkward load of burlap sacks being winched up by a crane, Bertram maneuvered to get out from under the desk and onto her feet with as much dignity as the situation permitted, which was very little. At least nobody was looking at her, as they'd all turned away in embarrassment shortly after she'd come to rest on the floor. Kroeger caught her as soon as her first attempt at walking acquainted her with her missing heel. In doing so, he noticed the tear in the back of her skirt, but wisely elected to stay silent rather than add to her current sea of woes.

Their earlier, interrupted conversation about her traveling to the war zone was temporarily forgotten as she walked unsteadily across the room to take the phone from the apprentice. Only later, when she would get home and discover the tear in her skirt, would it occur to her that the little prick could easily have switched the call to the table she'd been sitting at. Or, more correctly, under.

Taking the receiver and dismissing the apprentice with a glare, she said, "Mona Bertram" into the mouthpiece and listened for a response, frowning with concentration and anticipation. She already knew what the first problem was going to be, but she had a little speech worked out whose purpose nobody in the control room would guess without hearing the other end of the conversation, since she hadn't been exactly one hundred percent forthcoming with Kroeger back in his office, not completely accurate with respect to whom it was that Eddie was actually going to be calling. She'd been a teensy bit off on that part of her diatribe, but as long as she got the first sentence in, it wouldn't matter a whit, because that was all she'd need to let Eddie know that she was his contact, his main man, his go-to gal when it came to this—

"*Who the fuck're you!*" came squealing over the loudspeakers in the ceiling, rasping and static-laden but understandable

Bertram squeezed her eyes shut. She didn't need to look to know that Kroeger's lower mandible had just connected with his chest. Slowly, she took the now-useless receiver from her ear and dropped it back onto its cradle. "I'm the lead reporter on this for GNN," she said into the air, knowing now that it would be picked up by one of several microphones hanging from the ceiling, "and —"

"Where's Farley?" the disembodied Eddie Caminetti demanded. "And what 'this' are you the lead reporter on? Am I a 'this'? When the hell did I become a 'this'?"

"Mr. Cami—"

"Farley! You there?"

"I'm here, Eddie," Farley said reluctantly.

"How you doin?"

"I'm good. You?"

"Not so good."

"What'sa matter?"

"I'm about to get killed. I've only got—" Eddie's voice, barely discernible up to now, faded away altogether.

"Eddie?" Farley, who'd been sitting on top of a desk, came to his feet. "Eddie! What the hell's —"

" . . . get it back." Amid a flood of crackles, squeals and whistles, Eddie's voice came back. Then there were a series of hard, staccato popping sounds.

"What? What'd you say? Eddie, you're breaking up!"

"I only got a couple minutes! Gotta get . . . phone . . . missing . . ." More loud pops.

Bertram snapped a finger at the senior engineer. "Can you clean this up?"

The engineer dipped his head and looked at her over the tops of his reading glasses, then he turned toward Kroeger, who rolled his eyes at the ceiling and shrugged: *Don't let's even go there. I got enough troubles.* The engineer nodded his understanding, turned to his console and twiddled a few dials, then tightened his lips in immense frustration and turned back to Bertram, shaking his head in rueful despair. "He's broadcasting on the chrono-synclastic waveband. Completely infidibulized. Sorry, ma'am: There's nothing we can do on this end."

"Damn." Bertram chewed on her lip, then looked up and said, "Repeat every sentence twice! Exactly the same!"

Kroeger snapped his head toward her, then made a scrawling motion in the air at the engineering apprentice, who scrambled for a pencil and pad.

"Fighting . . . all over . . . place. Fighting going . . . the goddamned . . . . Can barely . . . who's . . . I can . . . tell . . . who. Captured . . . gunfight . . . slightest idea where . . . . Captured . . . escaped, except . . . once . . . where the hell to go. Piece of shit campsite . . . sneak back . . . grab this sat phone, but just . . . I don't even know who . . . me . . . shit!"

The pops came back, louder this time and more closely spaced. When they finally stopped, Eddie spoke again. "Hung around outside this piece of . . . couple of hours . . . grab this sat . . . few minutes, don't even know . . . the hell snatched . . ."

The loudspeakers went quiet, and all eyes turned to the apprentice, who tore the top sheet off his pad and began writing on a fresh piece of paper, with frequent glances back at his original notes.

" . . . the hell is . . . over there!" Eddie's voice demanded.

"Give us a second!" Bertram shouted, then made a hurry-up motion to the apprentice, who didn't see it but was hurrying on his own.

" . . . out of time!"

It was useless to respond, and nobody did, and another few seconds later the apprentice yelped "I got it!" and jumped up. "There's fighting going on all over the place," he said, paraphrasing his decryption. "He can't tell one side from the other." He looked up. "Sounds like he doesn't even know who's doing the fighting."

"Just read what he said!" Bertram ordered.

"He was captured during a gunfight and managed to escape, but once out, he didn't know where to go, so he stuck around the camp they'd taken him to. He can sneak back in every couple of hours to grab a satellite phone, which he can only use for a few minutes before somebody notices it's gone." Having finished his recitation, the apprentice took off his glasses. "He doesn't know where he is and he doesn't know who captured him."

"What were those popping sounds?" Kroeger asked.

"Gunfire," the senior engineer answered. "Or bombs."

"You sure?"

He nodded. "I was the sound guy for NBC during Desert Storm. By the way, it seems he can hear us better than we can hear him."

"Okay, Eddie, we understand!" Bertram said into the air. "What—"

"Rumors . . . atrocities . . . mass . . . " interrupted another transmission. "Rumors . . . refugees . . . graves . . ."

There was no need for the apprentice to piece it back together. "What language are your captors speaking?" Farley called up to the ceiling.

"Don't know. Sounds . . . fast Spanish . . ."

"Fast Spanish?" Bertram repeated.

"Portuguese!" someone said. "They're Brazilian."

Bertram snapped her fingers. "Right! So they're . . ."

"German . . . French . . . Ital—"

They looked up at the speakers, as though to wring more information from them. "What the hell is he saying?"

"Eddie," Bertram said, "we're going to get this out on the air ASAP. By four o'clock the whole country will know your predicament, and I personally guarantee—"

An excited burst of especially harsh static stormed out of the loudspeakers. "Nuts? Fucking . . . dead man . . . dumb . . . Want . . . repeat? Fine. Are you . . . crazy . . . slips out I'm a . . . jackass . . ."

The apprentice adjusted his glasses, ignored Bertram's outstretched palm and said, "He wants to know if you're completely nuts, totally out of your fucking mind, because if you leak a word about him he's a fucking dead man, you dumb—"

"I got it!" Bertram snarled. She thought it over for a few seconds, then said, "We have to say there was a source, Eddie. But we won't use your name. We'll—"

"Such deep . . . in deep . . ."

Bertram snapped her fingers again, causing several people in the control room to wince at the retro theatricality of it. "Deep Java!" she exclaimed. "We'll refer to you as—"

"I don't give . . . flying . . . what you call me!"

Kroeger, unable to stay quiet any longer, looked up at the ceiling. "Caminetti!"

"Wha . . . ? Who . . . hell . . . ?"

"We need somebody!" Kroeger shouted without bothering to identify himself. "Do you hear me? A contact, somebody to confirm! Give me a name!"

There was no answer, just the continual hiss of static.

"Caminetti!"

"Ay . . ."

Kroeger looked around the room. "What'd he say?" He got back only bewildered head shakes.

"Ay . . . CIA . . . Hay . . ."

"Hayne!" the engineer shouted as he unwittingly snapped his fingers.

"Who?" Kroeger demanded.

"The guy who does the president's daily briefing," the engineer answered. "I met him when we were doing the Taliban thing."

"Caminetti!" Kroeger called again. "Did you say Hayne?"

"Es! . . . Hay . . . !" came down by way of scratchy response, followed by more popping noises, "Shit!" and then nothing, save for a weak background hum that indicated only that the receivers in the control room were still tuned in, even though there was no signal to be processed.

The engineer looked at his console. "Line's dead."

"Hope Eddie isn't," Farley said into the eerie quiet that followed.

"Doesn't make any difference," Bertram announced. "There's still a story to be covered."

"There's still a story to be confirmed, first," Kroeger had reminded Bertram on the way back to her office, which is where they were now, along with one of GNN's international beat veterans, Jason Merriweather.

"You don't just pick up a phone and call a senior analyst in the Directorate of Intelligence in the CIA," Merriweather was insisting.

"Why the hell not?" Bertram asked.

"Because they're professional spooks, that's why not! These guys won't tell their own mothers if it's raining outside. There's a chain of command, protocols, rules of the road . . ."

"He's right, Mona," Kroeger said.

"First thing you do, you call State, the South American desk."

"State. You mean the State Department?"

Merriweather had received whispered instructions from Kroeger not to rub Bertram's face in the mud of her inexperience, but to be helpful, for the good of the team. "Yes," he replied, and tapped on his Palm Pilot to get the number.

"Horseshit," Bertram said, picking up the phone and punching "0."

"What do you mean, horse—"

"Bertram. Get me the phone number for a guy named Hayne at the CIA. Better yet, dial it and put me through."

"Mona!" Merriweather yelped. "Are you crazy?"

Bertram put her hand over the mouthpiece. "Are you? You want me to call some lower-level flunky desk jockey and spend half an hour listening to him bullshit me with diplomatic doubletalk while he tries to figure out the best way to keep me in the dark?"

There was no denying that this was what was going to happen at first. "What makes you think," Merriweather said, "that this guy is simply going to—"

"Those guys don't answer direct calls from reporters," Kroeger assured Bertram.

"Last time I tried to—"

"Neither of you is Mona Bertram," Mona Bertram pointed out, then she threw a hand into the air to quiet them. "Yes? Yes? Thank you very much." She covered the mouthpiece and said in a hoarse whisper, "What's his name?"

"What's his—what's whose name?" Merriweather asked.

"The CIA guy, for God's sake!" Bertram said. "His first name!"

"Joffrey."

"Jeff?" Bertram said into the phone prettily. "Mona Bertram. I'm fine, thanks, and yourself? Good. Glad to hear it."

She turned away, so as not to be distracted by the otherwise quite gratifying looks of astonishment on her colleagues' faces. "Jeff, the reason I called . . . we got a bead on a story and we're looking for some confirmation." She chuckled lightly. "Come on now, I think you know very well what I'm talking about." She sighed into the phone. "The war down in South America?" A pause. "Brazil? That Barabbas guy? Come on!"

Merriweather frantically scribbled something on the desk blotter and pounded it with his fist. Bertram turned around and read what he'd written, then said into the phone, "I said *Barranca*. The fighting that's going on down there? You don't. Are you being coy with me, Mr. Hayne?"

Merriweather wrote again. *Deny or stay silent!!!* Bertram frowned her noncomprehension, and Merriweather looked at Kroeger in frustration.

"Remember *All the President's Men?*" he whispered loudly.

Bertram nodded enthusiastically. "Well . . ." she said into the phone, buying time.

"Okay. Remember the scene where they call this guy, but the guy won't say anything, so Woodward . . ."

Bertram frowned again.

"Robert Redford?" Merriweather asked, and got another enthusiastic nod. "Okay. Robert Redford asks this guy questions, and if the guy doesn't answer, that means it's—"

"Tell you what, Jeff," Bertram said. "Suppose I tell you what I know, and you can tell me if I'm wrong, but if I'm not wrong, you just don't say anything, okay? Okay? Jeff? You can answer out loud for this part. Okay, here we go. You ready? Good."

Noticing that Bertram wasn't taking any notes, Merriweather fished a digital recorder out of his pocket, flicked it on and pointed its tiny microphone toward Bertram.

"Manuel Barranca launched an attack on the Brazilian army in the southwest." She waited, then looked at Merriweather and shook her head: No response from the CIA analyst. "The Brazilians reacted very strongly. There are reports of mass graves, atrocities, fleeing refugees." She waited, then shook her head again. "Confirmed reports." Still nothing, and now she was out of questions.

Merriweather wrote on the blotter: *Is the CIA involved?*

"We also heard the CIA is down there supporting the Brazilian regulars," Bertram said.

"No goddamned way!" came the reply, so loudly Merriweather could hear it.

"But the United States is, somehow, right?"

"No, we are not!"

Merriweather put one flat palm above the other and moved them both back and forth in opposite directions. Cut it off!

"Okay. Thanks very much, Jeff. Uh-huh. Uh-huh. I'm sure we'll be speaking again. And listen: Have a nice day." Bertram hung up.

"Not bad," Kroeger was forced to admit.

"Not too damned bad at all," Merriweather agreed. "What's your next move, Mona?" He knew they were under orders not to antagonize

Bertram, but he couldn't help himself. Now that their star "reporter" was in the middle of the story, it might be fun watching her grope around with no idea what she was supposed to do.

"My next move? Well, hell: I've got to get down there as soon as possible."

CHAPTER 28

AN UNNAMED BUILDING IN LANGLEY, VA

Despite, or perhaps because of, his close relationship with Thomas Eastwood, DCI Baines Gordon Wainwright knew that there were times when the president needed to be taken very, very seriously, when attempts to defuse tense situations with humor were simply not going to work, because the fuse was real, burning and connected to something especially volatile.

"You realize," he began, well aware that the president would have no patience at all with stalling or ass-covering but knowing this had to get said anyway, "my information doesn't even rise to the level of back channel. It's third-party, from dubious sources, transmitted with tin cans and string, and —"

"But you saw fit to redirect my motorcade to Langley so you could give it to me firsthand." Eastwood hadn't moved more than his lips when he spoke, the rest of his body having tightened up into a taut package waiting to spontaneously combust. "Therefore you have some basis to believe it's true."

"Well, sure." Wainwright squirmed uncomfortably, an especially uncomfortable thing for him to do. "But it's a percentage kind of thing, Tom—Mr. President. Some stuff we believe sixty percent, some seventy . . ." He waved a hand as his voice trailed off.

"But despite your lack of faith in the specifics," Eastwood pressed, "you've developed some confidence in the general overall picture. Is that a safe assumption?"

"I'd have to say it is."

"That a yes?"

"A qualified yes."

Eastwood turned his head slightly and peered at Wainwright from the corner of his eye. "Hayne have anything to do with this analysis?"

"The analysis, yes, but—" Wainwright quickly rushed on before the president could mount a protest "—the raw data, no. At least not the confirming sources. That came directly to me before it went to analysis."

"Directly to you," Eastwood echoed, and pondered what kind of foreign source would have direct access to the U.S. Director of Central Intelligence. Was that a note of pride he detected in Wainwright's voice, a subliminal message telling the president, without telling him, that his information could be relied upon? "Okay. I'm with you."

"Okay." Wainwright sat back and nodded with satisfaction. Eastwood stared at him, then at his chief of staff.

"Does there come a point," Conchita Ortega said, "when you actually tell us what this information is?"

Wainwright stopped nodding and looked momentarily nonplussed. "Of course," he said stumblingly, as he hunched forward in his chair and tried to remember the quick summary he'd mentally prepared.

"Because I have to tell you, Baines," Eastwood said, making it sound like a warning, "I've got everybody lined up behind us on this one. All the involved countries south of the border are practically begging us to come in and nip this so-called revolution in the bud, I've got troops literally in the air and on the water, I was ready to give the final okay when that call came in."

"I understand, sir."

"Fine. Then tell me why in the hell I'm sitting here talking to you when I should be ordering all the —"

"There's fighting going on down there. In South America."

"Fighting."

"Yes sir."

Eastwood, his ire with Wainwright suddenly forgotten, tried to figure out if he should be seeing implications beyond the simple words, then decided nobody had a right to test him, and found himself starting to get angry again. But before he could let loose, Ortega jumped in.

"You mean Barranca is fighting?"

"Yes."

Prompted by the DCI's continued reticence, Eastwood resumed control. "Baines, how much longer are you going to sit here pushing my patience?"

"Sir, I assure you I have no intention of—" He was stopped by the sound of Eastwood's fist slamming into the table with enough force to rattle the china ashtrays embossed with the agency's logo, a holdback from the days when smoking was allowed on the premises.

"Goddamnit! What the hell is going on down there?" Eastwood half-rose, shifted his seat around to face Wainwright directly, and sat back down. "I already know it's vague but stop farting around and just tell me!"

"Okay." Wainwright cleared his throat. "As best I can tell, and, as I said—no, okay. Best I can tell, Barranca has launched a major offensive, and an especially brutal one, against government forces in southwestern Brazil."

"Government forces?" Ortega echoed. "Which—"

"The Brazilian army."

"You must be kidding," Eastwood said.

"No, sir. I mean, yes, you're right. The Brazilian regulars are well equipped, well trained, have overwhelming numbers—"

"And they're probably going to get reinforced by Peru, Colombia and the others," Ortega guessed.

"That'd be my assessment as well," Wainwright agreed.

Eastwood, sporting a look mixing disbelief and confusion, rose and began pacing. "Has Barranca completely lost his mind?"

"Hard to believe it was a rational decision," Wainwright said. "Taking on a regular army with his ragtag band? Doesn't make a lick of sense."

Eastwood, frowning, scratched at the side of his head, tried to make sense of it and failed. "I don't get it."

"Neither do we, sir. All I can tell you is what appears to be happening."

Eastwood frowned some more, then sat down. "Okay, I need you to level with me, Baines, and don't fuck around, y'hear me?"

"No fucking around. Got it."

"Good. What parts are you sure of, and what are you guessing at?"

It was a reasonable question, and Wainwright didn't try to duck it. "We know there's fighting going on, we know Barranca's involved in it."

Ortega picked up on what was missing. "What about who they're fighting?"

"Has to be the Brazilian army."

"Because there's nobody else there," Eastwood surmised.

"Exactly." Wainwright shrugged at the obviousness of it. "What I can't be sure of, though, is who started it."

"What do your sources say?" Eastwood asked.

"That Barranca launched the offensive."

"And you doubt that because . . . ?"

"As I said, it doesn't make any sense."

"He's right there, Mr. President," Ortega said, and Wainwright looked grateful for her concurrence.

Eastwood was lost in thought, Ortega and Wainwright both happy for the peaceful interlude, however slight it was destined to be. "You don't suppose he thinks he can win?" the president said at last.

"Win?" Ortega and Wainwright said simultaneously.

"Yeah. You don't suppose his pride is finally getting the better of him?"

Ortega thought it over. "Well, he's had some pretty visible successes."

"Throwing the entire United States into chaos?" Wainwright asked rhetorically. "Yeah, I'd say that spells success for a terrorist."

"So now he thinks he can take on Brazil and a few others in an open fight." Eastwood smiled crookedly and without mirth. "You gotta admire the stones on that sonofabitch."

"Or the stupidity," Wainwright argued. "His offensive against us was highly leveraged. He had one weapon: withholding a staple of our economy. That's like a lone hostage-taker controlling an entire police force because he's got one big card to play. But taking on an army in a full-scale confrontation?"

"You're right. It doesn't make sense." Eastwood looked away as he thought about it. "But assume for a second that Barranca isn't an idiot. What could possibly be his game?"

"I don't know, sir. I've got people working on it. But it gets worse."

Eastwood looked back. "Worse?"

Wainwright nodded. "GNN's got wind of it. They phoned Joffrey

Hayne and he took the call."

As the president groaned, Ortega said, "How'd they find out?"

"I don't know. They won't say."

"Did Hayne confirm?" Eastwood asked.

"Had to. Their knowledge was very specific. But it was strictly a passive nonresponse."

The president nodded his agreement that Hayne had done the right thing. Any denial in the face of GNN's obviously accurate knowledge would have been disastrous. "Can you put a lid on it?"

Wainwright waved a hand in the air. "Absolutely."

On the way back to the G.E. a few minutes later, Ortega said, "Why don't you just pick up a phone, call the Brazilian prime minister and ask him what the hell is going on down there?"

Eastwood shook his head. "No way. Once I acknowledge the fighting, I'm practically bound to help him out, and I don't want to put us in that position."

"Kind of funny he hasn't called you."

"Not really. It's an internal matter, and he probably feels they can handle it just fine on their own."

Something was still hanging in the air unsaid, and it took Ortega a few moments to figure it out. "They're not fighting a very nice war, are they."

"No," Eastwood answered quietly. It was the kind of third world blood-and-pain fest the United States couldn't sully its hands with, which the Brazilian P.M. would understand only too well. If the Brazilians were crashing down on Barranca's troops with the kind of brutality that might normally arouse the interest of an international war crimes tribunal, they'd want the U.S. as far away as possible. "That's why we won't hear from Brazil unless they get into real trouble. And it's why I can't even pick up the phone and talk to the prime minister."

CHAPTER 29

"**I want to get an establishing shot** as soon as the plane stops moving," Mona Bertram said as she touched up the last of the makeup she'd been applying since they'd descended through 10,000 feet. She wasn't speaking to anyone in particular, assuming that whatever she said would be forwarded by someone to whomever it was that needed to hear it, in this case the cameraman. "And ask the pilot to keep the left propeller turning until we finish the stand-up."

Before the taxiing plane had stopped moving, she was up out of her seat and gazing out an exit door window to survey the situation. "There." She pointed toward a dilapidated two-story shed that looked as though it might be a control tower. "When you pan around, get that thing in the shot. Make sure some of these soldier types, the ones carrying the machine guns, make sure they're in there, too. I'll talk to them, and see to it they stay close. Who do you figure the head *kahuna* is . . . the guy still in the jeep? Yeah, he's Mr. Big. I'll get him sorted out first thing so he doesn't fuck us up. Come on, we're stopped! Somebody open up this goddamned door!"

An air stair was wheeled into place and the door opened from the outside. Bertram had a foot through it before the attendant could secure it against the fuselage, and was bounding down the rickety aluminum steps with a hand held up toward the soldier in the jeep. "Hang on a second there, fella. You and I need to talk about how we're going to . . . Hey! What the fuck . . . !"

Two of the machine-gun toting soldiers had stepped forward to block her path, and one of them was grabbing at the sides of her breasts and fondling them roughly.

She threw a forearm at his face in an effort to stave him off. "Listen, you slimy . . . !"

The other soldier unshouldered his weapon and put the barrel under Bertram's chin, which had the desired effect of making her go quiet. His comrade proceeded from her chest to her sides, back, crotch and legs. If he enjoyed the trembling he could feel beneath her clothes, the thoroughly professional soldier gave no sign of it, but stepped back when the frisking was complete and nodded to his superior in the jeep, who inclined his head in polite acknowledgment of her.

"Welcome to Brazil. I am Captain DaSilva. You were saying?"

Bertram wasn't saying anything, distracted as she was by the gun barrel still tickling the bottom of her chin. DaSilva flicked his little finger and the weapon was withdrawn. Bertram almost fell over in relief as the last dregs of adrenaline faded away and left her weak.

The others on the plane, more seasoned, were submitting to somewhat less aggressive body searches behind her. "Ready for the stand-up?" the cameraman called out.

"It can wait," Bertram replied. It came out as a feeble wheeze.

"What?"

"I said it can wait!" The unexpected shrillness of her voice embarrassed her, and she clamped her mouth shut.

"They're police," Jason Merriweather said.

"Huh?"

"Not soldiers. Police."

"Like I give a shit," Bertram muttered. She realized she was losing it in front of the people she needed to stay in control of, and forced herself to stride purposefully toward the jeep. "Where's Manuel Barranca?"

DaSilva pointed toward the nearby jungle. "In there somewhere."

"Why isn't he here?"

"Why should he be?"

"We came to interview him!"

"Ah." DaSilva withdrew a twisted, brown cheroot from the breast pocket of his uniform and stuck it between his teeth. "I don't think he's keen to be interviewed."

"But . . . but we're GNN! We flew all this way to meet him!"

"Did he invite you?"

"No, but . . ."

"Well, then!" DaSilva struck a match against the side of the jeep and touched the flame to the tip of the small cigar. "One can hardly hold him accountable."

"Listen . . . !"

"Captain DaSilva." Merriweather, who'd been content to let Bertram get flustered for a few minutes, stepped up behind her. "We understood you were going to take us to the scene of the fighting?"

"Me?" DaSilva removed the cheroot and blew out a thick cloud of smoke. "Are you mad?" He used the cigar to point to the jungle. "I'm a policeman. No reason for me to go into that madhouse. But these men—" He waved toward the half dozen soldiers milling around "—they will escort you."

"How come?" Bertram asked.

"Because you will pay them five hundred U.S. dollars a day to do so." He took another long puff on his cigar. "Each." Another puff. "And they can only take four of you."

"Five hundred a day?" Bertram snorted and folded her arms in preparation for the negotiation to come. She'd read about these third world desperados and their extortionary bribery demands, and knew they started out at five to ten times what they'd eventually settle for. "I don't think so."

DaSilva shrugged noncommittally. "As you wish. *Allez!*" The soldiers scrambled into the jeep and the driver started the engine.

Bertram, trying not to smirk, said, "Okay, Captain, let's get down to cases here. Seems to me . . ."

The driver ground the gears, pressed the accelerator and began driving off.

"Captain . . . ?"

And kept driving.

"Captain! Wait!" But Bertram's cries were ineffectual and the jeep, accelerating, continued down the runway. Nobody on it was looking back.

"Good one, Mona," Merriweather said as he watched the departing vehicle kick up a rooster tail of brown dust.

Bertram whirled on him, eyes flashing. "I wasn't going to pay those highway robbers three, maybe four thousand a day!"

"*You* weren't going to pay them anything," Merriweather pointed out. "GNN was. We spend more than that on coffee and Danish every day." He set down his carry-on grip, then shrugged off his backpack and let it drop to the ground.

"Where are you going?" Bertram asked.

"To get them back. Where the hell do you think I'm going?"

"How are you going to do that?"

"They need the money. They just don't like to be pushed around, especially not by women. It's about saving face." *So I'll tell them you're just an overpaid bimbo not worth getting insulted over and offer them another thousand a day for the whole bunch.*

"Okay. Go make it happen, and do it quick."

With a warning look from the cameraman—*Let it go!*—Merriweather headed for the control tower.

Twenty minutes later he was back, sitting on the tailgate of the overcrowded jeep, handing a flask to DaSilva, who took a swig and handed it back. Behind them was a second vehicle, with just a driver.

"Okay, let's go," Merriweather called out as the jeep ground to a halt. Whether it was intentional or not no one could say, but the small cloud of dust rising from the wheels perfectly enveloped Bertram, who coughed as she tried to wave it away.

DaSilva got out, capping the flask and sticking it in his jacket pocket. "As I said, I shall not accompany you. However"—he waved a hand toward the jeep—"these men will not approach any of the fighting, so do not take any more equipment than you can carry in the one vehicle they will leave you after they turn back."

"What!" Bertram, horror-struck, glanced back at the three suitcases, two footlockers and assorted duffels lying at the bottom of the air stair. They contained all her clothes and personal items. "I can't fit all of this into that truck!"

"You're going into a jungle, miss," DaSilva pointed out. "I assure you the opportunities for formal dining are rare." He bid farewell to his men and took off on foot.

Merriweather glanced at his watch. "Kroeger wants the first stand-up in fifteen minutes. Better do it right here."

A shiver rippled through Bertram. She knew that the plan was for GNN to interrupt all its broadcasts with a "breaking news" bulletin.

Even though for most of its viewers these breaks had become a giant yawn—they'd been used to report on arraignments that had been scheduled weeks in advance, expected news that hadn't materialized at all, which seemed to constitute news in itself, live reports in front of inanimate buildings that could more easily have been handled in the studio, and entire wars broadcast as one long, "breaking" story—she knew this would be different, an honest-to-God armed flare-up in a heretofore peaceful country, of which Americans had been completely unaware until GNN told them.

Bertram nodded her agreement rather than give the order, since the cameraman, sound guy and satellite engineer had already begun assembling their equipment.

"Problem," the engineer said as he touched a finger to his headphones.

All eyes turned to him. "What?" Bertram asked.

"We gotta hold off a couple minutes."

"You shouldn't air this story, Sparky."

"What story, Baines?"

"Very funny," the Director of Central Intelligence replied. "You need to hold off on the Barranca deal."

"You must be kidding," Kroeger said with a chuckle. "Why?"

Why, indeed? "It's a matter of national security."

Now that was funny. "Good one, Baines. You told my reporter the Agency wasn't involved, the U.S. itself wasn't even involved, and now it's a matter of national security?"

Wainwright, knowing how lame it was going to sound, nevertheless launched into a semicoherent speech about complex geopolitical pressures, regional instability, third-party aggression and interlocking relationships among fragile southern hemisphere economies. "That's why you have to hold off, Sparky."

"No."

"What?"

"No."

"What?"

"Look: You think we don't know that the golfer who got snatched down there was asshole buds with the president?" There was no answer. "So I'll tell you what."

"I'm listening."

"You tell me when the operation is going to launch, and we'll give you twenty-four hours in exchange for an absolute exclusive."

"I can't do that."

"Didn't think you could."

"Sparky—"

"Baines, listen. Neither of us is stupid. You know good and damned well that if we don't get this out in the next ten minutes, somebody else is going to do it within thirty."

There was a pause on the other end, then Wainwright said, "If you don't agree to hold off for at least a day, somebody's going to have it in less than that."

Kroeger slammed the phone back into its cradle, jumped up from his chair and ran to his office door. Yanking it open, he stepped out into the corridor and yelled, first in one direction, then the other, "Go! Tell Bertram to go! Right goddamned now!"

CHAPTER 30

The GNN logo burned brightly in the upper left corner of the screen. At the bottom, in large, bold letters of gold outlined in cobalt blue, was the title that had been assigned to this story, and which would accompany it until its conclusion:

THE COFFEE WAR: BARRANCA VS. BRAZIL

There was theme music, too, dramatic and swelling, to underscore the seriousness of war in general, but with a jarringly upbeat tempo to indicate that, after all, this was about coffee, not something more serious, like oil. As Mona Bertram spoke, her words were concurrently summarized in a kind of electronic flashcard below the story title: **Barranca launches bold assault; Brazil retaliates harshly; Atrocities, mass graves alleged; Refugees reportedly fleeing; Lakers 98, Knicks 96.**

Somewhere in the middle of all that screen clutter was Bertram's face. "Don't let the seeming serenity of the jungle behind me fool you," she warned. "Somewhere not too far from our present position an intense battle is being waged, between a mysterious, self-styled revolutionary and a government that has simply been pushed too far."

Then, as planned, Bertram paused as the cameraman, Ernie Bonnelli, zoomed in slowly on her face. Her expression morphed from excited but restrained intensity to deep solemnity, her eyes boring in on the camera to underscore the import of what she was about to reveal. "Manuel Barranca," she intoned as the zooming came to a halt and her face filled what was left of the screen after the logo, flashcards, sports crawls, story title, the current time on the East

Coast and the temperature in Houston, "refused to be interviewed." The dire implications of that refusal were alarmingly self-evident and she left them for her audience to ponder on its own.

"We're down!" the engineer called out from his portable console.

Bertram pulled out her earpiece and let it dangle from her shoulder. "How'd it look?" she asked her assistant.

"Great. Voice was nicely modulated, eyes held steady, very little blinking. It was great."

"Hope this asshole revolutionary sees it and decides to talk to us. Who the hell does he think he is, anyway?"

"Unbelievable," the assistant clucked sympathetically.

Over at the jeep, Jason Merriweather asked one of the soldiers who spoke passable English, "How far away is the fighting?"

The soldier conversed with his comrades, then answered, "Maybe eighty, eighty-five klicks."

"What was that?" Bertram asked him. She was still flushed from the glow of her first on-site report.

"He was just telling me how far 'not too far from our present position' is. You know, where that fierce battle's taking place?"

"Oh yeah? So how far is it?"

"About fifty miles."

"Well, there you go. That's not too far."

"Not like you were about to get hit by a rocket," the assistant mumbled from behind her.

"What was that?"

"Got some hairspray in my pocket. Need any?"

"You know," Merriweather said, "it's been a while since we heard from Deep Java. Wonder if the guy's alright."

"I wonder what it says about how the fighting is going," Bonnelli added. He looked toward the jungle with apprehension. "We're kind of blind without him."

Bertram followed his gaze, and appeared to be contemplating the advisability of heading for the battlefront absent any more information from Eddie. Then she looked up at the sky and shrugged. "Doesn't look like any wind's coming up."

"So what do you think?" Bonnelli prompted her.

Bertram handed the microphone to her assistant. "Don't think I'll need any just yet."

"Sorry?" Merriweather said. "Any what?"

"Hairspray. It can wait."

CHAPTER 31

"I read about this stuff in National Geographic," Jason Merriweather said, looking upward, "but I never would have believed how thick it really was."

He was in the second of two vehicles, the jeep, which was preceded by an ancient half-track that looked to be of World War II vintage. The vegetation was so dense that there was essentially no visibility at all beyond about twenty feet. The half-track was doing a reasonably good job of mowing down bamboo and other trees, but once in a while the stuff got so piled up the soldiers had to jump out of the vehicles and hack through it, at least enough so that the jeep could climb over the rubble the half-track was creating. It had been about four hours since they'd entered the jungle.

"How far you figure we've gone?" Bertram asked.

"Not six klicks," the English-speaking soldier answered. "My name is Guillermo."

"Less than four miles," Merriweather said.

"Four miles!" Bertram checked her watch, then looked around with newfound dread. "Are you telling me we might to have to sleep out here?"

Guillermo grinned, translated for his colleagues, then joined in as they laughed in gap-toothed pleasure.

"What's so damned funny?" Bertram demanded.

"Two, three nights," the soldier responded.

Bertram was distinctly unamused. "You mean it's like this all the way?"

"No, madam. Soon there will be some roads. Very old. Very bad. But better." He turned to one of the other soldiers and barked an order. The other man nodded, grabbed a small black case and hopped out of the half-track. The GNN crew watched, fascinated, as the man slung the case over his shoulder, took off his shoes and began climbing a large, thick palm tree.

"Where's he going?" Merriweather asked.

"Read GPS," came the answer.

"What's he need to climb for?" Bertram asked. "I've got one of those in my Mercedes and I don't have to—"

"Trees." Guillermo pointed upward. "Must to see sky."

"Is he shitting me?" Bertram said to Merriweather, who shook his head.

"Nope. Gotta have some clear sky."

Bertram, incredulous, looked from Merriweather to the canopy above and back again. "Do you mean to tell me," she said slowly, "that the greatest navigational device since the compass—" She was quoting a GNN science reporter who'd done a feature on the technology a month before "—doesn't work when there are trees?"

Merriweather shrugged. "What can I tell you, Mona? It isn't my fault, I swear."

Bertram reflexively turned to tell the engineer to take a note, then remembered that he and the sound man had to stay behind to make room for her assistant and her makeup cases. She reached into her fanny pack and withdrew a small pad of paper and a pen.

"What're you doing?" Bonnelli asked.

"Making a note. This is unbelievable. We have to do a story on this."

Merriweather held up a hand to forestall any imminent comments from Bonnelli. "Terrific idea," he said to Bertram.

"You bet!" she agreed. "People have to know about this!"

"Yeah," her assistant muttered, "in case they get caught in an Amazonian rain forest in their Mercedes."

"What was that?"

The assistant quickly grabbed up a camera. "Want a photograph in the rain forest? Say 'cheese.'"

The soldier up in the tree yelled down and pointed in a direction a few degrees to the left of where they'd been headed.

"Road," Guillermo translated. "Just ahead. It will go faster then."

"Let's get cracking," Bertram said, slapping her knees. "Next report we do, I want some goddamned mortar shells lighting up the background behind me." Taking note of the looks she was getting, she hastily added, "To show the viewers the harsh realities of war."

"Mortar shells dun' light up nothin," Guillermo said to Merriweather.

A few minutes later they were off again, the half-track crushing away happily as though reinvigorated by the thought of the nearby road. It took nearly an hour, then with one last groan of its ancient diesel the truck burst through a final wall of reeds and clanked down onto a well-worn pathway paved with flattened, rotting stalks. The driver turned the half-track sharply left to make room for the jeep. The smaller vehicle took the drop from the crushed reeds much harder, nearly tossing the GNN crew out, so jarring them that it took a moment before anyone thought to try to locate the source of a crackling, throaty whine that at first rose in pitch, then fell, then went silent just before it slammed into the jungle with a sickeningly concussive explosion.

Bertram, still smarting from her dive under the control room table two days before, wouldn't have ducked had she seen the rocket heading directly toward her, but the others did. Suspecting that this moment would someday be the highlight of her memoirs, she yelled, "Get me set up!" before any of her colleagues had picked their heads back up, then looked skyward to find the smoky trace of the missile's path. It was just above treetop level to the east, which meant the late-afternoon sun was directly opposite. The lighting would be perfect.

Happier doing something other than lying in the mud and feeding his fear, Bonnelli scrambled after his camera equipment and the satellite uplink gear the engineer had given him and began assembling a tripod. Bertram jumped down from the jeep and pointed to a high spot in the trampled undergrowth that formed the road. "There," she said. "Shoot up." With the camera down low, the upper half of the frame would be filled with the sky above the tree line, and if she was very, very lucky . . .

An arcing trail of smoke appeared parallel to the earlier one that was now nearly gone. It streamed majestically, the rocket moving so fast there was no sound until it was practically overhead. "Goddamnit!" Bertram screamed in near-hysterics, but it wasn't in fear of the rocket, it was in exasperation at Bonnelli.

"I'm almost there!" he assured her. Bertram grabbed the microphone from the assistant and headed for the high mound in the road. Turning to make sure nobody was watching, she bent and brushed her hand along the roadway, then patted her face with the damp moss she'd scraped up. The explosion as the second rocket hit the jungle was louder than the first.

"Fuck it!" Bonnelli shouted, kicking the tripod away and hoisting the larger of his two cameras onto his shoulder. "We'll tape it first. Let's do it!"

The assistant saw the green-brown smudge on Bertram's face. "Hold it . . . !"

"There's no time!" Bertram yelled back, bringing the microphone to her lips.

"How'd she know what I was talking about?" the assistant said to Merriweather.

"What was that?"

"Now we know what you're all about, Miss Bertram! Knock em dead!"

"Anytime," Bonnelli said. A small red light appeared on the front of the camera.

Bertram fiddled with the mike and blew into it several times. She tapped it. She scratched her shoulder. She cleared her throat.

Bonnelli took his eye away from the viewfinder and looked at her questioningly.

"Am I hot?" she asked.

He twisted the camera in his hands so he could see the red light. "Uh . . . yeah?" What the hell was she talking about? She'd stared into cameras half a million times and knew damned well when she was hot.

"Okay." She nodded a few times. "Okay, I got it." Then she started fussing with her hair.

Suddenly, everyone's eyes lifted to the sky behind her.

"This is Mona Bertram somewhere in the rain forest of western Brazil," Bertram said crisply, as the missile that she knew was now in the sky behind her zipped menacingly above the trees. "Just up ahead an epic firefight is raging, a war of blood and determination between—"

She paused as the crumpling, ripping sound of the rocket reached them and made Bonnelli jerk. She winced to emphasize the closeness of the attack, but never took her eyes from the camera. So what would they be calling her during the Emmy Awards . . . the Missile Vixen? Rocket Goddess?

The Mortar Maiden! "Mortar and RPG rounds have been screaming overhead for hours—" The sound from overhead halted abruptly, and Bertram discreetly tipped her microphone toward the jungle, waited for it to pick up the boom of the exploding warhead, then tilted it back "— but it's difficult to pinpoint exactly where they're being aimed. We're going to be pushing on in a few minutes and hope to bring you more details of this fierce engagement in our next report. Incidentally, Manuel Barranca still refuses to talk to us or even meet off the record."

"Nice," the assistant commented as soon as the camera went down. "How'd you find out Barranca won't meet with us?"

"You see him anywhere?" Bertram asked.

"Good point. You got some dirt on your face." He began swiping at it with a gauze pad.

"Did I?" Bertram touched a finger to her cheek and held it up to see. "Darn."

"No problem."

Bertram looked around as her face was being attended to. "So where'd all the soldiers go?"

"Huh?" The assistant poured a little more cold cream onto the gauze pad.

"The soldiers." Bertram waved a hand toward the beaten-down hole in the jungle wall they'd come through earlier.

The assistant turned around. Bonnelli stopped what he was doing and looked in the same direction, as did Merriweather. In addition to the soldiers, the half-track and the jeep were both gone as well.

"Uh oh," Merriweather said.

The silence following the noise of the rocket attack was more frightening than a banshee wail.

"That police captain said his men would leave if there was trouble," Merriweather recalled.

"Didn't say they'd take both goddamned vehicles," Bonnelli snarled. "I had most of my gear in the half-track, including a Sony DXC-D50 and the satellite stuff."

"My makeup was in the jeep," Bertram said forlornly.

"Over here," the assistant called from behind a large banyan tree. He was pointing to a pile of what would turn out to be all of their possessions.

As they pored through the pile trying to locate and retrieve their individual belongings, Merriweather said, "Hard to believe those guys would run out on what's probably two month's pay for two days' work."

"Musta been pretty scared," the assistant observed.

"You know what I don't get?" Merriweather straightened up and put his hands on his hips. "If those policemen were Brazilian, and—"

"I thought they were soldiers," the assistant interrupted. "They were wearing military uniforms."

"You sure?" Bertram asked.

"I worked costuming on this movie once? Supposed to take place around here somewhere? Looked just like what those guys were wearing."

"Either way," Merriweather continued, "if their own army is kicking Barranca's ass, what the hell were they so afraid of?"

"And another thing, Bonnelli said. "Somebody on one side of us was launching those rockets at somebody on the other side. So what do you figure—"

Bertram, with one hand on the first of her three hair-and-makeup cases, froze. "What was that?"

"What?" the assistant asked.

"Shh!" Bertram put a hand on Bonnelli's arm to get him to stop rummaging around in the pile. "In the jungle. I heard something."

"It's a jungle," Bonnelli said as he took his arm back and gently lifted an exotic-looking video camera out of a metal case, setting it down about ten feet away so no one would bump into it. "It's supposed to be noisy. Hey, get it? It's a jungle out there. A jungle. Don't you—"

But he didn't get to finish explaining his clever wordplay because suddenly half a dozen heavily armed men were standing on the opposite side of the road, even though none of the members of the GNN crew would later recall how or when they'd materialized out of the jungle.

"They don't look so bad," the assistant offered.

"Seen worse," Merriweather agreed. "Let me see if I can find out what's going on." He held up a hand in greeting and started across the road.

"You getting this, Ernie?" Another memorable Bertram line for her memoirs.

Bonnelli stood and turned toward where he'd set his camera down, but in the time it took to register that the sharp crack from across the road was a rifle shot, his $13,000 Sony DXC-D50 was reduced to scrap metal that might fetch twenty or thirty bucks if the gold in the circuit board contacts could be cleanly salvaged, which, judging from how badly some of the other innards had melted from the searing impact of the large-caliber round, was doubtful.

Less than two minutes later, the four of them were sitting on the ground in a tight circle, facing outward with their backs to each other. Their eyes were covered with handkerchiefs or bandannas, which were quickly becoming soaked with perspiration fueled by their bottomless dread.

"*Wir nehmen sie mit uns!*" they heard from several yards away.

"*Qu'a-t-il dit?*" someone else asked.

"*Di che cosa state parlando?*" another one challenged. "*Siete pazzeschi?*"

"*Was sagte er?*"

"*Nós não podemos fazer exame d com nós.*"

"*Che cosa ha detto?*"

"*Tous les deux vous soient silencieux!*"

"*Was sagte er?*"

Sensing none of the soldiers was very close, Bertram risked speaking. "What are they talking about? What language is it?"

"I heard some French," Merriweather said. "And German."

"Italian, trust me." Bonnelli countered. "At least some of it."

"Portuguese!" the assistant insisted.

"Oh, shit!" Merriweather barked. "Oh shit oh shit oh shit!"

"'Ey!" one of the soldiers yelled angrily. *"Fermez la bouche!"*

"Oh shit oh shit oh shit!"

"Jason, what the hell is wrong with you!" Bonnelli whispered hoarsely. "You trying to get us all killed?"

"You don't need me to do that!" Merriweather replied.

"What are you—" Bonnelli stopped suddenly. "Oh shit oh shit oh shit!"

Bertram, about to soil herself, was shaking so badly the others could hear dry palm fronds rattling beneath her. "What in God's name are you—"

"They're mercenaries!" Merriweather said, the words catching in his throat as he tried to modulate his whispering between making himself understood and not arousing any more of their captors' attention. "Soldiers for hire."

"That's how Barranca put his army together," Bonnelli concluded once he'd gotten hold of himself. "He just imported the manpower he needed."

"Is this bad?" Bertram asked, her voice just this side of a helpless keen.

"These people fight for whoever pays them the most," Bonnelli responded.

"So?" Bertram asked, with a hint of hopefulness.

"Prisoners just slow em down," Merriweather explained. A morbid silence followed.

Which Bertram soon broke. "Well, great!" she chirped brightly. "So they'll probably let us go, right?"

Somebody had to tell her, and it turned out to be Merriweather. "No, Mona . . . they'll probably kill us."

Bertram hoped that none of the others, all of them being blindfolded, would be able to tell which one was involuntarily urinating at the moment, and gave fleeting consideration to the notion that it might be better to just get shot through the head than have to eventually stand up and reveal a spreading stain on her khakis, a pair of Abercrombie's best, with eleven pockets, four zippers, four Velcro'd pouches and a canteen holder. When she heard the voices of the soldiers drop lower in both pitch and volume, followed by the seemingly reluctant cocking of

RUSH

GOLF
MAGAZINE

GOLF RENEWAL SAVINGS FORM

YES! Keep sending me GOLF Magazine.

( ) 3 YEARS (36 ISSUES) FOR $30.00
( ) 2 YEARS (24 ISSUES) FOR $20.00
( ) 1 YEAR (12 ISSUES) FOR $10.00

07/01/13 EXP   2451984294 GFAHAY3

☐ Payment enclosed.
☐ Bill me later.

**To renew online, go to
www.RenewGolf.com**

Plus sales tax where
applicable. GOLF Magazine
is published monthly.

0486
P692
204
317

#BXBCCJZ *********AUTO**5-DIGIT 44039
#2451 9842 9404#GF   E JUL13   0486
                      00166
MR DAN FOLINO
37828 AVALON DR
N RIDGEVILLE OH 44039-1086

half a dozen weapons, she decided that, no, she'd just as soon stay alive and be a little embarrassed. The increase in Merriweather's breathing rate as soft footsteps drew closer solidified that notion in her mind.

The footsteps, very near now, stopped. Bertram held her breath. A shot rang out. After determining that she hadn't been hit, Bertram tried to figure out who had. Merriweather was still breathing heavily. Bonnelli, to Bertram's left, was still shaking. But why were the soldiers suddenly shouting?

More shots, some from farther away. Cursing now, anger mixed with fear. Someone shouting orders in a language she couldn't identify, arguments coming back in French and German. More gunfire, the belly-whomping blasts of grenades, a staccato rat-a-tat of automatic weapons fired aggressively from off to the right, answered weakly from the left and getting farther away. Someone was attacking with order and discipline; someone was retreating in chaos and disarray.

"Brazilian regulars!" Merriweather said excitedly.

The gunfire died down, replaced by the occasional and gratuitous burst of rounds at nothing in particular. Men were calling to one another, but it was all Spanish now, and alarm had given way to the breathlessness that accompanies adrenaline withdrawal.

"Ernie?" Merriweather whispered.

"I'm good," Bonnelli answered, as did the assistant.

They could tell from the sound of violent retching that Mona Bertram was alive as well, but they didn't have time to think about it as the blindfolds were taken from their faces and they blinked against the light lancing into their dark-adapted eyes.

"Está usted bien?"

The question came from a dark-skinned man with an old rifle slung across his back. Well into his sixties, he was dressed in a work shirt, jeans and trekking boots. Merriweather looked around and saw that his comrades were similarly attired: no uniforms anywhere, just a ragtag agglomeration of what appeared to be ordinary work clothes and ancient weapons.

"Don't Brazilians speak Portuguese?" Bonnelli asked after listening to the chatter among the soldiers for a few seconds. They were smiling, some lighting cigarettes in a celebratory fashion, waving disdainfully in the direction that the troops they'd just routed had run.

"Yeah."

"Are you alright?" the man asked again, this time in English.

"I think so," Merriweather answered as a soldier cut the ropes binding his hands. "Who are you guys?"

"I am Pablo. That—" He indicated one of the men who'd lit up "—is Pedro. Next to him is Estefan, over there is José . . ."

"No, no." Merriweather shook his head. "I mean, who . . . what army . . . who are you guys fighting for?"

"Ah! Forgive. We fight with Manuel Barranca. And you are . . . ?"

CHAPTER 32

It took half an hour to get the shaky crew to its feet, make introductions, get their supplies sorted out and figure out how to carry it all.

"It is about ten miles," Pablo said, "but there is another trail not too far along."

He whistled, and more men appeared from the jungle. One, a relatively light-skinned man in his mid-twenties, said to Pablo, "Brush is clear. Those pansy-asses hightailed it the hell outta here. So who are these guys?"

"They are newspeople," Pablo explained. "GNN."

"No shit?" The younger man looked them over but didn't recognize anybody. "I dig that Mona Bertram chick. You guys know her?"

Bertram straightened up, poked uselessly at her scraggly hair, and turned around. "That would be me."

The man's eyes grew wide. "Get oudda town! You're Mona Bertram?"

"I am."

"Jesus, you look like shit! Whud you do . . . piss yourself?"

Pablo smacked him in the back of the head, knocking off his cap. "Young Lawrence has a good heart, but the manners of a goat."

"Where are we going?" Merriweather asked.

"To our camp," Pablo told him. "From there we will find a way to fly you home."

Bertram's heart soared. Home! She felt her feet get lighter, her shoulders and back get straighter, her stray hairs start to fall into place. Her entire outlook was suddenly and deliriously brighter and she thought—

"Home?" Merriweather said. "You must be kidding! We didn't

come all the way down here to turn tail at the first sign of trouble!"

Bertram felt as if the earth had opened beneath her feet and she was falling into a black abyss. She grabbed onto a tree to keep from toppling over.

"You were almost killed," Pablo said patiently. "Do you know who those men were?"

"Mercenaries."

"Yes. Only several of many thousands. Paid to kill us—"

"But we're not—"

"And they will not take the time to make sure their bullets pass harmlessly around you on their way to us."

"Pablo—"

"They are paid to kill us, Mr. Merriweather, but their pay is not docked if others are killed along the way."

"Who hired them?" Bonnelli asked, seeking to deflect the matter of the news crew's disposition, at least temporarily. "We thought they were working for Barranca."

Two soldiers, upon hearing this, unslung their rifles and took several steps toward him, anger flashing in their eyes.

Pablo held up a hand and they stopped. "The coffee growers hired them," Pablo answered. "With the cooperation of the coffee-growing nations. Why would you think they were working for Manuel Barranca?"

"It's what we'd heard," Merriweather said. "That Barranca had launched a major offensive against the Brazilian army."

"Heard from whom?"

Merriweather didn't say. "We also know you captured an American."

"An American."

"Yes."

"Who?"

"You know very well who."

"And this you heard where?"

When Merriweather didn't answer, the two soldiers started forward again, and this time Pablo didn't stop them. Merriweather looked down and shook his head, trying to ignore the soldiers who'd taken up position on either side of him. "Forget it, Pablo. I wouldn't tell you if the Supreme Court ordered me to. "

"If you are referring to Edward Caminetti," Pablo said, "then I'd be quite cautious about whoever gave you this information."

"And why is that?"

"Because Señor Caminetti came to South America at the personal invitation of Manuel Barranca—"

"We already knew that."

"—and was captured by the mercenaries, not us. We never saw him and do not even know if he is alive."

Merriweather hesitated, then said, "He is. At least he was two days ago."

Pablo's eyes narrowed. "How do you now this?"

"We spoke with him."

"Is there a bathroom somewhere?" Bertram asked.

"Whole fucking jungle is a bathroom," the assistant said.

"Actually," Lawrence said as he scratched at his ear, "he's right."

Bertram estimated the time it would take to walk the ten miles to Barranca's camp and decided that holding it that long was preferable to a potentially unpleasant encounter with some of the exotic and doubtless toxic local flora.

"Didn't you just go anyway?" the assistant mumbled.

"What was that?"

"We should just go on our way now."

"Quite right," Pablo agreed. He pointed to the various grips, cases and duffels on the ground before him and assigned them to various people among both his soldiers and the news crew.

"What about my makeup cases?" Bertram asked after everything else had been apportioned out.

"They stay."

"What!"

"Or you can carry them yourself," Pablo said as he whirled a finger in the air, then stopped to watch, incredulous, as Bertram bent to retrieve the cases. "What are you doing, señorita?"

"*Ella nos va nacer tarde,*" Pedro said.

"You're going to slow us down," Merriweather translated.

"I don't care! I'm not—" Bertram stopped speaking as the case farthest from her seemed to turn inside out, bright streams of Manhattan Hip Brown, Soho Nude, Uptown Taupe, Times Red Square and assorted other colors of nail polish spewing out in every direction, mixing in gay swirls with melted blobs of Burgundy Russet, Honey Rose and Ethnic Ochre lipstick. By the time she figured out that Lawrence had unleashed a burst of automatic rifle fire into the makeup case, he had already taken aim at the one she was holding, which she now dropped with a shriek.

When the remaining two cases had been similarly dispatched, Bertram's assistant folded his arms and said, "Well, guess you won't be needing me anymore. Mr. Pablo, I'll take that ride home."

About an hour into their trek through the jungle they came across the path Pablo had mentioned, which considerably eased their journey.

About an hour after that, Pablo, who'd taken up the point, suddenly stopped, causing the rest of the convoy to jostle to a halt behind him. Rifles were drawn as everyone dropped to the ground.

Everyone except Pablo.

He turned slowly and sought out Merriweather, at whom he curled a beckoning finger. When the veteran newsman had cautiously risen up and gone forward, Pablo said, "Señor Caminetti."

"What about him?"

"How did you speak with him?"

"How . . . what?"

"How were you speaking with him?"

Merriweather finally caught on. "Satellite telephone!"

"You have the frequency?"

Merriweather slapped at his back pocket and pulled at the zipper holding it shut, while Pablo unholstered a portable radio and pulled up the telescoped antenna. He barked some quick phrases into it in Spanish, and was answered in kind. After a moment, another voice came through. Merriweather handed over a piece of laminated paper and Pablo, following a rapidly delivered explanation of some sort, read off the numbers, first in Spanish, then in English, then in Spanish again.

"*Lo tengo,*" came the reply. "*Cuándo usted estará aquí?*"

Pablo looked at his watch. "We shall arrive in five, perhaps four hours."

"*Bueno. Adiós, Pablo, y viaje con seguridad.*"

"He tells us to travel safely," Pablo said as he re-holstered the radio. "The man is full of such useful advice."

"What man?"

"Manuel Barranca."

Some time later two of Pablo's forward scouts returned to the column, their faces grim. Pointing toward where they'd just come from, one said, "*Refugiados.*"

Pablo's own face darkened as he turned toward the GNN crew. "Refugees," he said somberly. "Just ahead. Running from the mercenaries."

"Who are they?' Bonnelli asked.

"Just coffee workers," Pablo answered. "Sympathetic to Barranca."

"What's his game, anyway?" Merriweather asked. "Barranca, I mean. Why's he holding up the United States?"

"He has only one objective, and that is to better the lives of those among us who work the coffee."

"That's it?"

"That is it."

"He doesn't want to take over? Install himself as president or something?"

"Of what?" Pablo smiled sadly. "Half of South America? Is this a reasonable or even a desirable thing?"

Ernie Bonnelli came up clutching his only remaining camera. "Yo, Jason," he said to Merriweather. "You realize we've got jack footage since we been here? What's she gonna talk about when she reports . . . her missing eyeliner?"

Merriweather looked back to where Bertram was still lying on the ground, face down, her hands over the back of her head. "She in any shape to even do a stand-up?"

Bonnelli held up the camera. "She sees that little red light aimed at her, it's like a shot of penicillin, amphetamine and Xanax all rolled into one."

"Pablo," Merriweather said, "let's go see those refugees."

Pablo looked at his watch. "If you insist, but quickly, ah? If your Miss Bertram is caught in this jungle after dark . . ."

Merriweather held up his hand. "I understand."

It was as bedraggled and pathetic a group as any of them had ever witnessed, two dozen people clutching rag-wrapped bundles, dazed children and battered suitcases, along with two donkeys.

Merriweather ran a practiced gaze over them, landing immediately on a young woman with the most dazzling violet eyes he'd ever seen. He nudged Bonnelli and pointed her out with his chin.

"Way ahead of you," the cameraman said as he brought up the digicam.

"Wow!" Bertram exclaimed, growing excited. "Those eyes! She's like that girl from Africa, the one on the cover of *Scientific American*?"

"Afghanistan," Merriweather corrected her.

"What?"

"She was from Afghanistan. And it was *National Geographic*."

"Whatever," Bertram said impatiently. "Ernie, you ready?"

"Yeah. I—" He stopped speaking when a hand came from behind him and switched off his camera. "Hey!" He whirled to face a smoldering Pablo.

"They are people," the coffee-worker-turned-soldier said, "not a story."

"Yeah, so?"

"So, you do not photograph them."

"Hold it a second." Merriweather stepped forward. "Listen, I appreciate you pulling us out of the fire and all, but who are you to speak for these people?"

"You are right." Pablo turned toward the shuffling refugees. *"Hoy, amigos! Desean ser fotografiados?"*

An elderly woman cried out and dropped to her knees, hiding her face in her hands. Several of the others stopped as well, pulling jackets up over their heads and grabbing children into their bosoms to hide their faces, too.

The violet-eyed woman angrily shouted *"Estás loco?"* before bending to console the elderly one.

The man next to her whirled on the news crew. His face, a strong visage flawed only by a jagged scar zigzagging down one cheek, was stormy with anger. *"Usted desea conseguirnos matados?"*

"She asks if you are crazy and her brother asks if you wish to see them dead," Pablo translated.

Bertram, peeved and petulant, said, "What are you talking about?"

"They're running away from the mercenaries, and you want to put their faces on television."

"We'll hide em with those little dot things," Bertram insisted, "so no one can recognize them."

"Then you do not need their pictures at all," Pablo reasoned.

"But—"

"We are not negotiating, Miss Bertram."

Bertram, pouting, didn't want to be seen as giving up too easily. "You ever hear of the First Amendment?" she asked Pablo.

"Certainly."

"Well?"

Merriweather walked up and leaned in close to Bertram. One hand cupping his mouth he said, "We're in fucking *Brazil*, Mona!"

"So what!" Bertram declared loudly, making Merriweather wince. "It's still the First Amendment!"

"She's got a point there," Bonnelli said delightedly, earning him a hard glare from Merriweather.

Bertram put her hands on her hips. "So what makes you the big king all of a sudden!" she said to Pablo.

"Well, señorita," Pablo answered patiently, "we are in the middle of a jungle, surrounded by wild animals and human enemies, and I have all the guns."

Bonnelli put a hand on Bertram's shoulder. "Listen—"

"Listen what!"

"Go talk to them, I'll shoot from a distance, and you'll report on what we heard, okay?"

"That's compromising, not reporting!"

"Right." Merriweather cleared his throat and threw his arm across Bertram's shoulders. "So here's the deal," he whispered. "You go along here or I'm going to shove my foot so far up your ass you'll be able to taste my toes. Now nod your head like a good girl and let's go get this over with so you don't have to sleep out in the jungle tonight with the snakes, okay?"

As Bertram considered her options, Merriweather said to Pablo, "How'd you know he was her brother?"

"Perdon?"

Merriweather gestured toward the refugees. "That girl with the purple eyes. How'd you know that other guy, the one with the scar on his face, how'd you know he was her brother?"

Pablo seemed momentarily confused by the question, then said, "I know these people."

"What people?"

"The coffee people. I know them."

"You know *all* of them? There's gotta be, I don't know, hundreds of thousands of them?"

Pablo turned and walked away, keeping one wary eye on Bonnelli and his camera. "Despite its size, it is a small community."

"This is Mona Bertram reporting live from an undisclosed location somewhere in the jungles of Brazil, where we're witnessing a humanitarian disaster of unprecedented proportions."

Senate majority leader Orville Twickham (R-NC) was deep into his third bourbon at the Mendel Rivers Memorial Bar in Arlington when the smiling if somewhat disheveled face of GNN's star reporter filled the screen. "Ha!" he exclaimed as he brought his hand down on the bar. "That's what I'm talking about!"

"What is, Senator?" a reporter for the Washington Post asked.

"A humanitarian disaster!" Twickham pointed toward the television with his glass. "Peasants and whatnot fleeing from the crushing grasp of the evil subjugators!"

"And—"

"Just what I warned em about, if they didn't put down this Barranca character!"

The reporter set down his Chivas and reached for his dictating machine. "You warned about a humanitarian disaster?"

"I think what the senator means," Twickham's aide intervened smoothly as the senator's attention was redrawn to the television screen, "is that—"

"Lemme ask you something, son," the reporter interrupted back. "Is your man here senile?"

"What? No. No, of course he—"

"Brain damaged, maybe? Old war wound, or played a little too long without a helmet?"

"Absolutely not! What on earth are you—"

"'Cause what I'm wondering," the reporter said, flipping his dictating machine on, "is how come every time he says something abysmally stupid or out of line, you're always there to tell me what he really meant."

"Well, that's not exactly—"

"I mean, when he told me pollution was good for the planet because it cleaned up the oceans, you said what he really meant was that a transit strike in Cleveland was in nobody's best interest."

"Well, now, I don't—"

"And when he told me that he never makes big decisions during a full moon, you said what he really meant was that it would take a tax cut of at least five percent to stimulate the economy."

"Now just a—"

"Come to think of it, you never let him off the leash, do you? Because I can't remember the last time the good senator was ever out in public without you right there with him. Now am I wrong there, or what?"

"This isn't—"

"What the hell're you two yammerin about!" Twickham scolded. "Can'tcha see there's some important shit goin on here!"

". . . unable to confirm earlier rumors that Manuel Barranca had launched a major assault against Brazilian army regulars," Bertram was saying. "A group of men claiming to be part of Barranca's movement told GNN earlier they were the ones who were attacked. They further claimed that the opposition soldiers weren't Brazilians but hired professionals brought in from as far as western Europe."

"Hey, wait just a goddamned minute . . ." Twickham said.

"Mercenaries?" Now the reporter was interested. "Did she just—"

". . . were viciously assaulted and captured by an armed group of men speaking a wide variety of languages, and were seconds away from being executed until the men claiming to be Barranca's troops pulled off a daring rescue at the last minute. We're being taken to an undisclosed location but along the way I personally witnessed terrified refugees fleeing from certain death at the hands of the same people who attacked our GNN crew."

"Who the hell attacked Barranca?" Twickham asked the air.

". . . a great deal of confusion down here," Bertram continued, "and extremely difficult to determine who is telling the—"

"How do those mercenaries understand each other," the aide asked the same air that hadn't answered Twickham, "if they're all speaking different languages?"

". . . be sure GNN will get to the bottom of it just as soon as—"

"What the hell is that freakin ditz Mona Bertram doing out in the field?" the reporter asked, but the air still wasn't saying.

CHAPTER 33

It was only a handful of outbuildings, small warehouses, equipment sheds, barracks and the like, but to Mona Bertram it looked like Givenchy Spa and the Ritz Carlton rolled into one.

"That smell is driving me nuts," Ernie Bonnelli sighed. "Give my left nut for a cup."

Pablo looked at his watch. "They are roasting. The aroma is intoxicating, no?"

"Is there a bathroom somewhere?" Bertram asked as she stepped back and forth from one foot to the other.

Pablo was about to point toward the facilities when a door burst open in the building that served as administrative HQ. A young man wearing a headset came running out, pointing skyward and yelling *"Aeroplano! Aeroplano!"* while clutching a portable radio and battery pack with his other hand.

"De dónde?" Pablo called to him.

"Del oeste!"

"Oh, dear," Pablo said quietly.

Bertram, already halfway across the courtyard to find the bathroom herself, hadn't heard the exchange and kept going, but Merriweather said, "A plane from the east. This is bad?"

"From the west. The direction of our enemy." Pablo looked on approvingly as people in the compound sprang into action and, within seconds, went from a seemingly random and chaotic collection of disparate parts to a single well-oiled machine. Wide doors were raised up over building entrances, tarps were thrown back from green-painted vehicles, and in short order, just as the first droning of a propeller reached the news crew's ears, a battery of well-worn but apparently functional weaponry was in place and aimed upward.

As the sound of the incoming aircraft grew louder, chatter among the readying troops grew quieter. "Single engine," Merriweather said, getting an agreeing nod from Pablo. "A drone, maybe?"

"Difficult to tell. If so, it must be shot down outside our perimeter." Pablo turned away and began yelling commands of some kind. He got answering gestures but nobody moved to do anything differently, so Merriweather guessed he was just bolstering their courage.

"Where should we go?" the assistant asked tremulously.

"It does not matter," Pablo replied, "unless you know where they plan to crash it."

"Lo tengo!" yelled a man seated atop a mobile antiaircraft gun of indeterminate vintage.

"Jorge has radar lock!" Pablo translated. *"Apunte buena, Jorge!"*

"Si, Pablo!"

"That thing has radar?" Merriweather inquired skeptically.

"Merely an expression," Pablo explained. "Jorge means he can see the plane with his binoculars."

Pablo turned to Bertram's assistant, taking in Merriweather and Bonnelli as well. "Most likely they will try for the middle. Your best course of action is to head out of here and back into the jungle."

The assistant was off like a shot, but the other two stayed. "Okay if I shoot?" Bonnelli asked, holding up his camera.

"As you wish. But our faces must be obscured, *si?*"

"Got it."

A whirring, wheezing, clanking noise, like someone trying to start the engine of a giant tank that had been rusting since the Crimean War, arose from the opposite side of the courtyard. Merriweather turned to see the antiaircraft gun swinging into position, its turret mount rotating haltingly as the dull green barrel, with an aching, arthritic stutter, rose slowly toward the clouds. Men with submachine guns assembled in a straight line across the middle of the yard.

"They will set up a wall of bullets," Pablo explained, "and hope that one or two of them hit the plane as it passes through."

"I take it you don't have any shoulder-mounted missile launchers," Merriweather ventured.

"Useless against a small plane. Not enough heat signature."

"Allí!" Jorge called out, taking the binoculars down from his face and pointing west. They all turned and could now make out the single-engine craft as a dark point against the sky.

"That's no drone," Merriweather muttered.

"Sure isn't," Bonnelli agreed. He had his camera to his eye and was shooting with a telephoto lens. "Drones don't weave all over the sky. Somebody's behind the wheel."

"A defensive maneuver," Pablo said. "To evade our fire."

Merriweather watched as the plane drew closer. "I don't think so. Looks more like he's drunk."

"What makes you say that?"

"He's not just turning," Merriweather answered. "He's skidding. Not using the rudder, just the ailerons."

They watched for a few more seconds, then Pablo nodded and said, "I understand. It is sloppy flying."

"Right. If he wanted to be evasive he'd make sharp turns. But he's just . . . whoa!"

The plane had skidded so badly it was almost sideways to them, and began dropping precipitously until the pilot regained some kind of control.

"He's wallowing all over the place." Merriweather folded his arms across his chest. "I don't think he's attacking, Pablo."

"No?"

"No. He's just in a lot of trouble."

"Perhaps, but I feel we must shoot him down anyway."

"Absolutely," Merriweather concurred.

"Hot dog!" Bonnelli said as he got down on one knee to steady the camera, visions of Pulitzer plums dancing in his head.

At a signal from Pablo, the men with the automatic weapons checked their ammunition cartridges, snapped the safeties off and cocked the firing mechanisms. The machine gunners squinted through their sights and swung the guns a few times to make sure the gimbals were loose. Jorge on the antiaircraft truck was completely still, two fingers on the trigger.

Pablo lifted his hand high into the air and turned to face the plane. *"Listo!"*

The little craft continued to flounder in the sky. "Gonna have to bracket him," Merriweather suggested. "He's all over the place."

"My men will know that. *Apunte!*"

Khaki clothing rustled as the automatic weapons were brought into position, then there was silence, except for the rising and falling sounds of the plane's engine as it continued to dip, skid and porpoise in the air.

Pablo's upraised arm tensed.

"Alto!" came a choked cry from somewhere.

Pablo whirled to find the source of the command to stop. It was the young man who'd come running out of the headquarters building with a portable radio. He was standing off to the side pressing one of the headset cups to his ear, listening intently.

"Qué pasa, Javier?" Pablo growled.

"Un momento, por favor . . ."

The plane's engine whined as the tail pitched up and the wings slewed crazily until the nose was pointed right at them. Then the engine took on a throaty growl as the machine stabilized and picked up speed.

"Holy shit," Bonnelli said, his eye still glued to the viewfinder of his camera.

"Javier!" Pablo insisted.

The radioman looked up, eyebrows raised so high they disappeared under his cap. *"Esta es Barranca!"*

"Quién es?"

Javier pointed to the plane, which was now barreling directly for them. *"En el avión! Es Barranca!"*

The men on the line with assault weapons lowered them and looked at each other, then at the plane. The name "Barranca" ricocheted around the compound until it reached the barracks area, then doors flew open and children ran out, waving their arms and calling for their leader, as though he might hear them up in the sky.

"Are you certain?" Pablo asked Javier.

The radioman tapped his headset. "I speak with him now. He says . . . he says . . ."

"Ó qué dice él?"

"He says he has the American with him!"

The GNN production department back in Chicago would later edit out the sudden shake and jitter of Bonnelli's camera. "An American?" he asked while trying to recapture the plane in his viewfinder.

Pablo turned away from the plane and looked inquiringly at his men. "What American?"

"That golfer guy," said a voice in accentless English.

"Lawrence." Pablo regarded the man quizzically. "What are you speaking of?"

"Eddie Caminetti, of course."

"I know who he is." Pablo jerked a thumb over his shoulder. "But why is he in that plane!"

Lawrence shrugged. "On account of Barranca went to get him."

"Alone?"

"What can I tell you, Pablo? He gave an order."

Pablo, unsure of whether to be angry or just more confused, chose to be both. "Where the hell does he acquire an airplane!"

"Well, now you mention it," Lawrence replied, "he didn't have one when we left here."

"So who is flying it?"

"Must be Caminetti."

"Nuh uh," Merriweather said, shaking his head forcefully. "I sat next to him on a plane once, to a Ryder Cup. White-knuckle flyer all the way, can't go from New York to Jersey without a few belts to calm his nerves. No way in hell he knows how to pilot a plane."

"Well," Lawrence said, scratching his chest, "by the looks'a things, I'd say you're right about that." They all turned to see the plane veer off to the left and level out momentarily.

"He is injured!" Javier called out. "The American!"

Bonnelli pointed his camera almost vertically as the plane passed by overhead, less than two hundred feet off the ground. "Can Barranca fly?"

"He has had lessons," Pablo answered.

"How many?" Merriweather asked.

"Four. Perhaps five."

Bonnelli snapped off the camera as the plane disappeared behind a stand of trees. The sound of the engine wound down precipitously, then stopped altogether.

"Let's go!" Merriweather yelled, and as one man the GNN crew and every other person in the compound headed for the jungle in the direction the plane was last seen. A few seconds later there was a sound like five hundred men with machetes slashing at bamboo at the same time, then a clash of crumpling metal, then nothing.

"Maybe all of this vegetation cushioned the crash," Merriweather said.

They kept running. After half a minute more, a searing flash of heat and a tower of flame shot up above the trees. Barranca's men picked up the pace, leaving the GNN crew in their wake, but then were themselves stopped by a second outpouring of flames.

The news crew caught up to them at the edge of a clearing. Great clouds of billowing smoke were sweeping upward, obscuring the flames that were still giving off enough heat to be felt at a distance.

"There was a delay after the crash," Merriweather said hopefully between deep lungfuls of air. "Before the flames. Maybe they got out in—"

"Look!" someone cried.

Out of the roiling mist of smoke a figure emerged, staggering under the weight of something slung across his shoulders.

"Es Manuel?" could be heard from several of the onlookers, a hopeful plaint as several soldiers darted across the field.

Halfway there, one turned around and shot a hand into the air. *"Si, si! Esta es Manuel!"*

"I got him in the telephoto," Bonnelli said.

"Is it really Barranca?" Merriweather asked him.

"Beats me." Bonnelli began walking forward, still aiming his camera. "Don't know what the guy looks like. But he's carrying someone on his back."

The soldiers reached him and grabbed the man off his back, setting him down on the grass. Someone called for a stretcher and Pablo sent two men back to the compound to get one. By that time the flames had died down and the smoke was dissipating.

As they neared, the news crew could see that the man who was being carried was sitting upright, cradling his left arm. One eye sported a fresh shiner and there was crusted blood above it. Barranca stood over him, talking to his soldiers, one of whom was examining the seated man.

"Is that Caminetti?" Bonnelli asked.

"Sure is," Merriweather answered. "Hey, Eddie . . ."

Eddie looked up at the sound of his name and spotted Merriweather. "Hey, yourself. I know you?"

"Slightly. Last Ryder, you and I—"

"Yeah, yeah." Eddie grinned in recognition, then grimaced as the man examining him touched his arm. "Same plane. You were knocking back shooters and hitting on that babe from ESPN."

"Musta been another guy."

"Yeah. So what the hell are you doing down here?"

"Might ask you the same thing."

"Playin golf, what else." Eddie looked down at his arm. "Least I was, till the shit hit the fan." He yelped and looked at the man who was examining him. "Hey, are you a doctor?"

"No . . . pero miro muchos de la televisión."

"He says no," Barranca translated, "but he watches a lot of television."

"Beautiful," Eddie muttered. "So what's wrong with me?"

The maybe-a-doctor leaned back and pushed the bill of his cap up. "Broken arm, sprained ankle, minor contusions . . . very sorry, Manuel, but I'm afraid he's going to live."

"Yes, but can he play golf?"

"You're all heart, Barranca," Eddie said.

Merriweather turned to Barranca and held out his hand. "I'm Jason Merriweather, GNN."

Barranca accepted the hand. "Manuel Villa Lobos de Barranca. *El gusto es mio.*"

"Likewise. So how come he got all busted up in the plane crash and you hardly have a scratch?"

"He was not injured in the crash," the doctor said.

"What?"

The doctor pointed out the dried blood on Eddie's facial wound and the color of the contusion around his eye. "At least twenty-four hours old."

"Then what the hell happened to him?"

One of the soldiers twisted open a thermos and poured a steaming cup of coffee into the dual-purpose lid, then handed it to Barranca, who passed it slowly under his nose with his eyes closed. *"Gracias, Pedro."* He took a sip, sighed appreciatively, and handed it to Merriweather. "He was kidnapped. You know . . . by those Brazilian army regulars your Ms. Bertram reported on with such authority?"

Merriweather took the proffered cup, reddening slightly. "Yeah, well . . . sorry about that. It was the best information we had at the time."

"If I had to guess, Mr. Merriweather, I would say it was provided by your government. Please . . . drink."

Merriweather brought the cup idly to his lips and took a small sip. Startled, he looked down at the brew and took a bigger one. "Wow . . ."

Barranca smiled. "Good, no?"

"Good?" He took another swallow, then turned around and handed it to Bonnelli. "Take a swig of this." Then, to Barranca, "What makes you say it was the U.S. government?"

"Because it is in their best interest to make me look like a swine. Tell me that I am wrong."

Merriweather didn't answer, but watched as Bonnelli set down the cup so he could film two men arriving with a stretcher. When they had it down on the ground Eddie sidled onto it without assistance, but before lying back said, "We have an agreement."

"What agreement?" Merriweather asked.

"Not to identify me."

"Oh, come on, Caminetti! This is the biggest—"

"I'm holding you to it, Merriweather. You can source me as Deep Java and that's it."

CHAPTER 34

s they trooped back into the compound, Mona Bertram came out of a barracks building, her head wrapped in a towel. "Jason!" she called cheerily. "Over here!"

"Mona. How you doin?"

"Great! They have a shower here and everything!"

"That right?"

"Uh huh! Hot water, the works. You should give it a try. Ernie! You can borrow my shampoo if you want!"

Bonnelli said, "You brought shampoo?"

"Absolutely! Conditioner, too, but, well . . ." Bertram scrunched up her face and rocked her head back and forth. "Actually, to be honest, there's really not that much left, and, uh . . ."

Bonnelli held up a hand. "Not a problem, Mona. Really."

The two stretcher bearers came by carrying Eddie.

"Who's that?" Bertram asked.

"Just some guy," Merriweather answered.

"Oh. Okay, I gotta get back, okay?" She rolled her eyes heavenward. "Wrong voltage for my gosh-darned hair dryer, can you believe that? What time's our next report?"

"Bout an hour," Merriweather informed her. "I'll have something written for you."

"You're a prince, Jason."

Half an hour later Pablo came upon Merriweather tapping on a pocket computer in a side corridor of the admin building. "Are you preparing your report?" he asked as he handed over a cup of coffee.

Merriweather eagerly accepted the cup. "Yeah. Thanks for this."

"*De nada*. Any chance I might read it?"

Merriweather had the cup halfway to his mouth. "You can read it, but you can't change it."

Pablo held up his hands in mock defense. "Nor would I wish to. A free press is something we ourselves wish for."

Merriweather tapped a few keys with his free hand to save his work, then handed the pocket computer over to Pablo. "Keep hitting this page down key."

"I understand."

As Merriweather savored the coffee and looked on anxiously, Pablo read his report, a blank expression on his face. "Central Brazil," he said after some minutes.

"Sorry?"

"We are in central Brazil, not western."

"Ah. Thanks."

"And the mercenaries are not only from Western Europe, but central Asia as well. Perhaps you did not recognize all of the languages while you were bound . . ."

" . . . **reporting live from an undisclosed location** in central Brazil. And, as is so often the case in today's confused world, things are not as they seemed at first."

Mona Bertram had been near-hysterical over the state of her hair, but the loan of a military-style cap had assuaged her anxiety. She'd also made some new friends among the local women by carrying out several hasty makeovers using extra supplies in her one surviving makeup bag.

"Earlier rumors of a major offensive by Manuel Barranca against the Brazilian army turned out to be . . ."

" . . . **dead wrong,**" DCI Baines Gordon Wainwright was reporting to his president at the same time. "What my guys found out, it was Barranca who was attacked, not the other way around."

"Attacked by whom?" President Eastwood asked.

"Mercenaries, sir. From damned near everywhere, including western Europe and central Asia. And what makes it worse—" Wainwright paused for emphasis "—it was apparently done with the permission, if not the outright cooperation, of the major coffee-growing countries of South America."

Eastwood rose up from his seat behind the big desk in the Gates Office and walked to the window. "How bad is it?"

"Bad, Mr. President. We don't have specifics yet, but it seems there was a terrible battle, with great loss of life, and . . ."

"And . . . ?"

"Reports of atrocities." Wainwright's voice grew bitter. "The usual kind of horror when these third world shitheels go after each other."

"You said the mercenaries were largely from western Europe."

"Yes. They're in it for the money, and could care less what they're paid to do."

"And this Barranca character. You're telling me he went into enemy territory and pulled Caminetti out? Single-handedly?"

"So it seems."

Eastwood grew quiet for a few moments. "So what GNN is going to be reporting," he eventually mused out loud, "is that Barranca is really . . ."

" . . . the first true freedom fighter of the new millennium." She stared at the camera for a few pregnant seconds, then said, "Mona Bertram, reporting live from the front lines in central Brazil." Then the picture faded from millions of television screens across the western hemisphere.

"Why won't he let us interview him?" she asked Pablo.

"Doesn't matter. He is not here anyway."

"Not here! Where'd he go?"

Pablo pointed toward the jungle. "Back to the front lines," he answered. He looked for some flicker in Bertram's face to indicate that she'd caught the insinuation that the front lines were someplace other than where she'd reported them to be, but saw only blankness.

"Then that's where we should be," Merriweather said as he came up behind them.

"I think not, Mr. Merriweather."

Bertram nodded her enthusiastic agreement with Pablo. "He's right, Jason. We barely made it through the—"

"It's what we live for, Pablo," Merriweather said, ignoring her. "It's why we're newspeople. To get where the story is, to bring it home for millions of people."

"Much too dangerous."

"That's why we have to go."

Pablo was adamant. "Barranca would be very angry with us. He risked his own life to save the other American, and now you propose to go there yourselves?" He pointed at Bertram. "With a woman?"

"We're journalists. It's what we do. For the most part, both sides of a conflict leave us alone."

"Leave us alone?" Bertram cried. "What about those shitheads in the jungle? They were going to shoot us, Jason!"

"I don't think so," Merriweather responded. "I think they were just trying to scare us."

"To what purpose?" Pablo asked. "Would it not have been in their best interest to befriend you, and gain some sympathy in your reporting?"

Merriweather shook his head. "They were mercenaries, remember? They wouldn't care a whit how we covered the fighting."

"In that case, they would not accord you the privileges of the press, either."

It was a logical wall, and Merriweather chose not to go through but around it. "Bottom line, Pablo, it's our call. Do you want to take us or should we go it alone?"

By then, Bonnelli had joined the group, and picked up on the discussion quickly. "You're on the right side of this, Pablo," he said. "Only nobody's going to know it if we don't tell it." He could tell he'd gained his attention, and hoped nobody else would jump in when silence was called for.

"We can tell it from here!" Bertram shrilled. "His men have sat phones! They can call it in from the front and we'll do the stand-ups right here."

"You mean where the showers are," Bonnelli muttered.

"What was that?"

"You and me where the soldiers are," Bonnelli said more clearly. "Getting the real story."

"Think of it, Mona," Merriweather said. "You in the jungle with rockets going off all over the place. They'll be calling you the, uh, the, uh . . ."

"The Missile Mistress!" Bonnelli blurted.

"No!" Merriweather shot back. "The Jungle Queen! Hell, you can start clearing space on your mantel for the Emmy!"

"Emmy, hell . . . the Pulitzer!"

Bertram bit her lip: Wouldn't Queen of the Jungle have a better ring to it, a kind of rhythm? Mona, Queen of the Jungle. It could even get her a full hour on Danny Prince. That'd show that Christiane Rain-and-Pour or what the hell ever that she wasn't the only goddess of hard news.

Pablo sighed. "I cannot stop you, and therefore will do all I can to assist. But first I must speak with Barranca."

A soldier walked up to Bertram and leered at her. "You should be in bed with us."

"What!"

He pointed at Bertram, himself, and the others in his platoon who were hanging back ogling the television star. "You should be in bed with us."

Bertram, in a panic, replayed in her mind Pablo's comment about them being in the middle of a jungle and his men having all the guns. Having saved their lives, would he really allow them to—

Pablo, smiling and shaking his head, said, "He means, you should be embedded with us." Bertram exhaled loudly and patted her chest.

As Pablo and his men walked away to begin making plans, the soldier who had approached Bertram said, "Bullshit, Pablo: We're lookin t'get laid, not interviewed!"

CHAPTER 35

QUAKER OATS CRISIS CENTER

President Thomas Madison Eastwood felt a vibration in his jacket pocket. "Excuse me," he said, and stepped out of the room.

When he was safely alone, he took the cell phone from his pocket and put it to his ear. "Smith," he said.

"Jones," Dalton Galsworthy replied.

"I told you never to call me here!"

"Very funny, sir. Am I interrupting anything?"

Eastwood considered the mass of brass gathered in the room next door: three Cabinet secretaries, all of the Joint Chiefs including the chairman, National Security Advisor Anatoli Kropotkin, chief of staff Conchita Ortega, Director of Central Intelligence Baines Gordon Wainwright, FBI director Bradford MacArthur Baffington, and a set of assorted hangers-on standing along the wall. The crisis center was as packed as he'd ever seen it.

"Nah, no big deal," he replied. "About time you checked in. How's it looking down there?"

BRAZIL

"So, Deep Java: How's it going?"

"Very funny," Eddie replied to Merriweather, then waved halfheartedly to Ernie Bonnelli and Mona Bertram as they trooped into his makeshift hospital room, an old office into which a bed and side table had been rolled. He was stretched out on the bed, his arm in a cast, lower leg in a splint, with a bandage above his eye. On the side table, a bottle of scotch of indeterminate origin shared space with a pack of cigarettes and an empty urine specimen container serving as a glass. "Why's he got his camera?" Eddie asked, inclining his chin toward Bonnelli.

"Force of habit," the cameraman explained as he set the camera on the floor. "Sorry."

"How are you doing?" Bertram asked airily.

"I've got a busted wing, twisted ankle and my head's been bashed to shit. How are *you* doing?"

"Still think you should let us put you on the air, Eddie," Merriweather said. "It'd sure make our story more credible."

"That's true."

"So you changed your mind?"

"Nope."

"But you just agreed it would make us more credible!"

"It would. But what would it do for me?"

"The people have a right to know, Eddie," Bertram said.

"Maybe." Eddie reached over painfully and grabbed the "glass," enjoying the barely suppressed look of disgust on Bertram's face. "Dudn't mean I got an obligation to tell em."

"Sure it does! What if everybody felt the same way, and nobody—"

"Fuck em."

"Excuse me?"

"I said, fuck em."

Bertram *humphed* and folded her arms across her chest. "Some attitude."

Eddie took a small sip from the specimen container, and as the onlookers winced he said, "Stuff tastes like piss anyway, so what the hell. Why are you here?"

"We're reporters, Eddie," Bonnelli said.

"Not you." Eddie held the cup out toward Bertram. "Don't think I ever saw you out in the field. This like a new thing?"

"I'm out here getting the story."

"Good for you. Why are you in my room?"

"We want to interview you. We don't know if Barranca is going to let us go to the front."

With that, Eddie's cynicism seemed to drop away. His face grew somber and he took another, longer slug of his drink. "The front?"

Merriweather nodded. "It's where the action is, so that's where we go. Why?"

"We've seen fighting before," Bonnelli said. *Or at least two of us have.*

"Not like this, you haven't."

"Bad?" Bonnelli asked tentatively, as though afraid of the answer.

Eddie took a deep breath, held it as he looked away toward the window, then let it out slowly. "Hard to describe. If Barranca hadn't come fish me out . . ." He let his words die away as he shuddered and tried to reach for the cigarettes on the side table.

Merriweather stepped forward to help him. "We heard rumors. Chemical weapons, maybe some bio . . ."

"I can't confirm the bio," Eddie said quietly.

So there were at least chemical, Merriweather's eyes said to Bonnelli. Bertram's own eyes were tightly shut as visions danced through her head of footage she'd seen from chemical attacks in the Middle East. It was one thing to be the Missile Babe or the Ack-Ack Chick or the Bombshell Bitch, with Fourth of July rockets lighting up the background in your stand-ups and nearby explosions making the camera shake every ten seconds. That was the fun way to cover a war, but who the hell ever wound up on Larry King because she got her face half-melted off from some godawful freakin chemical nobody could even pronounce and nobody was supposed to have in the first place, or golf ball size boils all over your neck from an alien life-form some half-crazed terrorist scientist duplicated in his lab and figured out how to powderize and stick in a shoulder-mounted missile?

"She okay?" Eddie asked, causing Bertram's eyes to snap open.

"She's had a rough day, poor thing," Merriweather replied. "What did you see over there? Specifically, I mean."

"I'm not an expert . . ." Eddie put the pack of cigarettes back on the table, then tried to roll over, gave up and closed his eyes. "Tanks. A lot of them."

"Tanks!"

Eddie shook his head, his eyes still closed. "Not like Shermans. Storage tanks. I don't know the lingo so I couldn't read what was in em. But . . ."

"But what?" Bonnelli urged.

"Symbols. Signs, like. Skulls and crossbones, things like that."

Bonnelli caught his breath and looked at Merriweather, who said, "How big?"

Eddie shrugged. "Like, I dunno . . .size of a refrigerator."

"We had a few other questions . . ." Merriweather began, but Eddie waved them away and put a trembling hand to his forehead.

"I don't feel so good."

"Just—"

"Oh, one other thing . . ."

"Yes?"

"The tanks were on wheels."

"Wheels! But . . . what do they—"

"Listen, I'm really tired. I think maybe I caught something . . ."

The others quickly backed away and were gone within seconds.

Out in the courtyard Pablo greeted them with a wave. "Seems you will get your wish after all," he announced.

"How's that?" Bertram asked him.

"I have spoken with Barranca. Against my better judgment he accedes to your request."

"He does?" Bertram asked, unable to hide the dread in her voice.

"Indeed. And seeing as I am unable to dissuade you from such foolishness, my men will escort you through the jungle, but the last miles are on your own." He watched as the three of them stood quietly, shuffling their feet and looking around nervously.

"Sounds great," Bonnelli said lamely.

"Great, yes," Pablo concurred with equal unenthusiasm. "Get as much sleep tonight as you can. Good night, and *vaya con dios*."

Merriweather thought Pablo had said it as though he never expected to see them again.

GNN BROADCAST CENTER

"Tell me, Mr. Director," said Forrest Arbuckle, "how should the Brazilian government and its neighbors deal with the mercenaries?" Arbuckle was doing his best to look cool and professional, and not to think about how his entire life was riding on the next few minutes.

CIA director Baines Gordon Wainwright smiled indulgently.

"Well, Forrest, that's not my decision. It's something the Brazilians will have to work out for themselves."

Arbuckle had been called in as a last-minute substitute for Derek van Dinman, who was supposed to substitute for Mona Bertram on her evening show but had come down with the flu. Van Dinman had scored this interview with Wainwright following his dalliance with Marguerite Swanson, a thirty-five-year veteran of the CIA's Office of Current Production and Analytic Support, who herself was now abed with the same affliction. The only person available to handle the interview had been Arbuckle, and he'd leaped at it with a vengeance, determined to show Lance "Sparky" Kroeger that he was made of the right stuff.

Wainwright sniffed and folded his hands in front of himself, prepared for the next question. But Arbuckle wasn't ready to ask it. "Sorry, Mr. Director . . . seems I didn't make myself clear."

"How's that?"

"I was simply asking what you thought they should do."

Wainwright smiled again and spread his hands. "Yes, well, as I said, that's a decision the Brazilians are going to have to grapple with, and something I can't decide for them."

"Let me be clearer. I didn't ask you to make the decision for the Brazilians, and I hope I didn't imply that I thought it was yours to make. What I was asking for was your opinion. What do you think they should do?"

Wainwright laughed good-naturedly. "I understood the question, Forrest, and I believe I've answered it."

"You answered *a* question, Mr. Director, but not the one I asked."

"I believe I did."

"What I was asking—"

"I know what you were asking, I've answered it, so let's move on."

"I wanted to know what advice you had for the Brazilians."

"And I told you."

"I'm not sure you did."

"The answer I gave was my answer."

"But—"

"I think we should move on."

Arbuckle paused. "So what you're saying, you'd rather not deal with this issue?"

"I—"

"Because if you'd rather not answer, that's your privilege, and I will move on. No problem."

"But I did answer you. I just think we need to get off this topic, which I've already dealt with, and move on."

A few minutes later when they exited the studio, Kroeger was waiting, standing beneath a small circle of storm clouds, his face dark with barely repressed fury.

Wainwright stuck a finger in his face. "I know he was a sub, Sparky," the DCI said with angry menace, "but the next time you put me on the air you better goddamned well make sure it isn't with some raw punk who can't follow a script and thinks he's Edward R. Fucking Murrow!"

As Wainwright stomped away, Kroeger turned to Arbuckle, who shook his head as he watched the departing DCI. "Can't believe he thought I'd let him get away with that bullshit answer."

Arbuckle, of course, was totally unaware that his career had come to a screeching, skidding, irreversible halt some ten minutes ago.

CHAPTER 36

It was a Democratic fund-raiser, but Sparky Kroeger, a staunch Republican, was there anyway, because even though he hadn't filed a news report in thirty years, to deny entry to the president, chairman and CEO of Global News Network in an election year would be like chopping off one of your feet before a marathon.

Besides, the president, who was the keynote speaker and the prize attraction of the event, wanted to see him.

"Mr. President, a pleasure," Kroeger said as he extended his hand.

"You're so full of shit," Eastwood responded, then turned them both toward the photographers for some happy-smiley shots. That the head of a purportedly objective news organization was hobnobbing with the president of the United States at a purely political event wouldn't even be cause for comment in the weekend's talk shows, not when investigative reporters routinely played tennis with the very Cabinet secretaries they were supposed to be casting a critical eye on and network news executives attended alcohol-fueled, back-slapping roasts for corporate executives currently under indictment.

"It's those waves of love washing over me that I enjoy the most about seeing you," Kroeger shot back as he flashed a big smile for the paparazzi.

"I need two minutes from you, Sparky."

"And who am I to deny my president?"

They managed to slip into a side room only after the president won a heated argument with the head of his Secret Service detail who'd wanted to first sweep the room for bugs, examine every inch of every electrical and phone wire for suspicious devices, have his men personally crawl through all the air conditioning and heating ducts, interview every hotel employee who'd been anywhere near the room in the past two weeks, secure every sightline within a ten-block radius and have the elevated trains of the Loop as well as all incoming and outgoing flights at Meigs Airport halted for half an hour prior to the planned meeting. As it was, within three minutes of the president and Kroeger entering the room, half a dozen Marine guards were stationed outside the door and four Ninja-style Special Ops officers had taken up station on the roof, complete with assault weapons and enough mountaineering gear to rappel an elephant down the side of the building, should the need arise.

"I know you're on to the story down in South America," Eastwood began with no preamble.

"Boy, that daily briefing you get is right on the money, Tom." The story had been airing on GNN every half hour for two days.

"You're a riot. I'm talking about the real story." Kroeger stayed quiet but Eastwood only had a few minutes. "I don't have time for the usual Bullshit Bolero, Sparky. The story about what kind of fighting is going on down there."

"Yeah, we know about it."

"Well, you don't know the half of it."

"That so?"

"Yeah, that's so."

"So tell me."

"I can't."

"Well, there's a big surprise. So if you can't tell me, what's the point of this—"

"You need to keep your people away from the front."

Kroeger felt a little thrill of fear at the base of his spine. He and Eastwood might have their philosophical differences, but he knew the president was a straight shooter not normally given to intricate game-playing. "That's not an easy thing for newspeople."

Eastwood nodded. "I know. But you're going to have to trust me on this one. It's nasty, and there's none of the usual diplomatic niceties in place, nobody to Rodney King what's happening. Stuff happens, it stays a secret, and that's not much motivation for people to play by the rules."

"But if my guys are there to report on it . . ."

"Your guys won't be reporting on anything."

"Are you telling me—"

"I'm telling you that if you allow that news crew to get to the front, you're going to have a lot of explaining to do when they don't come back."

A wild profusion of implications raced through Kroeger's mind and almost made him dizzy. Was the president telling him there were chemical or biological weapons in place? Nukes? Was he saying that there were covert U.S. forces in place, and that they themselves would take out his news crew to cover whatever nastiness they were up to?

Clearly Eastwood wasn't saying, but what he wasn't saying was clear: If Kroeger allowed his people to go to the front and they didn't come home, he'd been warned, by no less an authority than the president of the United States, and would suffer dire consequences. "I don't think I—"

"Conversation's over, Sparky." Eastwood walked to the door, opened it and left the room.

They'd packed all their gear and were waiting for first light. None of them could sleep and they were sitting around in various states of dread and anxiety. Jason Merriweather was writing letters home, wording them carefully under the assumption that they'd be read by millions if he cashed in his chips at the front. Ernie Bonnelli was snapping stills of him doing it, figuring that a posthumous Pulitzer was better than none, and Mona Bertram was secreting a knife into her makeup bag, fully intent on surreptitiously slashing her ankle out of sight of the others about a mile into the jungle and then claiming she'd been bitten by a snake. She'd settled on the inside of the ankle because the resulting scar would be less visible there than on the outside. There would be the question of where the snake had gotten to after the attack, so she resolved to come running back after a bathroom excursion into the thicket, screaming in pain with such intensity that nobody would be moved to go searching for the creature who, after all, was just doing what it is that snakes do and couldn't be blamed or punished for it. Then again, there might be some question about how a snake might have gotten positioned to bite her on the inside of her ankle in the first place, or how a pair of hollow-point fangs could leave a clean, three-inch gash. Maybe she'd better think of a different beast. Were there wild boars in Brazil? Tigers? A tiger would be extremely cool. That Christiane Rain-and-Pour had never gotten attacked by a tiger, that was for damned sure. But first it might pay to make sure there really were tigers in South America, because how would it look if there weren't and she—

"Phone."

The voice was quiet but it startled the GNN crew into an assortment of arrhythmias, from which Merriweather recovered first. "What?"

"Satellite phone," Pablo said from the doorway, holding out the cumbersome set.

"Who is it?" Merriweather said as he took it.

"Interesting how you Americans ask who is on the phone when you have it right in your hands and can find out for yourself. I will return to retrieve it."

Merriweather, aware of everyone else's eyes on him, put it to his ear. "Hello?"

"That you, Jason?"

Kroeger, Merriweather mouthed to the others. "Yeah. How you doin, Sparky?"

"Good. That little trip you have planned to the front?"

"Yeah . . . ?"

"Call it off."

"What?"

"You can't go."

Merriweather, whose letter-writing had gotten him worked up into a near-psychosis as he recalled and described everything he knew about the kinds of weapons that were made in laboratories, almost dropped the phone as a tsunami of icy relief surged through his gut. He was literally dizzy with it, the ground beneath him swaying and bucking as though he were standing on a ship in a storm.

"Jason, you there?"

Merriweather took a few deep breaths to steady himself, to find his voice, then spoke into the phone. "Bullshit!" he shouted. "What are you talking about, Kroeger!"

"It's too dangerous. You can't go. None of you can."

Merriweather stood up, slowly at first, then with greater confidence that his legs would hold. "Are you out of your mind here, or what? This is the biggest story of the year, maybe the decade! We're the only ones on the scene and—"

"What did he say?" Bonnelli and Bertram were asking, both speaking at once. "What's going on?"

Merriweather covered the mouthpiece with his hand. "He says we can't go to the front."

Bertram leaned against a wall. She thought her bowels were about to let loose. She listened to more of one side of the satellite phone conversation and when she was absolutely convinced that Kroeger wasn't going to change his mind, said to Merriweather, "Give me the phone!"

"Be my guest," he said, handing it over.

"Sparky? Mona. Listen here, this is outrageous! I don't—you can't—we're journalists, for Pete's sake! Of course it's dangerous! If it wasn't you could've sent a copy boy! What? What?" She tore the phone from her ear and handed it back to Merriweather. "I can't talk any sense into him!"

Bonnelli, no less relieved than Bertram but unwilling to acquiesce to her posturing, said, "So what? We'll just go anyway."

Merriweather hit the disconnect button on the phone. "Oh, cut it out. We're not going anywhere." He looked at his watch. "I asked Kroeger to put somebody on getting in touch with the top guys in the Brazilian government. Peru and Colombia, too. We gotta report in half an hour and we need some answers.

"Right." Bertram pushed back from the wall. "Ernie, better start warming up your gear."

Bonnelli flipped three switches on his fully transistorized camera, sound box and portable uplink. "Okay. It's warm."

"Things are different here," Mona Bertram said into the camera. "Outside the harsh glare of a free press, horrors are perpetrated that we can only imagine, and the perpetrators go unidentified and unpunished."

She walked slowly, the camera panning along with her, the dense jungle passing by dramatically in the background. "Regretfully, my crew and I have been forbidden to travel to the scene of the harshest fighting—"

"Or any fighting," Merriweather muttered as he watched Bertram's performance, which he had to admit was Oscar-caliber, at least if your objective was thinly veiled self-aggrandizement.

" . . . but an overwhelming preponderance of the evidence we've been able to gather tells us that a well-equipped gang of highly paid foreign mercenaries is crushing the hopes, the dreams, the very lives, of the ragtag troops of freedom fighters who have rallied to the worker's rebellion of Manuel Villa Lobos de Barranca."

The red light on Bonnelli's camera went out. "They're running footage of the plane crash," he said into his miniature boom mike.

Bertram nodded in acknowledgment. "GNN staff earlier today contacted the host governments in the area, but each of them denied emphatically that they were in any way involved in the suppression of Barranca's movement." As planned, she came back onto the feed and Bonnelli zoomed slowly into her face. "As a matter of fact," she intoned, her eyes boring into the lens, "they even denied that there was any fighting at all going on."

The red light went out again, and this time she was replaced on the outgoing feed by a shot of flames blooming high into the sky over the jungle.

"We were hoping to bring you a live interview with Barranca himself," Bertram said, "but he declined, with regrets, choosing instead to be on the almost impossibly dangerous and harrowing front lines with his men, where he has vowed to make a last, desperate stand against troops far superior in numbers and weaponry to his own cadre of citizen-soldiers. Reporting live from somewhere in the hellish jungles of Brazil, this is Mona Bertram."

CHAPTER 37

Television network MS-GNN had been running ads for its coverage of the Coffee War six times an hour since early in the morning East Coast time. "We have the exclusive on this story," the voice-over said as the MS-GNN Coffee War theme music blared over the MS-GNN Coffee War logo, a stylized, tripod-mounted machine gun being belt-fed not with conventional rounds but miniature sacks of coffee. "For the very latest critical information on this destabilizing conflict that threatens us all, watch the MS-GNN six o'clock news, sponsored by Crazy Debbie's House of Halters. You won't believe it."

Anchor Derek van Dinman was ready at the appointed hour. "MS-GNN is preempting some of its planned regular evening news coverage," he said, "for exclusive coverage of this destabilizing conflict that threatens us all. We begin our coverage with the results of an exclusive MS-GNN poll conducted this afternoon, in which we asked American citizens, Who do you think will win the Coffee War, Barranca or the mercenaries?"

Van Dinman's face was replaced by a graphic showing the results as his voice continued. "As you can see, forty-three percent of you believe that the mercenaries will win, forty-one percent think it will be Barranca, and sixteen percent had no opinion."

Van Dinman's face returned to the screen. "The margin of error in this survey was nine percent, and we need to remind viewers that this was not a scientific poll. Now, we move on with our coverage to a live, exclusive interview with GNN super-reporter Mona Bertram." He swiveled around to the flat plasma screen mounted behind him. "Good evening, Mona."

"Good evening, Derek. Nice to be with you."

"Absolutely! First of all, I wanted to let you know how much we here at MS-GNN appreciate you taking time out from what must be a punishing schedule to bring us up to date."

Bertram brushed away a stray hair and hitched her shoulders against the fatigue clearly etched on her face. "Happy to be with you, Derek," she said gamely.

"And we'd also like to thank GNN for allowing this unprecedented access to one of their top reporters." He declined to mention that MS-GNN was a joint venture of GNN, the GNN financial wire service, www.GNN.com and the GNN Radio Network, all owned by Global News Network. "Mona, tell us how it's going down there. How are you and your crew?"

"As well as can be expected, Derek. You never know what's going to happen from one moment to the next, and that's a little unnerving. But it's all part of the job, and we knew what we were getting into when we came down here."

"Are you getting enough to eat?"

"No complaints, and hey: who among us couldn't stand to lose a few pounds, right?"

Van Dinman laughed uproariously. "Heckuva way to go about it, though!"

Bertram idly waved a hand. "You play it as it comes."

"Absolutely! Now, we understand your assistant came home after you were captured by the mercenaries. Case of nerves, there?"

"Absolutely not, Derek. The man was solid as a rock. It was just our feeling that there was no sense subjecting more people to the incredible risk and hardship of being here than was absolutely necessary, so we cut it back to just me, my cameraman and one other."

"Incredibly decent and caring of you, Mona. You truly are a star in this business."

"No big deal."

"It most certainly is. And, of course, your incredibly insightful and detailed reporting has been a source of inspiration to all of us, and to all Americans."

"Thanks, Derek. Very kind of you to say so."

"Absolutely! Well, we're awfully proud of you, Mona. And, of course, your crew."

"Thank you. Just doing our jobs."

"And there you have it from an undisclosed location in Brazil," van Dinman said, swiveling back toward the cameras, "the very latest on that unbelievable situation. For comment we turn to MS-GNN's very own Bob Simpson. Bob? What did you think of that report?"

Bob Simpson was an extraordinary individual, and had to be, as he was qualified to declaim on a remarkably wide range of subjects, including but not limited to foreign policy, health care, election campaigning, the federal deficit, media responsibility, border conflicts, congressional ethics, the war on drugs, the war on poverty, the war on terrorism, teenage crime, white collar crime, inner-city crime, racial strife, state politics, Internet legislation, music piracy, abortion rights, consumer rights, immigrant rights, voter registration, constitutional law, infrastructure funding and environmental protection. "It was quite remarkable, Derek, and quite gratifying to see the lengths to which dedicated journalists will go to bring us stories of critical importance."

"Absolutely!" van Dinman agreed. "And there you have it on the situation in South America, as only MS-GNN can bring it to you. Coming up at nine o'clock, Danny Prince's exclusive interview with Mona Bertram, live, from an undisclosed location somewhere in South America. A full hour on the bravery, dedication and unprecedented expertise of America's premier on-the-air news personality."

As van Dinman stacked the papers in front of him and jogged them into order, the red light winked out on the main camera and the control room engineer swiped a finger across his throat.

"So who's winning?" a cameraman asked.

Van Dinman dropped the sheets of paper, all of which were blank, back onto the desk as he stood up. "Who's winning what?"

"The war. The one down in South America."

Van Dinman unwound the earpiece around his head and unclipped the microphone cord from his jacket collar. "Beats the shit out of me."

"How many more exclusives?" Ernie Bonnelli ask Mona Bertram.

She consulted her handwritten schedule. "Seven, then an hour with Danny. Why?"

Bonnelli looked at a meter on his belt. "Battery's winding down. I'll go grab a spare at the next break."

Something stirred at the far end of the camp: excited shouts, men running, lights coming on in upper windows. "What's up?" Bertram asked.

"No idea. Better go find out."

Bertram looked at her watch. "No. We got less than two minutes. Jason!"

Merriweather, who'd been writing in his journal nearby, looked up. "What?"

"Think you could find out what's going on over there?"

Merriweather looked toward where Bertram was pointing, then stood up. "Sure," he said, and walked off.

He came loping back a minute later. "Hey, you won't believe—"

Bonnelli held up a hand, keeping his eye on his viewfinder, and Merriweather stopped.

"As well as can be expected, Oprah," Bertram was saying to the camera as she wiped a stray hair from her weary face. "You never know what's going to happen from one moment to the next, and that's a little unnerving. But it's all part of the job, and we knew what we were getting into when we came down here."

Merriweather stamped impatiently from one foot to the other until the exclusive was over, then said, "Men are coming back. From the front. Pablo just took a patrol to escort them in. Caminetti's going with them, on crutches."

"How many?" Bonnelli asked.

"Not sure. Someone said about three or four hundred. Come on, let's go get em!"

"How far away are they?"

"About three miles."

Bertram did a quick mental calculation. "No hurry. We'll catch them on the way in."

"But—"

"She's got Danny Prince," Bonnelli answered for her. "For the full hour. And two, and one!" he said to Bertram.

"As well as can be expected, Danny," Bertram was saying to the camera as she wiped a stray hair from her weary face. "You never know what's going to happen from one moment to the next, and that's a little unnerving. But it's all part of the job, and we knew what we were getting into when we came down here."

CHAPTER 38

The first they knew they were near the returning troops was from the singing drifting up from the valley below their position. It was a strange melody, in a strange tongue, but while clearly a song of triumph, a minor key element of a dirge lay beneath it. Merriweather jotted into his note pad: *They have the unmistakable look of the reflective warrior caught between the delirious exhilaration of leaving the front behind and the gnawing concern for those still fighting.*

"I make it about two hundred and fifty men, minimum," said Lawrence, the light-skinned soldier, when he'd seen the entire column.

"Yeah." Merriweather walked to where Pablo was standing, nearly at attention. He'd just finished a conversation on a two-way radio. "Say Pablo: How many went altogether?"

It took Pablo a moment to realize he'd been asked a question, and another to play back in his mind what it was. "Over a thousand."

"Huh." Merriweather looked back down at the weary men still some minutes from where they were watching. "So there's maybe eight hundred still there. Not counting, um, you know . . . the ones who—"

"There is no one there," Pablo said.

"No one there? I don't . . . then who's—?"

"The fighting is over," Pablo said with finality.

"Over! It's over?"

"Yes."

Merriweather filled Bonnelli and Bertram in when they finally arrived, and the three of them stood staring at the slowly creeping column until Merriweather asked, "So what happens now, Pablo? Do these men return to their countries? Do they run for their lives? Does Barranca go into hiding?"

Pablo turned slowly toward him. "None of these things will be necessary."

"And that's because . . . ?"

"That's because Barranca was victorious."

Pedro, whom they'd not noticed standing some yards away, framed his mouth with his hands and called down as loudly as he could in Portuguese, "*Guerreiros! Heróis! Homens da honra!*" Warriors! Heroes! Men of honor!

The column, as one organism with three hundred pairs of eyes, looked upward toward the sound.

"*He terminado!*" someone yelled back.

"*Se acabó!*" called another.

"It is finished," Pablo translated, nearly in tears as the fatigued fighters below were suddenly reanimated, waving their hats, holding up their rifles, dancing spontaneous tarantellas.

Merriweather opened his notepad and made a few changes. *They have the unmistakable look of the reflective warrior caught between the delirious exhilaration of victory and the fathomless sadness at its cost.* "Are you telling me," he asked Pablo, "that this bunch of field workers with picks and shovels defeated a well-equipped, highly paid army?"

"This is how it is with mercenaries," Pablo replied, "as Barranca well knew. They will risk their lives for the money, but only up to a point. When the likelihood of death crosses a certain threshold, the money no longer sufficiently motivates." He waved a hand at the re-vivified snake of soldiers below. "The ones willing to die are not only usually the victors—" He turned to face Merriweather "—they are also usually on the right side of the fight. As witness your own revolution."

"Hey!"

The GNN crew turned at the sound of Eddie's voice. He was standing some thirty yards away, his good arm draped over a crutch, calling them over. Reluctantly, they left the view of the road to join him.

"Follow me," Eddie said when they'd reached him.

"Eddie, we want to—"

"Do what I tell you," Eddie ordered. "And try to look a little nonchalant, like it's no big deal, us just taking a walk for a better view."

He led them along a little-used path that was taking them to the rear of the column below. After a three-minute walk, Eddie working hard to grapple with the thick underbrush, they came to a small clearing. He stopped before entering the opening in the thickets and urged the CNN crew forward to do so alone. They did, and soon had a clear view of the road below.

Just coming into view were the first of what would emerge as some two dozen mud-caked, open flatbed trucks. On each one squatted four one-hundred-gallon tanks, each festooned with warning labels in five languages and unmistakable symbology: skull and crossbones, large exclamation points, red circles with lines drawn through the middles over pictures of human beings, farm animals and pets. "What the hell are those?"

"Fertilizer," Pablo answered from behind, causing them to nearly stumble in their surprise. He turned toward the jungle behind them and barked, *"Elimínelos! Inmediatamente!"*

Seconds later a squad of soldiers appeared and began hustling Merriweather, Bonnelli and Bertram away from the scene. It was clear that protest would be useless, and the three reporters didn't bother trying.

"So Barranca has chemical weapons," Bonnelli said excitedly when they got back to the compound.

"At least a hundred tanks that I could count," Merriweather said. "Could be bio, too."

"This is some twist," Bonnelli mused. "Wonder how President Eastwood would handle it if he knew that the good guys had that shit now!"

"What do you mean, if?" Bertram yipped. "He'll know it when I report it!"

The other two whirled on her as though she'd just grown another head, each vying to be the first to ask her if she'd completely lost her mind. "You're not reporting on shit!" Merriweather concluded for them both.

"Why not!"

"Because they don't want us to," Bonnelli said, pointing to Barranca's men, "and if we do, and they toss us out of here, we're out of a story."

"We don't do anything to piss em off," Merriweather warned her.

"But they have weapons of mass—"

"I don't give a rat's ass if they sacrifice children to volcanoes, Mona," Bonnelli admonished her sternly.

"You don't shit where you eat," Merriweather said. "Not if you want to be in the news business."

"Freedom fighter Manuel Villa Lobos de Barranca's extraordinary, almost unbelievable, truly mythical victory over the mercenaries whose very existence is still being denied by the same officials who deny importing them in the first place, and witnessed firsthand by this GNN reporter, has, as many such stories do, a bitter aftermath."

The picture dissolved from Mona Bertram's moronic smile to the downcast, anxiety-ridden faces of yet another pack of disheveled families arriving on foot, all their worldly belongings on their backs or on hand-drawn carts in hastily packed duffels, straw totes, pillowcases, battered cardboard suitcases and coffee sacks. "These are the newly displaced," Bertram said in voice-over, "families made homeless by the very victory they cheered only yesterday."

The camera zoomed in shakily on one woman's face, but she averted her astonishing violet eyes before her face could appear in full. Bertram had begged her to cooperate, as had Ernie Bonnelli, who carried a digital still camera with him at all times, knowing that the difference between a boring or uselessly blurred image and a Pulitzer could be a matter of half a second, but the shy, fearful woman had adamantly demurred.

"I saw this same family only days ago in the dense jungle," Bertram's voice-over continued, "when they were fleeing the scene of intense fighting and rumored chemical or biological weapons. Now they are on the move again, this time to the protective custody of Manuel Barranca because, like many thousands of others . . ."

The poignant footage of the shuffling families came to a halt, freezing on the face of an eight-year-old on which was painted a mixture of uncertainty, terror and a prescient anticipation that worse was yet to come.

The freeze-frame dissolved back to Bertram, still incapable of wiping away the incessant smile that splattered her face whenever she was on camera, as though her very presence before millions of adoring fans was the real story, surpassing in immediate importance whatever tragedy she might happen to be commenting upon at the time.

" . . . these are now people without a country. Their homelands don't want them back, suspecting them of colluding with Barranca against the mercenaries who supposedly don't exist, and they have no wish to emigrate, because they are coffee workers to the bone and know no other life. Who will replace these workers and restart the machinery of the great growing conglomerates is anybody's guess, and the fear among those who know the industry is that this vicious cycle of resentment and exile might decimate entire local economies."

Shift to a long shot of Barranca surrounded by several dozen men. "Manuel Barranca has assured GNN that he has plans to see to the needs, both short and long term, of all of the newly dispossessed. However, in his typical enigmatic style, and probably in order not to tip his hand prematurely, he has declined to discuss with us his plans in detail."

A small girl ran up to the group of men, broke through and jumped into Barranca's arms. He lifted her high into the air and smiled brightly as she giggled.

"Barranca also hasn't said whether he knows the location of chemical or biological weapons that might have been left behind by the mercenaries, but he has assured GNN in no uncertain terms that, should such weapons be discovered, he will personally take possession of them and see to their destruction."

Dissolve back to Bertram. "Reporting live from somewhere in Brazil, this is Mona Bertram." She turned her head to the side slightly and winked at the camera, ending up with a sly, come-hither grin.

"We can still make you a hero," Jason Merriweather said to Eddie Caminetti later that afternoon.

"A hero?" Eddie was throwing another shirt into his duffel with his one good arm but stopped. "For what . . . getting myself captured and having to be rescued?"

Merriweather, sitting by a wooden-slatted window on the second floor of a barracks building, laughed. "Are you kidding me,

Caminetti? Screwing up and getting rescued? Hell, that's an automatic *Newsweek* cover."

"Well, it's bullshit."

"Doesn't matter, pal. When there are no real heroes around, we'll make one out of anything. Dogs that bark when there's a fire? Little kids who dial 911, cops who do their jobs, fighter pilots who lose their planes and save their own lives? Evening news, an interview with Danny Prince and a presidential commendation, guaranteed."

Eddie dropped the shirt into the duffel and hobbled to the bathroom with his shaving kit. "All I want is to get the hell out of here."

"You're news, Eddie."

It had an ominous, slightly threatening ring. Eddie stepped out of the bathroom so he could see Merriweather. "And we had a deal, Jason."

"Yeah...but the fact is, without you we wouldn't have had a story."

"Now that you mention it, I didn't hear giggle-puss out there report those hundred vats of nasty shit moving along the road."

Merriweather shifted uncomfortably. "We saw no proof they were chemical weapons."

"What else would you do to get proof . . . crack one open and take a deep whiff? There was no proof that there were any mercenaries, either, but that didn't stop you from reporting it."

Merriweather pointed to an open pack of cigarettes on a table and raised his eyebrows, taking one when Eddie nodded his permission. "We had enough evidence to make a reasonable inference."

"Good." Eddie stepped back into the bathroom. "Then as far as I'm concerned you can take all the credit for some first-class investigative reporting and leave me the hell out of it."

He heard the sound of a match being struck and smoke being inhaled and stepped gingerly out of the bathroom holding the shaving kit. "You'll be doing me a favor, Jason. If the wrong people find out about me, I'm a dead man."

"Aren't you being a little dramatic?"

"Maybe."

"Eddie—"

"Jason, if you know anything about me, you know I don't make idle threats."

"I'll give you that."

"So trust me when I tell you that if this leaks, by the time I'm through GNN won't be able to get a confidential source to disclose where to buy a good ham sandwich."

Merriweather paled slightly. He didn't know Eddie all that well personally, but everything he'd heard from his buddies in the sports department led him to believe that this was not someone to trifle with. "Can I ask you one thing?"

"You can ask."

"What were you really doing down here in the first place? And don't bullshit me, okay?"

"Okay." Eddie, breathing heavily from the exertion of trying to pack with a broken arm, sprained ankle and an assortment of bruises, sat down opposite Merriweather. "I came down to play some golf with Barranca."

"Why?"

"Because he invited me to. For money."

"It doesn't strike you as unusual that you get invited down to play golf with a revolutionary who happens to be in the middle of a revolution?"

Eddie smiled and took a cigarette for himself. "Jason, I'll go anywhere, anytime, under almost any conditions to play golf if there's enough money involved."

"And there was enough money involved here?"

Eddie held out his hand and Merriweather dropped the book of matches into it. "Oh, yeah."

Merriweather grunted, and from the sound of it Eddie knew the veteran reporter would keep his word. "Why the hurry to go back?"

Eddie lit his cigarette. "Well, Jason, I'll tell you," he said through a blue cloud of exhaled smoke. "The president himself called me on the sat phone and said to me, he said, 'Eddie,' he said. 'Get your ass on back here. Your country needs you.' And by golly, when the president speaks, this citizen obeys."

"Very funny," Merriweather said grumpily as Eddie returned to the bathroom. He listened to the scraping of a razor for a few seconds, then said, "But tell me another thing, if you can."

"If I can."

The scraping continued. "Did Barranca win this war because he somehow managed to get those vats away from the mercenaries?" The scraping stopped. "And if that's the case," Merriweather went on, "are there mass graves out there somewhere because some of that stuff was used before it was captured?"

Silence, and then the sound of the razor on Eddie's face resumed, followed by the gurgle of water and then the squeak of a tap being closed. Eddie emerged from the bathroom one-handedly wiping his face with a towel, his shaving kit tucked under his arm. "I have no way to know any of that, Jason."

"I thought so."

"But one thing I can tell you with absolute certainty."

Merriweather, anxious to get something—anything—out of Eddie, stayed quiet, didn't push, but urged with his eyes.

"Barranca will never use anything in those vats," Eddie said.

"How can you be so sure?"

Eddie dropped his shaving kit into the duffel. "Because every one of them was emptied into the ground earlier today. And yes, I saw it with my own eyes."

Merriweather pursed his lips, then stood up. "Want to fly back with us?"

"No, thanks. Got my own ride."

"When?"

"Tomorrow."

"Tomorrow? Thought you wanted to get out of here as soon as possible."

Eddie held the duffel steady with his knee as he used his good hand to zip it up. "Off the record?"

"Okay."

Eddie got the zipper pulled shut, then lifted the bag and set it down near the door. "Promised the president I'd get Barranca to turn the coffee supply back on. Gonna take me at least the rest of the day."

Merriweather, knowing when he was licked, laugh good-naturedly. "You knock me out, Caminetti. You really do."

CHAPTER 39

AEROPUERTO DE ATAHUALPA—HUAMANQUIQUIA, PERU

"**A**eropuerto" **was a tad hyperbolic,** like calling a mud hut Grand Central Station. The runway looked like it might once have been the main street of a village whose houses and shops hadn't so much been torn down as simply allowed to erode to ground level over time. The control tower consisted of a kiosk the size of a Porta-Potty out of which a toothless old man sold last week's newspapers, magazines too old for a dentist's office and cigarettes only smokable because the contents had been deemed unfit for use as fertilizer. When the old man heard the sound of an approaching airplane, he "hurried" out to the runway with a broom to shoo away any wild pigs, llamas, capybaras, rare Andean night monkeys, pampas cats or sloths that might have chosen the warm asphalt on which to siesta. At least that was his purported job description, but by the time he heard an approaching plane it was probably already four feet from touchdown, and second of all, after once nearly losing a leg to an anaconda he mistook for a tree branch, he much preferred to let the noise of a landing aircraft dispatch as much of the indigenous fauna as possible.

Eddie decided that the kiosk in fact *was* an old Porta-Potty, and that it would be better to stretch out his remaining three cigarettes rather than purchase a pack from a "bin" he recognized as originally having been the urinal. Using his very limited Spanish, he tried to engage the old man in conversation but got nowhere, not realizing that the ancient dispenser of even more ancient tobacco was one of about seventy people left in the entire country who spoke only Guarani, a language thought by ethnographers to be long extinct. So as not to be unfriendly, though, he accepted a cup of freshly brewed coffee from the old man, and was pleased to discover that it was much like Barranca's private stock. It reminded him of the first time he'd had a sip of real scotch, at the private bar of the St. Andrews golf course clubhouse, and realized that he'd been drinking swill all his life without realizing it. He'd since made sure that his private island golf resort stocked nothing but brands like the smoky Lagavulin, and even named the place Swithen Bairn, after a single malt privately produced by a family in Achnahanat, Scotland.

The old man cackled in glee as Eddie's eyes grew heavy-lidded with pleasure and he took another sip. "Amehca, ah? You Amehca, ah?" Eddie nodded, and the old man's eyes crinkled up even more. "Café shit, ah? McDonna, Bogga King, ah? *Shit!*" He pointed to Eddie's cup. "Ah? Ah?"

Eddie nodded again, and smacked his lips appreciatively. "Not too bad."

"Fuckin'-A right, bubba," the old man said, and went back to his 1937 issue of *Popular Science,* clucking his skepticism over a car that could supposedly shift gears by itself.

Eddie returned, limping painfully, to the pecan tree that served as the *aeropuerto's* main terminal. The coffee was so good he hoped the plane would be late, but a few minutes later he heard the unmistakable sound of . . . propellers?

A DC-3 whose manufacture likely preceded that of Amelia Earhart's Lockheed Vega soon appeared over the hills to the east. It looked like it was coming in for a landing but paused in its descent about fifteen feet above ground level and roared down the runway. Dozens of lounging animals scattered before the sonic onslaught. Eddie had just enough time to realize that the plane's flyover was a clearing action before his attention was captured by some kind of very large cat heading his way from the opposite end of the runway. He looked toward the kiosk, the only structure in the vicinity, just in time to see the proprietor frantically slamming shutters into place, then considered trying to scramble up the tree when he remembered he had only one good arm and one good foot. He also realized that the cat was probably hoping he'd do just that. The coffee was still hot; maybe he could toss it into the charging animal's face at the last minute?

Right. As the DC-3 rose lazily into the sky and banked sharply, Eddie tossed the cup and his light wooden cane away and unzipped the cover of his traveling golf bag. He briefly considered a driver but changed his mind, figuring that if he had only one shot, he needed a better combination of heft and control and so he selected a five-iron instead. In the thirty or so seconds he had left until the lithe jaguar reached him, he took a few one-handed practice swings and gave some thought to which angle of approach would be best.

Planting his feet firmly and twisting slightly on the ball of his good foot in order to gain better purchase on the loose soil, Eddie steadied himself, watched the cat, and tried to figure the best time to start his swing, when a loud c-r-a-a-a-c-k sounded in the sky. A large puff of dust popped up right in the jaguar's path, about ten feet ahead of it, causing the fearsome creature to veer suddenly. Eddie looked up at the DC-3 and saw that its rear door was open. Someone on board had taken a shot at his attacker, and missed.

By that time the cat had slewed back around and was headed his way again. Another shot rang out and another puff of dirt arose, again about ten feet in front of the animal. This time the cat angled away and kept on going, and as the DC-3 made a perfect three-point landing Eddie realized that the shooter hadn't missed at all, but had put his rounds precisely where he'd wanted them.

Eddie still had the five-iron in his hand when the plane, kicking up a huge cloud of dust and small stones, swung around on its tail wheel and came to a stop about thirty yards away. The sound of the propellers dropped in pitch as the pilot feathered them and shut the engines down. Something about the way the props slowed down didn't seem quite right to Eddie but he couldn't put his finger on what. The uniform in the doorway handed the sniper rifle to someone inside, then jumped down onto the ground.

"Your stance is too wide, Caminetti. You'd be lucky to clip that cat on the ear and only lose a foot."

"I'll be damned," Eddie muttered, as he recognized the same Marine officer who'd picked him up by helicopter at the Wolf Creek golf course a lifetime ago. "Munson! You fly all the way down here just to win your crummy hundred bucks back?"

Colonel Jerome Munson returned the smile and held out his hand as he walked up. After shaking, he turned and held his other hand out toward the DC-3. "Your limo awaits, sir."

Eddie took a good look at the aircraft for the first time. It was a mess. Paint was peeling from the fuselage where it wasn't pitted or faded, light brown sprays of oil streaked the engine cowlings and leading edges of the wings, one section of the windshield was crazed with cracks and he swore he could spot several missing rivets. "You gotta be shitting me."

"Come on." Munson took the iron out of Eddie's hand, put it back in the bag and zipped up the cover. Pointedly picking up the lighter carry-on and leaving the golf bag, he started for the plane. "It's not so bad inside."

Eddie sighed and began to follow, then stopped. "Hey, hang on a second." Before Munson could mount a protest, he was limping back to the kiosk.

The proprietor was opening the last of the shutters when Eddie walked up and said, "Hi there. Thanks for protecting me from that goddamned Bengal tiger, you little prick."

The man grinned his toothless grin and pointed to his brewing machine. "Ah?" Eddie held up two fingers and waited while the coffee was prepared, then dropped a ten on the counter, smiled as he said "Go fuck yourself," and carried them away. At the plane he handed one to Munson.

"We got coffee on board, Eddie. Don't have to buy from the locals."

"Taste it."

Munson did. "Holy shit."

Eddie noticed that someone had picked up and stowed his golf bag. "I'm not really up for climbing into this crate, I gotta tell you. Where'd you find it, anyway . . . flea market in Chuchurras?"

"Aucayacu. Trust me, you're gonna love it. Besides, if you don't get in, I got orders to hog-tie you and throw you in." Munson again held out a hand toward the rickety air-stairs.

Eddie shambled up the first three steps as best he could and stuck his head inside the plane. "What the hell—?"

What looked from the outside like a bucket of spare parts held together mostly by hope, inside looked like anything but. A dozen plush and fully reclinable seats lined one side of the cabin; the other side was covered in a muted, green baize fabric, at least where a dazzling array of futuristic consoles loaded with blinking lights and blue-green readouts allowed the space. Rich wooden paneling throughout complemented the patterned carpet, the whole effect mimicking that of an elegant drawing room from some snooty British men's club.

Eddie felt a polite shove from behind and stumbled up into the cabin, which is when he noticed that two of the airborne Barcaloungers were occupied.

"Morning, Mr. Caminetti," said Secretary of State William Patterson.

"Coffee?" offered Director of Central Intelligence Baines Gordon Wainwright.

"Brought my own," said Eddie. "What the hell is this thing?"

Patterson, unable to contain himself, said, "So what happened?"

"Huh?"

"With Barranca."

Eddie stared at him for a second, then said, "Gee, Eddie . . . awfully sorry about your arm, and that golf match you never got to play."

As Patterson's jaw hung open, Wainwright said, "Sorry about your arm, Eddie. You look awful. Have a seat." He pointed to one close to himself and the Secretary of State. "We're about to take off."

"What the hell do you mean, a golf match!" Patterson roared.

"Easy, Bill," Wainwright said soothingly.

"Easy, my ass!" Then, to Eddie. "Listen, do you think we flew Air Force goddamned One down here just to have you blow us off like we were—"

"Air Force One?" Eddie looked around the plane. "What the hell are you talking about? I been on Air Force One and this piece'a—"

"That's what it is," Munson answered from the rear as the door closed with a thud. "Least when the president is on it. Go on, sit down."

Eddie did as instructed, placing his coffee in one of three cup holders attached to his seat. "I don't get it."

Munson helped Eddie on with his seat belt, then took his own seat, punched a button on his armrest, and less than three seconds later a high-pitched whine started up from somewhere. Eddie looked outside and saw the starboard propeller beginning to turn slowly. Something about it still didn't look right . . . "Say, isn't this a DC-3?"

"Sure is," Munson said. "Best damned all-around airplane ever built."

Eddie pointed toward the prop, which was smoothly picking up speed. "But that's not—"

"Few slight modifications. Like taking off the piston engines and slapping on a couple of Pratt & Whitney turbines. Stuff like that."

Munson and Wainwright enjoyed Eddie's confusion for a few more seconds—Patterson was too angry to be amused—then Wainwright said, "It really is the president's plane, Eddie. One of six like it, that look like aging pieces of shit from the outside but are rock-solid reliable and capable."

"But why?"

"Why?" Wainwright took a sip of whatever he was drinking, which looked to Eddie like a double scotch, neat. "Because a 450-ton Boeing 747 gussied up in bright blue and white paint with the presidential seal the size of a landing pad on its exposed belly is a flying target a brain-damaged orangutan with a slingshot couldn't miss if he was blindfolded, that's why."

"If there was a real crisis underway," Munson added, "instead of a junket to go shopping in Paris or drink schnapps in Berlin, who do you figure would waste a missile on this hunk'a junk?"

"I'll be damned," Eddie breathed, as the common sense of it sank in.

Wainwright leaned forward and tapped Eddie's knee. "And now you've been entrusted with one of the nation's most closely guarded secrets."

"Why?"

"Why?" Wainwright blinked. "What do you mean, why?"

"I mean, why are you telling me this?"

The two higher-ups looked at each other, then back at Eddie. "It's a mark of how much the president trusts you, Eddie," Patterson said. "Now, what the hell did you discuss with Barranca!"

"I told you, I don't know what you're talking about." Eddie picked up his coffee cup. "And if you got any more big secrets you wanna tell me, do the country a favor and keep em to yourself, okay?"

"Excuse me? Say again?" the two said simultaneously as Eddie took a sip.

"I didn't ask to be let in on this. And why do I care if the president trusts me or not?"

Patterson rose half out of his seat. "Listen, you low-life piece'a freakin—"

"Siddown, Bill," Wainwright said.

"Whaddaya mean, sit down! Guy tells me to have a nice big cup of Shut The Fuck Up and I'm supposed to—"

"And buckle your seat belt."

A minor jolt of the plane convinced Patterson to get back in his seat, but he wasn't through with Eddie. "Are you going to sit there and bullshit us for the whole flight?" he demanded, back in his seat but still unbuckled.

"I don't know what you're talking about," Eddie insisted. "I went down to play golf and turned into a goddamned POW instead. End of story."

Despite Patterson's towering rage, Wainwright couldn't help but smile. "You're good, Eddie. Could use a man like you in the Company."

"What company is that? You a CEO or something?"

Wainwright's smile faltered. "I'm the director of central intelligence. Head of the CIA."

"Oh. I thought maybe you were like, head of Sears & Roebuck or something."

A snort started up somewhere in Munson's throat, but was quickly cut short by a glance from Patterson.

The remainder of the flight was distinctly unpleasant, but Eddie, sleeping soundly through most of it, didn't really notice. When he transferred to the Gap Jeans presidential helicopter at Andrews Air Force Base, Patterson didn't even shake his hand to say goodbye.

CHAPTER 40

ot too bad."

"What?"

"Not too bad."

"What?"

"I—Mr. President, can we go inside? I'm freezing my—"

"What? Oh. Yeah, yeah, sure. Sorry. Come on in. Jeez, you look like shit."

Eddie stamped his good foot to shake off some loose snow and stepped inside the main lodge that was reserved for the president's exclusive use. He looked around and, as expected, there was no one else present. He shrugged off his coat and hung it up on a peg near the door, but kept his cane and a paper bag, which he handed to Eastwood. "Brought you something. Got anything to drink around here?"

Eastwood accepted the bag and set it aside on a table. "What do you mean by 'not too bad'? Is he going to play ball? Do we get the coffee back?"

"Well . . . yes and no. Can I get a—"

"What do you mean, yes and no!"

"Gonna take a little explaining. Now can I f'chrissakes get a beer or somethin?"

Eastwood nodded glumly and led Eddie into the main room, a nearly three-story open space with a massive stone fireplace at one end in which a fire crackled invitingly. The president pointed him toward one of several hide-covered couches facing the mantel. "Got some hot mulled wine, if you want."

"Just a beer, thanks."

Eddie sat down, rested his cane on the floor and held his hand out toward the fire, enjoying the warmth that instantly began wrapping itself around his fingers. "How come they make you walk all the way from the landing pad. Don't you have golf carts or something?" Eddie had been acutely embarrassed by all the respectful coming-to-attention and snappy salutes he'd gotten from Marine guards as he limped along the path with three Secret Service agents, one arm in a cast and sling, one hand on his cane, a bandage wrapped around his head. He half-expected a fife-and-drum corps to appear from somewhere and break out in a medley of Civil War ditties.

"Security thing," Eastwood said as he came back from the next room carrying two beers but no glasses. "Slows things down between the vehicles and the main house, or something like that." He sat down and handed over one of the beers. "What the hell happened, Eddie?"

Eddie accepted the beer, took a long swig, then set it down on the wide arm of the couch and resumed warming his hand. "Never got to play," he said, nodding toward his bad arm. "But shit happens, knowmsayin?"

"Eddie," Eastwood said, trying not to lose his patience, "this may come as a big surprise, but I don't give a hoot about your golf match."

"Sure. Wasn't your dough on the line."

"Did you get us a deal or not?"

"Yeah, I got us a deal. Just don't know if you're gonna go for it, is all."

"That good, huh?" Eastwood sat down slowly. "I keep forgetting that Barranca's not just a schoolyard bully waving his father's gun around." He looked away, pensive and distracted. "Is this the part in my memoirs where I explain how western civilization came to a screeching halt?"

"Doesn't have to be, Mr. President. I said I didn't know if *you* were going to go for it. Me, personally?" Eddie tilted his beer and regarded it with interest. "I'd take it in a heartbeat. It's not as bad as it's gonna sound when you first hear it."

Eastwood seemed to leap at the small glimmer of hope and turned his attention back to Eddie. "It isn't?"

"Nah." Eddie took another hit and set the bottle down. "Barranca's really not a bad guy. Kind of liked him, matter'a fact. He's a reasonable man."

"Reasonable, yeah." Eastwood folded his arms. "So what am I looking at?"

Eddie, who had to admit to himself that he'd been needling the president a little, saw no reason to keep it up, especially since there was important business to be transacted. "Pretty simple, really. What he wants is recognition, and for things to be set up so that his people are well treated from here on out."

"His people? Who are his people?"

"The ones that work the coffee: people who plant the stuff, tend it, pick it, process it . . . those are his people."

"I meant, which country?"

"Doesn't matter."

"Of course it matters!" Eastwood's voice lost its incipient timidity as he sought to gain control of the conversation. "You got any idea how complex and touchy that can be, interfering in the internal affairs of a sovereign? We don't phone up Brazil or Colombia or Peru and tell them how to handle their own citizens!"

"Who said anything about their own citizens?"

Eastwood snickered. "So where are these guys . . . the middle of the ocean?"

"No. They're in Brazil, Colombia, Peru . . . but they're not citizens."

Eastwood was beginning to get tired of Eddie's annoyingly enigmatic behavior, and let his frustration show. "I think we need to stop playing games. You and I both know that the United States is not about to get pushed around by some egotistical thug, even if GNN declared him the greatest freedom fighter since George Washington. We'll play his game up to a point, then we lay down the law and go in with guns blazing. The nations of the world will crap all over us for a while but we're the ones who always end up on top. So tell me what games this pissant wants us to play and I'll decide if we're willing to do it."

And thus was it clearly established where the real power lay. As smart and canny as Eddie might have been, he was also smart enough not to take on the commander-in-chief. Unless he was sure he could win. "Like I said, what he wants is recognition. Not for himself—trust me, he doesn't give a damn how he looks—but for the new country."

"What new country?"

"The United Farms of South America."

"Which is where, exactly?"

"Well —" Eddie hesitated, then drew in a deep breath and let it out as he answered "—pretty much everywhere, really."

"I told you, Eddie: Don't play—"

"It's a virtual country, Mr. President. A fluid nation, made up of all the coffee workers of half a dozen conventional countries who choose to be part of it, regardless of where they live or work."

"Very romantic." Eastwood closed his eyes and heaved a sigh, which was not lost on Eddie. "Really, I mean it. Some high school sophomore could get another petal on his good citizenship clover for coming up with that one for the World Peace bake sale."

"Mr. President—"

Eastwood opened his eyes and jumped up off his seat. "Bill Patterson was right, goddamnit!"

Eddie respectfully rose as well. "Right about what?"

Eastwood waved him back down. "Sending amateurs to do a professional's job."

"A professional would have gotten you into a shooting war, sir, except you wouldn't be able to define the enemy, wouldn't be able to find him even if you could, and the only thing you'd be shooting is yourself in the foot."

"Right." Eastwood headed for the doorway to the bedroom area. "The agent at the front door will show you out, Caminetti."

"What are you going to do, Mr. President?"

"Don't worry about it," Eastwood answered without stopping. "We'll handle it."

"Handle it how?"

"I said, don't worry about it."

"Mr. President!" Eddie called sharply.

Eastwood stopped, hesitated, then turned. "What?"

"If you're going to handle it the way I think you're going to handle it, you better have that agent out there kill me right here and now." Eastwood evinced no shock or surprise at all at that, which sent a small tremor of apprehension up Eddie's spine.

"And why do you think I should do that?"

Eddie fought down the bile rising in his throat; there was no turning back now anyway. "Because my first stop when I leave here is going to be *The New York Times*."

"Is that a matter of fact?" A kind of preternatural calm seemed to descend on the president. He was in his element now, and knew that Eddie was out of his. "And you expect them to believe you?"

"Well, once I get the lawsuit going, I'll subpoena the secretary of state, the CIA director, your chief of staff . . . and you."

Now Eastwood was grinning broadly, and there was nothing fake about it. "Good one, Eddie. You've got a lot of imagination. Except that you can't charge a sitting president with a supposed crime he committed while in office. I've got immunity, and there's not a damned thing—"

"Who said anything about charging you with a crime?"

Eastwood's smile dimmed slightly. "You just said—"

"I said a lawsuit, not a criminal complaint."

"A lawsuit."

"You heard me."

"Suing me personally?"

"Yep."

Eastwood now looked like he was on the verge of boredom, and he began inching slowing back toward the doorway. "And what exactly would you be suing me for?"

"Interfering with my right to make a living."

The president laughed out loud. "You kill me, Eddie! You know that? You really kill me!"

Eddie smiled back at him. "Yeah, I even crack myself up."

Eastwood walked off, and, after he disappeared around a corner and Eddie could no longer see him, called back, "How do you figure I interfered with your right to make a living?"

"Pretty simple, really." Eddie waited until he was sure the president had stopped to listen. "You sent me down as a representative of the government to play a round of golf at my own expense with a potential enemy of the state, based on my reputation as a professional golf hustler, of which you're personally familiar, as is the head of the FBI and two or three dozen other highly placed administration officials.

Remember, I have detailed records of every dollar I ever took from all of you guys."

There was no response, so Eddie continued unbidden. "Oh, by the way, I was fully authorized to negotiate on your behalf, represented the same to the adversary, did so in good faith and struck a deal, which you then reneged on, causing irreparable harm to my hard-won reputation and therefore to my ability to continue in my profession."

Eastwood slowly reappeared in the doorway. Obviously, Eddie wasn't just making this up off the top of his head, but had given it a great deal of thought. "You're full of shit."

"Never denied that, sir. But it doesn't mean I can't file a civil lawsuit against you, and you've got no immunity from that."

"Actually I do, as I was in office at the time. It'll never stick."

"I didn't mean immunity from the suit. I meant immunity from getting sued."

"The difference being . . . ?"

"Nobody can stop me from filing a suit. If you want it thrown out, you'll have to fight it. And that's not going to happen quietly."

"Is that so."

"That's what they tell me."

"Who?"

"My lawyers. We'll let it be known that, not only did you bet the economy on an amateur diplomat, but, even worse, you welshed when it didn't turn out the way you wanted. I've got character witnesses who'll testify that I'm the most honest person they ever bet a buck with, I'll subpoena everyone who saw me on the Blockbuster with you, I'll get the G.E. residence phone logs and if I can't, the special prosecutor will."

"What special prosecutor!"

"The one that'll get appointed ten minutes after my suit hits the papers."

Eastwood took several menacing steps forward, his fists clenched into tight balls. "You blackmailing me, Caminetti?"

"Of course not, Mr. President!" Eddie answered indignantly, then waited until Eastwood backed off slightly. "It's extortion, not blackmail. You shoulda paid more attention in law school."

Eddie was betting his life—perhaps literally—on years of experience reading people, but wasn't quite sure what to make of Eastwood, who, unable to speak, stood rooted to the spot, his breath coming in short, labored gasps that he struggled to suppress.

If there's one thing Eddie understood about negotiating—and this was definitely a negotiation—it was that if the other guy thinks you won, you've lost. Having already backed the president into a corner because there was no other way to get him to listen, Eddie had a ways to go to bring him back. "If you'll just give me a chance to explain, Mr. President, you'll see that this works out pretty good for both sides."

"And if I don't think it does?"

"Then you can assassinate Barranca, invade South America . . . I don't really give a shit one way or the other since I'll probably be dead."

Eastwood had managed to calm himself somewhat by now. "What *do* you give a shit about, Eddie?"

"Told you already: my reputation. Gave the man my word—and your word, too—and that's the only thing I own worth fighting for."

"What about your country?"

Eddie scratched the back of his head. "You want to keep this up, or you want to talk a little business?"

"America is my business, sir."

Eddie looked up at the ceiling, scanned it thoroughly, turned his attention to the far wall, then back to the president. "You got this place wired, or what? You gotta have it wired, am I right?"

"Why do you say that?"

"Because we know each other too well for you to be throwing this much bullshit at me unless someone's listening in, that's why."

Eastwood iced up, then his shoulders slumped and he shook his head. "Sometimes you really piss me off, Caminetti. You're the only sonofabitch in the western hemisphere who can talk to me like that and still keep his passport. You want another beer?'

"Yeah, but you sit down; I'm buyin."

"A virtual country?" Eastwood called out as Eddie puttered around in the kitchen.

"Yep. To an uneducated slob like me, it sounds like a great idea. With help from you, Barranca sets up a series of treaties with the growers whose asses he just kicked and whom he now forgives. Gonna drive up coffee prices, but compared to what people are paying now, it'll seem a bargain."

"What makes you so sure?"

"Think gasoline after '74. Right now a buck sixty-nine a gallon sounds like a bargain, but twenty years ago the pumps didn't even have a third digit."

"And what do we get out of it?"

"Long-term coffee contracts, no more than twenty percent over current prices."

"Current prices! Are you—"

"I meant, the prices before all the shit hit the fan." Eddie walked back in carrying two beers in one hand and a glass tucked under his arm. "And before you say it, I know it can't look like the U.S. lost out on this deal."

Eastwood accepted a bottle of beer and a glass. "That's nonnegotiable. You know that, all this other bullshit aside."

"Course I know it." Eddie held up his bottle, waited for Eastwood to pour some of his own into his glass, then they clinked and took quick swallows. "Barranca knows it, too. I told you, he's a reasonable man."

"A reasonable man armed with chemical weapons."

"Just a rumor, sir. But look at it this way: If he does have them, then it pays for us to stay on his good side, right? Because we really suck at trying to find these guys when they go off the radar screen."

"Speaking of sucking, how does it look for the U.S. to be sucking up to a potential terrorist?"

"Hell, they're all potential terrorists, Mr. President. But if we help him out, he has no reason to use any of that stuff, and therefore he stays a good guy, see? Besides, what if he gets attacked again? Since you won't offer direct military assistance—"

"We can't. Those countries he operates in are friends, and they still insist they had nothing to do with those mercenaries."

"Whatever. Point is, Barranca needs a means of defense."

"He beat them once without . . ." Eastwood looked up suddenly.

"How *did* he beat them, Eddie?"

"I have no idea. I was out of there by then."

Eastwood stared into the fire. "Suppose you're going to want the Congressional Medal of Freedom for this."

"Hell, no!" Eddie exclaimed forcefully. "All I want is my five million bucks." He steeled himself for what he knew was coming.

"The five million was for getting everything I wanted," Eastwood said. "You didn't."

"It was for getting the country—and you—out of a mess, which I did, even if it didn't happen exactly the way it was supposed to. And we wouldn't want it known that I was your *official* representative, would we?"

"Nobody would believe you."

Eddie pretended to think about that. "There was a great old story about Lyndon Johnson's first congressional campaign . . ."

"I assume this is going to have a point?"

"He told an aide to leak to the press that his opponent had slept with a pig. The aide said, But he didn't do that. And Lyndon said, Of course he didn't do it . . . I just want to watch him deny it." When Eastwood remained quiet Eddie added, "I'm a hero, remember? Never fuck with a hero."

"Some hero," the president said with a grimace. "Used to be, a hero was a guy who rescued someone else. Now it's the guy who got rescued. When the hell did that change?"

"Beats me, but you owe me five million smackers and then I can sink back into my comfortable obscurity." When Eastwood didn't respond, Eddie said, "Let me put it this way: If you don't pay me, you don't take Barranca's deal. It's that simple."

"How do you figure that?"

"Because if you do agree to it, that means you think it's acceptable, and that means I earned my dough."

Eastwood stared at Eddie for a few seconds, then shook himself loose with a shudder. "So how do we do this? And how do we manage how it looks?"

"Start with us coming to the aid of innocent workers who were attacked with universally banned weapons."

"But we have no proof. The talking heads are going to leap on that like—"

"So have the A.G. call em traitors on *Meet the Press*. Besides, you're not using it as an excuse to go to war, you're simply coming to the aid of a man and a cause Americans are already in love with."

Eastwood grew quiet for a few seconds, then said, "Did you know we arrested a suspected mercenary?"

"You're kidding!"

"I'm not. I promised to hunt them all down, in case you haven't heard."

"You did?"

"Had to. GNN's got the whole country up in arms over those imported killers. Seems they're afraid to return to their own countries for fear of war crimes prosecutions, and they're disappearing into the countryside. But we're not having much luck, including with this guy we nabbed in the Amazon."

"Who was he?"

"Claimed to be a biologist studying the rain forest canopy. Hey, you look upset."

"What?"

"This difficult for you to talk about?"

"Upset? Me? Sorry. I'm . . . I'm not . . ." Eddie took a deep breath. "What happened?"

"His supposed professor at Stanford stepped up and vouched for the guy. So we arrested him, too. Now it's starting to look like they're both really innocent."

"So what are you gonna do?"

"Let em go, than maybe invade Kazakhstan. But tell me more about how we play this thing."

Eddie, shaken by the president's news of the arrests, tried to compose himself. "Just call it like it is, Mr. President," he said, discreetly wiping a film of perspiration from his upper lip, "or at least like it's perceived, which is really the same thing: America standing foursquare behind a peaceful capitalist revolution whose only purpose is to better the lives of downtrodden people. Americans everywhere kicking in a few cents more for a cuppa on behalf of one of the great humanitarian efforts of the new millennium. Thomas Madison Eastwood ushering in a brave new world in which countries are no longer defined by physical borders, to the benefit of all humankind."

Eastwood had his glass halfway to his lips, and held it there. "How on earth did you come up with all that crapola?"

"Me? You must be kidding." Eddie reached into his back pants pocket and pulled out a folded square of paper. "Barranca wrote it himself," he said, handing it over to Eastwood. "Said to give it to you."

"He did, huh? Any message along with it?"

"Yeah." Eddie took another slug straight from the bottle and wiped his lips. "He said, Tell him next time send a professional."

Eastwood grinned crookedly. "Okay," he said as he kicked off his shoes and sat down in front of the fire. "Let's figure out how this is going to work . . ."

PART III

THE MIDDLE OF THE STORY

CHAPTER 41

ZAMORA CHINCHIPE, ECUADOR—THE WEEK BEFORE

As Eddie was hustled away from the airplane that had brought him to South America, he strained to see what was happening to the people who'd accompanied him down, but the jeep was bouncing crazily over the rutted field and it was all he could do to hang on. The car skidded to a halt in front of an aging Lockheed Vega twin-engine aircraft, and Eddie had just enough time to notice that its tail number was covered with a burlap coffee sack when two men reached up to drag him off the jeep.

A soldier approached him holding a black bandanna between his outstretched hands.

"No goddamned way," Eddie said as he shoved the man's hands away from his face. He then gritted his teeth and pressed himself back against the airplane in anticipation of getting hit or at least receiving a verbal lashing from the young light-skinned soldier who had tried to blindfold him.

"No need to get pissy about it," the soldier said, in perfect English.

Eddie stared at him.

"I mean, it's not like I'm planning to gouge your eyes out or kill your children, so why get your panties up in a bunch?"

Thoroughly taken aback, Eddie replied, "There's no need to blindfold me."

"How do you know?"

"What?"

The soldier folded his arms across his chest, letting the bandanna hang from his fingers. "Do you know why I'm going to blindfold you?"

Eddie had to admit he didn't.

"Hah!" The soldier spread his hands wide and smiled gleefully. "If you don't know why, then you can't say there's no need, can you?

Am I right or am I right?"

Still trying to figure out what could possibly be going on, Eddie, always a sucker for logic, admitted that the man was indeed right.

"Well, there you go. Now, will you let me put it on, please?"

"Why?"

"So you can't see where we're taking you."

Eddie's threat alert radar cranked itself down a few notches now that it looked like he wasn't going to get shot, and he allowed himself to relax a little. "Who are you, anyway?"

The soldier slapped himself on the forehead, then stuck out his hand. "Man, I'm sorry! Larry Bartholomew. Pleased to make your acquaintance."

Eddie ignored the proffered hand. "Eddie Caminetti."

"Well, *du-u-h-h . . . !*"

Good point. "Listen, I'm not sure I under—"

"It's for security," Bartholomew interrupted him. "We're going to take you to Barranca but we don't want you to know where he hangs out."

"That part I got, Larry, but—"

"Bart."

"What?"

Bartholomew shrugged sheepishly. "My friends call me Bart."

"Are we friends?"

Bartholomew shrugged again. "Don't see why not."

"So who are you? Because you sure as hell don't look like a South American coffee worker."

"Grad student at Berkeley. Or at least I was, before I joined up with Barranca."

"What made you do that?"

"He's a good man. I was going to do my doctoral thesis on his worker's movement, but I kind of got hooked into becoming part of it instead. So: Can we get this blindfold on you?"

"What are you going to do if I don't put it on?"

"Nothing."

"Fine. That's settled, then, so why don't—"

"But Enrique over here—" Bart jerked a thumb over his shoulder "—will shoot you through the head."

Eddie leaned to the side to look past Bart, and saw a very large, very heavily armed man standing quietly by, as if awaiting orders. Eddie suddenly felt queasy.

Bart grinned, bent over to slap a knee and came up shaking his head. "Ah, I'm just messing with you, Eddie. Listen, tell you what: We'll hang some shit over the cabin windows so you can't see out, okay?"

Eddie nodded dumbly, not trusting himself to speak until he'd had a moment, then Enrique and another soldier pulled him away from the plane and he felt a hand come between his legs from behind. "Hey . . . !"

Before he could twist away, other sets of hands had hold of his shoulders and waist as he was expertly frisked. Bart was still grinning as he watched.

"*Él está limpio,*" one of the men behind Eddie said.

"*Limpio?*" Eddie protested as he shook away the hands that were already withdrawing anyway. "Who says I'm *limpio!*"

"Means you're clean, Eddie."

Eddie turned to glare at his smirking examiners. "What'd you think I was gonna do . . . ice your great leader during dinner?"

"Nah." Bart waved it away as he motioned for others to get the plane ready. "Weren't looking for weapons."

"What, then?"

"Homing beacon, GPS unit . . . that kind of thing."

"Homing beacon," Eddie muttered. "Think I'd carry one in my shorts and fry my balls off?"

At the sound of a distant shout, Eddie turned to look across the field. Apparently an order had been given; all the Americans who had accompanied him to Brazil were turning around so they were facing away. "What's going on?"

"Don't want them to ID the plane," Bart said as he pointed toward the tail. A soldier clambered up onto the rear stabilizer and removed the burlap sack hiding the registration number. "So what do you say we get on board, okay?"

Satisfied that Bart intended to let his entourage go, Eddie turned and put a tentative foot onto the wooden ladder that served as an air stair. "It'll hold you," Bart assured him, and he climbed into the cabin followed by several soldiers.

As they settled themselves in, Eddie noticed something odd. "Uh . . . who's flying this thing?"

Bart had been stretching his seat belt across his middle but stopped. "Huh?"

Eddie pointed toward the empty cockpit. "Aren't we missing a pilot?"

Bart looked around at his compatriots, then frowned. "You're kidding me, right?"

"Kidding you about what?"

There was some angry muttering from the others as Bart continued to stare at him. "You're the pilot, Eddie."

"Come again?"

Bart let his seat belt go and twisted around to face Eddie. "They told me you were a licensed commercial pilot, rated in this model of plane. That's why we got it."

Eddie wondered whether he'd fallen down a rabbit hole. "You gotta be shittin me, Bart."

"You gotta be shittin *me*, Eddie!" There was genuine menace in his voice, and the other soldiers had gone silent. Eddie felt his recently restored stomach start to fall apart again.

Looking over Bart's shoulder, Eddie noticed that the cabin door and stairs hadn't been secured. "If I'm supposed to be the pilot," he said slowly, "then how was I supposed to fly with a blindfold on? And how was I supposed to fly us to someplace whose location I wasn't even supposed to know?"

A shadow appeared across the open doorway, then the floor shuddered as someone bounded up the steps and into the cabin. In one hand he carried a set of headphones, in the other a leather-bound book of flight charts.

"Sorry I'm late, Bart," the man said. "Had me some'a that local gazelle shit for breakfast and got a bad case'a the squirts." He jerked a thumb toward Eddie as he stepped into the cockpit and threw his gear on the copilot's seat. "This what's-his-name . . . Crackle Mammy?"

"Caminetti," Bart tried to answer, but he was laughing too hard and it came out garbled. The soldiers in the rear seats were laughing, too, and one of them reached over the seat back to smack Eddie on the shoulder.

"What's so funny?" the pilot said as he settled into the left seat.

Bart shook his head, unable to answer. Eddie, red-faced, said, "Your asshole buddies back here have a warped sense of humor." Then he twisted around to face the grinning soldiers. "Any'a you mugs at least got a cigarette?"

Two of them held out open packs, then somebody on the outside closed the door and a third soldier said, "*Nicht jetzt, Pierre. Warte ein paar minuten.*"

"*Ah, mais oui, Hans,*" the other man replied, taking back the cigarettes.

Bart motioned toward the sides of the plane and two other soldiers undid their seat belts, rose and began draping bandannas on the windows. Bart reached forward and slid closed a curtain that blocked their view of the cockpit. A few minutes later they were airborne, and the French-speaking soldier offered up the cigarettes. "*S'il vous plaît, monsieur.*"

"How the hell many languages do these guys speak?" Eddie asked as he took one.

"Never counted," Bart answered. "But we've got people from all over the world here, and—"

The plane lurched, rolled and underwent a series of more lurches and sharp banks.

"*'Ey!*" someone called out from the rear. "*Che cosa state facendo!*"

"What the fuck're you doin up there!" another soldier screamed.

Bart turned and said, "Couple of hard turns so our man here can't tell what direction we're going."

"Yeah, well give us some goddamned warning next time, you flaming dork!"

"*Certo, e va fa in culo!*"

Eddie waited to hear if there was to be a riposte from Bart, but apparently none was forthcoming. "You the leader of this unit?"

"That's me."

Eddie settled himself back on his seat. "Pretty freakin egalitarian revolution you got going on here, guys can talk to you like that."

"Kind of the whole point, isn't it? But when I say jump"—Bart leaned back, closed his eyes and clasped his hands over his belly—"they ask how high on the way up."

CHAPTER 42

SOMEWHERE, SOMETIME LATER

ddie looked around as he stepped off the plane. "Looks pretty much the same as the last place."

"You can walk five hundred miles in any direction and it's still going to look the same," Bart said. "Except it's cooler here. Feel it?"

"Yeah."

"Higher up. Coffee-growing country." He hitched a backpack up onto his shoulders as one of his soldiers did the same with Eddie's golf clubs. "About a four-mile walk. You ready?"

He didn't mention that the four-mile walk was also a seven-hundred-foot climb. By the time they reached their destination, Eddie was thoroughly winded and perspiring heavily despite the even cooler temperatures at the higher altitude and the fact that the entire walk had been along a paved and well-maintained road.

Relative to rebel encampments as Eddie had imagined them, this one was pretty upper crust. Instead of tents, there were some half dozen solid wooden structures of two and three stories each; two looked like barracks, the others like factory buildings. There were even power lines running into a small distribution yard, with other lines leading out and connecting to the wooden buildings. In addition to a handful of beat-up military-type vehicles, there were some pickup trucks and several ordinary sedans of less-than-ancient vintage parked in a lot next to what appeared to be the main building. Dozens of people were visible, not just soldiers but men in working clothes, along with a few women and children. The whole place had an air of purpose, but it seemed more commercial than warlike; it felt to Eddie like an industrial compound, and over it all hung the intoxicating aroma of coffee being roasted.

"Welcome to Java Central," Bart said. "Ready to meet the man?"

They walked toward the headquarters building, Bart greeting

various people with a nod of the head or a two-fingered salute. At the entrance to the building, two armed guards exchanged words with Bart in Spanish, then stepped aside, reluctantly, eyeing Eddie with some suspicion but no apparent enmity. Eddie stepped inside, waiting for Bart to lead the way, but instead felt a clap on his shoulder.

"Right up the stairs," Bart was saying as he pointed to the right.

"Aren't you coming?"

Bart shook his head. "I'm just transport today. You're on your own." And then he went back out the door.

Eddie walked along the corridor, noticing several posters along the wall. Instead of revolutionary slogans, they contained high-quality photos showing the various stages of coffee production: sowing the plants, watering operations, picking, roasting and packing. In each one, workers were featured in such a fashion that their faces were recognizable, and Eddie realized that the posters weren't about the coffee, they were about the coffee workers.

He reached the stairs and began climbing. The staircase was solidly built, not jury-rigged, evidence of competent carpentering, as were the tightly joined wall panels and the soundless floor. At the top of the stairs the room opened to the right. Sunlight streamed in through large windows and a skylight. On a low table away from the windows a man was fussing with a large pot of coffee. Although the man's back was to him, Eddie thought there was something familiar about . . .

"Carlos?"

Carlos Rivera turned and smiled in recognition. "Eddie! You made it!"

Eddie stared incredulously at the man who had caddied for him back in California and given him detailed information on Manuel Barranca's golf game. "Carlos, what the hell are you doing here?"

Rivera turned back to the pot. "Making coffee. Would you like a cup? A good roasting, and quite delicious. Believe me, you cannot purchase this in the States."

Eddie nodded dumbly, mindless of the fact that Rivera couldn't see him. He stepped closer and lowered his voice. "Isn't it a little dangerous for you here?"

"Why?" Rivera asked without turning around.

Eddie looked around to make sure they were alone. "F'chrissakes, Carlos . . . what if Barranca finds out you betrayed him?"

"Betrayed him? You mean by giving away his silly little golf secrets?"

Eddie was having trouble with the man's nonchalance. "There's an awful lot of dough riding on those silly little secrets!" He looked around again. "Where's Barranca, anyway? I'm supposed to meet him."

"Yes, well . . ." Rivera turned, holding two steaming cups, and handed one to Eddie. "Cheers," he said as he lifted his cup in a half-toast and took a sip, his eyes closing in pleasure.

Eddie ignored the cup in his hand. "What if he finds out?"

"He knows."

"He knows? What do you mean, he knows?"

Rivera took another sip. "Relax, Eddie. It is alright."

"How do you figure it's alright!" Eddie demanded, his voice growing fearful and strident.

Rivera went around behind a large oak desk and sat down. "It is okay because I say it is okay."

"And who the hell are you to—"

"I am Manuel Barranca. You may call me Manolo, as do many of my—Whaa-a! Calm yourself, Eddie! You'll spill that wonderful coffee all over yourself. Perhaps you had better sit down . . ."

About fifteen minutes later, Eddie finally decided that Rivera/ Barranca was telling him the truth. "But I don't get it."

"Get what?"

"Anything. Why all of that bullshit about pretending to be Barranca's caddie, giving up all of his—all of your—secrets, which I now assume was another bunch of bullshit?"

Barranca laughed. "I am compelled to admit, that part was fun. But the reason for it was quite serious. I had to convince you to accept the assignment from your president. It was my understanding that you were in the process of declining my kind invitation. And what better way to attract the great Caminetti to a money game"—He lifted his hands and let them drop—"than by convincing him he was going to win?"

Eddie grinned in spite himself. "Gotta tell you, Barranca . . . it's not too often I get outhustled. But you haven't won yet."

"And why is that?"

"Because we haven't agreed to play yet. Or under what conditions."

Barranca's aplomb seemed shaken for the first time. "What do you mean?"

"So far," Eddie explained, "there have been an awful lot of people speaking on my behalf, and yours as well. But I live in a democracy, and I don't take orders from anybody, not even my president. We don't have a game until we—that's you and me—until we say we do."

Barranca thought it over, then nodded slowly. "A point well taken. Okay, then, I propose you give me three strokes a side."

Eddie snorted. "Yeah, right. What are you, like scratch or something? Who gives three a side to a scratch golfer?"

"Scratch!" Barranca reared up. "I, scratch? You must have taken leave of your senses! I am a reliable eight, you are likely a two, which is why I request three and three."

Eddie held up a hand. "Not so fast there, pal. We're not exactly playing on my home course; we're playing on yours. And is it even rated?"

"Is it rated?" Barranca retorted indignantly. "Of course it is rated! You think because you are not in the United States you are dealing with peasants?"

"So what's it play from the tips?"

"Tips? Ah . . . you mean the rearmost tees."

"Yeah, the rearmost. So what's the rating?'

"There is only one set of tees, and it is officially rated as 'extremely difficult.'"

"Very funny. So?"

"I would be guessing, but seventy-four is probably a reasonable approximation."

"That's what I figured. And you know every blade of grass on it."

Barranca swiveled around on this chair and waved a hand toward his window. "So go and play it first. Become familiar. Perhaps"—he cackled with glee—"I will even caddy for you!"

"I think one loop with you is about all I can stand. Yeah, I'll play it first, but if it's really seventy-four, I'll tell you what . . ."

Barranca swiveled back and eyed Eddie carefully. "Yes?"

"Right now, without looking, I'll give you three a side . . ."

"Yes . . . ?"

"If you tee off first and putt first on every hole."

"And . . . ?"

"That's it."

"This is your only requirement?"

"Yep. Other than that, strict rules of golf."

Barranca thought about it for a few moments. "And you don't get a practice round."

Eddie pretended to think that over, but there was no need. He'd already secured a great advantage for himself. "Agreed."

"Now," Barranca said, sobering and leaning forward, "as to the stakes . . ."

"You said a million dollars."

"I did."

"Then that's what it is."

"If you wish. But . . ."

"But what?" Eddie said, wary now. "Are you planning to tell me you dragged me all the way the hell down here so you can renege on—"

Barranca screwed up his face and waved Eddie down. "Calm yourself, please. I am not reneging on my offer. Although, as you say, there is no wager until we both agree that there is a—"

"Yeah, yeah. So?"

"So, we will play, as agreed."

"And . . . ?"

Barranca smiled enigmatically. "I wonder what you might say to perhaps making our round a little bit more interesting . . ."

On their way out of the building a few minutes later, they ran into Larry Bartholomew. "So what's it to be?" the former graduate student asked.

"Eddie will give me three a side," Barranca answered.

Bart thought it over. "Sounds about right."

"Excellent. Well, we must be off."

"Hold it." Bart seemed to have caught something in Barranca's expression. "That it?"

"Is that what?"

"You get six strokes and that's all there is to it? The rest is straight up?"

"Not quite." Barranca explained that he would be both teeing off and putting first on every hole.

"Uh huh. Right. Got it." Bart shook his head, turned and began walking away. "I'm cutting your coffee rations in half, Manolo. That's all we need, the head visionary going into caffeine psychosis."

When he was gone, Barranca lifted his eyebrows: *What can I tell you?*

"Nice show you two put on," Eddie said sarcastically. "Why do I have the feeling I'm about to lose my life's savings?"

Barranca laughed and threw his arm across Eddie's shoulder as he led him away. "You are being coy, Eddie. You and I both know that you are here to, how do you Americans put it? 'Make this little problem go away?' Please do not tell me that your president expects you to risk your own money."

"Actually, he does. And it didn't look like much of a risk when a dead guy named Carlos Rivera showed up to give me some advice." *And if I lose the match and don't come back with a deal, there goes my $5 million fee and I'm still out the million.* But there was no sense trying to get Barranca to believe that.

"Oh, dear, you bear me a grudge. Well, let us have dinner and we will commence play in the morning."

"Not so fast." Eddie tried to relax, folding his arms as he walked and taking his time. "There's the matter of your caddy fee."

"Please?"

"I'm supposed to pay you ten percent for your advice, which advice is now useless, and if I win, I'm not kicking anything back to the same guy who has to pay me off."

"Ah." Barranca made a dismissive gesture. "Merely a ploy to entice you into coming."

"You thought me paying you a hundred grand was motivation?"

"Why, certainly. Had I offered my assistance to you gratis, you would have dismissed me without another moment's thought. By making it seem enormously valuable, you bought in completely." He mistook Eddie's blank stare for misunderstanding. "Would you buy a Patek Philippe watch for fifteen dollars? Certainly not. But price it at fifteen thousand and suddenly it becomes an object of desire."

Eddie didn't need it explained to him. What he needed explained was how he'd failed to latch on to Barranca's game in the first place. "I noticed you didn't tell Bart about our little side bet.'

"Side bet?"

"You know; the part about making our round a little more interesting?"

"Ah." Barranca paused in front of a small, one-story building from which was flowing a symphony of exotic cooking smells. "I rather think that is something we should keep to ourselves."

CHAPTER 43

THE SIMON BOLIVAR GOLF COURSE

The tee box was a hand-shoveled rectangle of fresh soil patched with squares of grass cut from the jungle. The fairway resembled an overgrown dirt road, complete with ruts from the wheels of heavy vehicles. The green, identifiable by a white bandana hanging from a bamboo pole, was a somewhat distorted circle that had been veneered with something that didn't look quite like grass. The rough, aptly named for once, looked liked a comfortable habitat for snakes and wild cats, and the crudely constructed bunkers looked more like mud pits than sand traps. The overall effect was that of a neighborhood weekend project, an amateurish attempt at emulating the work of professional course builders, using shovels instead of bulldozers, machetes instead of riding mowers.

Eddie thought it was the most beautiful golf course he'd ever seen in his whole life.

Barranca stood quietly as his guest's eyes roamed over the first hole and what was visible of the fifth and ninth. He was going to ask Eddie what he thought of it, but knew from the look on his face that he didn't have to, that the canny hustler had sensed immediately that every inch of the place was imprinted with the backbreaking labor of people who wanted to play golf so badly they'd beaten the environment into whatever submission their own hands could effect. Barranca had of course heard of the legendary Swithen Bairn, Eddie's private golf club in a secret location somewhere in the Pacific, a glittering jewel of fairways that looked as though they'd been cut with fingernail clippers and a ruler, and greens that rivaled pool tables in their manicured perfection. He also knew that Eddie hated that course, and kept it that way only for the benefit of pampered guests who thought that kind of flawlessness the pinnacle of golf, who'd forgotten that the whole point of the original game had been to battle the land as it came, not to tame it first and then claim empty victory.

Each of them knew that the other was near nerveless and immune to pressure, but Eddie was so happy to have a big money match in front of him that he had to concentrate on tamping down his elation. He'd already gone over in his mind a hundred times exactly how aggressively he'd play each hole, or as much as he could without ever having seen the layout, with variations depending on whether he was ahead or behind in the match, where Barranca stood on the particular hole, how the wind was blowing, how well or poorly he was putting, how Barranca's short game was holding up. He'd thought about it so often he had to fight down the feeling that actually playing the round was almost an afterthought as opposed to the great ocean of unknowns every round of golf always was.

"This a par four?" Eddie asked when he was able to find his voice.

"I have no idea," Barranca answered as he began stretching using a three-wood. "What difference does it make?"

"You said the course was rated," Eddie said accusingly.

"And so it is."

"How, if you can't even tell par for a hole?"

"Simple," Barranca said as he brought the club up across his shoulders and began twisting left and right. "I used myself as the reference. My best twenty rounds of the first forty I played. Knowing my long-consistent index, I imputed the rating and slope. I assure you that I am an eight on this course." At Eddie's skeptical look he added, "My self-assessment is doubtless at least as trustworthy as yours, wouldn't you say?"

He pointed down the fairway, where one member of a twosome dressed in jungle camouflage had just taken an ugly swing but somehow managed to get his ball onto the green. The man raised his hands in triumph while his partner applauded. Neither carried a golf bag, just a handful of clubs and a backpack Eddie assumed contained extra balls and maybe a sandwich and a canteen of water. "Do you see that boulder off to the right?"

Eddie followed Barranca's outstretched hand. "One-fifty marker?"

"Yes, and quite accurate. We used military GPS for the distances."

"Yards or meters?"

"Yards. Also, we allow the ball to be cleaned and placed within a club head's distance. Otherwise, the mud and debris would make most shots a random event. As you can imagine, there is only natural drainage here."

Eddie nodded his approval of the local rule. "How are the greens?'

"Unique. One is not required to use a putter, but please be diligent about repairs."

The two of them carried full bags, but they were joined by two of Barranca's comrades, Enrique and Javier, who carried backpacks and assault rifles instead of clubs.

Taking a driver out of his bag Eddie said, "So how'd you get to be an eight anyway, running around the jungle all the time?"

"Everywhere we go, I make it a point to play."

"What do you, like, liberate the course or something? Set up an occupying force?"

Barranca grinned at Eddie's easy presumption. "Much easier than that. I get invited."

That was a surprise. "Invited? By who?"

"Members."

"You're kidding."

"I have even been made an honorary member in some of the best clubs in four countries. At no cost."

Eddie had taken a few practice swings but now stopped. "What the hell are you talking about? You invade their territory and they comp you to their clubs?"

Barranca held his hand out toward the fairway. "Take your shot, Eddie. It will all become clear soon."

Eddie stepped away and held out his own hand. "You first, remember?"

"Ah. Indeed."

Barranca had been stretching using a three-wood since they'd set their bags down near the tee box, but now exchanged it for a driver. "Probably just a three-wood for you. All that is required is two-twenty, perhaps two-thirty in the center of the fairway."

The tee box was marked by two coconuts painted white. Barranca bent over to tee up his ball, then straightened up and took a long look down the fairway. He set his club head behind the ball and only then took his stance, as though the club were an anchor around which he centered himself. Once set, he lifted the club off the ground a fraction of an inch, took a deep breath and came to stillness. Motionless for some seconds, he took the club away slowly, paused at the top and then brought it down smoothly, his head so still it might have been painted against the trees behind him. A satisfyingly clean *click* sounded as he struck the ball, which flew crisply away in a shallow arc and came to rest with very little roll several yards to the right of the imaginary center line.

"Good one," Eddie complimented him. "Another twenty yards or so do me any good?"

Barranca retrieved his tee and stepped away from the box. "If you can do it safely, yes. But too much left or right and trees near the green will interfere with your approach.

"Got it." Eddie was holding his driver but hesitated before teeing up his ball. He couldn't quite put his finger on why, but he felt oddly exhilarated. Maybe it had to do with an imminent rediscovering of a purity of the game he thought he'd forgotten, here in a godforsaken jungle on a pathetically bedraggled track that no one in his right mind could possibly mistake for a real golf course. He was reluctant to step up and hit, as though to do so would shorten by one stroke those he had remaining.

"Everything alright, Eddie?" Barranca asked solicitously. "I am painfully aware that this is not Pebble Beach or—"

"How about a practice round first?"

"Pardon?"

Eddie worked the grip of his driver in his hands, looking down as he spoke. "A practice round, then we play. And you won't have to go first every time."

Barranca thought it over as Eddie sweated his answer. "I am sorry," he finally said. "I fear there might not be enough time."

Eddie nodded, trying not to let his disappointment show. He stopped working the grip and prepared to take his shot.

Barranca stepped back to give him some room. "In truth, I did not think you would want to play this course more than the once we—"

"Yeah, whatever. Pipe the hell down and let me hit, okay?"

Barranca held up a hand, palm outward, then let it drop. "Strict rules of golf, correct?

"By the book." Eddie set himself up, then took a look down the fairway as he inhaled deeply and slowly let it out. He squeezed his eyes shut and tried to put out of his mind all that had happened in the past few days, all that was likely to transpire in the days coming and what the consequences might be if anything went wrong. When he thought he might have managed that, if only for a few seconds, he opened his eyes again and swung, hearing Javier puff out a breath in admiration before Eddie himself looked up to find the ball. It was sailing a beautiful trajectory, drawing slightly from right to left, just as he'd planned, and when it landed smack in the middle of the fairway, he gave off no indication that it had been anything but routine, which, in fact, it hadn't.

Enrique whistled softly, and Javier shouted, "Mulligan!"

Barranca, who'd caddied for Eddie during his round with Charles "Chuck" Stevenson at Desert Falls in California, wasn't at all surprised by the shot, which he'd seen Eddie hit twelve times without a hitch. "Well done. Now you'll have an easy approach."

"Easi-*er*," Eddie corrected him as he returned the club to his bag. "Why'd he yell 'Mulligan'?"

"It is the only English word he knows," Barranca explained. He hefted his bag and slapped the grinning soldier on the back. Eddie picked up his own bag, and they were off down the fairway, stepping carefully to avoid larger rocks and the muddy ruts, chatting easily, pretending not to notice the men carrying submachine guns walking stealthily in the jungle to their right and left.

They both made the green on their second shots, but Barranca was within five feet while Eddie's ball was twenty feet away.

"Hey, what the hell is this stuff?" Eddie asked as he stepped onto the green. The surface was soft and far more uniform in texture than he'd expected.

"It is moss," Barranca said. "Gathered from the forest."

"Amazing. How does it break?"

"All else being equal," Barranca answered as he pointed, "away from that mountain."

Eddie finished plumbing the line and took up his position over the ball. "Looks like a pool table."

"Not as fast. The moss is never dry."

After one last glance at the spot on the green a few feet away he'd picked as a target, Eddie hit. Instead of bouncing and jiggling as balls normally do on grass, however finely manicured, his ball rolled cleanly toward the hole, but its path was eccentric, breaking first left, then right, then back again before coming to rest four feet short and well away from the line.

Off to the side, Javier made a farting noise with his lips that broke both himself and Enrique up.

Eddie looked up in some irritation. "The hell are they laughing at?"

Javier called out something in Spanish, and Eddie looked over at Barranca for a translation.

"He says his grandmother could make that putt."

"Bullshit," Eddie muttered as he walked to his ball and bent to mark it. "Like putting on a gravel pile."

Javier called out again, grinning broadly and pointing first to Eddie, then to himself, then to the spot where Eddie had putted from, Enrique nodding supportively so that he had to grab his hat to keep from losing it.

"He asks if you would care to place a wager." Barranca translated.

"On that putt?" Eddie said. "Tell him to name it."

"*Cuánto?*" Barranca called back.

"*Cien dólares!*" came the answer.

"He says—"

"Yeah, I got it. A hundred bucks. *Muy bien!*"

"Don't do it, Eddie," Barranca warned.

"Bullshit," Eddie repeated, then walked back to his original putting spot and set his ball back down. "OK?"

"You're going to lose," Barranca persisted.

"OK!" Javier answered. He bent down, untied his boots, then walked briskly onto the green and held out his hand.

Eddie handed him his putter. "There's a catch here, right?" he said to Barranca. "Some trick I'm missing?"

"Just that you have already lost one hundred U.S. dollars."

Eddie stepped back to give Javier some space to look over the green, line up and plan his putt, and had gotten about half a step away when Javier struck the ball. Hard. As Eddie's had done, it rolled smoothly but veered wildly, then seemed to settle down in some kind of groove as it got closer to the hole. Before it had come within three feet, Eddie knew for a dead certainty it was going in.

Javier held out his palm to Eddie while bowing deeply to an applauding Enrique, followed by even deeper bows and waves of his hat to an imaginary gallery. Eddie took out his wallet and counted out five twenties, all the while shaking his head and sneaking glances at Barranca, who shrugged helplessly. Javier thanked him in Spanish, walked off the green and put his boots back on.

"Damnedest putt I ever saw," Eddie said with genuine wonder. "He knew he was going to make it, too."

"I believe he did."

"Why'd he take off his shoes?"

"If he had his way," Barranca replied, "everyone would do the same before walking onto his green."

"Whaddaya mean, *his* green?"

"I will explain later. As I received a stroke, I am now up by one, yes?"

CHAPTER 44

Back in California," Eddie said as they walked to the next hole, "you were telling me about Castro's round with Che Guevara. Anything else exciting happen?"

"Many things," Barranca said.

"Gimme a f'rinstance."

Barranca searched his memory, then said, "On number seven Fidel landed near a flower bed. By then somewhat more familiar with the rules, he asked me for a five-iron and used it to measure a club length for his free drop. Then he cursed loudly, because he saw that the new position would place an overhanging branch directly in the path of his backswing. I asked him why he was using a five-iron to measure and he responded that this was the club he planned to use for his shot."

"And you told him . . ."

"That he was not required to use the same club to measure one length. Happy at hearing that, he asked me for his driver, but I stood still and told him that wasn't necessary, either. When Che drew near I called to his caddy—"

"Who was that?'"

"Carlos Rivera."

"What!"

"The real one. I'm afraid he is in fact deceased."

Eddie slapped his head. "Oh, brother."

"I asked Carlos to hand me Che's driver, which was several centimeters longer than Fidel's. I handed it to Fidel and told him to use it to measure his drop, and now he was well clear of the branch, much to Che's considerable ire, especially when Fidel won the hole."

"And where did that put the match?"

"At the end of the first nine holes," Barranca said, "Castro was up by two and feeling quite confident."

As they walked, Eddie heard a rushing sound that seemed to grow louder with every step. "So what's this next hole?" Eddie asked.

"A simple par three," Barranca answered. "One hundred ninety-four yards, but with a slight drop."

Eddie was mentally already picking a four-iron out of his bag when they turned along a sharp angle on the stony path and he got his first look at the second hole. Without thinking he stopped suddenly, his clubs rattling loudly as they banged into his back.

Directly in front of them danced a shimmering, vaguely defined and apparently stationary column of water some twenty feet wide. Curtains of spray bloomed and billowed all around it, and it took Eddie a few seconds to realize that he was looking at the middle of a waterfall, the source of the rushing sound he'd been hearing for the last few minutes.

As he slowly moved forward he saw that the water was not quite as close as it seemed, but was beyond the end of the path, which came to an abrupt stop some fifty feet ahead. Unhitching his bag and stepping carefully up to the edge, Eddie looked down to see a pool of water more than ten stories below him. The waterfall was crashing into it with such power that the entire surface was a churning cauldron of blue-white foam. He felt a strong, damp wind emanating from the column of water, and was so riveted by the sight that he didn't realize he was quickly becoming soaked.

And freezing cold as well, as tons of rapidly evaporating water sucked all the heat from the surrounding air. Unwilling to step back, though, he wrapped his arms around himself and looked up to see the source of the water high overhead. It was gushing from a large hole in the rock face of a sheer cliff.

He heard someone shouting behind him but was unable to make out the words, which were lost in the thunderous roar that seemed to come from everywhere at once. He backed away from the edge but kept his eyes on the water. Barranca stepped up and put his mouth next to his ear.

"It is fed from the river that runs near our compound," he shouted, Eddie nodding back his understanding.

Enrique clapped his hands. *"Estamos listos?"* he yelled.

"Ready to play?" Barranca translated.

Reluctantly, Eddie walked back to his bag. He lifted it up and had a strap onto one shoulder when Javier yelled, *"Adónde va usted, estúpido?"*

"What'd he say?" Eddie held up a hand. "And I got the *estúpido* part."

"He asked where you are going." Barranca reached for Eddie's bag, took it off his shoulder and set it back down. "This is the second hole."

Eddie looked down and noticed two white-painted coconuts on the ground. He pointed to them and lifted his eyebrows in inquiry. Barranca nodded back: *Yes, this is the tee box*. Eddie then turned back toward the waterfall and looked out across the chasm through the mist.

On the other side and some fifty feet below their present position there was a flat, green ledge fronting a thick stand of jungle foliage. It was roughly oval in shape and stretched along the rock wall, with about forty feet of it separating the water-side edge from the vegetation behind it. Planted about a third of the way from the left edge was a bamboo stick with a pennant-shaped piece of cloth on top, and Eddie realized it was the green. *A slight drop?*

After some seconds he pointed to the waterfall and yelled, "Don't tell me you have to hit through that thing!"

Barranca shook his head. "Impossible. It would be like hitting through a brick wall." Taking a few steps to the side, he motioned for Eddie to follow him and drew a bead on the far left edge of the green. "If you hit very straight," he shouted, "you can land there."

Examining the green more carefully, Eddie saw that it wasn't at all level but sloped down from left to right. Going for the safe shot meant a tricky downhill putt, but if you could somehow get to the middle you'd have a shorter, safer uphill one. Eddie was even more thankful than before that he'd insisted on Barranca hitting first on every tee. He held out his hand and invited him to do so now.

Barranca chose a six-iron, intending to skim the ball as close to the falling water as he could without its path being affected by the spray. He struck the ball well, but, in order to stay safe, had lined up a bit too far to the left. It was a beautiful, high arc that stopped pin-high on the green less than two inches from where it had first touched down, but Barranca had left himself the longest downhill putt possible.

When Eddie had seen Barranca take out the six-iron, he'd thought it a bit long for the distance and drop. But when he saw that the length of the shot was near-perfect, it occurred to him that the moisture-saturated air and whirling eddies of wind around the column of water would have a dampening effect on the ball. He reached for a six-iron himself, then hesitated. Barranca would very likely par this hole, and he got a stroke as well. In order to at least tie, Eddie would need a birdie. To do that, he'd have to go for the flag, and the only way to make that happen was to fade the ball around the waterfall. That would take an enormous amount of spin.

As he considered the likelihood of pulling off that shot he had another thought: While he hated to purposely introduce a deviation from dead aim at the stick into any shot, given that the odds of his knocking it right into the hole were about a hundred thousand to one, he thought he might as well err slightly in favor of the easier putt, which was from the right side of the flag. That would require even more fade, as well as a heightened trajectory to make sure the ball spent enough time in the air to arc its way all around the water. He would also need as much club head speed as he could possibly muster but if he hit a six that hard, he might send it into the jungle. He replaced the club and took out a seven instead.

He stood behind his teed-up ball just inches from the left coconut and picked out a bent blade of grass about five feet in front of it that lined up with a palm tree well off the left side of the green. He then took up his stance and aligned himself so that the club head would pass right above that piece of grass on his follow-through. With one last glance at the green, he set up, exhaled, and swung with everything he had.

Barranca knew after the ball had barely left the club face that it was a spectacular shot that was going to do precisely what Eddie had in mind for it. It started out alarmingly off-line to the left, but the tremendous rate of clockwise spin bit into the onrushing air and quickly began moving the ball to the right. The trajectory was very high, not only supplying plenty of hang time for the asymmetric drag to keep pushing the ball around the waterfall, but also ensuring that aerodynamic friction would largely halt the ball's forward movement at just the point when it was right over its target. Sure enough, its reentry path was nearly vertical, and when it finally touched down on the mossy green it remained nestled comfortably at the bottom of the depression it had created itself, less than three feet from the hole.

"Mierda!" Enrique breathed.

Barranca didn't say anything, just nodded as he looked at Eddie in admiration. Nothing about the shot had been at all accidental, no luck about it whatsoever. Had anyone in a PGA tour event hit something like that, it would have been replayed on television for weeks.

A few minutes later, after Barranca had missed his difficult putt, he graciously conceded Eddie's and they were even going into the third.

They played on in relative silence broken only by the occasional click of a golf ball being hit, the lazy drone of winged insects, a softly delivered compliment for a shot particularly well executed and the periodic mutterings of Enrique and Javier, who were analyzing every shot with the intensity of network golf commentators. The two soldiers occasionally took a shot for fun, and while Javier could barely hit an iron or a wood, his expertise with a putter was astounding. He was absolutely deadly from inside fifteen feet, and even from longer distances had only missed twice out of some dozen attempts, and even then by less than three inches.

Eddie won two of the last seven holes, Barranca won two and they halved the other three, and so were dead even after nine. Both of them were playing at the top of their games, and who would eventually emerge victorious looked to be as much a matter of luck—the rub of the green—as a function of ability.

Eddie had learned along the way that few players bothered to keep score, the eccentricities of the course rendering meaningless such conventional metrics. Instead, only holes won and lost were tracked. However, some quick mental calculating confirmed for Eddie that Barranca had been honest about his level of skill.

"I see you've gotten the hang of this pitiful excuse for a golf course,"

Barranca said to Eddie, as they sat on a stone bench taking a breather. Javier and Enrique had produced cheese sandwiches and bottles of water from their backpacks.

"I like it better than Pebble." Barranca laughed at that, and Eddie didn't bother to try to convince him that he'd really meant it. He was no longer distracted by the ever-lurking armed guards in the jungle and had even come to extract some comfort from their vigilant presence. "But where the hell did Javier learn to putt like that?'

"He's good, no?"

"Good? Most amazing putter I've ever seen. By the way, how do you keep the greens so firm when they're made out of moss?"

Barranca pointed to Javier and said, "Thank him."

Javier began chattering in rapid Spanish and gesturing with his hands. Barranca "translated" for him, with considerable editing: "He comes from a family of stone craftsmen. They build walls, and their pride lies in using no cement or cutting tools of any kind. Each piece of rock is perfectly interlocked with its neighboring pieces."

Javier nodded emphatically and made more motions with his hands: He put together a jigsaw puzzle in the air, fitting pieces, patting them smoothly into place, rubbing the surface . . .

"Beneath, the greens are a mosaic of flat stones," Barranca explained. "He worked mud into the spaces between, smoothed it all with his hands, then set down a layer of moss. Once it took hold, it became very resilient, and it never needs cutting. Walking on it keeps it smoothed down, and the drainage is perfect."

Javier stopped talking and gesturing and smiled in approval of Barranca's version, even though he hadn't understood a word of it.

"You telling me he built eighteen greens that way?" Eddie asked. "By himself?"

"Others gathered the stones, but Javier set every piece down with his own hands."

"No wonder they're so small." Eddie looked at the grinning Javier. "How long did it take him?"

"A year. Although he was rushed at the end, as developing events interfered."

"Unbelievable."

"Not really," Barranca said. "Where one chooses to expend one's energy is only a matter of what one thinks is important. Of course, Javier did get a little bit lazy toward the end, as you shall see."

"So where do you choose to expend your energy, Manolo?" Eddie said after several moments. "What do you think is important?"

Barranca lifted his sandwich and gestured toward Javier and Enrique, who were laughing over some private joke. "To see that men like these are treated as human beings. Nothing more." He took a bite from the sandwich, then looked at Eddie, his eyes suddenly gone hard. "Nothing less."

Eddie sensed the ominous change in the man's voice, and elected to remain silent. But it passed quickly. Barranca, looking slightly embarrassed for having suddenly taken such a serious tone, swallowed and cleared his throat. "I want to thank you for what you did on behalf of my grandson. He has not spoken of baseball even once since you brought him to golf."

"It was nothing."

"It was everything." Barranca balled up the wax paper that had held his sandwich. "The boy had a very hard life. America, as it is for so many, was the only hope of his parents for him. But it is not easy for immigrants these days, especially for ordinary people with no special talents."

"So I've heard. But it isn't easy for Americans either."

"Yes," Barranca agreed. "I understand the prices for big-screen televisions are making life very difficult."

"Hey—"

"There are two kinds of Americans, Eddie, regardless of what documents they carry in their wallets: *real* Americans and interlopers. The distinction is a profound one."

"It's like that everywhere, in every country. The ones who were born there, and the ones who came later."

"True. But how many countries claim to be the last refuge of the downtrodden, the great melting pot, a shining light beckoning all to her shores?"

Eddie wiped his hands on his pants and stood up. "You bring me here to run my country down, Barranca?"

"No, I did not." Barranca also stood up, but was more deliberate and took his time. "I brought you here to tell you about mine."

"Good idea." Eddie looked around for a place to throw the paper from his sandwich, but Enrique stepped up to take it from him and put it in his knapsack. "Speaking of which, what is your country? Seems to be a little confusion about that back in Washington."

"This is my country," Barranca said, waving to the countryside around him.

"And where is that?"

"It does not matter."

"Listen, are you going to start that—"

"I tell you, it does not matter. Come. Nine more holes to go."

"Manuel!" Javier called out.

Barranca turned to see his comrade pointing toward Eddie's bag, from which a high-pitched, warbling sound was emerging. Eddie walked forward and reached for a pocket on the bag, but was stopped by Javier's viselike grip on his forearm.

"*Permítalo*," Barranca said gently, and Javier let go.

Trying not be obvious as he shook his arm to get the blood flowing again, Eddie zipped open a pocket and withdrew an exotic-looking device that looked something like an oversized walkie-talkie. As Javier stepped forward, Eddie said, "Telephone call," and held it up. It warbled again. Even after Barranca's approving nod, Eddie made no move to put it to his ear. Then the phone chirped, a different sound.

"Ah!" Barranca exclaimed as he stepped away, pulling the soldier with him. "Our friend wishes privacy."

When they were well away, Eddie held up the phone and spoke into it. "Hello?"

The phone chirped again, then a loud burst of static hit his ear. He winced and yanked it away, waiting for it to die down. When it did, he no sooner started to bring it close again when a fresh gush of noise started up. After a few iterations of that he gave up and hit the Terminate Call button, but the periodic chirping continued.

When he rejoined the others, Barranca said, "Anything important?"

"Don't know." Eddie held up the phone. "Nothing but static. Must be in a lousy reception area."

Barranca shook his head. "It is a satellite phone, Eddie, and we are close to the equator. There are no 'lousy' reception areas."

"What can I tell you." He slipped the phone back into his golf bag. "Never used one'a these things before."

"We have sat phones at camp and you are welcome to use one at any time."

"Ah, forget it," Eddie said as he lifted his bag onto his shoulders. "Besides, it was probably just the president. Don't worry about it."

Barranca got a stroke on number ten and bogeyed it, keeping them even when Eddie made par. On the long walk to number eleven Eddie again asked Barranca about his plans.

"It is a bit complicated, Eddie. I hardly know where to begin."

"Start with telling me where we are."

"I told you several times. It—"

"Yeah, yeah, I know. It doesn't matter."

"That is quite correct." Before Eddie could protest, Barranca held up a hand. "Did anyone in Washington tell you the number of people killed so far in our revolution?"

Eddie shook his head. "I don't think they know. Not a lot of information flowing out of here."

"The answer is, no one. Not a single life lost."

"Excuse me?"

"Americans are killing themselves over a little caffeine, yet thus far our little movement is bloodless."

"You know . . ." Eddie stopped walking, set down his bag and turned to face Barranca. "I'm the first one to indulge in a little game playing, a little cat and mouse . . . I enjoy the give and take, see?"

"Certainly."

"But when people persist in talking in riddles long after it's stopped being amusing, well then, that crosses right over the fun barrier."

Barranca smiled. "And we have crossed it, have we?"

"We have."

"Okay."

"Okay?"

"Yes. Okay. I will explain."

Eddie tried to read Barranca's face, but couldn't. "Why'd you wait so long?"

"I wanted you to trust me first."

"You think I do?"

"I am not certain. But one thing I do know . . ."

"And what's that?"

"I trust you."

"Big mistake," Eddie said as he picked his bag up onto his shoulders and resumed walking.

"Probably," Barranca responded as he caught up. "But I do not think so. I feel I chose well when I asked for you."

"Gonna feel different when I kick your ass in eight more holes."

"We shall see."

"I'm listening, Manolo."

But Barranca wasn't saying, because they were momentarily deafened by a nearby gunshot. As Eddie reflexively dropped to the ground, Barranca held up a hand and said, "Do not be alarmed. I believe Enrique just shot our dinner."

The tee box for the eleventh hole was nestled in a bower made up of a wild variety of fragrant trees. Bees heavy with nectar and pollen hovered lazily above brightly colored flowers, songbirds competed lustily and Eddie could see at least one monkey eyeing them suspiciously from an overhead branch.

"Every new country happens at a cost," Barranca said as he zipped open a pocket on his golf bag and withdrew a metal cylinder. "Usually it is several hundred thousand people dead on the battlefield and a physical landscape bombed into something that looks like the surface of the moon. The new nation spends its first years grieving, bitter, broke and worrying about a reprisals from whoever it just defeated to get itself started. True?"

"I'll grant you that," Eddie said as he watched Barranca screw open one end of the cylinder and take out two cigars.

"Well, what kind of way is this to establish a nation? So I said to myself, how do we do this so everybody wins?"

"Yeah, but back up a second. A new country? I thought this was a revolution. Don't revolutions usually take over old countries?"

"Usually, they do." Barranca said as he handed Eddie a cigar. "But that is why our revolution is so revolutionary. I do not wish to kill anybody. To be quite truthful, I am not even very mad at anybody, at least if you exclude from consideration coffee growers flying to Monte Carlo twice a month while the people working their farms can barely send their children to school. But do I want to kill them? I do not." Barranca bit off the end of his cigar and spit it off to the side. He waited for Eddie to do the same and said, "I want to do business with them."

"Business! Why?"

"Because," Barranca answered, "if we do business, everything is, as you Americans say, on the up and up. In contrast, relationships among countries are filled with so much deceit and double-dealing that nobody ever really knows what exactly is occurring. Politics, spying, coups, wars . . . no matter how badly any nation behaves, there is always a way to rationalize it. And even if you cannot, there is nothing to be done about it unless one is willing to go to war, which few say they are but many are eager to do." He felt in his pockets, then turned to Enrique and made a flicking motion with two fingers.

As Enrique came up to them and handed Barranca a lighter, Eddie said, "Why do you say that?"

"Because no captain ever proved himself on calm seas. So the harsh reality is that you cannot trust anybody." Barranca got a flame and touched it to the end of his cigar.

"What's any of that got to do with business?"

"Everything." Barranca held the flame up and Eddie bent forward to light his own cigar. "It has everything to do with it. In business you have the three essential ingredients that make it possible to trust others."

"One has to be money . . . " Eddie said.

"To begin with, money, yes. The others are contracts and . . . can you guess the third?"

"Rules? Courts? Due process?"

"No." Barranca held up a finger and waved it back and forth. "The third critical element is naked self-interest."

"Is that so?" Eddie puffed at his cigar, drawing in the flame until bluish smoke filled his mouth.

"Yes, it is. Your President Eastwood could come down here and make a public speech with a television audience of a billion people, telling the world what a great friend America is going to be to my new country. A week later he could attack us based on some flimsy or nonexistent piece of intelligence. If he does that, our movement is over. There is nothing we can do to stop him, and we do not have anybody to complain to. Therefore it is critical that our existence be in his self-interest. If it is, then we know we can trust him."

"You could complain to the U.N."

"The U.N.? You cannot be—Eddie, please. Dozens of nations have been complaining about the United States for years at the U.N. and the consequences to your nation have been exactly nothing while your own complaints there have received the same treatment. When the vote opposing your last war was unanimous, you went ahead anyway."

"Good point."

"But listen to me—" Barranca subconsciously leaned forward. "If I sign a contract with General Electric? It is pure gold. If it turned out to be bad business for them they would cry and complain but they would honor that contract regardless, and why? Because if they did not, no one would ever do business with them again."

"Same is true of countries, isn't it?" Eddie asked.

Barranca straightened up and looked at him as if to see if he could really be that naive, but Eddie had already raised his hand to stop him. "Sorry. Dumb thing to say. It just slipped out." He shook his head. "Gotta tell you, Barranca, you sure as hell don't sound like a socialist."

"Socialist! My God, whatever gave you the idea I was a socialist?"

Eddie shrugged. "I don't know. Thought every revolutionary south of the border was a socialist."

"Well, let me hasten to assure you that I am not."

"So what are you, then?"

Barranca spread his hands, then brought them back together again. "If you must have a label, then call me a compassionate capitalist."

"You must be kidding."

"Again, I assure you I am not. I am a firm believer in the free-market system, that people should be able to rise to the level of their own skills and talents, that those who are more productive should be proportionately rewarded." He held up an admonishing finger. "But I also believe that there should be limits. Constraints. In order that the less ambitious or able do not suffer when rapaciousness and greed are allowed to flourish unchecked." He waved a hand toward a dormitory building in the compound visible in the distance. "As they have done in parts of the world such as this."

Eddie, who was not unsympathetic to what he was hearing, nevertheless tried to remind himself that he had a job to do. "Sounds good on paper, Manolo. So now tell me what you have in mind, because I still don't get it. I don't know all that much—*anything*—about cranking up a country or refurbishing an old one, but . . . I mean, what the hell is it you have in mind, anyway: a country or a corporation? Because eventually we're going to have to work something out here, and I'm damned if I—"

"It is both. A virtual country."

"Right, now I get it," said Eddie, who still wasn't getting anything. "What?"

"A virtual country, Eddie."

"A what?"

"A fluid nation, if you will. It doesn't truly exist, except as a concept, but the concept is very real and, therefore, so is the country. Which, by the way, is also a corporation."

"Is it."

"Yes. Ours will be a country without borders, but it will have citizens in control of their own political destiny and a vibrant economy to support that vision. Because economy is everything, and do not let anyone tell you otherwise. Where there is prosperity, there is peace. Where there is poverty and want, there is only strife."

"You're getting a bit academic now."

"Am I?" Barranca took another puff on his cigar and blew out a long stream of smoke. "Look at the minority subcultures in America. With all the talk of revolution and uprising from so-called visionaries, there has never been one whose central vision was an economic revolution. If the nonwhites in America were making the same amount of money as the whites, your economy would explode through the roof, and you would once more be the envy of the world. Everyone would win."

Eddie waited for Barranca to finish, gave him a few more moments, then tried to bring him back to the business at hand. "Which is what you're trying to do for the coffee workers. Okay. But tell me again about this new country of theirs. Or better yet, if you haven't invaded anybody and haven't taken over any coffee plantations, how is all of this going to work? And how'd you stop the coffee shipments to America?"

"Simple," Barranca replied. "I made an attractive proposal to the growers."

"And that was . . . ?"

"I offered to make them richer, and I took away their fear of a violent uprising."

"But you didn't do it with guns?"

Barranca shook his head. "I did it with contracts."

"I don't get it."

"But it's very simple." Barranca left the cigar in his mouth, folded his hands across his middle and leaned back. "In exchange for pushing coffee prices up twenty percent, my people—our new nation, actually—will own fifteen percent of nearly every major coffee plantation in South America. He removed the cigar and gestured toward the tee box. "Please be extremely careful on this hole."

CHAPTER 45

Eddie, still stupefied at discovering that Manuel Barranca's revolution consisted of peacefully buying up pieces of his former enemies, was having trouble orienting himself back to their golf match and badly sliced his tee shot. It landed with a humiliating *plop* in the mud beside a stream-fed lake.

By now neither of them saw any need to keep a close eye on the other. As fiercely competitive as they were, they were both also scrupulously honest owing to their deep respect for the game. So Barranca didn't bother to accompany Eddie to his ball, instead heading for his own in the middle of the fairway.

As Eddie approached the lake he wondered whether the real reason Barranca had held off on explaining his movement was that he had been waiting for the very best time to get Eddie rattled. They were dead even more than halfway through the match and one of them had to make a move, so had that been Barranca's? Eddie found himself starting to really like the wily old bastard and reminded himself that there was some serious business that had to get taken care of.

He got to the spot where he was sure his ball had landed but couldn't find it anywhere in the vicinity, nor were there any marks in the soft mud to indicate that it might have buried itself. There didn't seem to be any way it could have rolled into the water, but he looked anyway and, to his disgust, saw it beneath the surface about five feet out and a foot or so down. He set his bag down, sighed and reached for a putter, as he had no ball retriever. With a deft touch he managed to nudge the ball within two feet of land, but the soft bottom wouldn't allow him to get it any closer. He set aside the putter, rolled up a sleeve and knelt to go after the ball with his hand. His fingers were just above the surface when a scream diverted his attention. He turned to see Javier about eighty yards away, sprinting toward him, screaming again and waving his arms wildly. Eddie couldn't make out the Spanish but figured Javier was warning him about something, so he started to stand up when he heard a violent splash, turned back toward the lake and pulled his hand away just as several rows of long, closely-spaced and razor-sharp teeth boiled up out of the water and missed closing around his fingertips by about the width of an atom. He yelped something incoherent as he fell back onto the mud.

Seeing that Eddie was no longer in danger, Javier stopped running and leaned on his knees to catch his breath. *"Estúpido!"* he gasped as Enrique, still holding the bird he'd shot on the previous hole, jogged past him.

"What the hell was that!" Eddie said hoarsely when Enrique arrive, Barranca close on his heels.

Enrique peered at the water, then turned to Barranca and nodded.

Barranca grunted his understanding, pointed to Enrique's bird and then to the water. Enrique smiled and tossed the bird in.

Eddie watched as it floated serenely for a second, began to turn, then was surrounded by foam and disappeared amid a frantic flapping of black fins. A tinge of red stained the water within seconds, and less than a minute later feathers began floating to the surface followed by a skeleton of bones as thin as matchsticks. Very clean matchsticks.

"Caribe," Enrique said.

"Piranha," Barranca translated.

"Fuck *me*," Eddie replied.

Eddie assumed he'd lost the hole but Barranca had blown his second shot. Even with the penalty he took for going into the lake, Eddie managed to halve the hole and they were still even. Determined to regain and maintain his composure no matter what other surprises this course managed to provide, Eddie kept himself on an even keel even when an oddly painted fire hose he stepped across on fourteen turned out to be a twenty-six-foot anaconda boa constrictor.

The tee box on the par five fifteen was a small but magnificent cathedral of hanging vines and broad banyans facing onto an expanse of brilliant green hillocks. The right edge of the fairway, however, was a dirt path lined with trees and the rusting hulks of military vehicles badly damaged during a long-ago battle. Barranca, first up, slipped on the damp tee box during his downswing and sliced badly, his ball bouncing off an armored personnel carrier and then rolling behind a tree.

"Tough break," Eddie said with insincere sympathy.

Now at an advantage, Eddie hit a four-iron, which headed for the middle of the fairway but struck a rock, took a severe bounce and came to rest at the base of a rusted out jeep not far from Barranca's ball.

"Tough break," Barranca said, with about as much sincere sympathy as Eddie had earlier mustered on his behalf, causing both men to laugh.

"Mulligan!" shouted Javier.

Once at the path, Eddie surveyed the situation, then took a token swing to demonstrate that the crumbling hulk of the old vehicle was blocking his swing.

"Does not matter anyway," Barranca observed. "You have a free drop, as this lane plays as a road."

"Thanks," Eddie said. "Didn't see it on the scorecard."

"Most amusing," Barranca said, there being no scorecards.

Eddie picked up his ball and carried it to the edge of the dirt path. The area in which he could legally drop was a mess, littered with rocks of various sizes, tire ruts, dead leaves and twigs. There was even a sizable anthill, and that's what finally caught his eye. He stood up and held the ball out shoulder high, positioned it over the anthill and let it drop. It hit the hill just to the side of the peak and shot away, coming to land back on the road.

"I get another one," Eddie announced.

"Correct," Barranca agreed.

Eddie picked up the ball, carried it back to the anthill and let it drop in the same place. This time it kicked off and headed in the other direction, disappearing into an especially deep rut. "What bad luck," he said, walking toward it. He picked it up, then carefully placed it on the spot where it had first touched ground, but sitting up in a nice lie.

Enrique began protesting in rapid-fire Spanish, but Barranca held up his hand. *"Está correcto, Rico."*

"Verdad?"

"Sí." Barranca put a finger to his lips. *"Ahora silencio."*

"Sí," Eddie threw at him as well. *"Silencio."*

"Su madre, huero!" Enrique shot back, flicking two fingers outward from beneath his chin.

Eddie took a seven-iron but wasn't able to get off a clean shot and came up about twenty yards short of the green. Surveying the situation as best he could from his present distance, he asked, "What's a *huero?*"

"A term of respect reserved for those Americans who are especially esteemed," Barranca explained.

"Thought so." Eddie wiped off his club and put it back in his bag. "Let's go check your damage."

Barranca's ball was nestled in some roots on the right side of the tree almost up against the trunk. He stood facing the ball and the tree with the green off to his right and took a few imaginary swings. "I must hit it left-handed," he said, then got a three-iron from his bag, turned the club head upside down so he could punch the ball out left-handed, and set up for his shot.

Which put one of his feet on the dirt road. *"Gota gratis!"* Javier shouted. *Free drop.*

Barranca picked up the ball, held it out to his side and let it go. It came to rest on a level bit of ground about six feet from the tree. With a wary glance at Eddie, Barranca put the three-iron back in the bag, took out a six and prepared to hit the ball. Right-handed.

"Any problem, Eddie?" he inquired before taking up his stance.

Eddie, who knew the rules as well as anyone in the world and frequently used that knowledge to his advantage, pursed his lips into a tight line and shook his head. Once having taken his drop, Barranca was under no obligation to use either the same club or the same odd, left-handed stance that had put him on the road and made possible the drop in the first place, so long as that was how he'd truly intended to hit the ball had the road not been there. Eddie watched as his opponent made an easy swing and put the ball onto the back part of the shallow green, some fifteen feet from the hole. "Nice shot."

"Thank you," Barranca said, and then proceeded to win the hole.

Eddie, remembering who he was and where he was and why,

and having softened up countless numbers of easy marks with back-slapping camaraderie on many a fine summer day, got down to business and won the next one.

They were still even going into the eighteenth and final hole.

CHAPTER 46

ou're one hell of a golfer," Eddie said later that evening.

"High praise, indeed," Barranca replied. "Of course, I was already familiar with your splendid game."

"Splendid, right. Damned near lost an arm trying to save a two dollar ball."

They were sitting on the rear veranda of the main building in Barranca's compound. It overlooked a small valley filled with a deep green riot of bamboo, leafy palms and broad aloe plants broken only by a narrow river gurgling through its center, the same river that fed the waterfall on the number two par-three. The sun was only a few degrees above the horizon, and this close to the equator it was dropping so fast its motion could easily be discerned as its lower arc neared the trees fringing the rise on the opposite side of the valley.

Eddie had raised his hand and wiggled his fingers to make his point about nearly losing an arm, making Javier giggle and bare his teeth as he said *"Caribe!"* through his laughter. *"Piranha!"*

"Regular comedian, that guy," Eddie said.

Javier suddenly stopped laughing and turned his head, then stood up and walked back into the building. A second later he called out, "Manuel!"

Barranca twisted around in his chair. *"Qué?"*

Javier held up Eddie's golf bag. *"La máquina está cantando otra vez."*

Barranca turned back to Eddie. "He says your phone is singing again."

"Guess I better take it."

Barranca called Javier over, then started to get up, but Eddie waved him down. "It's okay, Manolo. Stick around."

Javier brought the whole bag over. In addition to the ringing, the chirping from earlier was still sounding, but it was more insistent now.

As Eddie pulled the phone from the bag, the mouthpiece protector fell off. "Whoops," he said as he scrambled to retrieve it. "Musta got busted when one'a your guys at the airport dropped the bag."

"My apologies," Barranca said.

"No big deal." As Eddie started to put the phone to his ear, he noticed the antenna was bent, and tried to straighten it. "Caminetti!" crackled the earpiece.

Eddie struggled to hold the phone to his ear, restore the mouthpiece and straighten the antenna at the same time. "That you, Mr. President?"

He was greeted by an answering swarm of static. "Sorry, sir, I can hardly hear you. It's not a good connection." He dropped the mouthpiece and bent to retrieve it. "I don't think I can hold this damned thing together."

"Can you hear me now?" came through the static. "Can you hear me now?"

"Barely, sir." He was trying not to laugh as Barranca and Javier covered their mouths and tried as well. "Got some trouble with this goddamned . . . shit!"

Barranca couldn't help himself and burst into open laughter as one of the antenna segments fell off completely and clattered to the floor.

"What's that, Eddie?" came through the phone. "What'd you say?"

"The connection is terrible and I got a major problem with this piece of junk sat phone!"

"Eddie, what the hell is going on?" they heard, followed by more increasingly desperate imprecations.

Then the chirping got even more insistent. Eddie took the phone away from his ear and peered at a small orange light blinking near the dial pad. "What the hell is this now?"

"What is what?" Barranca asked, practically in tears.

"Some freakin light blinking here."

Javier made a beckoning movement and Eddie handed over the phone. Javier looked at the light, then said to Barranca, "*Sin electricidad.*"

"What?" Eddie asked.

"El se olvidó de cargarlo," Javier added, and Barranca started laughing again.

"What!" Eddie demanded.

His eyes squeezed nearly shut in mirth, Barranca said, "It's running out of power."

"Eddie, what the hell is going on down there!" Eastwood's voice insisted.

"Ah, f'chrissakes. . ." Eddie put the phone back to his ear as best he could. "Can't talk long, Mr. President. I forgot to charge the damned thing."

"Stay with me, Eddie! What's going on?"

"It's falling apart, that's what's going on." Another segment of the antenna cracked off and hit the floor. "I can't hold it together much longer. Running out of power, too. Oh, shit . . . !"

Javier and Barranca finally lost it altogether as the back panel of the phone popped off and the battery fell out, dangling by three thin wires.

"Will you fuckers quit laughing and help me with this goddamned thing!" Eddie barked. Barranca, who was closer than Javier, got out of his chair and started forward.

"Eddie!" President Eastwood shouted back in the Gates Office. "Eddie!

"Hold your horses. Barranca's coming to shove the freakin battery back in. Some piece'a shit phone your spooks gave me."

"Caminetti!" Eastwood called again, but it went unheard, because by the time Barranca's hand was almost at the battery, it disconnected completely and landed with a thud on Eddie's foot.

As the last thin sliver of sun vanished behind the low hill, a soft female voice said *"Es usted listo?"* from behind them.

A woman in her mid-twenties, dressed in civilian clothes and carrying a large tray laden with food, came around in front of their chairs and set the tray down on a table off to the side. A man of about the same age was with her. He also set down a fully loaded tray, but said nothing and kept a watchful eye. He had a pronounced, jagged scar running down one cheek.

"*Gracias, Maria,*" Barranca said.

"*El gusto es mío, abuelo,*" the girl answered. She kissed Barranca lightly on the cheek, then turned and flashed Eddie a brilliant smile. "Good evening, Mr. Caminetti."

Eddie couldn't answer at first. First, he had to stop himself from falling headlong into a pair of brilliant violet eyes carrying all the promise of springtime, a newborn calf and a six-inch birdie putt all rolled into one. "Ma'am," he finally said with a barely suppressed stammer. And then she was gone, along with the man who was with her.

Eddie could barely hear her soft footsteps as she departed. "*Abuelo?*"

Barranca nodded. "She's my granddaughter. The sister of the young baseball player you assisted. Or, I should say, the young golfer. Beautiful, no?"

"Beautiful, yes. And those eyes."

"It stands her well in the theater."

"Theater?"

"She is the youngest professor in the history of the Yale Drama School. Currently on sabbatical."

"Who was the guy?"

"Her brother Rodolfo, my grandson. He likes to think he is her bodyguard, and in fact would be so should harm threaten her."

"How'd he get the scar?"

"Razor."

Eddie shuddered. "Tough guy, huh?"

Barranca smiled. "He is very tough, but it has nothing to do with the scar. That he received at the age of eight when he attempted to shave his beardless face using his father's straight razor. A stumble on the wet bathroom floor, and . . ." He shrugged and let his voice trail off.

Eddie, still under the thrall of those eyes, said, "Hell of a thing, bringing your granddaughter into a war zone. Or a potential one, anyway."

"I told you: There is no war here, and there will not be. At least not one of guns and tanks."

Enrique and Javier brought their chairs around and set them down on the other side of the table from Eddie and Barranca. Eddie said, "Those armed guys who followed us around today didn't look like they were tending the flowers."

"Bodyguards. For both of us. Even peaceful men are targets, if they attempt to tamper with the status quo. My daughter is here as well."

"Damn," Eddie said an hour later as he pushed back from the table and looked up at Maria Barranca, who had just rejoined them. "This revolution in the jungle business isn't all that bad."

"If you're going to fight for a culture," she said, "you might as well savor all its fruits."

Normally a moderate eater, Eddie felt giddily sated as he surveyed the table before him. There was the black beans and pork stew called *feijoada*, chicken *ximxim* with shrimps, lobsters in Brazil's northeastern style, *moqueca* fish stew, squash filled with shrimps, *mariscada, frango ensopado* . . . and for the life of him he couldn't see any sign that any of it had been eaten despite the slightly sleepy, thoroughly satisfied looks of Barranca, Javier and Enrique as the immensely pleased Maria looked on.

"Here, here," Barranca agreed as he tapped his knife against a ceramic water cup.

"I'll get the dessert," Maria said, evoking a groan from Eddie.

Barranca motioned to Javier and Enrique. *"Vaya y ayúdela, y toma tu tiempo."* They got up to go help Maria, knowing that they should stay away until called back.

Barranca looked at Eddie and turned up his palm. "What is troubling you, my friend?"

"Mm?" Eddie had been gazing out at the jungle beyond the compound entrance, but now turned his attention back to the table. "Sorry. I was just thinking . . ."

"My vision is a good one, but . . . ?"

Eddie sighed and rearranged himself on his chair as Barranca reached over and poured him another glass of the coconut milk, *cachaça* and groselha syrup concoction known as "Angel's Pee." It was dessert in itself, albeit a lethal one, and Eddie took a small sip before revealing his thoughts. "Without some heavy-duty motivation," he said, "the United States isn't going to recognize your country."

"Why not?"

"Because right now you look like an extortionist, and no American president is going to cave in to an extortionist."

Barranca had obviously already given that some thought. "But it is the humanitarian thing to do."

Eddie shook his head. "Doesn't matter if it's right, doesn't matter if you're Mother Theresa or Albert Schweitzer. You don't bully the world's only superpower, no matter how much sense your cause makes."

Barranca considered Eddie's words carefully. "I have not as of yet done anything, really. I've made no demands, no claims . . . I've not even had a formal communication with your government."

"That's true," Eddie agreed, "but again it doesn't matter. What matters is the perception, and right now the perception is that you're holding us hostage."

"That is a creation of your news media," Barranca said angrily. "They speculate endlessly and masquerade it as truth. There could be a dozen reasons why your coffee supply has been curtailed, and the fact is they simply do not know!"

Eddie held up his hands defensively. "Manolo, we've got movie stars who live their entire lives on camera, trials that are decided before the indictments are even in, politicians who spend more time with image consultants than policy advisors and entire countries whose idea of social reform is to hire an American PR firm to sell themselves to the American public. You think anybody in that world would cross the street for the truth? And besides . . ."

"Yes?"

"You *are* holding us hostage, remember?" When Barranca didn't respond, Eddie continued. "Look, right now the U.S. has no percentage in recognizing you. Not only do we end up with inflated coffee prices, it would also look like the U.S. knuckled under to a geopolitical extortionist."

At that point Barranca got dismissive. "It does not matter, Eddie, because we still have the upper hand. We control the coffee, and, as you have already seen, you cannot get along without it. U.S. recognition is not as key as you think."

"Yeah, well, about that . . ." Eddie sat back and scratched the back of his head. "Thing is, there's no guarantee that those plantation owners will stick to the agreements you made."

"But we have signed contracts!"

"In what jurisdiction, Manolo? Who's going to enforce them? Without some real fear of the consequences, there's no reason to believe the deals will be honored. Come to think of it, your 'virtual' country approach might be just the excuse they need to say the contracts weren't valid in the first place."

Barranca tried not to let his budding dismay show as he attempted to convince himself as much as Eddie that he'd thought it all through correctly. "But they are businessmen."

"That's the problem. Businessmen weigh the costs and the benefits of breaking contracts, and whether it's right or not doesn't enter into the equation. Hell, corporations willingly pay fines all the time if it's cheaper to do that than follow the rules. And if those growers break their deals with you," he concluded, "you're screwed."

"Then there will be a revolution," Barranca said definitively.

"Fine. And there'll also be blood and death and you'll end up as either a hero or a monster or, more than likely, both, like the guy you used to caddy for."

"Fidel," Barranca said flatly, that inflection betraying more of his ambiguity toward that mythical figure than he'd intended.

"You have to be a country," Eddie insisted after a decent interval, "and you have to have the U.S. recognize it or you'll get thrown to the dogs."

Barranca closed his eyes briefly, then at the sound of some stirring in the interior looked up and waved his hand. Maria, Javier and Enrique came in bearing plates of *brigadeiro* and *beijinho de coco* fudge candy, *quindim* coconut-and-egg pie, orange bars and sweet corn pudding. He waved them down into their seats; Javier and Enrique didn't understand English anyway, and there was no reason for Maria not to be a party to the conversation.

Barranca was disconsolate at Eddie's harsh reasoning but saw the truth of it. "So what is the solution, Eddie?"

"Basically, you have to go from being a terrorist to a freedom fighter."

"What is the difference?" Maria asked.

"Whose side you're on," Eddie answered.

"But who am I to freedom fight against?" Barranca protested. "At least as of this moment, the growers and we are on the same side. There is no enemy."

"That's a problem."

Maria got up and walked back to the kitchen, leaving Eddie and her grandfather to lapse into a strained silence, both lost in their private thoughts, searching through the maze of possibilities and obstacles.

In the evening calm, pungent with the smell of exotic flowers and a mesquite fire, Eddie and Barranca nursed glasses of Pirapora rum, the highest quality *cachaça* in Brazil.

"This is delicious," Eddie said as he drained the last of his rum. "Doesn't taste like any rum I know."

"The rum you know is distilled from molasses," Barranca explained, "a by-product of the sugar production process." He raised his glass and looked through it at the small fire burning across the yard. "*Cachaça* is fermented and distilled from pure sugarcane juice, and thus is a purer product than rum." He reached for the bottle but it was empty; he turned to call for his granddaughter but Eddie put a hand on his arm to stop him.

"I'll get it, Manolo. Just tell me where it is."

Barranca pointed to a small hut near the perimeter of the compound. "There, where it is cooler. You will find it in a wooden crate near the wine."

"A wine cellar." Eddie shook his head as he stood up, somewhat unsteadily. "You could single-handedly revolutionize revolutions altogether, Barranca."

A minute later Eddie pulled opened the heavy wooden door of the hut. He stepped inside, snapped on an overhead light and saw that it was constructed almost entirely of stone, with a single small window facing toward the jungle. The interior was indeed several degrees cooler than the outside air.

He saw a wooden crate on a stone shelf just where Barranca said it would be, but when he lifted it down and opened the lid, it was empty. He peered into the empty space on the shelf and saw that there was another crate behind it. With some effort, he jimmied it out and set it down on top of the empty one. The lid was fastened with several wooden dowels that had apparently been driven home with some force; he couldn't budge them with his hands. As he looked around for something to hit them with, Enrique and Javier entered the hut. Enrique tugged on Eddie's arm to move him away, then set the crate down on the floor. Eddie saw that Javier was carrying a rock about the size and shape of a brick. As Enrique gripped the crate to hold it steady, Javier raised the rock high and brought it down sharply. It slammed into the end of one of the dowels, driving it out of its rope enclosure. That loosened up the other dowels and Enrique was able to push them out with his fingers and open the lid. He lifted out a fresh bottle and handed it to Eddie with a flourish, then turned at a sound from the jungle, a rustle of palm fronds.

The three grew still but the sound ceased as abruptly as it had begun. Javier shrugged and said, *"Mono,"* then stood up, shut the light and led the way out.

"What's a mono?" Eddie asked Barranca when they got back to the veranda.

"A monkey. Why?"

"Heard something move in the brush." By then Eddie had gotten the bottle opened and poured two glasses.

Barranca ignored his. "It is an unusual problem I am faced with, Eddie."

"What's that?"

"That I have no enemy."

"Ah," Eddie said, remembering their conversation before the president's call came in. "Guess we'll have to invent one."

They talked some more, trading ideas, working through the ramifications. It started out with neither of them believing any of it was possible, but the more they spoke, the more they felt the stirrings of real potential.

"What would be our specific objective?" Barranca asked at one point.

"To get the American media to sympathize with you," Eddie said. "Once you have a news network eating out of our hand, the rest of the country will follow suit."

"Why is that?"

"Because they have no one else to believe. Your average American has no other sources of information than the one newspaper he reads and the nightly news on television. He doesn't know anything first-hand, and he doesn't trust his elected leaders even though he elected them. No matter how many times the news media fuck up, we still refuse to believe they're telling us anything other than gospel truth." Eddie seemed to think of something partway through the last sentence. "Come to think of it," he said, "we don't even know they fucked up unless *they* decide to tell us."

Barranca, more concerned with his present predicament than idle philosophizing, was interested in how they could win over the media.

"The best way," Eddie mused, "is to start off with them hating you, and then turn them around. Then they get like reformed sinners, not just repentant but zealous as hell to get the world over to their way of thinking."

"So what is it I do?"

"First thing you have to do is play hard to get. An interview with you has to be the coup of the year, something someone could hang a Pulitzer on. You'll start out as the bad guy: They'll imply you're guilty of everything from murder to child molestation, and when you won't do an interview, they'll make you look guilty of everything they've already implied when they report that you refused to meet with them."

"And how do I know when they're on my side?"

"When they say you 'declined' to be interviewed instead of 'refused,' and they make up an excuse for you." Eddie, satisfied with his analysis, took a sip of his rum. "Once you have them, so long as it's an exclusive, they'll imply that whatever you say is true."

"Why is that?"

"Because if it isn't true, their exclusive isn't worth dick."

"Ah." Barranca smiled. "I thought the American media were supposed to be objective."

"Right. You believe in the tooth fairy too? They couldn't be objective if they tried."

"Why do you say that?"

"Because every editorial decision is an editorial comment, that's why. Even if all you do is take somebody's hour-long speech and report on it in three minutes, you've editorialized. You decided what was important for people to hear and what they could ignore. And consider this: If a presidential candidate spends all afternoon laying out his plans for tax reform, foreign policy, health care and arms reduction, and thirty seconds on what a lousy dresser his opponent is, what do you figure is going to make it to the nightly news?"

Having realized he'd started lecturing, Eddie tried to relax and gather himself. "That's the key, my friend. Get the press on your side and your cause is practically won."

They talked some more. During a lull Barranca said, "Don't you need to get in touch with your president?" He pointed to the remnants of the sat phone. "Surely he will be worried. We have other phones."

Eddie considered the pile of junk that used to be a high-tech communications device. "Let's hold off for a while."

"Why?"

Eddie shrugged. "Beginning to get an idea."

"Truly?"

Eddie nodded, then looked away, turning some thoughts over in his head as Barranca stayed quiet. Eddie had pulled a thousand scams in his storied life but was starting to wonder if this situation wasn't completely beyond his abilities. No matter what avenue his scheming mind took him down, there was always an element missing, one that he couldn't fill in by himself.

He exhaled loudly and looked down at his glass. "Also beginning to get the idea that I can't pull it off alone."

Several seconds later they both turned at a sound coming from the other side of the building. "That ain't no *mono*," Eddie observed as they got up and headed for the steps of the veranda.

CHAPTER 47

The sounds of men shouting in the distance drifted toward them, babbling voices overlaid with a mixture of anger, surprise and fear. In short order more voices joined the excited chorus.

As Eddie and Barranca turned the corner of the building, peering into the night to try to ascertain the source of the commotion, the clatter of palm fronds and bamboo increased, soon followed by the emergence from the thicket across the yard of a group of men with someone in their midst. Machetes were being waved, some over the head of the captive, who was blindfolded and trying as best he could to feel for his next step despite being urged forward by the press of many hands on his back and shoulders.

The group slowed to a halt in front of the building, and Barranca waved them around to the back where he and Eddie had been sitting. Once there, Barranca didn't say anything, but jutted his chin toward the hapless prisoner by way of question.

"We caught him in the jungle," Larry Bartholomew said, throwing down a canvas tote topped with parallel wooden slats serving as handles. "He had this on him."

Bartholomew upended the tote, spilling out three sets of socks, a shaving kit, two shirts, two pairs of pants, an automatic pistol, a digital camera and a satellite phone.

"*Quién es él?*" Barranca asked softly.

"No idea," Bartholomew answered. "He won't tell us, and he's got no ID." He looked at the prisoner, who was standing fully erect and facing as forward as he could estimate with his head covered. "Don't even know if the guy speaks English."

"I speak English," the bound man said.

"Good," Barranca responded. "Then you will be kind enough to tell us who you are."

The man turned his head toward the sound of the voice. "Are you Manuel Barranca?"

"I am."

"Fine. So how about taking this smelly piece of shit off my head?"

Barranca waved at Bartholomew to do so. When the burlap bag was finally off his face, the man breathed deeply of clean air, then opened his eyes. He found Barranca first, looked at him appraisingly and coolly, then turned to Eddie, frowned for a second, and lifted his eyebrows. "Well, whaddaya know."

Eddie tried to read the man, but got nothing. He was of average height, average build, some sixty or so years of well-preserved age. He gave off no indication of being frightened or anxious, nor was he overconfident, although a trace of arrogance was evident due simply to the fact of his being so at ease in the face of his obviously dangerous circumstances. Eddie squirmed uncomfortably at what felt like having his photograph taken by a stranger. "Whaddaya know yourself, pal."

"You're Caminetti."

"What's it to you?"

The man looked from Eddie to Barranca and back again. His eerily expert visual survey took in the two men, the comfortable chairs behind them, the drinks sitting on the table and the deference his captors seemed to pay to them both. "Well," he said with a genuinely amused laugh, "I came down here to find you. Among other things."

"Then you're a genius," Eddie shot back, "'cause you found me right out of the box."

"Guess I did at that." He shifted his shoulders and twisted his head back and forth. "You suppose you can untie me, or do you figure I can take out this whole encampment without any weapons once my hands are free?"

Barranca gestured again at Bartholomew, who pulled a knife from his belt and sliced through the ropes binding the man's wrists. When the newly freed prisoner let his hands drop to his sides, everyone realized they'd been subconsciously expecting him to rub his wrists once the ropes were gone, but he didn't.

Barranca sat down. "Now will you be so kind as to tell us who—"

"Would you ask your men to back off?"

"Why?"

"Rather not announce myself to half of Brazil." He paused, then added, "Or Cuba."

Barranca waved his men away. Reluctantly, they obeyed.

The man stepped forward. "Dalton Galsworthy," he said softly. "Ordinary U.S. citizen, former CIA, now personal emissary of the president of the United States."

"And your assignment, Señor Galsworthy?"

The man pointed toward Eddie. "To rescue this guy—" He then waved a hand toward the compound. "—and to find out what the hell is going on."

"I see." Barranca touched a finger to his lips, thought for a moment, then slapped his thighs with both hands and stood up. "Well, my friend, there is nothing going on. My men will accompany you to our modest airport in Atahualpa, and you may return home." He turned to go.

"What about him?" Galsworthy said, pointing to Eddie.

"Him?" Barranca stopped and turned to regard Eddie. "He is a guest here. He may do as he wishes."

"Not sure I believe you."

Barranca now turned to Galsworthy. "Your beliefs are of surpassingly small consequence, Mr. Galsworthy. And your president agreed to my request that Mr. Caminetti come alone. Have a safe flight home."

He turned once more to leave, but something in Galsworthy's acerbic tone had piqued Eddie's interest. "Hang on a second, Manolo. Fella came all this way, it wouldn't be polite not to invite him in for a cuppa, now would it?"

Barranca sighed, and said without turning around, "I suppose not."

"How about taking his toys," Eddie called to Bartholomew, "and let the man sit a while?"

"Suits me," Bartholomew said agreeably. He walked forward and bent to retrieve the pistol, camera and sat phone, then kicked the bag over to Galsworthy and waved at his men to disperse. Galsworthy pointedly ignored his belongings, stepping over them as he approached the porch, grabbed a log handhold and swung himself up. "Wouldn't mind a cup of hot joe, now you mention it."

Barranca signaled for someone inside to bring out the coffee, then gestured Galsworthy to a seat. "Was your government under the impression that we had kidnapped Mr. Caminetti?"

Galsworthy shrugged, indicating that this was exactly what had been surmised. "Sure looked like it. And when he broke off right in the middle of a phone call with the president, they figured for sure he was in some kind of trouble." He didn't mention that he had been watching as Eddie went to the hut to get more rum, and had apparently completely misinterpreted what he saw. When he allowed himself to be captured, he'd fully expected to find Eddie with a crushed skull.

Eddie frowned, trying to reconstruct the sat phone conversation, but couldn't imagine what about it might have given that impression. He reached under a bamboo side table. "Only thing that was in trouble," he said as he brought his hand out, "was this piece of government issue piece of shit." With that, he dropped onto the larger coffee table a broken *piñata* of wires, circuit boards, shattered plastic housings, a battery and a bent telescoping antenna.

Galsworthy contemplated the tangled mess, cocked his head to get a better angle, then said, "Looks like it used to be a sat phone."

"It was," Eddie confirmed. "Fell to pieces in the middle of that phone call."

"Huh. Well, seems to me you could've found some other way to get in touch with your president."

"Maybe I didn't feel like it."

The ex–intelligence officer looked at Eddie with renewed interest. "And why might that be?"

Eddies stole a covert glance at Barranca, whose blank expression contained no clues as to their next move. "Mind if I ask you something?"

"Not at all." Galsworthy sat back as Maria Barranca came onto the porch carrying a tray, a small urn and three cups. It was dark, but it didn't stop her eyes from capturing his.

"My granddaughter, Maria," Barranca said.

"Nice to meet you," Galsworthy said, tearing his eyes away from hers only when another sense demanded attention. "Damn, that smells good. What'd you want to ask me?"

"What? Who?"

"You," Galsworthy said to Eddie. "You said you wanted to ask me—"

"Yeah. If you don't report in on time, what happens?"

Galsworthy went quiet as he watched Maria pour the coffee and hand him a cup. He passed it beneath his nose and closed his eyes appreciatively. Then he did it again.

"Aren't you gonna drink it?" Eddie asked.

"Eventually. But one thing about coffee . . . it's like chestnuts. Smells a lot better than it tastes. So let's see now: The president sends one guy into harm's way in a godforsaken jungle at the personal request of some *bandito*—" If Galsworthy was worried that Barranca might take offense, he didn't show it "—and when that guy goes quiet, he sends one of his most trusted covert operatives down to find him, and then that guy fails to report in."

He stopped waving the cup and held it a few inches from his lips. "Now, he's already pissed off that some third-rate, self-styled revolutionary is holding his country hostage and making him look like a limp dick in front of the whole world . . . sorry for the language, Maria." When she did nothing to indicate she'd even understood, he said, "And please don't tell me you don't speak perfect English."

"How—?"

"You've been following every word of this conversation, that's how. So anyway, after all of that, how do you suppose the president, a mere human being after all, is likely to react?" His eyes firmly planted on Barranca, he finally took a sip of the coffee, at which point he shifted his eyes to the cup. "Good Lord . . ."

"It's just a cup of coffee, spook," Maria said lightly.

"Ex-spook," Galsworthy said, taking another sip. "And Caruso was just another lounge singer." Reluctantly, it seemed, he set the cup down and folded his arms across his chest. "So why don't you just tell me what the hell is going on?"

In one of those rare, ineffable moments that can never be explained, a thousand disparate elements ricocheting around in Eddie's brain suddenly coalesced into a single, crystal-clear plan that, while risky and dangerous, was probably the only chance they had. He glanced at

Barranca, who nodded his permission as Maria drifted away quietly. "We're gonna fake a war," he said to Galsworthy, "turn Barranca into a hero and trick the United States into recognizing a new country that doesn't really exist."

Galsworthy didn't blink. "Why?"

"So Barranca's people can win their revolution without anybody getting killed for real."

"Because . . ."

"Because it's the right thing to do."

"Who loses?"

"Nobody. Price of coffee goes up a few percent and a couple hundred thousand people start living decent lives. Everybody wins, and the crisis is over."

"How does it work?"

Eddie laid it all out for him at the same time he laid it out for himself, anticipating questions and answering them before they were asked. Galsworthy occasionally glanced at Barranca to see if his expression indicated agreement.

"So there it is," Eddie said at last.

"Huh." Galsworthy picked up his coffee cup. "Okay." He took a sip. "I get it." He took another. "I'm in. Which, of course, you already knew."

"I took a chance."

"You had no choice," Galsworthy pointed out, having been the architect of one or two intricate plans himself. "And now I understand why you want the president to think you're in trouble."

Eddie didn't answer—he knew enough about Galsworthy already to know he didn't need to. He let the veteran intelligence officer have all the time he needed to think through the implications.

"You're going to need the press on your side," Galsworthy said at last.

Barranca and Eddie exchanged pleased glances, both at Eddie's prescience and Galsworthy's confirming insight. "What I don't know," Eddie said, "is how to get them there."

"For another cup of coffee, I'll tell you." He held up his cup and waved it toward Maria, who was standing by on the far side of the room adjoining the porch. *"Señorita, pour some more!"*

"What?" she called back indignantly as she walked forward.

"I said, *por favor!*"

"That's what I thought you said." Maria, smiling, picked up the coffeepot and walked out onto the porch. "You sonofabitch," she said easily as she poured the coffee.

Eddie shot a quizzical glance at Barranca. "Somethin goin on here we should know about?"

Galsworthy grinned as he held out his cup. "I saw this sly wench in a play. Back when the Company was recruiting at Yale."

"A piece of junk," Maria said, wiping the tip of the spout as she tilted the pot back up. "Written by one of our graduate students who eventually went into real estate."

"But you were splendid," Galsworthy said as he set the cup down. "And that was a funny line."

She curtsied, then turned to go. "Why, thank you."

When she was out of earshot Galsworthy said, "An actress. Perfect. She in on your little cause, Manuel?"

"Wholeheartedly. But I will not put her in harm's way."

"Understood."

Eddie picked up his glass and jiggled it. "The press. You were saying . . ."

"What I—" Galsworthy stopped talking and looked at his watch. "I need to make a sat phone call."

Barranca sat forward. "To whom?"

"The president."

Galsworthy waited for Barranca's permission to use his phone, and when none appeared forthcoming he turned to Eddie.

"What do you need to call him for?" Eddie asked. He knew he had no right to ask such a question but had a strong feeling Galsworthy would be willing to explain.

"To tell him not to launch an attack."

"An attack against whom?" Barranca asked.

"You," Galsworthy replied as he got up to get his phone.

When he was out of earshot, a shaken Eddie said, "Jeez. Guess it's a damned good thing your men captured him."

Barranca snorted. "My men are amateurs. Coffee workers." He gestured toward Galsworthy. "One such as this is not captured by amateurs unless he wishes to be."

Galsworthy returned and resumed his seat. "We were talking about the press," Eddie prompted him.

"You've got one huge advantage here," Galsworthy said to Barranca, "and that's your isolation. What we do, we get to one of the news networks and give them an exclusive. Nobody else gets so much as a disposable camera in here."

"Yes . . . ?"

"That way, they're so far up your ass you can tell em dog shit is gold and they'll report it as gospel."

Barranca thought it over, then said, "But will they believe that this situation is important enough?"

"That's the beauty part!" Galsworthy exclaimed, the first time Eddie or Barranca had seen him at all excited. "They'll *make* it important! If they have the exclusive, they'll build it up into the biggest story since O.J., because the more important the story is, the more important *they* are."

"But if they are investigative reporters," Barranca persisted, "will they not feel compelled to investigate?"

"Not necessarily," Galsworthy said. "What they're going to want is great visuals, and what they're going to want even more than that is their own people right smack in the middle of them. You give them that, and you let them know you can take it away at a moment's notice?" He held his arms out, palms upward. "It'll be like having your own personal news network, because sources are more important than truth."

"How about we throw some weapons of mass destruction shit in, too?" Eddie suggested. "That ought to get their juices flowing."

"Good!" Galsworthy said. "Especially if we can get them to find out about the weapons themselves, tip off somebody in the Agency, and then afterward they can beat the shit out of him for acting on false information."

"So which one do we go for?" Barranca asked.

"Only one will do," Galsworthy said as he reached for his cup.

"GNN," Eddie volunteered.

"Yep." Galsworthy took a sip and set the cup down. "Go high or go home, I always say. Besides, if somebody else has it and GNN doesn't, they'll either launch an invasion of their own to get here themselves or sic every reporter they have onto the story to show where the other guys got it wrong." He pointed a warning finger. "And you do not want them looking too close."

"So how does it work?" Eddie asked.

"Might be a little dicey," Galsworthy said, "but what we should do is plant the seeds of a story with the news guys, then have them call some government higher-up to confirm it. Since there's nothing going on, the government guy doesn't know shit, but he thinks the news network does, so what he'll do, he'll try to get as much information out of them as possible and give as little as possible back."

"Which is easy," Eddie said, "because he hasn't got anything."

"Right. But he has to let the news guys think he does, or they'll hang up on him and search for somebody else. So he kind of lets them know they're on the right track, just to keep them talking, and now the news guys think they're on to something real, so they give the government official everything they have, and while he doesn't confirm anything, he doesn't deny it, either, which to a reporter is like confirmation from the pope. And as a bonus—"

"You've now planted it with the government as well," Eddie finished for him, shaking his head in wonder. "That's too beautiful."

Galsworthy held up his hand. "But it's only good for a few days," he said, "because eventually they're going to find out it's all horseshit." He turned to Barranca. "Which means we've got about four or five days at the most, maybe six, to wrap this whole thing up and then get rid of the evidence so nobody gets wise."

Eddie nodded his understanding, but Barranca looked troubled. "What?" Galsworthy asked him.

"We have one obligation. A business delivery, due in five days."

Galsworthy looked confused. "A business delivery?"

"Yes, señor. We have promised to deliver a rather large number of drums of fertilizer."

At the mention of fertilizer, Galsworthy lost his faint air of wise cynicism; his eyes went hard and his lips went bloodless, like a feral cat ready to lunge. "Fertilizer." Bomb-making ingredients.

"Easy, Dalton," Eddie said, sensing the man's sudden, and potentially dangerous, alteration. "He means it literally."

"Fertilizer for who?"

"El Barristo Industries."

"The largest coffee grower in Brazil?"

"*Sí*. They were integral to our ability to secure contracts with other growers. For them we make a special effort."

Galsworthy exhaled and dropped back against his chair. "Still can't get over this, Barranca. I came down here expecting to find you guys fighting the growers and instead you're in bed with them. So what are we looking at?"

"One hundred drums, four hundred liters each. A trip of some sixty kilometers."

Galsworthy whistled softly. "Gonna suck up a lot of manpower."

"Not necessarily," Eddie said, then paused as the other two looked at him. "Let's just make the stuff look like chemical weapons. We give the news guys a peek and get us some major sympathy."

"Good idea." Galsworthy turned to Barranca. "Then we leak to the CIA that you captured all of it. Throw a little scare into them and get you some respect."

"Freedom fighters do not use such weapons," Barranca declared.

"Yeah, right," Galsworthy sneered. "But don't worry about it. The U.S. government doesn't ask too many questions of its friends. Once you're written in the Good Book, you can have secret police and corrupt officials, you can fund terrorism . . . hell, you can even have the bomb, and we won't give a shit."

"But what if your government reveals that I have them?"

Galsworthy and Eddie both laughed. "You nuts?" Galsworthy said. "They wouldn't mention that stuff unless they had a bottle of it sitting right on the president's desk. Look what happened the last time."

Barranca, less enamored of the excitement of the venture than his two compatriots, seemed uncomfortable. "It seems a trifle hit or miss," he observed with a sigh, "especially with respect to who the newspeople call, and how he responds."

"You're exactly right," Galsworthy agreed. "But we've got some backup." He went strangely quiet.

"What backup?" Barranca asked.

"I can't tell you."

They could see he meant it. While Galsworthy's eyes were averted, Barranca looked at Eddie questioningly, and Eddie answered with a barely perceptible shake of his head: *Let it go.* For better or worse, they were now dependent on Galsworthy.

"This call from the news guys to the Agency," Eddie said, redirecting the conversation. "Has to be just the right guy, doesn't it?"

"Definitely," Galsworthy answered, glad to get past the awkward lapse. "Has to be somebody who's hugely ambitious, who'll take a chance and be a little sloppy in order to be the guy who lays this coup in front of his superiors." He wiped a hand over his mouth several times as he thought it over. "Preferably somebody who's in the doghouse and is looking for just the right opportunity to get himself back on track . . ."

As his voice drifted off Eddie said, "You've got a guy in mind."

Galsworthy didn't seem to hear him at first, but a smile slowly made its way across his face. "Oh, have I got the guy . . ."

What Galsworthy would later tell Eddie, but which he wasn't willing to share with a non-citizen, was that CIA senior analyst Joffrey Hayne had three deep contacts in South America, named Hernando Vasquez, Nicholas Peron and Ricardo Sabista. He trusted them implicitly, paid them handsomely and used them sparingly so as not to risk blowing their cover. Hayne reported their information to no one other than DCI Wainwright himself, although he did occasionally leak watered-down versions of their intel to major news media when his personal Q rating needed a little boost. What Hayne didn't know was that Hernando Vasquez, Nicholas Peron and Ricardo Sabista were all pseudonyms for an Argentinean postal clerk named Isaiah Jefferson, former gardener at the home of DCI Wainwright, who had resettled the man in his parents' native Buenos Aires and used him not only as a source but whenever he needed to leak some information to the press via the supremely ambitious and predictable Joffrey Hayne.

What Wainwright didn't know was that Galsworthy used him whenever he needed to leak some information to Wainwright.

"Hey, Barranca," Galsworthy said suddenly. "You caddied Castro's match with Che Guevara, right?"

"Did he ever," Eddie said. "Got some great stories, too."

"I bet. So tell me how it ended."

Happy to take a break, Barranca turned his glass of rum a few times, then said, "The hole you see in the photo of Guevara putting is the sixteenth. Castro was up by three strokes when we reached it, and had already made a nine on this hole. Ernesto was lying seven, and needed this putt to keep the match going. Unless he won this hole, Fidel would be up three with only two holes to go, and that would be it."

"And they were taking the game pretty seriously?" Galsworthy ventured.

"Oh, indeed. Everyone was. You can see the tension etching lines in the faces of the onlookers, Fidel himself standing on the opposite side of the hole, his own putter still in his hand, anxiously watching Che's every move. Che examined the green from every angle, as though observing bacteria under a microscope. He held the putter up so it dangled from his fingertips and tried to assess the slope of the green, bent his head to change the angle of the light, ran his hand over the grass to read the grain . . . but eventually he ran out of ways to gather more information and had no choice but to actually hit the ball. You see can see the intensity of his concentration in his strained posture, the stiffness of his hands and how tightly he appears to be gripping the putter. Fidel, looking on, was just as anxious, focusing as though to deflect the path of the ball as hard as Che was trying to keep it on a straight path."

"So he hit it," Eddie said impatiently. "Then what?"

"It was well struck, skidding only slightly before taking hold of the grass and rolling smoothly. The speed seemed perfect, and all of us were certain it would only run out of velocity at the exact moment it reached the lip of the hole, and it was so, but that was also its undoing. Barely moving when it reached the hole, there was no momentum left to resist the sideways pull of the grain, and at the very last possible moment the ball veered ever so slightly, no more than the width of a few dimples on its surface, and came to rest with some if it hanging over the edge of the hole, but most of it still on the grass."

Barranca took a sip of rum, swirled it around in his mouth and swallowed. "And there it stayed, Che remaining hunched over in disbelief, Castro exhaling with an audible sigh, I still holding the flag, uncertain whether I should replace it right away or wait until Che picked up his ball. I chose the latter, and it seemed a very long time before he finally stood up straight, walked to where Fidel was standing and held out his hand. Fidel, trying not to betray his elation, grabbed him in an embrace—" Barranca set the glass down on the table with a definitive *clunk* "—and that was the first and last time the two ever played golf together."

They spoke far into the night, long after the soft murmurs of other conversations around the compound ceased to drift their way through the heavy night air. Sometime after midnight Maria came out with a glass of rum and, unbidden but with no objection, took a seat.

"So what historic campaigns are you aging warriors launching?' she asked as she slipped off her shoes and tucked her feet under her.

"Have some respect," Galsworthy said. "We're making your grandpa a hero."

"He already is a hero," she said. "All you're doing is telling the world."

"You're wrong," Eddie countered. "Nobody's a hero until the news media decide he's a hero. And even then it's more about image than substance."

"That's a very cynical attitude, Eddie."

"In a world like this one, the only clear thinkers are the cynics."

"Chris' a'mighty, Caminetti," Galsworthy slurred. "I was a little less drunk, I'd write that down."

"Is that cynicism what lets you pull off such a hoax as this one?" Maria asked. She'd only caught bits and pieces of the conversation but had managed to get the gist of the plan.

"A hoax?" Eddie said with mock indignation. "How can you call it a hoax?"

Even in the dark they could see Maria's eyebrows rise. "You can't be serious! What else would you call it?"

"An event," Eddie answered.

"Ah. I see."

"I don't think you do." Eddie held out his hand and Maria handed him her glass. He took a sip and smacked his lips. "Saving the good stuff for yourself, I see."

"An event, you said."

"Most of what we see in public is just a series of bullshit events." Eddie took another sip and handed the glass back. "Stage-managed, calculated, carefully orchestrated."

"What are you talking about?"

Eddie tilted his head. "Political conventions, for instance. Every second is planned and rehearsed. They know who's going to say what, when they're going to say it . . . they even light up signs telling the audience when to applaud. They have platforms nobody ever looks back on, make poll-friendly speeches drafted by dozens of committees and consultants, they time entrances and exits according to television station schedules, do the boring stuff in the afternoon and the staged fireworks during prime time, and yet"—he held up his hands and let them drop—"the networks cover the whole thing like it's real news, like it was naturally unfolding right before our very eyes. And nobody says boo about it."

"But everybody knows that's theater," Maria protested. "They're not putting on a phony war."

"What's the difference?" Eddie argued. "If a candidate mumbles some Spanish and eats a taco in the barrio or parades down Mulberry Street during the Feast of San Gennaro, what's he telling us . . . he's really a Mexican or an Italian?" Eddie shook his head. "No. He's telling us he's a better bullshit artist than the other guy, and that's why we should vote for him. And we do, too, because we're so used to being fed bullshit and told it's the real thing, we can't tell the difference anymore. We literally can't separate image from substance. At every Wayne Newton show in Vegas he says he's having the best time of his life, and every night eight hundred people go home believing they shared a moment with him that's never happened before. A president says it's not about oil and there are enough people who believe him to put him back in office. Osama bin Laden was our hero when he fought the Russians and now he's Satan, Qaddafi used to be Satan but now he sees the light . . . you think those guys really changed?"

Maria was absorbed, but not intimidated. "So you're saying that all you're doing is what everybody else is doing?"

"Pretty much."

"And you justify it because . . . ?"

"It's the right thing to do."

"That's what they all say."

"True," Eddie agreed. "But in this case I'm right."

Maria laughed and reached over to pat her grandfather's arm. "I know you are, but is that the real reason?"

"Nope." Eddie yawned and scratched his chest. "I'm gonna make four million bucks on the deal."

"Very funny." Maria stifled her own yawn. "So what will be your role in the charade, Mr. Galsworthy?"

"He will be one of my lieutenants," Barranca informed her. "As our Mr. Caminetti is purportedly in distress somewhere, it remains to Mr. Galsworthy to guide our friends in the press to the light of truth and reason."

Maria eyed the ex–intelligence officer carefully. "You can pass," she decided, "with enough makeup and the right clothes. But somehow I don't think 'Galsworthy' befits a Latino revolutionary."

"Ah, no" Galsworthy agreed. "I've been thinking of a suitable pseudonym."

"So what's it gonna be?' Eddie asked.

Galsworthy looked up at the ceiling fan, pushed his chin up to stretch the skin on his neck, then looked back down:

"How does 'Pablo' sound?"

EPILOGUE

CAMP TRUMP (FORMERLY CAMP DAVID), MARYLAND

The grizzled Marine veteran watching the house from the nearby woods glanced at his watch. Although he was anxious at the amount of time this had gone on, to all outward appearances he was as unconcerned as one of the implacable trees that dotted the snow-covered forest floor.

Through the windows of the main house he could see the president and his visitor as they talked. The visitor, carrying a cane and with his arm in a cast, arose from his seat before the fire only once, but the president, by turns agitated, calm or simply restless, had gotten up and down several times, once even disappearing into another room for a few minutes before slowly wandering back, either at the behest of the visitor or because of something provocative the man had said.

At long last the visitor got painfully to his feet, limped toward the door, and allowed the president to help him on with his coat. They shook hands, the president as was his custom clasping the visitor's shoulder with his left hand, and a few seconds later two Marines took up positions on either side of the man as he shuffled away from the house.

The veteran Marine took one last hit of his cigarette and threw it to the ground, where it melted a spot of snow with a sizzle and drowned itself. When he got to the house the door was ajar, and he walked in unbidden.

"So?" he asked as he unbuttoned his uniform overcoat.

The president, who was standing in front of the fire and hadn't heard him come in, whirled on him. "Criminy, Galsworthy . . . you should wear a goddamned bell or something, people can hear you coming."

"Must be your hearing, sir. I wasn't even trying to be quiet."

Eastwood grunted and turned back to the fire. "I think it went okay. You can listen to the tape if you want."

"I will, later. Did you shut if off?"

"Shit!" Eastwood strode to a nearby cupboard, opened it and pressed a button on the faceplate of a glowing machine. "You or I say anything I should erase?"

Galsworthy shook his head. "I wouldn't worry about it."

"You never worry about anything."

"To the contrary, I worry about everything. Got anything to drink?"

Eastwood jerked a thumb toward the wet bar. "Help yourself."

On his way across the room, Galsworthy spotted a brown paper bag on a table. "What's this?"

"Huh?"

"I saw Eddie give it to you. Didn't you look inside?"

"Ah, jeez . . . no. See what it is."

Galsworthy picked up the bag, rustled the top open and reached inside, pulling out a squat brown bottle, which he rested on the paper in his hand as he held the label toward the light. "I'll be damned . . . this is good stuff."

"What is it?"

"Pirapora rum. Best damned *cachaça* in the world." He held up the bottle. "You mind?"

"Help yourself."

Galsworthy set the bag down and began picking at the seal on the bottle with his thumbnail. "Caminetti going to play ball and stay quiet?" he asked casually.

"I think so. I should've gotten an Oscar for that acting job I pulled on him."

"You got the presidency for an acting job. I saw all of the debates."

"You always this cynical?"

"Have to be." By this time Galsworthy had gotten the foil seal off, and he went to the kitchen for a corkscrew. "My job depends on it. Besides, the appropriateness of my attitude is confirmed on a daily basis."

The president called out, "You want to talk about cynical? How do you feel about Caminetti getting five million out of me?"

"Good one," Galsworthy called back from the kitchen. "Especially now that you don't have to pay it."

"Course I'm paying it, but imagine the master hustler getting out-hustled. Dalton? Hey, you there?"

Galsworthy walked out of the kitchen, bottle in one hand, half-inserted corkscrew in the other. "You're paying him?"

"If I take the deal he worked out, I pretty much have to. You having trouble with that cork?"

"Huh?" Galsworthy looked down at his hands. "Oh. No, no trouble." He went back into the kitchen, set the bottle down and clamped his hands over his mouth so the president wouldn't hear him laughing. That wily sonofabitch, Caminetti . . .

Getting hold of himself and picking the bottle back up, he gave the corkscrew another turn but didn't speak until he could trust himself to keep his voice steady. "If you're paying him, what did you mean about him getting outhustled?"

"Just that he didn't glom on to the fact that you were reporting everything back to me. Not a big deal really."

"Yeah." *Almost everything, Mr. President.* Galsworthy willed his hand to stay steady as he poured two fingers of the *cachaça* into a pair of crystal brandy snifters, then carried them into the sitting area.

"Thanks," Eastwood said as he accepted his and waved Galsworthy to a seat. He held up the snifter and said, "To Eddie."

Galsworthy clinked his glass against the president's and echoed, "To Eddie," adding *If only you knew* in his mind.

They both stared into the fire for a few minutes, each lost in his own thoughts, until Eastwood said, "One thing I still don't get, though."

"What's that, sir?"

"Eddie's injuries. I couldn't ask him where he'd really gotten them, since I was supposed to think he'd gotten hurt when the mercenaries supposedly captured him, so tell me: How'd he get so banged up in that plane crash when Barranca walked away without a scratch?"

Galsworthy waited for a sip of the potent rum to sear its way down his throat. "There was no plane crash, Mr. President. We had a Cessna crop duster flown in over the trees and behind a hill, then set off some ground explosions to make it look like there'd been an accident."

"I see. So when was Eddie hurt?"

"The night before."

"How?"

"You wouldn't believe it, sir, so I suggest we just leave it at that."

Trusting Galsworthy, Eastwood assumed he was being kept in the dark for good reason, and didn't press for details. Except . . . "Barranca didn't rough him up when he first got there, did he?"

"No!" Galsworthy assured him quickly. "He'd already been there for nearly six days when he . . . when the accident happened."

"Ah. That's right. So you said." Eastwood was dying to know, but let it go. "One last thing, Dalton." He slouched on the easy chair and propped his elbow on the armrest, rubbing his forehead as he stared contemplatively into the fire. "I would have done the right thing by the coffee workers if I'd known what was going on. He should have known that. Instead he pulls this fake man stunt and believes he forced my hand, which you and I both know is bullshit. Hell, the only reason I agreed to pay him the five million anyway was to keep him from going public and to make sure he didn't suspect I knew what was going on all along."

"I figured that."

"So how come he didn't trust me?"

It was a good question, and Dalton knew that Eastwood wouldn't figure it out. The president, as do all presidents, tended to think in lofty, geopolitical terms, high-flying motivations layered with rational, long-range thinking, but they often forgot about the baser impulses that drive individual men and women. If Eastwood would just come down to earth, Galsworthy thought, and remember who and what Eddie Caminetti was, he'd have his answer in a flash. "I don't know, sir, but I wouldn't assume he didn't trust you." *In fact, he trusted you completely. It's just that trusting you to do right by Barranca had nothing to do with it.*

The president stayed silent, his mind in a rush. "Another thing I can't figure," he said, "is how the hell Caminetti put together this deal with Barranca. I mean, what was his negotiating strategy? He refused to be briefed by the State Department, so what cards did he think he had? My God, no wonder he let Barranca push him around like that!"

When no answers were forthcoming from Galsworthy, Eastwood said, "Ah, well," stood up, yawned and stretched his arms over his head. When he let his arms back down he waved the issue away with a flick of his wrist. "It all worked okay, didn't it?"

"You bet it did, Mr. President," Galsworthy concurred, silently breathing a sigh of relief that there were to be no more questions.

He wasn't sure how he would have gone about explaining to the president of the United States the real story behind the phony Coffee War, which was that Eddie and Barranca had bet the entire outcome of the revolution on a single game of golf.

SOMEWHERE IN BRAZIL—DAY FOUR OF THE COFFEE WAR

Eddie was going nuts.

When they'd laid all these plans out, it hadn't dawned on him that everybody would have something to do, some active participation in the elaborate scheme, but that his only job for two solid days would be to stay out of sight until the newspeople arrived and Barranca came to "rescue" him. The revolutionary himself was off in Peru and Colombia finalizing arrangements with the coffee growers, assuring them that it was just a matter of days until they could begin shipping again, at the escalated prices he'd promised. Galsworthy was running around in the jungle playing Pablo to the GNN crew, Enrique and Javier were happily shooting off rockets trying to convince the reporters that a full-scale war was under way, and Maria Barranca was off somewhere turning a few dozen coffee workers into a pathetic band of rudely uprooted refugees.

At least they'd left him at the golf course, but they'd neglected to also leave at least one guard who knew a putter from a head cover and had more than two Brazilian *reals* in his pocket to rub together. Sure, he had the run of the course and could play as much as he wanted, but for an Olympic-caliber hustler like Eddie Caminetti, playing solo golf was like playing solo poker. There was just no point to it, so he'd spent the afternoon standing in one spot hitting hundreds of balls with his sand wedge, producing a cluster of landings so tight it wasn't likely he was going to improve much if he kept on going, and trying not to think about Barranca's rescue of him they were supposed to stage the following morning but hadn't yet figured out how to accomplish.

So now he was tense, anxious and irritable, and the last thing he needed was Dalton Galsworthy, near-catatonic and staring stupidly out into space, busting his balls over a harmless little golf wager.

Pieces of his brain snapping and arcing like a downed power line, Galsworthy turned slowly toward Eddie. "You had the full authority of the president of the United States," he said with some effort, "and bet it all on a fucking *golf match?*"

They were sitting on lawn chairs in front of a supply building some two miles east of the main compound. The night air hung heavy and still, as though inside a protective bell jar that trapped within itself the smells of jacaranda and hyacinth and the sounds of cicadas. Fireflies blipped against the radar-screen darkness, in no hurry to get anywhere but compelled to periodically announce their presence regardless. It was hard to imagine in that bucolic setting that there were people elsewhere in the world who were anything but at peace. They'd already been through one bottle of rum, and Barranca had gone to fetch another one.

"Why the hell not?"

"You were supposed to negotiate, that's why not!"

"I did."

"What do you mean, you did!"

"The president just told me to work something out. He didn't tell me how."

"But a golf match?"

Eddie straightened up in his chair and turned toward Galsworthy. "That's what I do, Dalton," he said with exaggerated patience, as though explaining rudimentary multiplication to a slow nine-year-old. "Barranca knew that and so did President Eastwood. What the hell did you expect me to do down here . . . debate macroeconomics with the guy?"

"But you lost!"

Eddie shrugged. "Hey, it happens, what can I tell you. Can't win all the time. If I did, who the hell would play with me? Besides, it kind of worked out pretty good all around, didn't it?"

"So you say."

"You, too. You agreed to be a part of it."

They stopped talking when they heard Barranca approach. He was carrying cigars and a fresh bottle of rum, which he set down on a low table in front of them.

"How'd you figure it out, anyway?" Eddie asked Galsworthy after he'd lit up.

Galsworthy eyed Barranca slyly. "Fearless leader here told you all those great stories about Fidel Castro's golf match with Che Guevara, right? But you didn't tell it all, did you, Manolo."

"Perhaps not every last detail."

"Right. So start with Fidel coming to you for lessons. When was that?"

Feeling Eddie's eyes on him, Barranca said, "Right after Che came to him and proposed that they play together."

"Which was?"

"Two days before their match. First he swore me to secrecy, then we met several times each day and I taught him as much as I could."

As Eddie stared, Galsworthy said, "So this was supposed to be a match between two guys who'd never picked up a club before, and Castro had himself some secret lessons?"

Galsworthy didn't wait for him to answer, but reached into his jacket and pulled out a small manila envelope. Handing it to Eddie he said, "Remember these?"

Eddie took the envelope and opened it. Inside were copies of the photos of Castro and Guevara's golf match. "Sure. So?"

Galsworthy reached over and took the photos, then pushed aside the bottle of rum and laid them out on the table. "Take a closer look," he instructed. As Eddie did so Galsworthy said, "You see anybody smiling anywhere? Does anybody look happy, like they're having a good time?"

Eddie, bleary-eyed as he was, tried to focus on the faces. Galsworthy was right: To a man, everybody in the pictures looked tense, agitated . . . almost desperate. "I don't get it," Eddie said. "Why'd they all look so grim?"

Galsworthy leaned back and bit off the end of a cigar. "The CIA always suspected," he said enigmatically, "but you know for sure, don't you, Manolo?"

Eddie looked up at Barranca, who lifted his chin and scratched his neck. "I liked Ernesto Guevara very much," he said. "He took life seriously. Did you know he was a doctor?"

"A medical doctor?" Eddie asked in surprise.

Barranca nodded. "He received his degree in Argentina in 1953—"

"I thought he was Bolivian."

"No." Barranca's voice grew soft and wistful. "He died in Bolivia. His nickname, Che, is Argentinean slang for friend, much like chum or mate. He graduated from medical school the same summer that Fidel led an attack on the Moncada Army Barracks in Santiago de Cuba. It was a terrible, misguided operation, and most of the attackers were killed, but Fidel was arrested and sentenced to fifteen years in prison."

"And released two years later," Galsworthy said.

"Yes, as part of an amnesty ordered by Batista. Fidel fled to Mexico and from there began planning his revolution. Che, restless and idealistic and looking for adventure, joined him there, and a few months later the two of them loaded sixty would-be revolutionaries onto a yacht called *Granma,* sailed it to Oriente Province in Cuba and tried again to launch a rebellion."

"With sixty guys?" Eddie exclaimed.

"Foolish, no? Most of them were of course killed, but Fidel and Che fled to the mountains and continued to press their cause. Now that they were folk heroes, they were able to organize considerable support among the Cuban people."

"Fidel was a pretty good PR man, too," Galsworthy said. "Spent a lot of time rallying support overseas." He tapped the side of his head. "Like I was telling you guys: Get the press on your side and the battle is half won."

"Dalton is right," Barranca said. "The more heroic Castro and Che appeared to the world, the worse it became for the Batista regime. Urban terrorism increased, the middle class became alienated and United States support of Batista began to cool. In the last days of 1958 Castro and Che attacked from the Sierra Maestra Mountains. The Cuban army fell apart and on New Year's Day Batista fled to the Dominican Republic. A week after that, Ernesto entered Havana."

"Ernesto?" Eddie, who despite his considerably inebriated state had been listening with rapt attention, frowned. "Che Guevara entered Havana?"

"Yes."

"Huh." Eddie frowned in concentration. "Didn't realize he'd played such a big part."

"Oh, yes. Both he and Fidel took charge of the country, along with Fidel's brother, Raul."

"Which left them with a little problem," Galsworthy said. "Because once things settled down only one of them could be the big *kahuna*."

"Imagine the problem facing them," Barranca said, "especially now that they were very close comrades who'd fought and struggled side by side. They'd both been bloodied, had lost dear friends, been in hiding together. They were weary of the killing and the heartbreak, and weren't about to let their deep friendship disintegrate over the matter of who would hold the reins of the new government."

"Neither of them wanted to fight for it," Galsworthy added. "It would make no sense and could only damage the revolution. They had to settle it peacefully."

"Like gentlemen," Barranca explained.

"And quickly."

"Yeah, I get it." Eddie's cigar had gone cold. He reached for Barranca's lighter, lit it and held the flame to the tip of his cigar. As he rapidly puffed to draw the flame in, he said, "So whud they do?"

Galsworthy and Barranca didn't answer.

"I mean," Eddie said, snapping the lighter shut and dropping it on the table as he blew out a cloud of smoke, "how'd they decide Castro was going to get the job?"

Still getting no answer, Eddie, puzzled, looked from Galsworthy to Barranca and back again, until Galsworthy pointed down at the photos on the table. Uncomprehending, Eddie picked up the pictures, leafed through them without seeing anything new, then froze and looked back at Barranca, who folded his hands in his lap.

His besotted mind reeling and dizzy, Eddie said, "Are you trying to tell me Fidel Castro and Che Guevara played that golf match for the presidency of Cuba?"

Barranca shrugged and said, "Where do you think I got the idea for our little competition?"

They gave Eddie some time to get over his shock and then tried to get back to the matter of how they would stage his rescue for the GNN news crew the next morning, but none of them had any great ideas and they felt themselves in danger of growing despondent.

Suddenly, Eddie sat up straight. Thinking he'd come up with a brainstorm, Galsworthy and Barranca sat up as well, and waited to hear what Eddie had to say.

"I gotta go to the can," he announced.

Galsworthy slumped back in his seat. Barranca said, "The facilities this far out are, to say the least, spartan."

"Shitter's a shitter, Manolo, so point me to it."

"Drunk as you are, let me show you."

"No drunker'n you, but lead on."

They left Galsworthy to the sighing palms and reeds of the humid jungle and made their way across a field. In a tiny clearing amid a stand of *mpingo* trees, Eddie saw a ramshackle structure that looked kind of like an outhouse, but without the charm and structural integrity. "Don't tell me . . ."

Barranca stepped forward and opened the door with a flourish. "Your limousine awaits, sir."

Eddie tried to peer through the darkness outside and the fog in his brain but, try as he might, he couldn't make out a throne. "Someone stole your crapper there, Manolo."

"No, it is there. Come."

Eddie walked up and peered inside, but all he saw in the otherwise empty facility was a hole in the ground, two footprint-shaped indentations on either side of it and a catalog from *Lojas Americanas*, Brazil's largest department store, hanging from a wire on the wall. "That's the john?" Eddie groaned. "That's it?"

"It is actually a much healthier way to do your business," Barranca assured him.

"Healthy wasn't high on my list of priorities right now."

Eddie swayed as he grabbed hold of the door, and Barranca reached out to steady him. "Will you be okay?"

"What're you gonna do, help me?" Eddie drew a deep breath and straightened his posture, as though preparing to fight Mongol hordes rather than enter an outhouse. "Now get the hell out of here."

"As you wish." Barranca made sure Eddie had a firm grip on the door before making his departure, and also made sure the American had successfully negotiated the foot-high ledge leading into the interior.

It wasn't easy, but somehow Eddie managed to keep his balance, keep his pants clean and achieve a reasonable line-up on the hole. After divesting the *Lojas Americanas* catalog of the pages describing pigeon coops, pillows, pimiento recipes, pistols and Pilates equipment, he struggled to his feet but badly misjudged the traction of the damp ground. His left foot slid out from under him and slammed into the wall. Underestimating the damage, he tried to stand in order to pull up his pants, but the freshly twisted ankle betrayed him and gave out, sending him crashing into the opposite wall, where his face struck the wire to which the department store catalog was attached. The sudden pain caused him to reflexively pull up, at which point he banged the side of his head against a cross-member below the roof.

Now anxious to get the hell out of there as fast as he could, he reached down to grab the front of his pants with one hand while swinging the door outward with the other, ready to step outside into the fresh night air.

But Eddie had forgotten that his pants were still down around his ankles and that there was a ledge at the bottom of the door he had to get over. Both of these elements of the exit path conspired against him, and while the upper part of his body did indeed manage to get through the door, his feet didn't, sending him crashing forward with nothing to stop his fall except either the hand and arm holding the door open or the one holding his pants up. The microsecond he allowed himself to make the decision was too long, and by the time he did get a hand out in front of him it was too late for him to do much about cushioning the blow that his falling body insisted on dealing to it. A terrific pain lanced through his forearm just as he hit the ground.

He didn't move much after that, unsure of which part of his anatomy had come through in good enough shape to trust, and that's how Barranca and Galsworthy found him some fifteen minutes later after he'd failed to return. The sight of him sprawled on the ground with his pants down, moaning and holding his arm, was too much for them, especially in their rum-induced haze, and there were a few minutes of laughing before they realized that Eddie's injuries were more than merely embarrassing.

"Think my fuggin arm's broken," Eddie murmured bleakly.

"Holy shit," Galsworthy said as he looked at the arm. "I think he's right. Hey, you're bleeding, too."

Eddie touched a finger to his head and looked at it. Even in the pale moonlight he could tell that he'd touched fresh blood. "Ah, shit . . ."

"Can you stand?" Barranca asked him.

Eddie started to nod, then remembered something about a sharp pain when he'd tried to stand in the outhouse, and how that attempt eventually turned out. "Not sure."

Barranca went for some men to carry him and it was a good half hour before they had him back in the shack on the other side of the field and on a sofa. Enrique, who'd been part of the litter detail, held a hurricane lamp up to Eddie's face and whistled softly.

"Not as bad as it looks," Galsworthy said as he took a clean napkin and wiped away some of the dried blood. "Facial wounds always bleed like hell. But somebody needs to look at that arm."

"We have a doctor in the camp," Barranca said. "He is on his way."

When the doctor arrived, he confirmed that Eddie's arm was indeed broken, but that the fracture was not displaced and no resetting would be required. "But he must have a cast. I have the materials in the camp."

Barranca started to dispatch somebody to go fetch the supplies but Galsworthy held up a hand and said, "Wait."

"Fug y'mean, wait?" Eddie slurred.

"We can use this," Galsworthy said.

"Use it?" Barranca asked. "How? Use what?"

Galsworthy rested an elbow in his opposite hand and stroked his chin. "You're supposed to rescue him tomorrow . . ."

"Yes . . . ?"

Galsworthy stayed quiet for a few seconds, then said, "Okay. So let's put on a real show."

"Whuh kin'a show?" Eddie mumbled.

Galsworthy ignored him and turned to Barranca. "You got a light plane around somewhere?"

"Several. Mostly for crop dusting."

"Perfect." Galsworthy put his hands on his hips and said, "You're going to rescue Eddie, fly him back and then carry him away from the wreckage of a burning plane."

Barranca shook his head. "I cannot fly a plane, and we are in no position to purposely destroy one."

"Don't worry about it." Galsworthy sat down on a chair next to Eddie. "You're not even going to be in the plane. And neither is Eddie here. Hey, buddy . . ." Galsworthy leaned on the sofa and peered into Eddie's eyes. "We'll set your arm tomorrow, okay?"

"Why?"

"So Barranca can snatch you from the very jaws of gruesome death at the hands of the mercenaries and deliver your broken and bleeding body to the GNN news crew."

Eddie blinked a few times—he was having some trouble following the conversation—but it was his kind of thinking and it eventually sank in. "I like it," he said with a weak grin.

"You should," Galsworthy said. "You might be the first guy in history to get the Congressional Medal of Freedom for smashing himself up in a Brazilian shithouse."

EDDIE'S GOLF MATCH WITH BARRANCA FOUR DAYS BEFORE THE EIGHTEENTH HOLE

With the match even after seventeen holes, it all came down to number 18, which would have been a par-five had the course been officially rated. The *bonhomie* that they'd enjoyed at the beginning of the round faded to a distant memory as, grim-faced and focused, both of them made it to within a hundred yards of the green in two shots.

Eddie was away and hit first, lofting the ball cleanly with a sand wedge and setting it down about six feet from the hole.

"*Buena balla*," Barranca muttered, which good golf etiquette compelled him to do despite his dismay. He chose a pitching wedge for his own approach shot. Its lower loft wouldn't produce as steep a trajectory, but he wouldn't have to swing as hard as if he used a sand wedge. He'd have to set the ball down well in front of the green and let it roll to the pin, a much trickier proposition than getting it to a target spot and nailing it there, especially on these uneven, handcrafted greens.

In his eagerness to bring perfection to his shot, Barranca had a moment of indecisiveness at the top of his backswing, faltered for a fraction of a second and, unable to stop himself in the middle of the swing, came down too steeply and hit the ball at the bottom of the clubface instead of in the middle. The "bladed" shot caused the ball to spring out at much too low an angle, with too much velocity. Eddie winced as he watched the ball fly over the front edge of the green, land well past the flag and continue on a fast roll all the way to the back. It was a terrible shot; even a two-putt from that distance on that moonscape of a green was a long shot, whereas Eddie had a reasonable chance of getting down in one.

"*Mierda,*" Javier volunteered needlessly. Barranca tried not to betray any emotion as he dutifully picked up his bag and began the desolate trek to the green.

Eddie slapped a hand on Barranca's shoulder. "To be truthful, Manolo, it really doesn't matter."

"Sorry . . . what do you mean?"

"It doesn't matter." The sun was getting low behind the green and as they walked Eddie squinted to try to make out the exact position of his ball. "I mean, sure, there's a million bucks on the line, but I know you don't care about that. Fact is, even if you win, the United States isn't going to go along with you."

Barranca stopped walking and looked at Eddie, his eyes a mixture of disappointment and budding anger. "I am not a naive man, but I did not expect to hear this from you. Not from Eddie Caminetti."

"Hear what?"

"That you would renege on an agreement made in good faith."

Eddie took the bag off his shoulders and craned his neck to ease some of the strain. "I'm not reneging on anything, Manuel. If you win"—he jerked a thumb at the green—"and we both know that's not gonna happen, I'll go back and tell the president exactly what you and I agreed to."

"Yes . . . ?"

"That doesn't mean he's going to honor it."

"But why would he not?" Barranca asked plaintively. "You believe, as I do, that he is a fundamentally decent man. You know that what I am proposing is best for all concerned, so how is it possible that—"

"It doesn't matter, Manolo. Right now, in the eyes of the American public you're an economic terrorist who's holding us hostage. Right or wrong, you don't get to win under those circumstances."

Unable to formulate a reply, Barranca picked up his bag and resumed his march to the green, where Javier and Enrique, having seen his approach shot, waited glumly. "It seems to me," he said to Eddie without conviction, "that you would be obligated to ensure that your government honors the terms of our agreement. Anything less would be dishonorable."

Eddie thought it was a ridiculous conversation given that Barranca winning the match was a virtual impossibility anyway, but he was willing to play out the scenario as a hypothetical. "I have no such obligation, and you know perfectly well I don't have that kind of clout. Not to mention I'd be out a million bucks, which would kind of ruin my day." Even as the words left his mouth, though, the faint beginnings of an idea were making themselves apparent somewhere in the back of his mind.

"Do you mean to say," Barranca asked, "that if I were to win, there would be no way you could convince your president to agree to our terms?"

"I'm not saying there would be no way," Eddie replied. "But it would be difficult."

"How difficult?"

"Extremely."

Barranca stepped around a small puddle of water. "But not impossible."

"No, not impossible."

"How much is President Eastwood paying you?"

"Sorry?"

"Please, Eddie. Do not insult me."

Eddie, who liked the way this conversation was going, had no intention of insulting Barranca. "Five million dollars. But only if I come back with something close to the deal he wants, which is you calling off your revolution. On the other hand, if I were to lose this match, I'd be out the five million as well as a million out of my own pocket."

Barranca went quiet as he considered something. "Suppose I were to offer to compensate you for the five million dollars, but purely on a contingency basis, if you can get the United States to recognize my country. Would you help me then?"

"Assuming you win this hole, you mean."

"That is correct."

"*Que pasa!*" Enrique shouted impatiently from the edge of the green, but Barranca waved him to silence.

"Well," Eddie said, "that wouldn't be much of a deal for me, would it, Manuel."

"Explain."

Eddie looked at Barranca's ball, which seemed to grow more distant even as they got closer to it. "Right now I'm going to get a sure five mill from President Eastwood. If I agree to your proposal and lose, then *maybe* I'm going to get it from you, and maybe I'm not, depending on what the president does after I get home. What's the benefit to me of taking a risk like that?"

"I see your point. But I would not offer you the money without assurance that you would be successful."

"Perfectly understandable, and I don't blame you a bit. But you can see why I'm not interested."

"I do. So what would it take?"

As they neared the green, Eddie pointed from Barranca's ball to the flag and the huge amount of real estate in between. "Doesn't hardly matter, Manolo. We both know you can't sink this putt. Besides, where would you get money like that?"

"Out of first profits of our new enterprise."

They'd reached the green and, as they doffed their bags and set them down, the worst of Barranca's fears were confirmed. His ball was over seventy feet away from the hole, and this green was not Javier's best piece of work, having been finished hurriedly when more important events overtook his project. It looked like a large family of moles had been boring just beneath the surface for months. Eddie decided to putt out, but was a little too casual and missed his first. Barranca conceded the next putt and Eddie was down in par. For all practical purposes it was over, because for Barranca to achieve even a three-putt on this disaster of a green would be a miracle, and he would need to do it in two just to force a playoff.

"If I win," Barranca said, "I will pay you ten million dollars in cash to convince your government to accept my new nation." He hesitated, waiting for a response. Getting none, he walked onto the green to begin the task of assessing his miserable putt.

Eddie went in the same direction, but more quickly, and got to Barranca's ball first. He bent over and reached out a hand for it.

Enrique let out an angry yell and began running toward Eddie, who ignored him, picked up the ball and tossed it to Barranca.

"That's a gimme," Eddie said, bringing Enrique to a skidding halt.

Javier shot his hands into the air, kicked off his shoes and danced onto the green. "Mulligan!" he shouted happily as a delighted Enrique applauded loudly in approval.